ROGUE WARRIOR®

DESIGNATION GOLD

Photograph by Roger Foley

ROGUE WARRIOR®

DESIGNATION GOLD

Richard Marcinko
and
John Weisman

POCKET BOOKS
New York London Toronto Sydney Tokyo Singapore

Many of the Rogue Warrior's weapons courtesy of Heckler & Koch, Inc., International Training Division, Sterling, Virginia

 POCKET BOOKS, a division of Simon & Schuster Inc.
1230 Avenue of the Americas, New York, NY 10020

Marcinko, Richard.
    Rogue warrior—Designation Gold / Richard Marcinko and
John Weisman.
        p. cm.
    ISBN 0-671-89673-3
    1. Rogue Warrior (Fictitious character)—Fiction. 2. Special
forces (Military science)—United States—Fiction. 3. Terrorism—
United States—Prevention—Fiction. 4. Commando troops—United
States—Fiction. I. Weisman, John. II. Title.
PS3563.A6362R635   1997
813'.54—dc20   96-42436
                                                               CIP

First Pocket Books hardcover printing March 1997

10   9   8   7   6   5   4   3   2   1

Printed in the U.S.A.

The only trustworthy spy is a dead spy.

—*Old Russian Proverb*

THE ROGUE WARRIOR'S
TEN COMMANDMENTS OF SPECWAR

- I am the War Lord and the wrathful God of Combat and I will always lead you from the front, not the rear.

- I will treat you all alike—just like shit.

- Thou shalt do nothing I will not do first, and thus will you be created Warriors in My deadly image.

- I shall punish thy bodies because the more thou sweatest in training, the less thou bleedest in combat.

- Indeed, if thou hurteth in thy efforts and thou suffer painful dings, then thou art Doing It Right.

- Thou hast not to like it—thou hast just to do it.

- Thou shalt Keep It Simple, Stupid.

- Thou shalt never assume.

- Verily, thou art not paid for thy methods, but for thy results, by which meaneth thou shalt kill thine enemy by any means available before he killeth you.

- Thou shalt, in thy Warrior's Mind and Soul, always remember My ultimate and final Commandment. There Are No Rules—Thou Shalt Win at All Cost

Contents

Part
One

ZAPODLO

Chapter

1

BORIS, LOOKING LIKE YOUR EVERYDAY RUSSKIE ALIEN IN HIS THIRD-generation night-vision driving glasses, slowed the blacked-out Zhiguli to about thirty kliks an hour as we eased into the gentle curve.

Misha, who had a similar pair strapped around the northern hemisphere of his ugly Ukrainian puss, raised his left arm like a proper jumpmaster. He half-swiveled his bull neck, licked his thick, droopy mustache, and stage-growled, "Ready, Dicky," out of the corner of his mouth.

He hadn't needed to say anything. Even *sans* night-vision equipment, I could make out the rear of the old dacha through the windshield—a cedar-clad shadow among shadows, its crude shingle roof slightly concave in the cloud-obscured, last-quarter moonlight, sitting squatly atop a low ridge a hundred or so yards west of the single-lane, north-south, gravel service road on which we were driving.

Our car pulled abreast of the first gate, moving south, its tires scrunching on the packed crushed rock roadbed as Boris decelerated slightly. So far as I could see, there were no lights on inside the dacha. That was promising news—maybe they were all asleep, or drunk, or both. Less work for mother. That, of course, is as in mother . . . fucker.

We passed even with the second gate. That was my cue. As the rough-hewn wood fence flashed by I began counting the telephone-pole-size fence posts, slapped Boris on the padded shoulder of his distressed black leather jacket, threw Misha the bird, put my shoulder against the rear left-hand door, cracked it open, and—twenty-seven posts, twenty-eight posts, twenty-nine posts, *thirty*—rolled out into the unseasonably cool late September night, at precisely the spot I'd circled on the high-resolution aerial surveillance photo Misha had taken less than eight hours ago from a borrowed Russian Navy Kamov "Hokum" chopper.

But as I know from having traveled so many miles with Mr. Murphy of Murphy's Law as a constant (and uninvited) companion, while every picture tells a story, it doesn't necessarily tell the right story. No one, for example, had bothered to notify a certain stolid, solid, thick, and wholly unforgiving birch tree that grew uncomfortably close to the side of the road that I was coming and perhaps it should get out of the way. Nor was I aware of the tree's precise location. So, with the first few bars of Ray Charles's rendition of "Georgia on My Mind" playing in my brain, I tucked and rolled (expertly, I might add with justifiable pride), and was savoring this clandestine tactical infiltration triumph—even as my big, wide Slovak snout made forceful, emphatic, and painfully intense contact with the rough bark and dense wood of our aforementioned tree.

My friends, let me not go hyperbolic on you here—but geezus, that *smarts.* Of course, I didn't have time to think about discomfort right then. The impact skewed my perfect tuck-and-roll, I careened to starboard and began to tumble uncontrollably. In the process, my right calf was snagged by a thicket of blackberry bushes. In case you didn't know, the thorns on blackberry bushes are just as wire-lethal as razor or barbed when you roll into 'em at fifteen-or-so miles per hour.

Okay, okay, so shredded, faded jeans are all the vogue these days. But I ain't no vogue rogue, bub—I like my jeans the old-fashioned way: dark indigo and in one piece. In any case, having completed a passable Brer Rabbit-tossed-through-the-briar-patch imitation, I spun along the shallow ditch that ran alongside the road, chipped a front tooth on something hard, slammed the point of my elbow against something else hard, bounced through another thicket of thorns into the woods, and finally came to a stop in the middle of what I hoped wasn't a clump of poison anything.

4

I lay there listening to my heart, which was pounding out a reasonable simulation of the el-oh-en-gee version of *In-A-Gadda-Da-Vida*—played at 78 RPM (or 160 pulse beats a minute, take your pick), and took half a dozen d-e-e-p breaths.

Now, those of you who already know me understand that I savor pain. I appreciate pain because it tells me that I am still alive. As that other old Frog Rogue, Descartes, might have said, "I hurt—therefore I am."

But friends, *this* kind of pain was fucking ridiculous. Talk about too much of a good thing. You want specifics? Okay, let me give you a little geography lesson. I currently resembled either a fucking rag doll SEAL or a bowline knot, because my legs—still wrapped haphazardly in strands of blackberry thorns—were going east, while the rest of me was twisted in a more or less northwesterly direction. Blood from my newly mashed nose coursed southward into my mustache. Below the equator of my tactical nylon belt, my nuts throbbed *ka-boom, ka-boom,* as tender as if they'd been flagrantly fondled by the fingers of a fucking feminist bodybuilder. Still farther south, there was more blood on my right leg—oozing down into the ankle-high Adidas GSG-9 tactical boot whose guaranteed unbreakable lace had somehow disintegrated in the last thirty seconds or so.

I untangled and dethorned myself, groaned, rolled onto my side, checked for broken body parts, and received some slight measure of welcome news as I pawed, probed, and poked my abused corpus. Dings there were aplenty. My ankle was going to be tender for a week. My nose—well, let's just say I never had a pretty nose to begin with, I don't have much time to smell da flowers, and my nostrils seem to get wider and flatter with age. My right knee was sore, my left elbow ached, and there was, I discovered, a knot the size of a chestnut blooming on my forehead, just above my Bollé SWAT goggles. But there was nothing broken—and like they always say, if it ain't broke, don't fix it.

With nothing to fix I did a quick equipment check. The suppressed Heckler & Koch 9mm MP5-PDW submachine gun in the padded scabbard on my back had survived its rough landing—and mine. I eased it out, loaded a magazine, and—quietly as I could—let the bolt slip forward.

Yes, I know that the good people at HK's International Training Division recommend slapping the bolt down and forward *avec panache,* thus letting it slam into place with a satisfying *ker-*

raacchhet! But what you can do on the range in Virginia, when you don't give a rusty F-word who hears you lock and load, you can't always do out here in the field, where sound counts.

I unbuttoned my tactical jacket and adjusted the lightweight bulletproof vest I wore underneath. Then I inventoried the jacket pockets. The contents were all present and accounted for. I pulled a coil of black parachute line from my left breast pocket, cut thirty-six inches from it with a Spyderco folder, replaced the broken lace in my right boot, and fastened it as tightly as I could to give me some extra support for my bruised ankle.

I ran my hand along the butt of the USP 9mm pistol in its tactical thigh holster to ensure that neither it nor the mag had come loose during my roller-coaster descent. Next, I made sure I still had the two spare fifteen-round magazines I'd stowed in horizontal mag-sheaths on my belt. They were there—filled with the same SEAL Team Six formula hand-loaded 147-grain Hornady XTP bullets in a Plus-Plus-P configuration that have more stopping power than a .45-caliber Silvertip hollowpoint. I rubbed my face and the backs of my hands to respread the dark camouflage cream. I retied the tiger-stripe "Do" rag around my head, the better to keep my French braid in place. Finally, my equipment check completed, it was time to move on out.

I checked the black, nonreflective Timex on my left wrist. There were nineteen minutes until OMON hit the front gate. I was six minutes behind the OPSKED—that's SEALspeak for operational schedule—I kept in my head. But now was no time to rush. So I lay in the swale by the side of the road and waited, listening for anything untoward. My breathing slowed. My pulse did, too. I held my breath and opened my mouth slightly to help amplify the sounds in my ears.

It was all quiet—only night sounds. That's when you know it's okay to move. Because when you can hear a chirp here, a falling something-or-other there, things are normal. When it's all quiet, something is always wrong. Because the critters know better than you when it's safe. With the forest sounding like a forest, it was time to go.

Cautiously, I rolled to my right, came up into a low crouch, and crabbed across the road, the sharp gravel cutting into my forearms and knees as I edged forward. It was slow going. At night, you can't be quick. Since sight is all but lost, you have to rely on sound. So you have to take it low and slow. You move. You stop. You scan. You listen. That's how you do it—if you want to stay alive. The technique had worked for me all over the world and I wasn't about to rush things now just because I was a little behind schedule.

My progress was counted in inches, not feet. And I was glad of it—because, as my night vision grew stronger, I could make out the sentries as they leaned against trees, perhaps thirty-five or forty yards from my position. There were three—no, four—no, five—of them.

Doubly cautious now, I made my way across the road and up to the fence. It was made of rough wood boards, stained or painted black or dark brown. What I hadn't seen in the darkness (nor picked up on the surveillance photo) was the heavy wire mesh affixed behind it. I thought about the pair of Navy-issue wire cutters sitting in their ballistic nylon tactical sheath that I'd left back in Moscow, rolled my eyes skyward, and cursed myself in six languages. My old shipmate Doc Tremblay is right: sometimes I do have fartbeans for brains.

I did a quick inventory—and came up empty. Oh, sure, I could go over the top. The fence was only about six feet high. But I'd make a hell of a silhouette if I clambered athwart it. It would be like advertising. I rolled onto my back. Something hard prodded my kidneys as I did. I reached behind me—and felt the Gerber Multi-Plier that I habitually wore on my belt. I was so used to having it there that I'd forgotten about it. The Multi-Plier is a handy little gizmo. It's got three screwdriver bits, a knife, a small file—even a can opener. Best of all, there are all-purpose pliers—with a tiny wire cutter placed just below the jaws.

I pulled the tool out and quietly extended the plier head, slipped the cutters over the first strand of wire, and squeezed.

One of the facts you should understand about the Multi-Plier is that while it is a handy all-purpose tool, it was not designed as a wire cutter. Its handles are small and narrow and hollow—the better to accommodate all those tools. And hence, they leave little room for error, especially if you have size ten hands with size twelve fingers, a genetic legacy from my thick-fingered, coal-mining forbears in Lansford, Pennsylvania. What I'm trying to tell you, my friends, is that every time I applied pressure to the jaws, the handles bit nastily into my hands.

Yes, I was carrying gloves. No, I wasn't wearing them. Why? Because they were leather gloves. Thick-as-your-tongue, regulation, by-the-book Russian Army leather gloves. There is a Naval

Special Warfare technical term to describe such gloves. Get out your pencils so you can write it down. The term is: "useless."

Have I told you about my special relationship with pain? Then you must realize that I was feeling very much alive by the time I cut a hole large enough for me to squeeze myself through. I was now twelve minutes behind schedule. But I was making progress.

Now, you folks out there are probably asking WTF right now, right? Like what the hell is Dickie Marcinko, the old Rogue Warrior®, radio handle Silver Bullet, doing outside a dacha forty-seven kliks west of Moscow in the first place. And how come he's so friendly with a couple of Russkies named Boris Makarov and Misha Stroyev.

Okay, before I head across the road to sneak & peek, snoop & poop, and then (I hope I hope I hope) commit the sort of murder & mayhem that gives me both professional satisfaction and emotional release, lemme give you a quick sit-rep.

Our story begins three weeks ago, when my old friend and shipmate Paul Mahon was assassinated. Paul is—was—a one-star—that's rear admiral (lower half)—submariner, an Annapolis grad (one of the few I've ever really liked and respected) who'd been assigned to Moscow as the defense attaché. Now, I just told you that Paul was my shipmate. That is not literally true. By which I mean, Paul and I never served together in a ship of the line. But shipmatedom is a metaphysical state as well as a physical condition—it speaks of sharing risks, working together as a team, and achieving goals. In this particular case, our shipmate relationship goes back to the days when we were a couple of anonymous 0-4s—lieutenant commanders—working in the bowels of the Pentagon.

That was when Paul and I were charged by our respective bosses, a pair of E-ring admirals (those are admirals with offices on the Pentagon's E-ring, where the chief of naval operations, among others, has his 4 rms riv vu office suite) with one of the most difficult, sensitive, hazardous, and covert missions the U.S. Navy has ever devised. To wit: stealing the U.S. Army mascot, a mannequin dressed as a Special Forces master sergeant, from the grand foyer of the Pentagon's Mall entrance the week before the Army-Navy football game.

Anyhow, that escapade (which succeeded, I must add) made us friends, and we've stayed in touch over the years. Paul was one of the few officers who wrote me during my year in prison. In fact, not three weeks after my release from Petersburg Federal, when I was as depressed as I've ever been, Paul called to ask if I'd be willing to be his newborn son's godfather. He didn't have to do that—there were more than enough Mahon relatives around for the job. But he gave it to me because he thought I needed somebody to love and dote upon—which was absolutely correct. Not so very long ago he gave me a timely heads-up when the secretary of the navy tried to get me indicted for murder.

Anyway, roughly three months back, Paul began an accelerated, two-year stint as the CDA—that's Chief Defense Attaché, the top-ranking U.S. military officer—Moscow. The job can be largely ceremonial: you can fulfill your mission requirements simply by going to large numbers of diplomatic receptions, giving cocktail parties, doing lunch, taking meetings, and writing lots of empty-calorie memos detailing what you've seen and heard and noshed upon.

Not Paul. He took the job seriously. He actually went out into the field and collected information—the kind of stuff the folks at the Defense Intelligence Agency call Level One Grade-A HUMINT, or HUMan INTelligence. From what I was told, he was doing a terrific job, too.

Obviously, his success rubbed some local no-goodniks the wrong way, and they rubbed back. Three weeks ago, Paul, his wife Becky, their two kids—my godson, Adam, and the two-year-old Louise—and an enlisted female Navy driver were coming back from a weekend at a rented dacha in the lake district near Odentsovo, the same region northwest of Moscow where I was currently hurting. Their car was intercepted by a "group of persons identities unknown," as the diplomatic cable I saw so coolly put it, and all five were murdered.

According to the report, the car was rammed from behind—the Navy driver hadn't taken any tactical driving courses and evidently panicked—then pushed off the road. Once it had been stopped, Paul, his family, and the driver were machine-gunned. Then the car was set on fire, no doubt to make such things as identification of the passengers harder for the authorities.

Now, you probably know me well enough by now to realize that I would have found some way to get here on my own to exact revenge for my friend's death—not to mention my godson's. But fortunately, Paul's boss, a submariner named Kenny Ross, opened my cage and turned me loose with a trunkful of small arms, and a diplomatic USG—that's U.S. government—passport. It's a lot more complicated than that, of course, but there's really very little time to explain it all right now. Anyway, I arrived here in Moscow—lemme check my watch—four days ago and began making inquiries. At nine yesterday morning, Boris, who is a captain in the Moscow Police Department's organized crime squad to whom I'd been clandestinely introduced, walked me up to a holding cell at the aging, puke yellow brick departmental head-quarters on Petrovka Street, pointed at a huge, ugly, tattooed, white-walled, buzz-topped goon in Le Coq Sportif sweats, who was manacled uncomfortably to a length of galvanized steel pipe almost as thick and long as my dick, and asked, "Is he wearing anything you recognize?"

I looked. The haircut was UM—that is, universally military. I peered at the bruised, bloated face. Yeah, sure it had been worked over by the cops, but it could still be defined as U_2—that is, Ugly and Unfamiliar. The size fifteen shoes were $200 Nike Air cross-trainers. The currently grimy extra-extra-large threads were the real thing—the kind of country-club athletic gear that seldom sees sweat. The fingernails were dirty and raggedly bitten. Then I saw what Boris had been getting at. There was a chunk of gold and semiprecious stone jammed onto the thug's goon-size pinky.

I knew all too well what it was, too—an Annapolis class ring. I asked Boris WTF.

"He tried to sell it to an American tourist outside the Metropol Hotel," the Russian explained. "As luck would have it, the tourist, a retired Navy officer, complained loud and long to his tour guide about Russians selling U.S. Navy artifacts. The tour guide—he was very reticent, I might add, and if it hadn't been for the American tourist making such a stink he would have let it all go—finally called the police."

"So why is he still wearing it?"

Boris shrugged. "Look, it's not against the law to own such a thing. But if you can prove it was your friend's, then we can start to make a case."

I pointed at the ring and stuck my hand, palm up, in Vassily's face, making the universal sign for "hand it over."

The goon spat neatly in the center.

"Boris," I said, "would you give me a set of handcuff keys, then leave us alone for a few minutes?"

He grinned. "No problem, Dicky."

When I finally pried the ring off (unfortunately, I broke a couple of fingers in the process), I looked inside and saw Paul's initials, and his graduation date: 1973.

Now, despite the obviously spirited interrogation that followed (they don't have the same rules about cop-prisoner physical contact in Moscow police stations that we have in the United States. In Moscow, Rodeniy Kingski is the rule, not the exception), the GIQ— that's Goon-In-Question, and pronounced *geek*—whose name was Vassily Chichkov, had, Boris said, stuck with the story that he'd found the ring on the street, and wanted to make a quick pile of hard currency selling it to the first American he'd come across.

Yeah. Right. And if you believe that, I have some beachfront property to sell you in New Mexico. According to Boris, this GIQ worked as an enforcer for a Georgian *vor v zakonye*—that's Russian for a mafia Godfather—named Andrei Yudin. According to Misha, the cops had been trying to get their hands on Andrei for months.

But they'd been unsuccessful, Boris interjected, because, first, Andrei lived in the Yasser Arafat style—which is to say he moved from secret residence to secret residence on a weekly, sometimes daily basis, and second, because Andrei always managed to procure enough tactical intelligence about police activities to keep his Georgian butt from being busted.

Yudin. Andrei Yudin. Lightbulb. I recognized the name because Andrei the *vor* was one of a dozen Russian mafiyosi mentioned in the sheaf of notes, memos, reports, and other documents I'd taken from the Navy Only safe in Paul's office two days ago.

According to those notes, Andrei was one of the more dangerous and enterprising local mafiosi—tied into a wide range of activities that ranged from protection scams, to smuggling weapons, to drug dealing. There was a star next to his name—and it wasn't because he was a nice guy.

Then Boris walked me back to his office, pulled a yard-square sheet of posterboard out of his closet-size safe, and showed me Yudin's pug face on a well-worn, often-revised organizational chart of Russian Mafiya (which as you can probably guess is Ivan for *Mafia*) crime families—a chart that looked very much like the ones up in the U.S. Senate's Permanent Subcommittee on Investigations, the high-ceilinged room in the Russell Office Building where a mob hitman-turned-stoolie named Joe Valachi once gave Bobby Kennedy enough inside information about American organized crime to put two hundred soldiers and *capos* from La Cosa Nostra behind bars.

Double lightbulb. I'd seen Andrei's face before—Paul had taken a covert snapshot of the guy. He was celebrating something or other, wineglass raised, mouth open and laughing, at a sardine-packed table in a bustling restaurant or club. Except, Paul hadn't labeled the picture. Of course he hadn't—*he* knew who the fuck he'd photographed. Now, in Boris's office, I put the face and the name together.

I inquired as to whether I might spend some quality time with the prisoner, so I'd be more able to appreciate his lifestyle and his weltanschauung—that's his worldview, for those of you whose *Deutsche* ain't decent. Boris chuckled, gave me the key to the handcuffs, and I returned to the cell and had a few choice words with Vassily—a reflective, thoughtful, philosophical interlocution about the sorts of commitments and responsibilities one owes to one's friends and one's godchildren. Shortly before Vassily departed for the prison hospital, he saw things my way—they generally do, y'know—and I gave Boris the location where Andrei Yudin was currently holed up—the selfsame dacha that was right now so near yet so far.

Now, it may sound somewhat strange to you at first (it certainly did to me), but I learned by going through Paul's papers that from the day he'd arrived, Paul had spent much of his time collecting information on Russian (and Georgian and Armenian and Chechen) organized crime.

Bizarre work for a defense attaché, you say. You're right. Until you learn, as I had, that Russian organized crime deals with everything from money laundering and drugs, to the marketing of purloined nuclear warheads and the sale of chemical and biological warfare components.

In fact, even though Ken Ross had not said anything about it to me, I believed that the mafia—or mafiya, as they call it here—was the reason Paul's assignment here had been stepped up. He was a Russian speaker—fluent and *sans* accent. Equally important, he was an operator—a guy who could change his clothes, slip out of the embassy compound, and work the streets without attracting undue attention to himself. That ability is rare. It is even more remarkable in one-star admirals. So Paul had been sent here early because the Navy was concerned enough about Russian organized crime activities to place a one-star in harm's way. And Paul and his family had paid the ultimate price.

Now you know why I had Georgia—that's the country I'm talking about, not the lady—on my mind tonight. I'd come to pay a polite social call (I'm using literary understatement and stylistic irony here, in case you didn't catch on right away) on dear Andrei the Georgian Godfather. He, judging from our evaluation of Misha's afternoon surveillance photos—the Mercedes limo and two Volvo security cars in the front driveway, the Volga trucks going in and out, and the dozen bodyguards in the woods were all pretty convincing clues—was, just as Vassily had told me, holed up in the dacha across the road.

I wanted to ask Andrei a couple of questions before I put my foot across his throat and stepped down hard. Starting with, "How come your ugly goon happened to be wearing my friend's Annapolis class ring?" Yeah—I tend to ask direct questions. And God help you if I don't get direct answers—especially when people I love and respect have been killed.

Lest you think I've taken leave of my senses, I wasn't doing this all by myself. The cavalry was out front. As usual, I'd volunteered for the back-door entrance—the sneak-and-peek assignment. Boris had been only too happy to let me handle this part of the mission solo.

To be honest, it would get me out of his hair. You look surprised. You're about to ask what the hell I'm talking about. After all, aren't I Demo Dick Marcinko, Shark Man of the Delta, the old Rogue Warrior, and shouldn't I be able to do my hunting under any conditions and in any company?

Well, the answer is yes and no. Yes, I can pursue my lethal trade under most any circumstances. But I have never seen the sense of fucking up someone else's op just so I can say "I vas dere, Cholly." Yeah, in *Red Cell*, I elbowed my way into Grant Griffith's war game. But that was different: I had an objective to achieve, and I couldn't achieve it from the outside. And yes, I once beat the shit out of an incipient faggot named Major Geoff Lyondale, Royal Marines, when he managed to kill a bunch of his own men through a degree of tactical stupidity I haven't seen since the planning of the Tehran hostage rescue back under Jimmy Carter. But that was different, too—because when Major "Cawl me Geoff, old man" put his men in jeopardy, he also put *my* men in jeopardy, since we were operating jointly. And that sort of irresponsibility is something I will not allow.

However, in most circumstances, when I'm a visitor, I'll stand aside and let the home team take the field. I'm content to watch and learn. Warriordom, after all, is not a static art. The Warrior is constantly searching for ways to make himself better, more capable, and more deadly. That's what cross-training is all about—it's why I sent my SEAL Team Six shooters all over the world to see how the other guys did it.

So, in cases like this one, I'm happy to play backup. It was Boris's game, after all, and he knew the rules, the players, and had a sense of the whole operational gestalt far better than I.

As the ancient *Ch'i* master General Sun wrote in *Way of the Warrior* more than two thousand years ago, "Since the key to victory can often be found in that instant when the Warrior commits his troops, it is important to be neither early nor late. The Warrior uses timing as his fulcrum to victory."

Right on. I've always found that knowing when to commit—which can also be interpreted as when to play—is just as important as understanding the game itself.

Therefore, I was happy with my lonesome end role tonight. Moreover, I can't speak Russian and I've never operated *with* any Russians (only *against* them during the Cold War). Hence, I don't really know how they work, and I'd probably get myself shot. 'Nuff said.

Anyway, while I did my covert entry, Boris would charge the front door, accompanied by a squad of black-bereted OMON shooters. OMON, which is an acronym for *Otdel Militsii Osobovo Naznacheniya,* or Special Purpose Militia Detachment, is the Ministry of Internal Affairs' special reaction team—the Russian equivalent of a police or sheriff's department SWAT unit. OMON is made up of volunteers who regularly train in unconventional warfare tactics. It is one of the few police units that, according to Boris, hasn't been penetrated by organized crime—yet.

Cradling the MP5, I crawled forward. The ground was soft—it was covered with a thick coating of pine needles, which helped me maintain silence discipline as I moved. I progressed eight, nine, ten yards and stopped to check out the landscape and the bad guys. Even in darkness, there were no major differences from what we'd seen in the surveillance pictures eight hours ago. The dacha itself was nestled atop a slight knoll, the thick grove of pine trees running up to within a few yards of its roof. The rear of the house had a narrow wooden door and a rustic, railed porch and a wooden deck that led down to a smaller structure with a single metal chimney—Misha'd said it was probably the sauna. From the dacha itself, the land, thick with evergreens, white birch, and poplar, sloped gently down toward the road. The slope was roughly bisected by a small, spring-fed stream that ran north/south.

So much for topography. Now let's talk about the opposition. The sentries were spread out in a rough crescent between me and the dacha. If you're looking at the same clock I am, you'll see what I see: that one was at 0930, another at 1100, a pair at noon, and one at 1330.

Taking them out was going to be a problem. I had to hit 'em so that they'd go down—silently, without warning each other. Or, make 'em clump up and eliminate them all at once.

It is at times like this that I would have liked to have Stevie Wonder, or Doc Tremblay, or Gator Shepard—any of the five-man band of shoot-and-looters I'd brought to Moscow with me to help out. But that was impossible. Oh, my merry marauders were here—in the Russian capital. But they were doing their own thing tonight—which is, they were covering for me. They were setting up a little diversion back in the city so that nobody back at the embassy, particularly the DCM, or Deputy Chief of Mission, would know I was out here with Georgian (and murder) on my mind.

Oh. You mean I haven't mentioned before that tonight's little excursion in the country is off the books? Unauthorized? A rogue operation? Silly me.

Yeah, despite the fact that I am a duly constituted representative of the United States Navy and do not fall under his purview, the DCM has nevertheless specifically forbidden me on his thick, watermarked, Department of State letterhead (let me quote directly from the memo here, friends, so that you can experience the true flavor of his writing style and ability) to

generate, occasion, induce, provoke, elicit, or activate any sort of incident, event, or action whatsoever during your temporary assignment to this diplomatic post, without having notified the undersigned party in writing, at least twenty-four hours before such planned occurrence or episode is to take place. Further, you may not interact with any FN [Foreign National] without the specific permission of this office in general, and the undersigned in specific.

In the sort of simple, declarative English I understand, that means I'm not allowed to do fuck-all. According to the DCM, I can't operate with any Russian unit, either military or police, without his prior authorization. According to his official memorandum (CC: To the File; CC: Rear Admiral Kenneth Ross, USN; CC: Bureau of European and Canadian Affairs, U.S. Department of State, Washington, D.C.), I'm not allowed to prowl and growl on my own.

Now, friends, that's ludicrous. You know as well as I do that I don't have to answer to any deputy chief of mission or any other change-jingling, heel-rocking diplomat for that matter. After all, I'm anything but diplomatic. I'm a shoot-and-looting, hop-and-popping, hairy-assed SEAL. And I report to admirals—specifically to Rear Admiral Kenny Ross.[1]

Of course, even though I was clear about my chain of command, it seemed that the DCM held an opposing view. That view was that I was not to be allowed to do squat, unless I'd appeared before himself, himself being a slick-haired, cold-blooded, pinstriped professional change jingler heel rocker cookie pusher named— well, let's just call him Bart Wyeth, just in case he ever wants to sue for libel—with my wood begging bowl in my calloused hand and received his (this is his word) "endorsement," something he has told me point-blank will never be given.

Bart, incidentally, is short form for Bartlett Austin Wyeth Jr. His initials form the acronym BAW, which as you all know means Big Asshole Windbag in SEALspeak. He certainly manages to live up to it, too.

---

[1] I've mentioned this kind of chain of command structure before. Like my old boss, CNO Arleigh Secrest, I call it "stovepipe" chain-of-command because each separate command structure goes straight up and down, which means there is no interaction among them. Most of the time the system works to my detriment and the bad guy's favor because no one outside my particular "stovepipe" shares information. On this occasion, however, I am happy to report that my "stovepipe" was entirely separate from the DCM's. The good news was that the motherfucker couldn't lay a finger on me, and we both knew it. The bad news was that he could make my life miserable, because it was he who controlled the environment—e.g., everything that went on at the embassy.

And y'know come to think of it, from the way he's acting, you'd think that he was being paid by the Russkies instead of by our American tax dollars. I mean, it was *our* fucking defense attaché who got waxed. It pisses me off, friends, to see those charged with flying Old Glory overseas posturing as if they were officials of the place they've been posted to, while acting as if the United States is some third-world country not worth defending. Or worse, instinctively sticking up for the other guy instead of safeguarding Americans.

Moreover, since *we* are the only remaining superpower, I'd like to think that we'd act like one every now and then. But that wasn't the case here in Moscow, where timidity was the order of the day. I mean, you'd think that Paul's death was *his* fault, at least from the way the people at the embassy had dealt with it.

There was no outrage. There was not even any real indignation at what had happened. Only a bunch of diplomatic (yes, friends, I know I'm repeating the word—it is used here ironically) Diplomatic Demarches from the State Department deploring and decrying, and a similar set of replies from the Russian Foreign Ministry, regretting and lamenting. It's just a game to them—a fucking game of untruths and no consequences.

It was almost the same as when Freddie Woodward, one of the CIA's gumshoes, was assassinated in the Georgian Republic a few years back. Remember that incident? If not, here's a nutshell: an American official—Freddie was traveling under diplomatic cover— was murdered in cold blood. Repercussions? Hardly a ripple. Why? Because somewhere, a deal had been made. Between whom? Nobody knows.

It struck me that this was a remarkably similar case. My friend and his family had been murdered, and no one is doing anything about it. Makes me think that somebody is covering up. Was I being paranoid? I didn't think so—because Paul's murder had struck Ken Ross in the same way. After all, Ken had opened my cage so I could prowl and growl.

I decided to take the sentries out separately. They were spaced far enough apart so I knew I could drop them quietly. I crawled south, to come up on the man at 0930, from his blind side. It took me three and a half minutes to crab my way into position. Then I settled in, got myself a good cheek and shoulder mold, aligned his head with the neon green "finger" of the MP5's Trijicon front sight blade, and squeezed the trigger. The only sound I heard was a knuckle-crackloud *click* as the hammer fell, and the muffled thump of his body collapsing onto the thick bed of pine needles. Damn, the MP5 is an effective weapon.

I crawled to where he lay. There was a clean, dime-size hole in one side of his head. When I lifted it off the ground, I saw the silver dollar-size hole opposite, and brain matter on the ground. Even so, I reached down and checked his carotid artery. Yeah—he was dead meat. I ran a quick body search. He carried a semi-auto pistol, which was stuck in a cheap nylon waist band holster clipped to his warm-up suit trousers. In his jacket pocket was a portable radio, which was switched off, and a pristine matchbook. I looked at the cover. It bore an embossed, cartoon drawing of a raffish, fifties-styled Harley Davidson chopper, below which were the English words DYNAMO CLUB. *I'd seen that logo before—on something I'd surmised was a receipt—in Paul's files. On the bottom of the page he'd written the word* Yudin. The matchbook cover bore no phone number, and no address. I looked inside. The number 2130 had been written there and underlined. I slipped the matchbook into the breast pocket of my combat jacket, and finished patting the corpse down. There was no other ID. That told me this place was his turf. You don't have to carry a wallet around your own home.

The next two were equally easy. I think I've already told you that standing sentry duty is harder than it seems. You don't remember? Let me give you a quick refresher. Personally, I hate standing watch. It is monotonous. It is tedious. It is boring work, which demands a lot of concentration. Yet, despite all the temptations to smoke, day (or night) dream, or succumb to boredom, you must remain alert and on guard.

Why? Because if you don't pay attention and remain alert, you get dead when fatal folks like me show up to play pernicious. Which is exactly what happened here. These guys were so lackadaisical you'd have thought the dacha was empty.

I was on my way to deal with the final pair of watchdogs when all hell broke loose out front. I heard a heavy vehicle approaching, its engine grinding as it approached from my left to my right, beyond the dacha. Then came the sound of ripping metal followed quickly by explosions. Judging from the concussion, there was nothing subtle about the way OMON did its business. I guess they didn't care about prisoners.

Huge yellow-orange flashes from the front of the dacha ruined my night vision—but not before I saw my two targets go into defensive posture. One of them, an Ivan in a terrible suit, called out to his friends—and when he didn't get an answer he pulled something out of his pocket. I snapped a three-round burst in his direction.

Ivan dropped, but it wasn't because he was hit—in fact, he returned fire vaguely in my direction and screamed at his buddy to get the leadski out. I could see his arms move and I knew what the hell he was saying even though I can't speak the language. He was saying something to the effect of, "It looks like there's only one of 'em out there, so get the fuck around to your right and flank the sonofabitch—we'll catch him in a crossfire."

I, of course, was the AS—that is, the aforementioned sonofabitch.

"When weak," says Sun Tzu, "appear strong." Or, to put it in the Frogspeak bellowed by Roy Boehm, the godfather of all SEALs, the instant you're attacked you counterattack. "You go and fuck the fucking fuckers," is how he piquantly puts it. So I slammed a fresh mag into the MP5, put my best War Face on, and went straight for the belly of the beast, screaming, "Yaaaaaahhhhh!" like a goddamn Marine.

Ivan-in-the-terrible-suit hadn't expected that. It brought him to his feet. He was silhouetted against the dacha for an instant as a flashbang went off somewhere behind him, and I tagged him—a ragged burst that caught him in the leg, thigh, groin, belly, and chest of his bad threads. Okay—so it wasn't pretty shooting, but it did the job. Four down.

Except I didn't have time to admire my handiwork, because the tree trunk adjacent to my head splintered, something nasty slashed my cheek, and I dropped for cover. Yeah—there was that other Ivan out there, and from the blood on my cheek I gathered he was probably mad by now.

He'd fired from my left. So I'd go around him and take him from the side. The best way to get there was the stream. So I slipped the MP5's sling over my head, slung it on my back, scrambled forward, shoulder-rolled (unmindful of ankles, knees, and other sore body parts), and pitched myself headlong into the black water.

Geezus. Talk about your fundamental scrotum-shriveling cold. I lay there for a few seconds, letting the water course over me, waiting for my nuts to redescend from my throat. The stream was six feet wide, and roughly three and a half, maybe four feet deep in the center. The bottom was a lot firmer than I'd thought it would be. It was covered in large, flat, water-smoothed rocks. I made my way three meters left, moving toward where I thought Ivan might be lurking, and came upon what seemed to be a subsurface breakwater or dam, built of what felt like worn concrete. I eased myself over it. Now my feet sank into soft muck, decaying leaves, and other crud. Okay—that told me I'd just been in the sauna's dipping pool and now I was in the stream proper. It was slippery here—and much deeper, too.

I would have gone back to admire the work, but there was no time. Three quick shots caromed past my right ear and slammed into the bank, two feet behind my exposed head. I dove and bulled my way underwater for a few meters, fighting the current every inch of the way. I surfaced. A bullet smacked the water much too close for comfort, driving me back under. I moved forward again. This was definitely getting to be a drag.

Now a beam of light flicked over the water's rippled surface, searching for me. I pulled myself as close as I could to the bank where it had come from and stayed put. The light swung back again, passing directly over my body. After it moved on, I surfaced as quietly as I could, grabbed a lungful of air, and waited. Then I sensed it coming back in my direction. As the beam arced toward me, I slipped underwater again, holding on to a tree root about as thick as my wrist for support. The light sliced past me without wavering.

Looking up through the coursing water I could make out where it was coming from—off to my left. It slid past me again, moving right to left, playing on the opposite, empty bank. I bided time, then slid surfaceward and stole another helping of oxygen. (No oxy moron I. I know you gotta breathe to live, even if you're an amphibian—read Frog—like me.)

I sat there, freezing my *yaytsa* off, waiting the sonofabitch out until he came closer. He'd have to come closer if he wanted to check the near bank. And I'd be waiting. I lay there, the memory of my murdered godson Adam keeping my body white-hot, even though it was Arctic cold.

Finally he showed. Yeah—it was Ivan. He was silhouetted against the bank, leaning over, trying to peer down into the opaque water. He'd obviously been taught by a pro. His pistol was in his right hand, the flashlight in his left. The backs of his hands touched, so that his left wrist provided support for his firing hand, and the sight picture of his gun paralleled the beam of his light.

It is an effective technique. But it only works if you light up your target. He couldn't see me hunkered next to the bank. So, I waited until his flashlight beam passed two feet beyond my right shoulder, and he stepped smack up to the edge of the water so he could check the bank itself. The light began to move from horizontal toward vertically perpendicular.

Right then, like a big, angry croc, I smashed through the surface with a roar, reached up, grabbed him by his belt and his crotch, and brought him smack headfirst down into the water.

He struggled, but he was too surprised to react with any effectiveness. He lost his pistol and his light, and I was on him like the fucking hungry gator I am, my hands on his throat, my legs wrapped around him, holding him under in a death roll, squeezing all the breath out of him while he struggled as if his life depended on getting loose from me.

He had no chance to survive. Even so, it took a lifetime to kill him—maybe forty-five, fifty, even fifty-five seconds. If that doesn't sound like a long time to you, then *you* try wrestling with a big, strong Ivan who don't wanna die, for almost a minute, underwater, without losing any of your own air or drowning yourself in the process.

I struggled up onto the bank and collapsed on my back, exhausted. That was a double-ouch, because the goddamn submachine gun's bolt caught me right in the fucking kidneys. So I lurched onto my knees, retching water. If there are easier ways to earn money, please tell me about them, okay? And guess what, friends—this was only the beginning of my evening's fun. I still had to hit the fucking dacha.

But first, there was the sauna house. I unslung the MP5, drained it, slapped a fresh mag into the breech, then moved cautiously up the bank, edging to my right, using the trees for cover. The sauna had a three-by-three-foot window, which I slid underneath, and a narrow, cedar-sheathed door. I tried the knob. It turned. I pushed the door inward. It opened slightly. I nudged it all the way with the MP5's suppressor, kept real low, and "cut the pie." Cautiously, I peered inside. I could make out two rustic benches in the ambient light, and a half-dozen pegs on which hung huge towels, as well as a small, neat pile of hardwood and a brass bucket filled with kindling. But the dressing room was empty.

Immediately to my right was a second doorway. I repeated my sequence. The sauna, too, was empty except for the square steel sauna stove atop which sat a pile of stones. From the stove, a single, four-inch exhaust pipe went straight up into the ceiling. Opposite the stove was an L-shaped bench the width of a double bed. It was big enough for two people to lie on. Atop its smooth surface sat a wooden bucket of water. In the corner, someone had tossed a small bunch of birch branches bound together with rough cord.

I opened the stove. There were cobwebs inside the door, which told me it hadn't been used recently. The floor was coated with a thin layer of dust. I closed the stove door and ran my fingers underneath the metal box on its squat legs. Nothing. I dipped a finger inside the bucket. The water felt as cold as I did and there was an opaque film on top of the surface. Another sign the place hadn't been used in a while.

Time to leave. There were lights moving all through the dacha now. Explosions, too. And shots—magazine-long bursts of automatic weapons fire. Didn't these guys have any fire discipline at all? Then I heard guttural shouting. The words themselves I couldn't understand—but the meaning was plain: they were screaming the Russian equivalent of "Police search warrant—get the fuckski down, get your fucking armskis out, put your fucking palmskis up, and don't fucking move!"

I lumbered up the deck toward the back door, my MP5 in low ready as the door shattered outward. My muzzle came up and my finger moved from index to trigger.

So did Boris's. We locked eyes. We both breathed deeply. Then we lowered our weapons.

I managed the first word tumble. "Where the fuck's our target? Andrei what's-his-face—the Godfather?"

"Yudin?" Boris's wide shoulders hunched and he extended his arms, palms out. "Gone. Nothing but *byki*. Bodyguards. Cannon fodder—left behind to confuse us and maybe kill a few cops." He shook his head in disgust. "We have no fucking operational security anymore, Dicky. He was here when Misha taking surveillances this afternoon. I just know it. But now—gone. Somebody has to tell him we were coming."

While the OMON shooters pulled the bodies outside and pawed them over for evidence, Boris, Misha, and I went through the dacha with your proverbial fine-tooth combski. Not that we expected to find anything. First, OMON had done a pretty good job of wrecking the place when they'd come barreling through the door. Moreover, despite my short time in Moscow I'd already determined that these mafiya types were SUCs—Smart, Unpredictable, and Cunning. They acted as if they owned the streets—which, in effect, they did. You couldn't walk into a store, restaurant, or first-class hotel without running a gauntlet of sweat suit-clad hoodlums flexing their muscles outside. The mobs controlled everything from garbage collection to caviar distribution. Their enforcers ranged from goons like the one wearing Paul's ring, to former officers—SpecWarriors like me. Except they hadn't authored a bunch of bestsellers and had no pensions.

So a number of things occurred to me, none of them very encouraging, as I stood in the dacha and pondered the possibilities. First, the bad guys had known we were going to stage a hit. I wondered how they had gotten the word—that is, until I took a close look at the Ministry of the Interior colonel in charge of the OMON unit. He was very self-consciously rubbing his left wrist. On that wrist was a gold Rolex President watch. I sidled up, said hello—he spoke a *leetle beet engleesh*—and took a closer look. It was obviously brand-new—not a scratch on the crystal or crown. Those watches go for between seven and eight grand each. Now I knew how the bad guys had managed to get away clean.

And I mean *clean*. There was, so far as the Russkies could tell, no evidence left behind. Nothing. Nada. Worse, so far as I was concerned, was the fact that Yudin and pals had slipped away despite the fact that, so far as Boris had been told, the dacha had been under continual surveillance by the Ministry of the Interior for the past eight hours.

Yeah, right—you saw the colonel's new solid gold Rolex, too.

Knowing that there was little if any OPSEC—that's OPerational SECurity—here in old Mother(fucker) Russia meant I'd have to watch out for my own well-worn butt. You know, friends, I've often been accused of operating in a rogue fashion—to be specific, without getting the permission of my superiors before I initiate action. But that tactic has kept me and my men alive, confused my enemies, and made me a highly successful warrior.

Yes, there is a time for going through channels. But there is also a time and a place for silence—and for stealth. And Russia, I decided, was a country in which I was going to play things very close to the old *gilet*.

Now, just because the Russians hadn't been able to find anything of consequence in the dacha didn't mean it was an evidence-free zone. So despite complaints from Boris and Misha I methodically examined the dacha's interior, working my way from the splintered front door to the kicked-out rear in a classic pattern search. Much of what I found was puzzling. Indeed, the situation here was a new one—and it presented a series of fresh, tough, and unsettling problems for me.

As you know I've been fighting terrorists for the past few years. Well, terrorists are real bureaucrats when it comes to record keeping. They annotate *everything*. From Mao Zedong's notes made during the Great March, to Che Guevara's diary of his disastrous Bolivian expedition, to the Tamil Tigers' expense accounts, FMLN supply catalogs, Islamic Jihad ordnance requisitions, or Kahane Chai bomb manuals, every terrorist group I've ever come up against has been a prodigious keeper of paperwork. They keep itemized records, lists, inventories, diaries, journals, notebooks— all filled with a mixture of hard facts about what they have and where it is, to political musings (most of that is bull puckey), to tactical theories (ditto), to detailed notes about where they've been, what they've seen, and—this is the part I always like the best—the names and contact numbers of the people who help them.

You might wonder why they perform this scribbled ludicrousness—and have done for as long as I can remember, when it is so dangerous. That, my friends, is a question I cannot answer. All I can say is that I'm glad that tangos, which is how I most commonly refer to terrorists, are writers as well as fighters. Because it makes my job, which in broad terms can be described as hunting and killing as many tangos as I can lay hands or bullets on, much easier.

But that, as they say, was then—and this is now, and now there was nothing of note (yes, that word is used sarcastically here) to discover. The few sticks of furniture were early rustic—old and very well used. The rugs were cheap and mud encrusted. The closets were empty—cleared out except for the odd wire or plastic hanger. There was a film of dust in the hallway closet. But that dust had been caused by the concussion of the flashbangs—I knew that because the closet shelves in what must have been the master bedroom were clean.

In fact, the entire place was pretty bare. Oh, there was a shot-up Sony TV set hooked up to one of those new, half-meter satellite dishes. A shattered ghetto-blaster with integral CD player sat on the kitchen sideboard. The OMON team in their black clothes pawed over a box of pirated Chinese CDs[2] of American, English, and French rock and roll, and Russian popski music, stuffing souvenirs in their pockets.

I worked my way through the basic kitchen, whose tiny, two-burner stove was powered by a four-foot high steel bottle of gas—maybe propane—parked outside. There was half a loaf of hard black bread, half a dozen tins of pressed caviar, several cans of sweet condensed milk, and a bunch of half-empty bottles of vodka, Chivas, and Remy Martin in the cupboard. But the few dishes were chipped, and the thick drinking glasses looked as if they'd originally been filled with grape jelly.

There was a double bed with an old bare mattress, two moth-eaten pillows, and a single bedside table in what had to be the master suite. I went through the small drawers. Nada. I lifted the ragged pillow on the ladder-back chair. Nothing. The three smaller bedrooms were each stripped bare. No beds. No furniture. Even the floors had been swept clean—not a single dust bunny in the corners or inside the built-in cabinets. There was something strange with this picture; something terribly awry. And it troubled me that I had no idea what it might be.

Nevertheless, I kept up with my search. I pawed through the fireplace. The ashes were consistent with wood, which meant that no sizeable quantity of paper had been burned recently. Paper leaves a much different residue than wood. Still, the stones were warm—which meant somebody'd been in residence here in the not-so-distant past.

After about an hour of continued fruitlessness, Boris decided I'd seen enough. He picked up an unopened decanter bottle of Remy Martin Louis XIII cognac from the crudely painted rustic pine

---

[2]Despite all promises and treaties to the contrary, the Chinese are still making hundreds of millions of dollars from pirated compact disks. They manufacture bogus CDs in China, then ship 'em via a clandestine pipeline that runs through North Korea, Japan, and Brazil.

sideboard, smacked me on the back, then put his hand in the small of my back to guide me out through what was left of the front door frame. "Come on, Dicky," he said. "Nothing here for us. Let's go get drunk."

"Give me a few more minutes, huh?"

He sighed in resignation and saluted me with the cognac bottle. "Okay, okay, boychik, take as long as you want—we'll be outside."

I gave him an upturned thumb. "Thanks, Boris." Now I was able to be specific about what had been troubling me about the place. The surveillance photos had indicated movement. We'd assumed that people were coming to call on Andrei. Now I realized that premise was flawed. They'd been cleaning the fucking place out. Shutting it down. Taking evidence away. But evidence of what? The dacha had been swept clean.

Maybe. But maybe not. There was no way I was going to leave until I'd turned this place inside out. I've been doing this kind of work for a long time—and I know that it is virtually impossible to sweep a place absolutely clean. Remember this fact, because you're going to see it again. It is a truth: bad guys always leave something behind. A single shard of evidence. A fragment. A sliver. A shred. A fleck. But you cannot find it if you are rushed. So you must take your time and be methodical. And then, if you have gone over everything three times and the location is still absolutely vacuum clean, then you know you're dealing with real professionals, and you react accordingly.

I found my evidentiary fragment in the dented, tin-lined copper washtub that served as a log bin, next to the stone fireplace. I pulled out the chunks of wood and set them on the floor. A half sheet of wood-stained scrap paper they were probably going to use as kindling lay covered with wood chips and other detritus in the tub's tin bottom. I turned the page over to discover it was a blurry photocopy of the upper half of an Air France *lettre de transport aerien*—an air shipment waybill. The sheet bore the waybill number 059-5391-1572, but no date. The shipment was addressed to a Limon, Limited, in Mustique, the British Grenadines, by way of a Banque Lasalle in Geneva, Switzerland.

The original sender's name wasn't legible. But the shipment had been represented and insured through a company called Lantos & Cie, Paris XVI. The value: just over five-and-a-half million francs— about a million and a quarter dollars. The shipment was comprised of—and here I quote to you: "components for environmental testing chamber, crane, crane accessories, trollies, hot-freon tanks, heating tubes." Total weight, 24,500 kilos—just about 54,000 pounds.

An incongruous coincidence, huh—an Air France waybill used as kindling in a Russian dacha. Yeah, well in my long and ding-filled career, bub, there have been very few instances of coincidence, incongruous or otherwise. What the hell did a company named after a Spanish (or Italian) lemon need an environmental testing chamber for in Mustique, British Grenadines, anyway?

And who the hell were the Banque Lasalle of Geneva and Lantos & Cie of Paris XVI? These, I knew, were questions that I would spend the next few days answering to my own degree of personal and professional satisfaction. Why? Because they were associated with Andrei Yudin. And Andrei Yudin was connected to the death of my shipmate Paul Mahon. I see you out there. You are saying that the chain of evidence here was very tenuous. Well, you're right. It was. But it was all the evidence I had—and so I'd follow it until I couldn't go any further.

I peered down at the paper in my hand. From the old creases, it looked as if the photocopy had been folded in half horizontally, then into precise vertical thirds—maybe stuck in someone's suit pocket. It had been torn along the center crease when it was discarded. I refolded the sheet and stuck it in the pocket that already held the matchbook. I replaced the firewood in its tub, and headed for the door.

Yeah, I'd have a cognac or two with Boris and Misha on the way back to town—just to be sociable. But I had other things on my mind tonight besides doing shots of five-hundred-dollar-a-bottle booze. I wanted to check up on the folks, locations, and supplies mentioned in the waybill and amalgamate that information with certain other documentational slivers I had in my possession. I also wanted to goose things along by taking a gander at the Moscow club scene—in particular, a spot called the Dynamo.

Chapter

2

I REALIZED JUST AFTER I GOT BACK TO THE HOTEL THAT A FORAY TO THE Dynamo would have to wait a day. First, Boris and Misha had insisted on finishing the whole damn bottle of cognac. So we did. And since they were the ones with the car, I'd been trapped, wasting precious time, sitting in the dacha's deserted courtyard sucking on Louis Treize. Why didn't I protest? I'd considered it. But after today's security lapse, I wasn't about to say anything to anybody—not even the barest hint that I might have come upon something. Besides, it was long past 2130. And what was 2130, you ask? That was the military time written inside the matchbook cover. I knew that by the time I cleaned myself up, got dressed, and (more to the point) found the place, it would probably be closed—or closing down—for the night. Besides, I had no idea whatsoever what precise day the time referred to. It could have been tonight. But it could also have been two weeks ago—or two months.

Not to mention the fact that there were more immediate problems to attend to. Like my soggy weapons, which had to be cleaned, lubed, and stored in the heavy steel diplomatic lockbox we'd brought with us and kept under the bed. My lacerations, lumps, sprains, and bruises needed first aid, too.

But I also wanted to put the Air France waybill in some sort of perspective. It was, I realized instinctively, one small piece of a very

28

large puzzle. I had a few other pieces of the puzzle in my hands right now—the papers, notes, and pictures that I'd removed from Paul's desk and safe. If you examined each one separately, they presented no greater significance—no "big picture." I, however, had learned how to peruse, study, and evaluate evidence from a great teacher. Arleigh Secrest, the last of the warrior CNOs, who was murdered by Islamic fundamentalists, showed me the path to enlightenment.

Ah, tadpoles—you are clamoring out there. You want to hear the old master's words. Well, I will repeat them for you.

"Intelligence organizations are stovepipes," CNO Secrest had said in his wise, simple declarative fashion. "Treat them as such, and you will persevere."

And why, Master Marcinko-san, are intelligence organizations like stovepipes?

Because, tadpole, they stand parallel to one another, and the smoke (and mirrors) inside them go only one direction: up.

First, the parallel principle. CIA people report only to CIA people. DIA people report only to DIA people. State Department people report only to State Department people. Nobody pools information. Moreover, Christians In Action, which is what SEALs call the CIA, doesn't *want* to share any of its sources and methods with DIA, the State Department, or anyone else. Why? Because it is afraid it will get ripped off—that other agencies will steal its agents as well as its secrets. Now, the logic of that outlook escapes me. Why DIA or State would want to steal an agent like Manny Noriega from the Agency is something I cannot understand. King Hussein of Jordan, okay. The late Anwar el-Sadat of Egypt, sure. Guys like them are real assets, because they run countries. But most of the agents recruited by CIA overseas are, to put it bluntly (and kindly), scumbags.

For its part, DIA and State are convinced that CIA is riddled with moles. *They* won't share information because they believe whatever they tell the CIA goes straight to our enemies. Now, while there is some hyperbole to this outlook, I can't argue too strongly against it, given the CIA's recent history of fiascoes, busts, bombs, turkeys, and goatfucks. Are you getting the picture?

You are? Good—then let's add the other stovepipe element. Smoke—and intelligence—both rise—just like the hot air out of which they are all too often composed. Now, the more refined—or rarefied—intelligence is, the fewer people get to see it. That may be all right for strategic planning, but it doesn't help poor tactical assholes like me, who need to know things sooner rather than later. During the Gulf War, for example, the generals in Norm Schwarzkopf's bunker all knew where most of Saddam Hussein's mobile Scud missiles were. But by the time that information was trickled back down the line to the knuckle-dragging Scud-hunters in the field, the missiles had moved on.

Okay. Now, what CNO Secrest preached to me was to go around the goddamn stovepipes—to obtain every bit of intelligence I could lay my hands on, borrow, purloin, or appropriate. Then, he told me, "Overlay it. Look for patterns."

And that is exactly what I intended to do with the material from Paul's office tonight. In fact, the scope of the documents I'd found made me wonder whether Paul had been taken under CNO's inculcational wing the same way I was. Paul had never mentioned anything about CNO Secrest to me—but then, I hadn't said anything to him either.

Let's take a look at what I had in hand. There were the memos on the Russian Mafiya that I've already told you about. There were some miscellaneous papers—including the receipt I now realized was from the Dynamo, on which Paul had written the word *Yudin.* There was a Post-It on which Paul had written the words *Sting, Mafiya—cover, Agcy/Mos,* and *Call KR.* What it had originally been attached to, I had no idea. There were a handful of unidentified pictures—like the one of Andrei Yudin. There were news magazine clips (one was a story about U.S. Customs agents tracking down a businessman in suburban Virginia for shipping accelerometers to Jordan. Accelerometers, in case you don't know, are used to measure nuclear detonations. Jordan don't need 'em. And guess what? The BIQ—that's businessman-in-question—had a Russian-sounding surname.

There was a DIA memo detailing break-ins at a dozen NATO installations, from the HQ building in Brussels to air bases in Italy and Turkey, over the past five months. Remote sensors had been discovered near perimeter fences; electronic jammers had been tried on secure communications networks. The NATO security force had been at THREATCON (CONdition) Charlie for six weeks—which is category three (of four), and was getting stressed.

A copy of a two-month-old Department of State e-mail message between the assistant secretary of state for legislative affairs and the assistant secretary of state for politico-military affairs classified SECRET-SENSITIVE chronicled a quartet of false flag recruitments of low- and mid-ranking embassy employees that had been uncovered recently. A false flag is when the recruiting agent makes you think he's working for a friendly government, when in fact he is in fact working for a hostile power. The Israelis, incidentally, have enjoyed great success with false flag recruitments in the Arab world. Anyway, the State E-mail bemoaned the budgetary consequences if Congress ever found out. A communications clerk in Vienna, the DCM's secretary in Paris, a junior consular officer in the visa section of the London embassy, and an administrative section chief in Rome had all been discovered passing documents or papers to folks they thought were American counterintelligence officers, but who had turned out to be impostors. Who the real bad guys were, State had no idea—but somebody was out there, trolling and prowling.

Another State memo, equally classified, noted that "thrice in the last thirteen-week cycle" (I guess that's the bureaucratic way of saying once a month) the U.S. Mission to the Organization for Economic Cooperation and Development, known as USOECD, had been the subject of an (let me quote this one for you, too) "unauthorized access during light-duty time sequencing, probably nocturnal." In English, that means that some asshole broke in over the weekend, at night, when nobody was looking. And where had the break-in occurred? Paris—home of the Air France waybill, and Lantos & Cie. The memo did not state something that I knew: the building housing the USOECD is also the location of the Pentagon's largest European counterterrorism operations center.

There was an internal memo (it was stamped "unclassified with removal of Tab A") from the technology directorate of the Defense Technology Security Administration, properly acronymed DTSA, but pronounced and written by most folks at the Pentagon as "DITSA." The memo, which had been written by the chief of the Strategic Trade Technology Division, recounted an eyewitness in an unspecified Middle Eastern country stating that he had seen, during a visit to a metallurgical plant, a metal-casting furnace being unloaded from a shipping container bearing French and Swiss markings. The eyewitness stated that the furnace had "a parenthetical legend underneath indicating it had a charge capacity of 25 kilograms and a vacuum capability of 10^{-5} BAR." The last five words had been highlighted. And below, in Paul's handwriting, was the phrase "Dual use—nuke refinement—embargoed IL 1080 (d)."

Okay, tadpole, what do you make of all of these fragments?

They make no sense at all, Master Marcinko-san. It is simply a confusing collection of documents, collected randomly, and stuck in a file for convenience sake.

Ah, tadpole, let us go back to the ancients. The *Ch'i* dialogue described by the great warrior T'ai Li'ang in the seminal *Li'ang Hsi-Huey* asks, "How can reality be known?" The answer, responds the Master, is simple: "To succeed in The Way is to know all things. The significance of the pebble is no less than that of the boulder. Reality is what is."

You are giving me gibberish and pseudowarrior psychobabble bullshit, Master Marcinko-san.

If you believe that, tadpole, you are unworthy pond scum and you have no right to be in my temple. Now listen—and learn.

- Item: the fragment of waybill I found at the dacha mentioned France and Switzerland. There were French and Swiss markings on the container mentioned in the DTSA memo. Happenstance? Coincidence?
- Item: Paul, a submariner whose degree at Annapolis had been in nuclear engineering, believed the material mentioned in the DITSA memo was embargoed nuclear dual-use technology, which meant the furnace could be used for either commercial or military purposes.
- Item: the news magazine clip mentioned accelerometers— another nuclear-weapons industry device. Happenstance? Coincidence?
- Item: the half dozen more-than-a-year-old newspaper clips in the files showed that the Russian Mafiya had already been caught trying to smuggle nuclear weapons to the West. Paul was making notes and organization charts on the mafiya. Happenstance? Coincidence?
- Item: Like most SpecWarriors, I am good at breaking into places. My training allows me to come and go virtually at will—and leave no tracks. I only leave tracks when I am probing a target and want to see how the security forces react. So the DIA memo detailing the incursions at NATO

installations told me that somebody was nosing around—and probing the readiness of the security force. The State messages told me the same thing: somebody—maybe the mafiya, maybe the Russkie military, or maybe a combination of the two—was testing our counterintelligence capabilities (e.g., the false flag recruitments), probing our security apparatus (e.g., the incursions at U.S. and NATO facilities), and eliminating anyone who discovered that this-all was part of a coordinated effort (e.g., murdering Paul). Now here is a lesson for all of you aspiring SpecWarriors out there: you generally do not test, probe, and kill unless you are about to go on a major offensive.

Now all of the above, when taken into consideration with what I'm about to tell you, made me nervous. What am I going to tell you? It is that the Russkies had taken a huge step backward in the most recent parliamentary elections. Remember? The Communists took more than 20 percent of the vote, the ultranationalists got another 11 percent, and the fringe parties—the real crazies—received 6 percent. Coalesced, that comes to 37 percent of the Duma. The progressives were running scared these days—and they were making concessions. So, I had a troubled and instinctual premonition that these probes were neither random nor unplanned but part of a bigger, covert scheme that Paul had somehow uncovered a part of.

Why? Because Paul had understood the often ambiguous dynamics of this convoluted, contradictory, confusing country as well as anybody. Moreover, the simple fact that he had put all of these seemingly miscellaneous fragments in one manila folder told me that he was looking at them as parts of a whole.

And tonight, I get to add the Air France waybill to Paul's folder. Why? Because I think it belongs there. Said document tells me that there are concrete French and Swiss connectiors—the Swiss bank Lasalle; the Paris-based company called Lantos & Cie. And, given the evidence already in the folder, it means that the equipment therein listed—widgets whose applications I have no idea about—is probably going to be similar to the dual-use widgets Paul wrote about.

Okay, okay—I hear you out there. You're asking me what it all means.

Answer: I don't know yet. But if you know me, you know that I'm gonna find out. My friend and his family were killed because of it.

I eased into the room, turned on the single bare lightbulb that hung from the ceiling, dropped my weapons on the bed, and started to pull off my still-damp (and thoroughly frigid) clothes when I saw a small pile of messages, all of them, I noted, marked URGENT or MOST URGENT, sitting on the small, shabby table in the small, shabby third-floor room I shared with Machinist's Mate First Class Stevie Wonder, who groaned, rolled over, and looked upon me with a nasty expression.

Ah, yes. You ask, perceptive readers that you are, why the old Rogue Warrior was residing in a small, shabby hotel room. I shall tell you. We were here because the embassy's acting deputy assistant sphincter to the acting assistant deputy colon to the acting chief administrative asshole in charge of housing had stashed my guys and me in a small, shabby, fourth-class hotel, located just off the twelve-lane-wide Garden Ring Road, a twenty-minute walk from the huge mustard (or puke, depending on your philosophical stance) and white U.S. Embassy compound.

Now, there are guest quarters aplenty inside that walled compound. In the heyday of the Cold War, nobody wanted official delegations staying at Moscow's hotels, where they were at the mercy of KGB eavesdropping, honey traps—those were the legendary Soviet sex enticements, targeted at visiting businessmen, politicos, and military attachés—and other nefarious activities. And when I say eavesdropping, I'm being diplomatic, if you catch my drift. I mean, we're not talking about your everyday radio transmitter in the flower vase or the high-frequency tap on the telephone. I'm talking about impertinent, rude, surly bugs here. Cameras in the showers to catch you whacking off. Cameras above the beds to catch you *in flagrante delicto* (which, those of you who read *Green Team* and *Task Force Blue* know, means flagrant pussy licting). And microphones everywhere—cars, trains, elevators, hallways—you name it.

Here's another piece of Cold War trivia for you folks out there. The KGB used to position mikes next to the urinals in public bathrooms at the hotels where platoons of diplomats stayed during the big ministerial sessions, and also in all the pissoirs at the Foreign Ministry building. Why? Because when diplomats take their drain-the-lizard breaks during negotiations at the Metropol, the Intourist, or the Rossiya hotels, or head for the head at the Foreign Ministry, they tend to (a) go in pairs, and (b) they tend to forget all about OPSEC, and whisper secrets whilst they whizz.

That ain't all, folks. If a real high-ranking VIP showed up, the KGB even bugged the johns—sluiced the water off the toilets so that fecal and urinalysis studies could be performed. Well, to be honest, *that* behavior was common practice all over the world. Christians in Action did the same thing when Nikita Khrushchev stayed at a Washington hotel back in the sixties. And what did they learn by their tough shit-detection? I can now reveal they discovered that he needed more fiber in his diet.

But I'm digressing. The bottom line here is that the embassy of the United States of America has ample guest space for official visitors. Currently, in fact, more than a dozen class-B rooms (for guests at or below FS-1 or GS-13), three class-As (for your FS-1s and GS-14s and 15s), and two ministerial-grade town house suites were vacant.

So, why is it that we didn't stay there, you want to know. Well, the answer is that *they*—they being the diplomats—obviously didn't want us Navy security types around. *They*, you see, wear bespoke suits, carry hundred-dollar pens (with which they write lots of polysyllabic, fifty-dollar words), and have manicured nails. We dress in early prole, tend to say *fuck* a lot, make our notes using stubby pencils, and do manual labor with our calloused hands. Allowing us accommodations inside the compound would have been like the Romanoffs inviting a bunch of grimy serfs from Narishkino sur Volga to stay at the Winter Palace.

Still fuzzy or confused? Then let me give you some additional background. And, as the old chiefs at Organized Chicken Shit (which is how I refer to Officers Candidate School, or OCS) used to tell us incipient ensigns, do not skip this material, because—as you will see—it has a good chance of becoming reasonably essential as the novel progresses.

Okay. If there is any caste system more insidious, noxious, or demeaning than the Navy's caste system, it is the State Department's caste system. In the Navy, there are the Annapolis grads— ring-knockers we call 'em—and there is everybody else. If you didn't go to the Academy, you are at an automatic disadvantage when it comes to assignments, promotions, and other career enhancements. Annapolis grads—think of 'em as Naval Academy Mafiosi—always look after one another. They do it whether they were friends at the Academy, or not. They do it simply because they are all part of the same ring-knocking fraternity, and they consider the rest of the world nothing but pond scum. That means outsiders like me are put at the end of a long, long line when the goodies are being passed out.

Of course, as a mustang—that is, an officer who came up through the enlisted ranks—I've learned how to deal with the ring-knockers. I do it the same way I did when I was a radioman first-class. I smile, and I grin, and I say, "Yes, sir." But I spell *sir* with a *c* and a *u*, and then I do exactly what the F-word I want to do. Or, if I have to be somewhat more devious, I employ the safety net of chiefs I've built over my career to thread my way around the caste system. And if that sub-tile Machiavellian tactic doesn't work, I will bust right through the motherfucking system and bore it a new goddamn asshole. Occasionally, you will recall, I have been known to do *that*, too.

It is harder to circumvent the folks at State, especially if I am operating outside CONUS, which is how SEALs commonly refer to the CONtinental United States. (We Frogs, incidentally, are not the only governmental types to engage in rampant acronymism. The Leader of the Free World is nymed POTUS by the Secret Service in all its message traffic. I've always found that term humorous sounding. I mean, somehow, POTUS doesn't quite have the same high-flown cachet that President Of The United States does. Moreover, that particular acronym lends itself to crude, rude, lewd, but nonetheless sometimes appropriate jokes.

Bill Clinton, who early on suffered a rash of what one of his press secretaries yclept "bimbo eruptions," was, for example, sarcastically referred to as IMPOTUS—the IMprobable President Of The United States—by his own Secret Service detail.) Anyway, my point is that it's harder to diddle the State system as an outsider. First, I don't have a safety net of chiefs at State, which puts me at a tactical disadvantage operationally. Second, the cookie pushers, which is how our heel-rocking, pocket-change jingling, cotton-fluff memo-writing diplomats are commonly known, *do* control their turf efficiently. Well, they should—because most of 'em are dyed-in-the-pinstripe bureaucrats. Professional apparatchiks in the worsted way. Anyway, when one be overseas and assigned to an embassy, one operates at their mercy. They control the access, the housing, the credentials, and all the other facets of life necessary to do business in a foreign land. And they do it in the sort of high-handed manner that makes one want to commit murder.

Overseas, these very same diplodinks, who during their infrequent Washington tours live in tract housing an hour-and-a-half commute from main State and whose idea of gourmet dining is Mickey D's or Wendy's big and juicy, now get spacious, government-furnished quarters, servants, entertainment allowances, and chauffeured cars. It gives all too many of 'em a case of the grandiose self-importants, which is the most dangerous symptom of the dread diplomatic disease affluenza.

Yeah, I know that there are probably some devoted, hardworking Foreign Service State Department types out there, doing the Nation's business overseas and helping keep the world safe for democracy. And when I finally meet one, you'll be the first to hear about it.

In the meanwhile, however, I have to spend most of my time overseas, *not* planning unconventional warfare against tangos or other bad guys. I have to spend most of my time and energy trying to work my way over, under, around, or through the State Department assholes who've thrown roadblocks up all around me.

Take my current situation. (Please—take it off my hands right now.) I'd been assigned to Moscow as the head of an NSMTT, a mouth-filling acronym that stands for Naval Security Mobile Training Team. As usual, the military was playing catch up. Since Paul's driver hadn't known how to react when the car was attacked, the powers that be had finally decided that perhaps it might be a good idea for a security team to go to Moscow and teach all the enlisted drivers about evasive and defensive driving techniques, countersurveillance, and other tradecraft that can save lives in hostile environments.

Let me give you a bit of background here. Diplomats have their own protective agency, the Diplomatic Security Service. It is a part of the State Department's Bureau of Diplomatic Security. DSS protects embassies. Its Regional Security Officers, or RSOs, oversee what goes on in their geographic regions. Teams from its MSD, or Mobile Security Division, come in-country to train local personnel in everything from SWAT-type assaults, to evasive driving skills, to street-smart antirape techniques. But DSS's bureaucratic responsibilities exist only between Twenty-first and Twenty-third, and C and D Streets, Northwest—that is to say, inside the State Department's doors. The panjandrums at the Department of State will explain this by saying that State, by its very charter, can neither protect nor train any U.S. military personnel assigned to an embassy.

So in Russia, the ambassador's driver and the DCM's driver (both of 'em Russians, or FNs—Foreign Nationals—in State Department parlance, I might add) had received extensive counterterrorism driver training from a visiting Department of State MSD within the past six months. The defense attaché's driver, however, was an American military personnel type. As such, she had not been eligible for that training—even though the senior trainer in the State Department's MSD had asked that she be allowed to join the group. Our old friend Bart Wyeth, the DCM, had rejected the request. Ludicrous? Of course. But that, friends, is life in the real world, where competing bureaucracies often cost lives.

Now that Paul was dead, however, the Navy woke up. Ah, said the system, perhaps we should send some folks to Moscow to teach the military drivers how to stay alive if they are attacked. My five men and I were the lucky FIQs, or folks in question.

Why us? Well, I could say it was because we're the best suited for the job. But, to be perfectly honest, we're here because Rear Admiral Kenneth Ross, the newly appointed Director of Operations, Plans, and Politico-Military Affairs in the office of the Deputy Chief of Naval Operations for Plans, Policy, and Operations (let's just call him the DOPPMA/DCNOPPO, okay?) insisted.[3]

Twenty-four hours after Paul was killed, Ken assigned me to lead a six-man NSMTT to Moscow on a Designation Gold priority. In other words, he wanted us there yesterday. The ostensible reason was to train the military personnel in ways to stay alive. The real reason (remember, I told you I'd get to this sooner or later) was that Ken Ross had been getting backchannel messages from Paul Mahon that worried him. When I asked for specifics, Kenny told me they'd be in Paul's safe, gave me the combination, and ordered me to keep every bit of information I discovered on a close-hold basis. Paul had been working on his own, Ken Ross said, developing intelligence he'd hinted was critical to the Russian-U.S. relation-

---

[3]Kenny Ross and I had worked together once before. As the captain of the USS *Humpback,* a nuclear attack submarine that had been retrofitted as a SpecWar vessel, he had watched me and my Red Cell team as we infiltrated North Korean waters and took down a supply ship in Chongjin Harbor.

ship. But he'd been killed before he was able to pass on any precise data.

Despite my Designation Gold priority, and Rear Admiral Ross's concerns, it took another two and a half weeks before we were able to wheels up. The reason, friends, is twofold. First, it takes time to obtain diplomatic passports and ask the Russkies to stamp the sorts of diplomatic visas that would allow us to bring all kinds of normally verboten materials into the former Soviet Union. Second (and perhaps more relevant), the system's wheels grind exceedingly slow when there are turf wars to be fought—and the Department of State, or more specifically, AMEMB (AMerican EMBassy) Moscow did not particularly want an NSMTT anywhere near their home field.

AMEMB's feelings became obvious from the moment we arrived. Everyone from the top-ranked diplomats on the ninth floor, to the working stiffs who run the embassy's security, made certain we knew that they didn't want us around. Why not? Because I guess we six SEAL serfs represented an outside threat to the embassy's sovereignty. Much the same thing happened when I ran Red Cell, a group of fourteen shooters—the best of the best—I recruited from SEAL Team Six. Red Cell's overt mission was to probe the security conditions at Navy installations all over the world. (Our covert mission I will expound on when I'm not in a hotel room that might be bugged.) Anyway, back in the mideighties, it occurred to my then-boss, Admiral Ace Lyons, that Navy installations were vulnerable to terrorism. He told me to form a unit that would help base commanders assess their vulnerabilities, and plug the holes. It was a great idea. But when we actually took the field, I discovered that the vast majority of COs didn't want any "help" from Red Cell.

In fact, we were perceived as a more dangerous threat than the real terrorists. Why? Because, when we penetrated a base's security (and we always did), the can't cunts in charge took it personally. Instead of learning from us, they took our report and our suggestions, round-filed 'em, and breathed huge sighs of relief when our plane was finally wheels up. They believed, you see, that their fitreps would suffer because of Red Cell. And bad fitreps mean no promotions. And in today's Navy, promotion is more important than counterterrorism, right?

Ditto now, ditto Moscow. We were treated like personae non fucking gratae. Which meant *we* had to be watched carefully. Our quarters were far removed from the embassy compound. The minute we came through the gates, we had all been assigned permanent chaperons. We'd been given passes with a big red *V*— visible at ten yards—on them, the better to identify us as outsiders. We were not allowed to walk the embassy halls unescorted. Our conversations were monitored. Our schedules were rigorously scrutinized. Obviously, my men and I were considered more dangerous than Russkie spies.

So, of the dozen messages awaiting me, eight of them were rockets from the nasty man who ran the embassy. No, they were not from the ambassador. Ambassadors are all too often political appointees these days. They know nothing of statecraft, or history. They have bought their jobs by fund-raising for the president's campaign, or slipping him some kind of other under-the-table help. That was the case here. The ambassador to the Russian Federation, Throckmorton Limpdick Numbnuts the Fourth, or some similar moniker, was a nice enough fellow—a billionaire from the awl biz, or bond markets, or whatever-the-fuck—who had his own private Gulfstream III, which he used to commute to Saint Andrews, Scotland, every other week or so to play eighteen holes of golf with his pal Prince Charles and bring back two or three cases of twenty-five-year-old single-malt Islay Scotch, which he drank *sans* ice, in a Baccarat crystal tumbler, with a splash of branch water, commencing at 0900. Yes, 0900. Diplomacy? Don't be silly. But did he ever give great parties.

Meanwhile, the real business of realpolitiks in Russia was carried on by the rezident éminence grise, the DCM, which, as I explained not so long ago, means deputy chief of mission.

And you already know about the DCM here. Nutshell: he's an asshole, and. . . . Hey, do *you* hear all that commotion in the hallway? It's that dweeb of an editor, screaming he's heard enough fucking backstory already. Okay, okay, okay, every now and then he's actually right about something. So—let's move on.

I pulled off my still-damp clothes, stood under the lukewarm shower for ten minutes, toweled off, applied Betadine where necessary, then pulled on a pair of running shorts, donned my half glasses, sat on the edge of the narrow bed, a towel on my lap, fieldstripped and cleaned my weapons and magazines, lubed them carefully, rubbed them dry, and then cleaned and dried each round of ammunition I'd carried with me. The submachine gun and USP pistol went into the steel lockbox.

In exchange, I pulled out a slim-framed P7 9mm autoloader, two eight-round magazines, and a well-broken-in small-of-the-back holster for daytime wear. I filled the magazines with Winchester's Black Talon ammunition, loaded one, chambered a round, then topped off. Yes, Black Talon is restricted for civilian use these days. But then, as you know, I ain't no civilian.

That done, I arranged the messages into their proper chronological order, and scanned them. The first one queried where I was and why I hadn't checked in with the embassy security officer in more than six hours. Each subsequent message, delivered, I noted, on the precise quarter-hour, was more pompously hysterical than the preceding one. The final one—which had been received at about the same time I was discovering the Air France waybill at Andrei Yudin's dacha—demanded that I present myself at Bart's office first thing in the morning to explain, "in microscopic detail," my actions of the past twenty-four hours. "It has been brought to my attention that you have exceeded your authority and mission parametrics," the message concluded. "Therefore, I must be brought up-to-date immediately in order to evaluate what consequences should be undertaken." Have you ever heard such fucking gibberish, friends?

Stevie Wonder, who had wrapped himself up in the room's only extra blanket and tucked himself securely into bed, was wide awake now, studying a CIA street map of the Moscow suburbs so he'd know where to take his pair of Navy drivers for their defensive countermeasures instruction.

He watched my reactions as I went through my message traffic perusal with characteristic Wonder amusement. "I guess Bart's the nervous type," he said. He gave my mashed face and black-and-blue-splotched, Betadine-accented body a critical once-over and grinned at me. "Geez—what the hell happened to you? You look like you've been through the kielbasa grinder."

He knew exactly what had happened to me and so he was being a smartass. "Fuck you," I said by way of reply.

He shrugged and swiveled his head in his trademark right-left-right, left-right-left imitation of . . . Stevie Wonder. "Hey, no pain, no gain, *Dolboeb.*"

I was gratified to see that he'd learned to say *dickhead* in Russian. Wonder always treats me with such respect. Well, he's allowed to be irreverent. He's killed almost as many Japs, which is how we SEALs refer to bad guys, as I have. More to the *pernt,* as they say in his part of Noo Yawk, he has pulled my singed Slovak butt out of a bunch of fires. My extended middle finger told him that he was still Number One with me. "Yeah, well tonight I had a lot of goddamn pain but no fucking gain. Our friend wasn't home. He skipped. Clean, too, from the look of it."

I was leery about using proper names or virtually any other specifics in a Moscow hotel room. All those years of Cold War paranoia, y'see, have had their cumulative effect on me. I still have a problem trusting Russkies and anything to do with them—you saw the OMON colonel and his brand-new Rolex. Not to mention the fact that most Moscow tourist hotels still have the bugs that were installed by the old KGB as a way of targeting the odd agent of influence every now and then. The KGB loved agents of influence. They were businessmen, artists, politicians, and journalists recruited to covertly push Moscow's line all over the world. Anyway, do those chandelier mikes, phone taps, and parabolic pickups still work? Probably not—but then, I wasn't about to take any chances.

Wonder let the map and his magnifying glass drop onto his lap and pulled the blanket up around his shoulders. "So, nu, what's next?"

I pointed at the light fixture and gave him the silent signal for We'll talk later. Then I said, "Dealing with all this message traffic crap."

"Cool," he said, pronouncing it *"kuul."* He went back to his map.

I took the messages and tore them into little pieces. "There," I said, "all done."

Wonder glanced up and saw me pulling on dry clothes. He put the map and glass down, groaned audibly, looked at his own clothes, which in true, chaotic, Dennis the Menace fashion were heaped haphazardly atop a creaky chair.

He gave me an RDL—a Real Dirty Look, pulled himself out of bed, unwrapped himself from his precious blanket, slipped into his skivvies, his T-shirt, and as thick a pair of socks as he could find, stuck a leg into a rumpled pair of jeans and slipped an S.O.B. holster on his belt. He dropped the magazine out of his compact Glock 27 9mm onto the bed, pointed the muzzle in a safe direction, unchambered the round in the barrel, reset the mag, chambered a new round, then released the magazine, topped it off, slid it back into the pistol's butt, and placed the now cocked and locked weapon into its holster. *"Fuuuck you,"* he said, searching through the clothes pile for a sweater.

As an ex-Recon Marine who has seen more than his share of the cold, wet boonies, Wonder really hates the great outdoors.

0251. I rousted the rest of the team and after a suitable litany of grousing we headed out. At first, our path was seemingly random as we cut down one, two, three, four narrow side streets, walked past the rear entrance of the Minsk Hotel, then strolled around the corner and past the Baku, an Azeri restaurant that served great Turkish food. In the old days—pre-perestroika according to Boris—Baku was where fashionable young Kommies from the old Komsomol used to eat. From there we headed north, checked our six as we passed the Moscow Cinema, then began circling through a series of narrow, one-way streets.

Yes, we were checking for surveillance. Once I'd determined that no one was following, we cut back the way we'd come, and began walking eastward alongside the twelve lanes of the Garden Ring Road, our shoulders hunched against the moist, cold wind that blew in our faces. The traffic was light—an occasional Mercedes blew by, its back windows curtained. There were a few trucks, their diesel engines grumbling in the cold, and a couple of Zhiguli police cars, blue lights flashing. But the sidewalk was deserted.

Master Chief Hospitalman Doc Tremblay's right arm rubbed up against my left. I've known Doc since I was a wet-behind-the-balls tadpole, getting my butt busted by Chief Everett Emerson Barrett's big boondockers in his Second-to-None Platoon at UDT 21. To my right, Stevie Wonder, whose real name as you probably know is neither Stevie nor Wonder, muttered rude imprecations about my parentage as he marched with his hands in his pockets. He was doubly upset: first, because he was out here in the cold, and second, because he'd left his gloves in the room.

Just behind Wonder, Duck Foot Dewey's short legs churned to keep up the pace Doc and I had set. Duck Foot—given name Allen—is a barrel-chested hunter from Maryland's Eastern Shore. When he's not stalking geese, grouse, doves, or deer, he's hunting tangos with me. Duck Foot was flanked by the rest of the menagerie I'd brought to Moscow. On his starboard side was Gator Shepard; on his port, the Rodent.

As we walked, we talked. I gave them a quick sitrep on the evening's largely unproductive enterprise. There were groans when I described OMON's clumsy tactics. Gator Shepard's pace quickened. He nudged his way between Wonder and me. "Do you trust Boris?"

It was a good question. I'd been put in touch with Boris Makarov by a man I *do* trust (you will meet him shortly). He'd vouched that Boris was a good guy—one of the few good guys in the Moscow police. But there are good guys you trust, and there are good guys you don't trust. For example, I hadn't shown Boris and Misha either the matchbook (if anyone knew where the Dynamo was it would be them), or the waybill.

To be honest, I'd been uncharacteristically uneasy since we'd arrived here; anxious and restive in a way that was new, unexpected, and frankly unsettling. Being in Russia was like being on an alien planet. I have always thought there was no place on earth I could go, and not fit in. Until, that is, I came here.

The fact that I felt as stuck out as your proverbial sore *khuy* bothered me. Because if you feel like an outsider, you are going to act like one—and that is going to put you at a tactical disadvantage.

I'd run the possibles without finding a solution. Finally, I rationalized that, since I'd spent virtually my entire professional life trying to hunt and kill the Soviet Bear, my us-or-them mind-set would naturally be hard to change, and therefore I'd just have to live with it.

So I told Gator the truth about trusting Boris. "I don't know yet," is what I said. And I didn't.

By the time we circled back toward the hotel, I had passed around the matchbook—no one had heard of the Dynamo Club, which told me it wasn't anyplace frequented by the Americans in Moscow. The guys also pored over the air waybill.

Wonder kept it the longest. "So?" I asked.

He did a passable Jack Benny. "I'm thinking, I'm thinking." We walked on. "Hot freon tanks," he said. "I've seen that before. The question is, where." His face scrunched up in concentration. "Iraq, I think," he finally said.

"Iraq?"

"When I was there on the UN inspection team." About five years ago, Wonder, whose nominal job cover was machinist's mate first class at the Washington Navy Yard, had been slipped undercover into Baghdad by DIA—the Defense Intelligence Agency—to monitor the Iraqi nuclear program. He'd gone as part of a United Nations inspection team. He therefore knew a lot about nuclear facilities, and how they are put together. "Hot freon is what they call dual-use technology, Dickhead. That means it can be used for legitimate chemical processing—like in high-quality metal refining. But hot freon can also be used to clean the high-speed vacuum centrifuges they use to make nuclear weapons grade plutonium." He scratched his chin like a twelfth grader pondering a geometry question. "From what I can recall, it's a critical part of the final refining process."

That was not welcome news. "How do you know whether the freon is being used militarily or not?"

"You don't. That's why you have to watch carefully where it goes."

"That fits," I said. "Paul was looking at dual-use shipments, too. And the mafiya."

"Makes sense," Doc said. "Russian organized crime's been caught trying to sell surplus Soviet nukes—so why not the technology that makes the weapons, too."

"Besides," Wonder interjected, "the drop point is fake."

"How do you know?"

"Because Mustique is about five square miles in size. There's no industry. It's a private resort—maybe a hundred or so million-dollar homes and one hotel."

How Boy Wonder knows this sort of trivia I cannot fathom. But I am grateful that he does.

"Which means . . ."

"Which means," he continued somewhat pedantically, "that this"—he shook the waybill under my sore nose—"is a phony."

I round-robined the guys to see what embassy gossip they had picked up and was happy to hear they'd each managed some bit of helpful recon. Duck Foot had no specifics but nonetheless perceived something was awry. His instinctual hunter's sensibilities were disturbed. The vibes around the embassy, he said, were bad. He wasn't the only one to notice. Morale among the Marine guards was low, Wonder said. Lots of resentment, and not a lot of discipline. The gunny in charge was a weak s.o.b. who deferred to the powers that be. Wonder shook his head dejectedly. This wasn't the Corps he knew and loved.

According to Gator, who is an ex-cop and attuned to law-enforcement's distinctive gestalt, things weren't much better in the LEGAT, or LEGal ATtaché's, office. Gator and his lowly FS-3 (Foreign Service Grade Three) political officer escort had stopped by the cafeteria for a cup of weak coffee and sat two tables away from the FBI special agent who was posted to Moscow as the embassy LEGAT. Gator had made small talk with his minder—and listened as the disgruntled gumshoe complained to a fellow diplomat that it was getting harder and harder to do his job because of the fucking ninth floor's interference. The ninth floor was where the ambassador and DCM had their offices.

From my aft port side, Rodent chirped that the second class petty officer he'd been teaching countersurveillance techniques to had waited until they were alone on the street, then he confided that Paul's driver—the one who'd been killed—had told him Paul was getting a lot of flak from the DCM about his intelligence work in nonmilitary areas. "He said that Terry-Ann—that's the dead driver, Skipper—overheard the admiral and his wife talking one night, and that Becky Mahon told the admiral he should cut Bart Wyeth off at the knees—complain to Washington about him before things got out of hand."

Now, remember I said I'd explain Red Cell's covert mission when it was all clear? We're getting close to our hotel now, so let me give it to you fast. It goes like this: Red Cell's security assessment mission was a cover for its real assignment: active counterterrorism. While one contingent of Red Cell shooters did the security training, another—much smaller—could slip off and neutralize the bad guys. It didn't happen every time we went on the road. But it happened often enough (and was so effective that no one ever caught on) to make all the headaches caused by C²COs (those loveable Can't Cunt COs) worthwhile.

Why do I tell you this? It is because the same dynamic was in place now. My guys were doing official NSMTT training. By the numbers. And, I can add with justifiable pride, they were doing a great job, teaching the military personnel how to stay safe in this potentially hostile environment.

And while they taught, I'd gone hunting.

Now, however, it was time to expand our covert activities. I had a slim lead on Paul's killers, and I wanted to exploit it in the few days we had left here.

A light snow began to fall as we strolled and made our plans. Doc, Gator, Duck Foot, and Rodent would finish out the training cycle full-time, Wonder would do double duty, and I would work the stealth side of the house.

Yes, they complained that I'd be having all the fun. And yes, they bitched and pissed and moaned about their sorry lot in life. And I had to grant them their point: it *is* more fun to hunt than to train. But if we were to be successful here—and I was willing to accept no less—then they would have to do their jobs while I did mine. Let's all say this mantra together: *Thou hast not to like it—thou hast just to do it.*

Besides, they'd get ample time to play. Tomorrow night, we'd all go out and enjoy ourselves at a place called the Dynamo, sometime after 2130.

Chapter

3

THE LIGHT SNOW HAD TURNED TO A HEAVY, INSISTENT, BONE-chilling sleet by 0600, when the alarm in my head went off and I got up from my short combat nap. I pulled the curtain aside, and peered down into the hotel's sooty courtyard, barely able to make out the dirty ice crust forming on the brickwork four stories below. I put my fingers to the window and cracked it a couple of inches higher to let in some fresh air. It was well below zero out there—perfect weather for an invigorating day on the Moscow streets.

Wonder's bed was already made. No maid service for him. He always did his bed himself—Marine-style. You could bounce a damn quarter off the blankets, too. I knew he was already long gone. His pretraining assignment today was to locate, then recon, the Dynamo club and its environs, so we'd be well prepared for the evening's festivities. Given the weather, and the fact that his cold weather boots were back in the States, he was probably cursing me in eight or nine languages right now. Well, he didn't have to like this morning's work—he just had to do it.

Suitably attired in a long, black nylon raincoat buttoned up to my throat, a visored Greek fishing cap hiding my French braid, and a pair of black nylon and Gore-Tex boots with thick rubber soles, I presented myself and my black-covered, gold-sealed, diplomatic passport at the embassy gate at 0646. First thing in the morning—

just as Bart's message had instructed me. By 0656, in the company of a DSS agent whose expression told me he'd rather be doing other things, I'd deposited an UNODIR—that's UNless Otherwise DIRected—message in a plain white sealed envelope on the secretary's desk that sat directly outside the DCM's office suite.

The message, which I'd written on a piece of scrap paper, told Dear Bart (he detested to be called Bart, so Bart, of course, is how I always addressed him) that since I had shown up as ordered, but he wasn't around when I'd come to call, I was not going to waste my time by sitting and waiting until he showed up. Instead, I was going to go out and do a series of security site surveys of a few locations throughout the city where U.S. military personnel might, at one point or another, find themselves, and that I'd check in with him later. Maybe.

It didn't really matter to me what he thought or did. To be perfectly honest, he had no chain-of-command authority over me (although he could make my life miserable in the bureaucratic sense so long as I remained in Moscow). Besides, I had a comfortable margin of time in which to operate this ay-em. I knew, you see, that my message would be read only after Bart's early-morning pile of urgent cables and other message traffic from State had been dealt with.

An explanation for those of you who haven't spent much time in American embassies: the United States is eight hours behind Moscow. The time difference means that a steady stream of comms—communications—had been arriving here throughout the night. Those messages would have to be handed out to each of the embassy's offices—political section, commercial section, LEGAT (that's the LEGal ATtaché, remember?), economic specialist, and so on, to deal with. Only after that had happened would Bart get to the extraneous material, which most certainly included the message from *moi*.

Even the location I left my missive—outside the DCM's suite—would delay his receiving it. You see, when the ambassador is away, the DCM moves from his own office into the ambassador's suite, so he can assume the ceremonial trappings of acting ambassador. The folks at State are big on protocol, and Bart was fond of the ambassador's huge office and all the panjandrumcy it represented. So by the time he got my little notandum I'd probably have finished my day's work and be heading out to visit the Dynamo.

Oops—that meant I wouldn't see dear Bart for a whole day. *C'est dommage.* You don't know what that phrase means? Well, look it up in the Glossary.

My dour DSS escort rode down the elevator in silence and walked me back to the outer gate without a word. I returned my visitor's pass to the saturnine Russian security guard with a friendly "thank you," eased around the metal detector so that the HK P7 pistol in its holster nestled against the small of my back didn't set the bells and whistles off, pushed open the bulletproof glass door, and hit the bricks.

Well, let's be honest. I hit the concrete. I scrunched northward toward the metro stop about three blocks away, ostensibly paying rapt attention to the ice on the sidewalk as I trudged.

It took all of half a minute to pick out the gumshoes on my tail. There were three of them—all lookalike males. That was a mistake. Women actually make great surveillants because they can change their outward appearance more easily than men can. You want to know why? Okay—it is because it's not unusual for a woman to carry a big handbag or tote that can hide a number of disguises. A man with a big knapsack or tote bag is more easily picked out of the crowd, and being picked out is a no-no when you are working surveillance. Thus endeth the lesson.

Meanwhile, the trio following me could have been in uniform. They wore matching black leather three-quarter-length coats, Russian fur hats—extra large, and size fourteen galoshes. There were bulges—radios, cellular phones, or pistols, perhaps—in their pockets. I dubbed my retinue Vynkenski, Blynkenski, and Nodyev. Were they Russians or Americans? If Russkies, were they official or mafiosi? Who cared? Not me, certainly.

We convoyed through slush to the Krasnopresnenskaya metro stop. I slalomed my way through the small army of grandmothers, pensioners, and other poor souls gathered at the mouth of the subway station, shopping bags filled with pencils, hair bands, old teakettles, worn sneakers, and old clothes to sell. I galumphed down the stairs to the Koltsevaya line, flashed my monthly pass at the barrier, and continued onto the crowded platform. Three minutes later the train arrived, and we all climbed on together— one watcher elbowed his way onto the far end of my car, the other pair caught flanking cars. At the Belorusskaya stop, I waited until the heavy metal doors were hissing closed, then used my hips and thighs to squeeze through them and out onto the platform at the very last instant.

Vynkenski, the man in my car, was left behind, trapped helpless in a clump of unyielding rush-hour Russkies. I resisted the temptation to give him a smile and a friendly finger as the train pulled out. Besides, I wasn't in the clear yet. My peripheral vision told me that my other traveling companions had made it onto the platform. I caught a glimpse of one of them as he radioed his stranded comrade. Oops, I guess I shouldn't be using *that* term anymore, huh?

One down, two to go. I made my way through the *correspondence* to the Zamoskvoretskaya line and caught the first southbound train, squeezed aboard, and rode, sardined, two stops to Puskinskaya station. I detrained, got my bearings, and headed for the *correspondence* that led toward the Chekhovskaya—it was a long walk down an ornately tiled tunnel crowded with bustling rush-hour commuters, panhandlers, and guitar-strumming buskers. Yeah, there were panhandlers and buskers—it's amazing what *kapitalizm* will do for a country, huh?

I was about two-thirds of the way there when I saw a familiar face approaching me. Doom on Dickie (which is the Vietnamese way of telling you I was in the process of being fuckee-fuckeed). The asshole I'd left behind at Belorusskaya station was coming straight in my damn direction, the hint of a shit-eating grin on his huffy-puffy Vynkenski puss. He'd gone one stop and caught a southbound train on a parallel line.

Have I mentioned that the Moscow subway is as good or better than any subway in the world? Well it is—and there are lots of trains, too. Vynkenski's easy progress was ample evidence of that. His pals had no doubt kept him apprised of my movement, and here he was—coming back just like a bad kopeck.

Now I had the full contingent on me again. Well, what's life without a little challenge every now and then, right? Besides, in a situation like this one, it is the quarry—that's me—not the surveillance team—that's them—who has the advantage. But there are more of them, you say. And they have radios. Phones. And maybe they have friends in cars shadowing us all on the streets above.

True, all true. But since I know where I am going, and I can take my own sweet time about getting there, I can run my pursuers ragged. They're the ones who have to stay alert. They're the ones who have to react—and despite the fact that we all know that we all know about one another, *they* still have to do their jobs without being obvious. And all of that, friends, is tiring. Tiring—shit, it is absofuckinglutely exhausting. I know, because I've been on the pursuing end of things often enough.

Still, as the quarry, there is certain tradecraft to be followed. All that movie fluff—the checking in store windows to keep an eye on your pursuers, or peeking around corners, or the quick reverse of direction on a crowded street—is just Hollywood horse puckey. It doesn't happen in the real world. Out here, there are three or four techniques that you can use to shake your shadows loose. Since I am currently, ah, engaged, I will elucidate, indoctrinate, and inculcate you about only one of them.

In fact, since the most effective way of teaching is by demonstration, I am now going to display the most effective ploy for shaking surveillance, so you can see for yourselves how well it works. The maneuver in question is known to the trade as "cleaning." To clean yourself, you enter a large and busy location that has many entrances and exits. Railroad stations are perfect for this exercise. So are department stores. Hotels are good, too—but not in totalitarian countries where the exits are all watched closely by the secret police. I prefer stores. When I commanded SEAL Team Six and Red Cell, we played "Take Me to the Cleaners Tag" all over the world: at Bloomies, Saks, and Macy's; at Harrods in London; Au Printemps, and Galeries Lafayette in Paris; and La Rinascente in Rome. It was the best way of teaching my men how to shadow—and how to lose their shadows.

Here's the principle: you go into the location—the more crowded, the more better. You ride the elevators and escalators up and down and all around. You climb stairs. You wander through the jam-packed aisles, moving indiscriminately. You take an unexpected turn down a fire stairwell. And then, suddenly, you perform a well-executed, two-legged absquatulation, exiting directly into a crowded pedestrian route, or descending into a subway with multiple entrances.

Such behavior can stretch a surveillance team past its tactical limits. Especially if the opposition doesn't have unlimited resources. You can make things even harder for them by altering your appearance as you move through the store or the station. See, surveillant teams keep you in sight, not by staying on your butt and looking straight at you. If they did that, they'd be unmasked in no time and their usefulness would be over. So they don't look at you directly, but instead, they watch your silhouette. By that, I mean, they keep their eyes on your hat, jacket, coat, and other distinctive features that they can spot from a distance. It also means that if you have the wherewithal by which to change your shape and your silhouette, you can screw 'em up.

Okay, now that you have a general idea about methodology and process, let's take Vynkenski, Blynkenski, and Nodyev to the Rogue Cleaners.

First, I ran them ragged through the subway system. I switched lines four times in the crowded rush-hour underground, making my transfers very abrupt. That kept them guessing. It may, incidentally, occur to you to ask how the F-word I knew where I was going, since I don't speak Russian and I don't read Cyrillic.

The answer is: I'd done my homework. This type of op is not a seat-of-the-pants kind of thing, although you might think that it is. You have to memorize a primary route, as well as a number of secondary and alternative routes, and be able to act instantaneously. That takes the three "shun" qualities all Warriors need to strive for constantly: organiza*tion*, prepara*tion*, and concentra*tion*. (And if, incidentally, the Warrior does not practice that trio of "shun" attributes in preparing for his mission, there is a fourth "shun" he *will* achieve: masturba*tion*.)

Moreover, I had written out the Cyrillic subway stops I'd be using (as well as a couple of spares in case Mr. Murphy rode along) in waterproof marker on the palms of my hands. So all I had to do was glance down at my hairy-palmed cheat sheet, and I was good to go.

Okay—first we ride to a stop where there was no transfer available. So I climbed back onto a crowded train at the Lenin Library stop, rode northeast until I got to Sokol'niki, got off, and reversed direction by going up the exit stairs, crossing over to the opposite platform, and jumping on the first available train. I jumped off again just as the doors began to shut—and then squeezed back on the train as it started moving. That left Vynkenski on the platform. One down. That cut their efficiency by a third.

I changed lines two stops later, sprinting down the *correspondence* and playing the old "on/off" game again (nobody bit—so I still had two shadows on my tail), then changed lines once again and rode to the metro stop closest to Red Square. There, I got off and sprinted up to the street. I threaded my way through another huge crowd of babushka mamas and papas selling military trinkets, toilet paper, cigarettes by the piece, drugs, and whatever else they could, to try to make ends meet. Lemme tell ya, folks, ruble inflation is tough.

Anyway, I shouldered my way through, crossed to the eastern side of Red Square, darted around the corner, and went directly into the *1 ya liniya*—Line Number One—entrance of the huge, three-story GUM (they pronounce it *"Goom,"* which rhymes with *tomb, gloom,* and *doom)* department store.

I pushed past the Benetton stall, declined the offer of aftershave from the Estée Lauder demonstrator, and headed for the stairs, my pursuers hard at work about thirty yards behind me. I slowed down to let them get a good look at me as I started up the stairs.

Then I bolted—three steps at a time. Blynkenski also took off at a gallop. But he was too far behind me to keep an eye on me all the time. There were turns in the stairwell, and as I made the first of them, I began unbuttoning my raincoat. As I reached the first-floor landing (don't forget that in Europe the first floor is what we in America call the second floor), my coat and hat came off, and my French braid came tumbling down. Without pausing, both the coat and the hat were stuffed into the small Reebok carry bag I was wearing underneath, slung over a lightweight waterproof parka of royal blue.

I cleared the first-floor door and started down an aisle displaying heavy winter coats and piles of Russian-style hats in rabbit, squirrel, lynx, and bear. I turned right, picked up a big, bear-fur hat, size humongous, and stuck it atop my head. I hunched slightly to lose three or four inches of height, pulled a thick wad of five-spots from my pocket and walked toward the kiosk, waving my fistful of dollars like your typical Americanski tourist.

You should have seen the smile on the kiosk lady's face when she saw me holding my big, hard . . . currency in my paw. She welcomed me like a long-lost uncleski. I even tried a smattering of Slovak on her (to no avail). As I paid up, I caught Blynkenski's arrival out of the corner of my eye. He'd come bursting through the door and was looking wildly around. Within seconds, his *koresh*— that's his pal in Russkie—Nodyev made a Kramer-entrance through the door (that is to say he twirled twice and performed a

7.3 Richter-scale triple-take). He was doing nicely, too, until he caught his galosh on something and tumbled ass over teakettle into a rack of coats. That's right, boys—break Rule One of surveillance: the one that goes, don't attract undue attention.

Nodyev picked himself up and started scrambling in ever-widening circles. But he didn't see me even though he looked right at me. Of course not. Why? Because he was looking for a big fella in a Greek cap and a long black nylon raincoat. Not some long-haired tourist in a bright blue parka and a bearskin hat.

I was still finishing my transaction as the two of 'em headed back toward the stairwell, confused and panicked expressions on their faces. Smiling the dumbass smile of the blessed and the lucky, I walked down an aisle of badly made, imported Chinese winter coats, looked for the closest fire exit sign, and took the indicated stairwell down to street level, where I shimmied the big steel door open and slipped into the crowded street. *Schastlivovo puti—sayonara*, assholes—and it was nice having you visit the Rogue Cleaners.

I cut back to Red Square and, carefully checking my six, walked south, past St. Basil's Cathedral. I circled the huge Rossiya hotel. No, I didn't go inside, because the police stake out all the first-class hotels, ostensibly to keep hookers and mafiyosi away. In reality, it is to make sure they get their piece of the action. It didn't take long for me to make sure I was, in fact, traveling alone.

Good. I cut south again, strode across the Bolshoy Moskaretsky Most bridge spanning the Moscow River, a small island and the drainage canal beyond it, onto the narrow, seventeenth- and eighteenth-century road known as the Ulitsa Bolshaya Ordynka. Two blocks on, I passed a gilttopped church on my right. Straight ahead was a metro stop. I dug in my trouser pocket and came up with two *zhetony*—Russia's ubiquitous brown, plastic tokens—found a public phone, dropped both *zhetony* in the zhlot, and dialed a seven-digit number I'd committed to memory.

A woman's voice said something I took to be "Good morning, embassy of Israel," in rapid Russian.

"Extension seven two four, please."

Rapid language transition. "Yes, of course. Good morning to you."

The phone *bring-bringed* twice. Then: *"Pree-vyet*—hello?"

"Y'know if they hadn't lopped off so much of your big Jew dick when you were eight days old, you could actually go fuck yourself these days, you worthless pus-nutted Hebe asshole."

There was a pause, then the sound of laughter erupted in my ear. "Good morning, Duma Deputy Zhirinovsky, you loudmouthed, fascist sonofabitch. I was wondering when you'd finally unscramble your brains long enough to make this call."

Chapter

4

We met at our prearranged rendezvous—an anonymous little konditorei around the corner from the Novokuznetskaya metro stop. I got there first and claimed a small, round-topped marble pedestal table against the rear wall of the narrow, wood-paneled shop. First, however, I pointed at a slab of thick, sticky, honey-drenched cake filled with prune puree, and asked—*pazhalstuh* (please) for a *koffe bez sakhara s'molokum*—coffee with milk, no sugar. It was one of the first Russian phrases I'd memorized on the flight over and I was happy to see that I'd gotten the sullen pronunciation down well enough so that despite the parka and gym bag I raised no tourist flicker from the thick-framed, brooding babushka behind the counter until I paid with two one-dollar bills that bypassed the cash register and disappeared into deep cleavage. Hey—maybe I didn't stick out like such a sore *khuy* anymore.

I was on my second *koffe* when he came through the door. I hadn't seen Avi Ben Gal in almost a decade. He looked much the same as I remembered him—just a little bit older and maybe a touch grayer around the edges. He's an olive-skinned, short, slightly built man, diminutive in the way that doesn't grab attention when he enters a room. Today, he was wearing a long, thick, double-breasted wool coat over floppy dark gray flannel trousers, which were tucked somewhat haphazardly into a pair of fleece-topped, oiled leather, rubber-soled hunting boots that looked as if they'd come directly from L.L. Beanski.

He nattered at the babushka behind the counter in full auto AK-47 Russian. Her glower turned to smile, she put hands on hips, threw head back, wiggled her wattles and laughed, displaying half a dozen or so Stalin-era stainless steel teeth in the process. Her head nodded vigorously. *"Da, da, da."*

He shrugged himself out of his coat on the way to the table, dropped it over the back of the closest chair, then thrust his right hand in my direction. "At last we get to meet face-to-face again," he said warmly. "Welcome to the *dikiy vostok*—the wild, wild East. I'm sorry it's taken us so long to get together."

"Me too." I *was* sorry—and not only because I'm fond of Avi. I'd called him from Washington and we'd scheduled a working session for the evening I arrived, only to have to cancel because he'd been suddenly called back to Tel Aviv on urgent business the day before I arrived. Even so, he'd managed to arrange my introduction to Boris Makarov by long-distance.

I was grateful for that, and told him so, grasping his size seven hand in my size ten paw and shaking it warmly, looking down as I always had, my eyes drawn to the stubby nub where his little finger should have been. The pinky was two-thirds missing. It had, as I recall, been shot off during an altercation with a bunch of nasties in south Lebanon when Avi was a greenhorn—a young lieutenant serving with a *Saye'eret* (reconnaissance) platoon of the Golani Brigade's elite *Egoz* battalion.

Instead of releasing my hand he kept hold of it with both of his, turning it over critically so he could examine the inked Cyrillic crib marks on my palm and wrist with some obvious amusement. Nothing gets by Avi. "Good tactical idea," he finally said. "Mind if I borrow it sometime?"

"I thought you speak Russian."

He grinned at me. "Yes, but I might be caught in *real* unknown, hostile territory some day—New York, or maybe Washington."

"Go to hell." I knew that Avi knew New York and Washington as well as he knew Tel Aviv or Haifa. I resumed my seat and picked up my coffee. "Been keeping busy?"

He shrugged and dropped into the chair to my right with a sigh. He kept his back to the side wall. "A little of this, a little of that," he said, a mischievous twinkle flickering in his gray eyes. "The boring life of the agricultural attaché."

Yeah, right, agricultural attaché. And me? I'd come to Moscow on a Martha Stewart Fellowship to deliver lectures about flower arranging. "Well, that's what you people get for making the deserts bloom. Now you've got to go out and teach other folks how to do it, too—even in countries where there ain't no deserts and very little bloom, right?"

"You got it, Dickie." He chuckled, and started to continue, pausing as a shadow fell over the table. Avi lapsed into his mother tongue: *"Biduke*—exactly right." All conversation stopped as the babushka waddled over *(pa-doom, pa-doom)*, her felt-swathed ankles and slipper-clad feet scraping across the dirty tile floor. She was bearing a tray on which sat a huge, two-handled cup of frothy black coffee, a plate with half a dozen thick slices of crusty black bread, a pile of oily herring topped with chopped onion and a big cracked ramekin filled with what looked like a quarter-pound chunk of sweet, white butter. She clucked like a fucking mother henski as she set it all in front of him.

His round face beaming, Avi smiled up at her like a grateful kid—I honestly thought she was going to ruffle his hair and pinch his cheeks. He slipped her a five-dollar bill, and she withdrew, beaming, tucking the money into the huge bosom of her white smock.

He took a handkerchief from his pocket and carefully wiped his knife, then slathered two pieces of bread with the butter, forked some chunks of herring onto it, sprinkled some salt on top, carefully added chopped onion to the pile, then cut the bread in half, and took a huge bite.

Finally he paid me about half the attention he was paying to the food. "So—how did it go last night with Boris and the boys?"

"Do you want the quick sit-rep or the detailed one?"

He sipped his coffee. "The quick one. I have an appointment tomorrow and I know how verbose you can get."

I was glad to see that he hadn't lost any of his sarcasm in the years since I'd seen him. "It was a complete goatfuck."

He chewed some more of the black bread and herring. "Do you know how they say *goatfuck* in Russian? *Ya veh pizde.*" He wiped a smear of butter from the corner of his mouth and cracked a smile. "It means, 'I am stuck in a very deep vagina.'"

"The Russian equivalent of being fucked very much."

"Yup." Still smiling, he chawed on another slice of the herring, onion, and bread and washed it all down with a big swallow of coffee. Then his expression grew serious. "Look—like I told you Boris is probably still okay. The question is why, and I guess it's because they haven't met his price yet."

"But you say 'Yet.'"

"*Da.* Yet. The reality is that I haven't met a Russian who can't be bought. So I can't really vouch for Misha, or any of the rest of 'em. Fact is, boychik, the whole damn country is like a sieve when it comes to leaking information, or just about anything else."

If anyone should know about information—or anything else—it would be Avi. Like I said, here in Moscow he was accredited as an agricultural attaché. In fact, he was a colonel in *Zahal*—which is how they refer to the Israeli Defense Forces in Tel Aviv—and he worked for AMAN, an acronym that stands for *Agaf Modiin,* which translates from the Hebrew roughly as "The Intelligence Branch of the General Staff." (Y'know, thinking of that, I just realized the Israelis have always been able to take huge mouthfuls of English words and stuff 'em into real tight Hebrew jackets. How the hell do they do that? Maybe it comes from living in such a small country.)

While Avi's finishing his breakfast, let me give you a little interpersonal history to put things in perspective. Avi Ben Gal and I met in the mideighties, just after I'd been infiltrated into Lebanon through Cyprus. My assigned task, as outlined by the then-CNO, Black Jack Morrison, endorsed by the national security adviser, and sanctioned by the president's scrawled signature on the bottom of a national security finding, was to perform some discreet neutralization upon the leadership of a small, fundamentalist Islamic tango cell that had become both nettlesome and lethal while operating against Americans in the region. That, at least, was what Black Jack had told the National Security Council, the CIA liaison, and the Senate Armed Services Committee staff.

In reality, I had a more complex and covert assignment, one known only to the president, the secretary of defense, CNO, and the Chairman of the Joint Chiefs of Staff. I was to infiltrate into Syria and map as much of the Soviet communications network as I could. Having done that, I would incorporate my findings into a METL—that's a Mission Essential Task List—so that, in case of what the politicians call a Serious Conflict, a SpecWar unit could be quickly deployed and destroy all the Soviet C³I (which is pronounced C-cubed-eye, incidentally, and stands for Command, Control, Communications, and Intelligence) capabilities in Syria, blinding the Sovs and incapacitating them, which would make them much easier to kill.

You see, back in the seventies and eighties, the Soviets used Syria as their main listening post in the Middle East, sweeping the skies for U.S., Israeli, and NATO SIGINT (SIGnals INTelligence), ELINT (ELectronics INTelligence) and other COMINT (COMmunications INTelligence). We used bases and listening posts in Turkey and, until the shah was kicked out, Iran to do the same to them.

By ship and by plane, the Soviets brought in thousands of tons of electronic equipment. Ostensibly, it was all used to build the Syrian military communications system. But there was more (there always was, with the Russkies, which is why I'm so suspicious even these days). At the same time they were providing military aid to the Syrians, they were piggy-backing their own communications and eavesdropping networks onto the Syrian system. Our SIGINT capabilities allowed us to narrow the Soviet C^3I nerve centers to a dozen locations. But satellites can only tell you so much—and what DIA learned through a human source was that three-quarters of the C^3I installations were dummies—set up as diversions.

Which ones were real? That's why I'd been put on the case. It was my job to pinpoint the real eavesdropping centers. That meant I had to actually inspect more than a dozen Syrian military installations. It was the only way to see which bases the Soviets were using as camouflage, and which ones they'd actually built their systems in.

The sneak-and-peek aspect wouldn't be hard—not for me. But maintaining cover in Syria over an extended period might pose a certain problem. Arabic is not one of my strong languages. It isn't even one of my weak languages. And while I may resemble your archetypal swarthy Syrian, amber Arabian, or earthy Egyptian, I can't talk like any one of them—except, of course, to tell you to go fuck yourself and the camel you rode in on.

The problem was solved way above my pay grade when someone with four stars on his collar and a great respect for the Israeli military decided to hitch me up with an Arab-speaking Israeli officer who was performing a similar task in the AO—or Area of Operations. Enter Avi Ben Gal, stage right.

Avi was a young captain at the time, detailed to Lebanon by AMAN. He headquartered out of the Alexandre Hotel in East Beirut and made long, unaccompanied trips to the terrorist-controlled areas of the Chouf mountains and Bekáa valley, busily (even ostentatiously) assembling dossiers on terrorist factions and compiling lists of possible tango targets in conjunction with the Lebanese Forces, the Christian militia, which controlled East Beirut. But Avi's outward task, just like mine, was simply a cover story. His real mission was to get inside Syria and evaluate the level of Soviet Army staff penetration of Syrian combat troops stationed in the rough quadrant between Damascus, Beirut, Homs, and Highway 7. The Israelis wanted to learn how well the Sovs were able to operate inside the Syrian military structure—and so they'd sent the officer who, according to CNO, was probably their greatest expert on Soviet tactics for a firsthand look. Why? Simple: because when the next Middle East war occurred, the Israelis wanted to know whether they'd be fighting Syrians, or Soviets.

Now, the reason behind all this subterfuge lay in the unpleasant but incontrovertible fact that neither the Israeli military intelligence apparatus—the folks at AMAN—nor their American military equivalents, the generals at DIA, trusted their civilian counterparts. Hey, hey, hey—don't skip this material and go looking for the next action sequence, because what I'm going to tell you here will take on a shitload of significance in about 150 pages.

So read and learn, tadpoles, okay?

- Fact: from the early eighties on, DIA began to pare down its relationship with the Central Intelligence Agency.
- Fact: DIA mistrusted CIA's Soviet military assessments because DIA believed they were totally unrealistic.
- Fact: DIA suspected that the Agency had been drawn into a political role by a series of ideological directors, and that its data reflected political bias, not dispassionate, objective intelligence.
- Fact: most of all, DIA feared that CIA had been devastatingly penetrated by the KGB and was being fed disinformation.

On each one of these counts, history has shown that DIA was correct in its assessment.

For its part, AMAN had a similar set of problems with *Mossad Letafkidim Meouychadiym* (the Central Institute for Intelligence and Special Duties), more commonly known to the trade as Mossad. Mossad is the Israeli equivalent of the CIA. In the years that followed Israel's 1982 invasion of Lebanon, the generals who ran AMAN believed that Mossad was becoming too political in its assessments—telling the prime minister's office what it wanted to hear, rather than what it needed to know. They resented Mossad's considerable involvement in the Iran-Contra affair, because they considered Oliver North and the rest of those concerned in the matter well-meaning but naive bunglers who would, in the end, screw things up.

They also thought that certain employees of the Israeli spy agency made a huge mistake when they became peripherally entangled in the recruitment and running of the American traitor Jonathan Pollard as an Israeli agent. Pollard, a U.S. Navy civilian analyst with access to raw intelligence materials (that is a polite way of saying he had the run of the fucking farm), supplied a rogue Israeli intelligence operation with 360 cubic feet of documents— yeah, that number, which sounds incredible, is absolutely correct. The pile of paper he turned over was six feet deep, six feet high, and ten feet wide—of highly classified, code-word sensitive documents, photographs, and signals intercepts. Including sources. Including methods. Raw effing data. The whole nine fucking yards—except in Pollard's case, it was the whole thirteen (cubic) yards. The data ostensibly went to an Israeli techno-intelligence organization known as LEKEM (*Leshkat Kesher Madao,* or Bureau of Scientific Relations).

But a number of those documents somehow (!) found their way into Mossad files. Mossad, in turn, traded some of their newly acquired gems to other intelligence services. One of the recipients was the KGB, with which Mossad has had a long and troubled relationship.

Moreover, AMAN suspected for many years that Mossad had been heavily infiltrated by the KGB.[4]

And so, because neither his bosses nor mine trusted the civilian intelligence apparatus, Avi Ben Gal and I were ordered to work together, share information, and keep what we discovered from

---

[4]The analysts at AMAN, just like their colleagues at DIA, turned out to be right. In 1991, a highly secret internal investigation in Israel uncovered a KGB penetration of Mossad that would make the Aldrich Ames case look tame by comparison if it were ever to be made public. Luckily for Mossad, the Israeli prime minister at the time, Yitzhak Shamir, was Mossad's former deputy director of operations. He officially rejected the conclusions and had the damning report sealed.

falling into either Mossad or CIA hands, so the details would not become compromised. Our initial sessions were not easy—for either of us. I did not like the fact that I'd been assigned a partner whose operational capabilities were unknown. In fact, for a long time I'd enjoyed the luxury of being able to select those with whom I worked. For his part, Avi wasn't overjoyed at being forced to work with an ugly American who didn't speak, read, or write the language of the AO—that's the Area of Operations—and whose reputation for attracting attention to himself made the quiet Israeli justifiably nervous.

But, as is so often the case, we soon developed the kind of deep mutual respect and rapport that successful two-man patrols in hostile environments can (and indeed must) enjoy. After three weeks in close proximity, we could act—and react—without thinking. We'd bonded into a unit, despite the fact that two more disparate personalities would probably be hard to find.

Avi is diminutive, quiet, bookish, and given to introspection. I am large and somewhat flamboyant, in case you haven't noticed. He is happily married and monogamous. I am divorced and libidinously impetuous. But operators come in all shapes, sizes, and personalities. And Avi was a hell of an operator. You already know that his Russian is fluent and unaccented. Well, his Arabic was perfect, too—in fact, he had a hell of an ear for it.

I discovered that on the third day we worked together. I'd insisted on getting out of the city, so against his better judgment we were in his beat-up Datsun, about eight kliks east of the highway (and what an overstatement that depiction is!), which winds east and north up the Bekáa valley from Zahle to Baalbek. We'd turned off the main road onto a rutted dirt track leading toward the Biquar salient—a kind of promontory from which you can look down into Syria—to watch a Syrian Eighth Armored Corps FX, which stands for Field Exercise. We bypassed a small town called An Nabi Shit (I noticed unmistakable signs of tango activity there and made a mental note to ask the folks at the National Reconnaissance Office to assign a satellite to the area), then fishhooked south, along a series of small wadis, or dry stream beds, until we came to a village whose sign, Avi told me, read Janta. From there, we turned the Datsun eastward again, paralleling a decrepit narrow-gauge railroad line that ran between the foothills, climbing slowly into the Shariq mountains.

Just over halfway to the top, we came upon a dozen fifty-five-gallon drums that had been rolled out and strung haphazardly across the narrow road. Behind the drums, a dozen lanky preadolescents in ragtag khaki holding AK-47s flagged us down. We had no weapons in the car. I wasn't even carrying a knife. Oh, we had papers—but I wasn't sure that anybody behind the barricade was old enough to read.

Now, lemme tell you something, friends: there are few things as frightening in this world as a roadblock manned (childed?) by twelve-year-olds. Because twelve-year-olds will kill you as soon as look at you because they have no concept of death. They kill. Not for fun. Not for sport. Not for challenge. They simply kill.

"And keep your mouth shut," Avi whispered through clenched teeth as we pulled up slowly—not that he had to cue me. My lips were sealed.

He stopped the car short of the roadblock by eight or nine yards. He'd already rolled his window down without being asked. The biggest kid of the bunch, a redhead who wore a blue and gold UCLA T-shirt above his stained BDUs and stowed a half-smoked cigarette behind his left ear, nonchalantly stuck the barrel of his AK over the windowsill, even with Avi's chest.

Without looking directly at the kid I checked him out. He had the kind of dead eyes that told me he was extremely dangerous. I could see his finger on the trigger just above the window line.

There was a pause that made my heart catch. Then the kid asked Avi an insolent question. Avi paid neither the insolence nor the AK any mind at all. He nodded matter of factly, then rattled off a bunch of quick Arabic gibberish.

The kid must have liked what he'd heard, because the AK's muzzle rasped off the sill, scraped down the door of the car, and came to rest pointed at the ground.

Avi pulled a bunch of Lebanese pound notes out of his pocket, rolled them into a wad, and thrust them across the window at the kid, who took the money without a word. Then he threw a thumb toward the roadblock. The knot of kids dissolved. They slung their weapons and rolled the drums out of our path.

I didn't ask Avi WTF until we were a full klik up the mountain.

"He gave me the salad test," Avi said.

"What?"

"He asked me what I put in my salad. I told him."

"And? So?"

He looked at me with the same incredulous expression that

instructors back at Basic Underwater Demolition/SEAL (BUD/S) training look at stinking trainees when they ask a dumber than dogshit question. "Dick, if you're a Maronite, you pronounce the word *tomato* one way—*benadura.* If you're a Druze, you most likely pronounce it another way—*bendura.* If you're a Palestinian it's a third pronunciation—*bandura.*

"Yeah, so?"

"So, say it the wrong way in these parts and you're whatchamacallit—dead meat." He downshifted as we bounced rudely into a huge pothole. "From the way young master UCLA with the AK talked, those kids were obviously Palestinians from south Lebanon—Tyre, maybe, or Rashediye. So I spoke with a Nabetiyeh accent."

You could have fooled me. But I know when to take "yes" for an answer—and so, from then on I kept my big Slovak mouth shut and let Avi do all the palavering as we bluffed our way through the unexpected roadblocks that we occasionally came across on our travels.

For his part, while he's deadly with an Uzi submachine gun when absolutely necessary, Avi is not an in-your-face kind of guy. So when it came to the up-close-and-personal rough-and-tumbling—and there were a couple of times it did—he let me take the lead.

We made a good team. Belay that. We made a terrific team. And six weeks after I'd slipped into Beirut, I exfiltrated south, courtesy of an AMAN chopper, to Sde Dov, a small airfield on the Mediterranean just north of Tel Aviv that is frequented by Mossad and military intelligence flights. My canvas briefcase was full of sketches, pictures, and notes that would be used to design the heavy METL campaign for destroying the Soviet CommNet.

Avi told me "B'bye, b'bye" and stayed on. Seven months later, when he returned to the deceptively fortified complex in central Tel Aviv that is AMAN's main headquarters, not only had he obtained the Syrian order of battle, but he also had managed to identify, by proper name, and down to the rank of captain, every Soviet officer attached to every Syrian unit in the quadrant lying between the oil pipeline just south of Homs, Beirut, and Highway 7. His accomplishment earned him his third *Tzalash Shel Ha'Ramat'kal,* or Chief of Staff citation—the tiny, crossed daggers that are Israel's second highest military decoration.

So, nu, you ask, what was this Arab-speaking Soviet Army specialist doing in Moscow, since the self-same Soviet Bear was extinct these days? The answer was that more than a million and a half Russians had made their way to Israel in the past six years alone—Russian immigrants comprised almost one-third of the Israeli population these days. El Al, the Israeli airline, flew eight nonstop round-trips a week between Moscow and Tel Aviv—and they flew 'em at 100 percent capacity on the southbound leg.

And you don't have to be a rocket scientist to realize that some of those Russians who emigrate to Israel aren't really all that kosher. Some of them aren't even Jewish—they travel on forged documents. So Avi, the Russkie expert, had been assigned to keep an eye on developments in Moscow. Reluctantly, he had accepted a six-month assignment. That had been a year and a half ago. You get the picture.

Avi listened as I told him about Paul's file, nodding silently, his fingers intertwined and clasped together as if in prayer. "Seems as if we're on the same track once again, old friend," he finally said. "I wish I'd met Rear Admiral Mahon—there was a lot of information we could have shared."

"Shared?"

"It seems we are interested in keeping track of the same people."

"That doesn't stop *us*, Avi."

The Israeli's knuckles rapped the table. "You're right," he said. He tapped the copy of the Air France waybill remnant I'd given him with an index finger, his expression exhibiting considerable frustration. "And right here's the key," he said. "Lantos. Werner Lantos."

"As in 'Lantos et Compagnie' of Paris?"

"The very same."

"But what about Andrei Yudin?" It was Andrei, I was pretty certain, who'd had Paul killed.

"Yudin is smart, and dangerous. But he's a *vor*—a gangster. One of the new 'expediters' in this society. That gives him muscle, and it gives him clout. But he doesn't wield any power, or real influence, at least not much beyond the Ring Road. Werner Lantos does."

So, who was Werner Lantos, anyway? "'Splain me, Avi."

"My people—the ones I work with—have been following his activities for years now. When Mossad isn't getting in the way, that is. In fact, every time I turn around, I seem to bump into the *ben zona*—the sonofabitch," Avi said, the irritation in his voice evident. "He calls himself an 'investment banker.' Whatever the hell that means. Been going in and out of Moscow since the sixties. He pulled off a bunch of joint projects with the old Kremlin bosses, and got rich in the process. Then he got a contract to build half a dozen new hotels for the 1980 Moscow Olympics. The project went belly up—and somehow everybody but Lantos lost money. Even so, he stayed real tight with Brezhnev and that crowd. Then, when Brezhnev died, he cozied up to Andropov. You'd have thought he was KGB he was so hard-line. But when Andropov croaked and Gorbachev came into power, suddenly Werner Lantos was all for glasnost and perestroika."

"An opportunist." I detest opportunists. Today's Navy is filled with them.

"Yup. So, these days, of course, he's a big proponent of democracy and capitalism. Promotes joint ventures. Sets up lots of deals. Finances a lot of projects."

I wondered aloud why I hadn't heard about Werner Lantos before.

"You wouldn't have—unless you're an Israeli intelligence officer, a Soviet expert, or an economist. He's one of those run silent, run deep guys with lots of *protekzia*—juice, I think you call it—and no profile. Came out of the Second World War as a hungry teenage orphan from somewhere in Eastern Europe."

"Somewhere? C'mon, Avi."

Avi wagged his head negatively. "That's as specific as it gets, Dick. Look—millions of documents were destroyed during the war. Birth certificates, marriage licenses, deeds, loan papers—the whole fabric of society was expunged. Turned to ashes. Face it, between the Germans and the Allies, most of the records everywhere between Moscow and Paris were wiped out by one side or the other. So there's no way to tell precisely who Werner Lantos is, or where he's from."

"What's your interest in him?"

"Like I said—he has a lot of *protekzia*."

"There has to be more than that."

Avi shrugged. "Look—he carries an Israeli passport—when, that is, it helps him to do so. He's got a Senegalese passport, too—a gift from the president there for moving a couple of billion dollars out of the country. He has friends in high places in our government as well as here in Moscow. Nobody's told me, but I'd guess he was used by Mossad as a diplomatic backchannel during the Cold War."

"So, he rubs a lot of shoulders."

"Yes he does—and some of them may not be such nice shoulders. Mossad doesn't like us to nose around his business—but my bosses still like to keep track of people like Werner, just like yours do."

I looked over at my old friend. It wasn't enough. Not enough to justify one of Israel's top military intelligence officers being detailed to track one man. Believe me, friends, that just doesn't happen. It wasn't the whole story. Avi knew it and I knew it and now you know it—and don't you forget it, because like the old chiefs say, you will see this material again.

But Avi's expression told me it was as far as he was going to take things right now.

Since it was time to shift gears, I pulled half a dozen photographs I'd taken from Paul's files out of my pocket and laid them on the table facing Avi. If I'd had the use of a secure fax I would have transmitted them back to my old friend Tony Mercaldi at DIA. But the only secure faxes in Moscow were those in the embassy. And if I used one, I could be sure that the DCM would hear about it. And I didn't want to have to deal with any more of Bart's meddling than I absolutely had to.

"How many of these guys do you know?" I asked.

Avi stared down at a magazine picture of a bunch of tuxedo-sporting notables at some kind of opening or art exhibition. One figure—it was partially hidden at the very edge of the fashionable crowd—had been circled by Paul.

He pointed at the circled face. "That's Werner Lantos," he said. "Look—" Avi extracted a pocket calendar wrapped in a rubber band from beneath his sweater. He unwrapped the rubber, sorted through a wad of perhaps a dozen passport-size color photographs, and selected one. "Here's a better shot."

I looked down at the passport picture; at the tanned, creased face and the wavy, slicked-back, gray-turning-white hair. "Can I keep this?"

"Sure." He concentrated on the other pictures I'd brought. "This one's nice—"

I peered at the upside-down photograph. It was a grainy surveillance photograph of Andrei Yudin, taken at a boisterous party. One of Yudin's arms was clasped around the shoulder of a large man holding a champagne glass. The other hugged a very uncomfortable-looking Werner Lantos. "That's the deputy defense minister," Avi said. "Probably taken at the Dynamo."

The Dynamo. Oh, really?

"A Georgian nightclub near the Ulitsa 1905 Goda metro stop. I'd be willing to bet Andrei's *organizatsiya* has a controlling interest in the place—the owner never charges any of Andrei's *byki* sonofabitches, no matter how much they eat or drink. And the drinks— *ouuah!* A bottle of champagne costs more than I make in a month."

"He's a regular."

"Andrei? Of course. He does most of his entertaining there. It's dead in the middle of Georgian turf—the cops won't go near it. Not even Boris and his crew." Avi saw the expression on my face. "What's up?"

I told him about the matchbook I'd found, and the Dynamo receipt in Paul's files.

"Makes sense to me," the Israeli said. "You're going to pay a visit, right?"

"What do you think? Want to come along?"

He shook his head. "Nah—my face is too well known in those parts. I'd spoil your fun. But listen—you watch your back there."

"That's a roger." I finished the last of my coffee and waved off the babushka, who picked up the pot and started to head in my direction. "So—finish the sit-rep on our pal Lantos."

"We really don't know as much as we'd like. The name Lantos is Hungarian. But he could have simply assumed it. He's never been specific about where he came from—makes him more the man of mystery, I guess."

I was incredulous. "C'mon, Avi—you and the 'Ministry of Agriculture'—you've got lots of sources . . ."

He interrupted me, his voice tinged with irritation. "Yeah, maybe we do, but to tell you the truth, even *I* haven't been able to fit a complete true legend to this one. He's a real piece of work. The best I've been able to do is track some of his business dealings. I know he's into everything from arms smuggling, to art dealing, to venture capitalism. These days he lives mainly in Paris. In fact, he's there now. I know that because he flew out of Ben Gurion airport two days ago—he was visiting his office in Tel Aviv. Like I said, I'm watching him."

Noted for the record. "So he shuttles between Moscow, Tel Aviv, and Paris."

"And Britain, and Italy—he has offices in London and Rome, too."

"Nothing in America?"

Avi shook his head. "Negatory—he doesn't do business in your country because your banking laws are more stringent than most."

I tapped the copy of the waybill before sliding it over to Avi, who slid it into his pocket. "So now this guy's bank is financing dual-use equipment—stuff that's critical to the final stages of nuclear weapons manufacturing—which is ostensibly being shipped to some company, probably a front, on a five-square-mile island in the Caribbean—an island that has no industry."

"There's something else," Avi said.

"Yeah?"

"The company name."

"*Limon*—lemon."

"Lemon in Spanish or Italian," he said. "But here in Moscow, *limon* is mafiya slang for a million bucks—isn't that a remarkable coincidence, Dickie?"

I wriggled my eyebrows at him because as you all know by now, in our trade there is no such thing as remarkable coincidence.

"And," Avi continued, "there's another remarkable coincidence that scares the hell out of me, too." He pulled a thin envelope out of his jacket pocket and slid it across the table to me. "These are for you."

"What are they?"

"A gift. A few souvenirs. Waybills, receipts, customs documents. A picture or two. A fragment of a map. All parts of some damn jigsaw puzzle that neither of us have all the pieces to. When you told me about Paul Mahon's files I went back to my own. Found this stuff—things I've collected over the past six months or so. I made copies. Maybe they'll help you convince your people more than they helped me convince mine. It's like I'm beating my head against a damn wall. I haven't been able to persuade my bosses to do anything. It's like they've been paralyzed, politically. They make a move, and Mossad stymies it. I try to act, Mossad screams, 'Sources and methods will be revealed.' You know the drill."

I do know the drill. "What crap!"

"*Biduke*—exactly. And the worst of it is that every scrap of Mossad paper I see—and it's hard to wring anything out from those sons of bitches, believe me—but I've seen some notes, and a few maps, and one or two memos. And that, when you add

71

everything else I've been able to get my hands on, convinces me that Mossad is absolutely positive a lot of the dual-use stuff Lantos has been financing and Andrei Yudin has been skimming from the Ministry of the Interior is ending up in the same region you and I once spent some unpleasant time together."

"That doesn't make sense."

"I know—that's the part of the equation I can't figure out."

"I mean, Avi, why the hell would the Russkies want the Syrians to build a bomb—unless they want to destroy the peace process."

"But that's exactly what Mossad has to be thinking, Dick," Avi said. "That the Russians are allowing the bad guys to build a fucking bomb out there. Moreover, I know in my bones the damn thing is almost completed. Like your man Wonder said, hot freon is part of the final stage of assembly, not one of the preliminaries. But it makes no sense. I try to talk about it, and Mossad tells my bosses, 'He's wrong. There is no problem—everything's under control.' I can't seem to be able to convince anybody but you there's a problem."

Chapter

5

GATOR, BEING THE FNG—OUR PIQUANTLY SEAL WAY OF SAYING HE was the newest and most junior member of the team—pulled the evening's guard duty assignment. After last night, I wasn't about to leave the lockbox and its contents unguarded, even though I'd bound it with wire fastened with a small, imprinted lead seal, which told people it was official U.S. government property. In the box, Paul's files were now augmented by the materials Avi had given me. We'd agreed to meet in twenty-four hours and pool information once again.

While Gator played watchdog, the rest of the boys and I grabbed a quick dinner of lamb shashlik, rice pilaf, a couple of deceptively strong, fifty-dollar bottles of Mukuzani red, and inexplicably bad coffee at the Crazy Horse, a boisterous café attached to an expensive (and formal, judging from the number of Armani suits, patterned silk shirts, and Ermenegildo Zegna ties going through the door) Georgian restaurant. Crazy Horse was about a fifteen-minute walk from what the Russkies call their World Trade Center, but Wonder had selected the place because of its proximity to the Dynamo—about seven blocks away—and he wanted to walk us through the neighborhood he had so painstakingly researched.

We finished at about ten. I paid up, then we all strolled south, walking toward the Moscow River, through a neighborhood that was once working class but now was filled with big, expensive blocks of flats—which is what they call apartments almost everywhere but the United States—that housed many in the city's growing expatriate population. Moscow is a city defined by its colors—the color of soot, the color of mud, and the color of unwashed brick all come to mind.

In this neighborhood, however, the usual monochromatic landscape had been replaced by vibrant swipes of primary colors in the storefront windows. There were, in fact, a totally unexpected number of small, exclusive bars, cozy restaurants, and designer shops that catered to the well-heeled residents. Invariably, outside each of these new establishments, one or two hoods who (judging from the whitewalls and the buzz tops) were probably ex-Spetsnaz shooters or former KGB border guards, stood sentry duty in the cold. As the hard currency customers came and went, they performed the unique foot-shifting, arm-folding, head-swiveling choreography that is common to loitering cops all over the world.

With Wonder the ex-recon Marine leading the way, we made a slow, seemingly aimless tour of the district. It was not aimless: by eleven, we had seen every alley and passageway, walked every street and checked every building in the six-square-block area around the Dynamo. By then, judging from the amount of grousing I was hearing, We Were Getting Thirsty Already, Daddy.

I told Wonder to Move It toward cold beer.

"Your every wish is my command, oh great, wise, and all-powerful Dickhead, sir," he said, spelling it as usual with a *c* and a *u*. Happy in his work he steered us around the corner of a narrow, dark street bordered on one side by a small, neglected cemetery and on the other by a well-built nineteenth-century block of apartments, and emerged—*voilà*—onto a wide, brightly lit sidewalk, onto which dozens of Mercedes and BMW sedans had been pulled up and parked. I said *voilà* because it was like being dropped onto the goddamn Champs-Élysées about a block from Fouquet's. There were knots of well-dressed people moving up and down the street. Chauffeurs stood at parade rest, awaiting their bosses. A line of taxis, engines chugging, spewed exhaust fumes into the cold night air.

We worked our way between the cars until we came to a low, black painted storefront that was unremarkable except for the nineteen fifty-four Harley Davidson chopper that had been mounted above the industrial-strength metal doorway. The chopper matched in style and color the one on the matchbook in my pocket. This was the front door of Andrei's hangout.

A door, I should mention, that was vibrating from the sound inside. In front of said door stood an industrial-strength bouncer, dressed entirely in fifties black leather, right down to his square-toed black motorcycle boots with silver studs and spur straps and a Harley emblem between his shoulders. He looked us up and he looked us down. Then he smiled a big, friendly smile and said, in pseudo-English, *"Velgum, velgum*—Go een, go een."

Always willing to take *"da"* for an answer, I pulled on the door handle and een we went.

It was like climbing into a sardine can. A very noisy, hot, smoky, booze-soaked sardine can. Being, however, highly trained and field-tested SpecWarriors (and therefore tactically proficient), we immediately formed ourselves into a human wedge and moved, en masse, toward our right, where I could see the bar. Wonder was on point. From the look on his face, he was enjoying himself, too, as he squeezed past a knot of NYLs—nubile young lovelies—in tank tops, who were gyrating to the music while bouncing tambourines off their remarkable hips.

Have I mentioned the music? Have I mentioned the fact that it was loud? If not, let me tell you—it was loud. Obstreperous. Tumultuous. Rowdy. It matched the crowd. The crowd was dancing on the fucking tables.

Two dozen or so excuse me's and ooh, that felt goods later we'd managed to get within a thirty-six-inch sleeve's length of the beer taps. I saw they were serving Dortmunder Union and Russian brewski. I waved a trio of twenty-dollar bills at the sweating, overworked bartender, mimed a big, cold mug of beer, pointed at the Kraut spigot, held up five fingers, and shouted, *"Piat pivo*—five beers."* He nodded in agreement, reached out, took the money, and disappeared. A short time later, five one-liter mugs were hoisted in my direction. We took possession and worked our way toward the bandstand. You wonder where my change was? Dream on.

I nudged, pushed, and shimmied toward the rear, taking point as my boys dropped back one by one, deserting me to make nonverbal conversation with the knot of NYLs by the bar. I glanced over my shoulder and saw that Doc was already in love. Ah, youth is wonderful in its exuberance, ain't it?

As I proceeded, the place began to take on some proportion for me. It was wider than it was deep, with tables jam-packed jowl to jowl. The tiny bandstand was up against the back wall. As I faced it, I saw a kitchen door to my right, and a long corridor that—judging from the women working their way up and down it—led to the head.

The tables were set up family style—that is to say, there weren't no deuces in this place. It was what I call grab-ass seating—you grabs your ass and you sits down where you can. The crowd was as raucous as the band—dressed in everything from suits and ties to jeans and sweaters. There were guys on the prowl and single women trolling. Over there, in the far corner, a couple well into their seventies clapped along with the music. Mostly, however, it was groups—four, six, or eight couples, obviously out to have a Good Time—and proving it, too. I will say this for the Russians: they like to party, and they are good at it.

The band was smaller than I'd expected, given the decibel level, which was somewhere just under a Pratt & Whitney F100-PW100 afterburning engine (that's the one they use in the F-15) in full-throttle climb. There was a Jerry Garcia look-alike with an electric guitar. A second, equally hirsute musician stood in front of the mike with a small, amplified accordion strapped to his chest, and a humongous, computer-driven synthesizer console laid out in front of him. That was it—except they sounded like a whole fucking band.

They were into a rousing version of the theme from *Zorba the Greek*. Accordion watched as we made our way along the side wall just past the kitchen door. He waved at me. I waved back. He threw something in my direction. I started to duck—then caught the missile, a tambourine, just before it would have smacked a table dancer in the head. I shook it a couple of times, then handed off to a Russian with rhythm.

I drained my beer, set the mug down on the rail to free my left hand, and continued my rearward shimmy. The biggest table in the room—it was right in the center of the place—caught my attention. More than a dozen sweaty goons in shiny, Italian-cut suits, their arms around gold-bedecked women in tight knit dresses, were standing on chairs, whacking themselves with tambourines and gyrating to the music's infectious beat. The vibrating table itself was too crowded to dance on—it was filled with an assortment of vodka, champagne, wine, Scotch, and brandy bottles, and strewn with dozens of plates, salvers, trays, and bowls all piled high with food. There were probably people sitting there, too—but there were too many frenzied, chaotic things happening to see them right now. Overworked waiters in stained white aprons hovered as best they could, trying to keep out of the way of the flailing knees, elbows, and hips.

One loving couple of standees was simultaneously dirty dancing and drinking huge tumblers of what looked like either brandy or Scotch, their arms interlocked as they drained the glasses and their companions egged them on with shouts and applause.

I watched, transfixed. I'd never seen a woman drink like that before—I mean, we were into real chugalug land here. Finally, the beast with two backs separated. Their arms unlocked and their bodies parted. As they did, her eye caught mine and she leered at me, her tongue moving port to starboard across her lips. He watched her performance—and then his eyes fought for focus and veered vaguely in my direction.

Hey—I *knew* that big broad sweaty ugly face. It was Vynkenski. He knew me, too. His eyes went wide—then he shouted at an Ivan down the table, who turned, and peered quizzically. I knew him, too. He was the one I'd labeled Blynkenski. I watched a big grin spread over Blynkenski's fat red face. He jabbered at the rest of the table, gesticulating as he did. Then he clambered down off his rickety chair and staggered in my direction.

Blynkenski was a big man—six three, maybe six four. He weighed in somewhere around an NFL offensive lineman or center's 275, 280. He was a drunk big man, too. Glassy-eyed, he lumbered directly at me, cutting through the crowd and pushing over everything in his path, his big arms spread wide. He vaulted the rail, grabbed me, and hugged in a more than passable Frankenstein monster mash imitation, kissed me wetly on each cheek, and told me, laughing, in his drunken gravel voice, *"Yob tvouy mat* Dickie Marc*hinko*—fuck you, Dickie Marc*inko!* You giving us good run today."

Now, I found it somewhat (yet not altogether, given the past twenty-four hours) remarkable that he knew my name even though we hadn't been properly introduced. I was about to ask him his own when he preempted me. "I Volodya," he explained matter-of-factly, his left forearm slapping his fifty-five-gallon chest, his right arm wrapped securely around my waist, the hand drunkenly but nevertheless expertly checking out the pistol in the small of my back as he nudged me inexorably toward the raucous table. "Come meet Sergei, your other friend from metro."

It was like being inserted into one of those slo-mo scenes from Clint Eastwood movies. Those early Spaghetti Westerns he did, in which he played the Man with No Name. As I got closer and closer, I began to see more and more of the gritty detail. The circles of sweat under the women's arms. The creases and stains on the men's suit coats. The hand-painted, chipped earthenware plates holding chunks of rough-ground sausage and cracked olives laced with hot red peppers. Bulges in trouser waistbands where pistol butts or the round handles of leather saps protruded. Cracked and cemented white serving platters of meat pies, now cold, lying in congealed puddles of fat. The twelve o'clock shadow on Vynkenski's broad face as he climbed off his chair to greet me. Huge metal saucers piled with mayonnaise-laced salads made of boiled vegetables. The overwhelming, sweaty odor of unwashed bodies. A tray of sliced, pungent smoked fish. And over *there*, dead center, hidden by the chair dancers and the piled plates, his back to the bandstand—sat Andrei Yudin. There is a SEAL technical term for times like this when your intel has been good and things work out. It is: *Bingo.*

He looked so much more like The Accountant than The Godfather that I thought he was going to make me a ledger I couldn't refuse. He was dapper, delicately boned, and so petite that I wondered whether he was sitting on a telephone book, because the well-trimmed beard on his chinee-chin-chin barely cleared the tablecloth. His minute size was doubly accentuated by the fact that he was utterly dwarfed by the oversized *byki* who surrounded him. He wore round, wire-rimmed glasses. On his wrist was one of those thin, gold Patek Philippe watches that goes for somewhere between seven and eight grand. His thick salt-and-pepper hair— the one indication that he was probably in his midforties—was cut long and moussed stylishly over his ears and collar. He was dressed in a white-on-white-on-white shirt with its long-pointed collar button undone. The knot on his wide, deep red challis necktie, which was slightly askew, was a triple or quadruple Windsor about the size of a small child's fist. The tie disappeared into a loud, gray-on-gray checked wool vest that sported notched lapels and was edged in dark suede.

Next to him was Mrs. Yudin. I knew that because of the, oh, 7.5-

to 8-carat, marquise-cut diamond engagement ring, the matching gem-encrusted platinum wedding band on her third finger, left hand, and the possessive way he had his arm around her well-turned shoulders. Not to mention the huge *IY* monogram in cherry red, embroidered on the small but well-shaped, aroused, and obviously braless left tit of her clingy, Oxford gray, turtlenecked cashmere dress.

She wasn't a day over twenty-five, judging from the kitten face and the artful makeup, and she sported the kind of metallic copper-toned, chemically amplified red hair that is *le bec fin*—which means the latest craze when you're in Paris—among French aristobrats, trophy wives, and high-priced tarts. She was probably six or seven inches taller than he. Looking at her, I thought back to the vocabulary lesson Avi had given me earlier in the day. Yeah—she was a real Russian goatfuck.

And next to Mrs. Yudin, a glass bottle of Evian water and a glass sans ice placed directly in front of him, sat Werner Lantos. In the flesh, his skin was tanned perfectly, and even more remarkable, reptilianly wrinkled, the creases on his face and neck as uneven yet symmetrical as the back of a massive croc's tail. His curly, gray-turning-white hair, accented by his deep skin tone, was slicked back in such tight waves that it looked almost permed. Below a pair of intimidating white eyebrows that would have done Brezhnev proud, his eyes were as soft and gray as Mrs. Yudin's cashmere dress.

Andrei stopped playing with his wife's tit long enough to arc his head behind her and whisper something to Werner Lantos, who nodded imperceptibly, sipped his water, and stared up at me. Then Andrei leaned to his right and murmured to a huge Ivan sitting behind a liter bottle of Moskva vodka and a shot glass that looked as if it had been originally made for King Kong.

The tablecloth in front of the Yudins was clean—a pair of napkins had been spread out to hide any blots, blemishes, smudges, or stains. On the creased and starched napery sat two short-stemmed champagne coupes, and an ice bucket containing a half-empty magnum of Dom Perignon. That figured. Dom is what people who don't know the difference between good and great champagne drink when they want the expensive stuff.

I allowed myself to be guided up to the table and inserted between Blynkenski and Vynkenski, who up close and personal turned out to be another equally humongous *byk* with equally humongous *byk*-odor. When the hell did these guys ever take a bath? The rest of Yudin'z boyz had all climbed down from their chairs, now—they were sitting at the table like well-behaved hoods, eyes on their boss, waiting for Andrei and me to get it on.

Doc, Wonder, Rodent, and Duck Foot were nowhere to be seen. That was good—I wanted everyone at this table, especially Andrei and his goons, to think I was here on my own.

I stood opposite them. Andrei's tiny hand gestured, graciously, palm up, for me to sit, which I did. A napkin was unfolded and placed atop the greasy tablecloth to mask the stains. Immediately thereafter, a clean plate was slid in front of me, and utensils rolled in a napkin slapped gently atop it. As I moved the knife and fork to the side, shook the napkin out to place it on my lap, an unopened bottle of Bombay Sapphire gin appeared, along with an Old-Fashioned glass and a bucket of ice.

I could feel the hair standing up on the back of my neck the same way I did when I led my men into hostile territory. Somebody had done his fucking homework. But that was to be expected: old Andrei had access to good intel.

From whom, you ask? Well, from the Rolex-wearing OMON colonel, for one. And from any cops who'd spoken to Boris and Misha. And then there were all those folks at the embassy, including hundreds of FNs—Foreign Nationals—who understood more English than they let on and kept their Russkie ears open. It's amazing what money will buy these days.

Andrei put his index finger on the champagne coupe that sat in front of him and nudged it perhaps a quarter of an inch. Instantly, a waiter materialized in the crush, leaned over, and filled the shallow vessel with fresh, chilled champagne.

The Georgian hesitated while I took ice, opened the Bombay, and filled the glass in front of me. Then he picked his champagne glass up by the stem. "Welcome to my city, Richard Marcinko," he said, leaning forward to speak above the noise, and reaching across the table to touch the rim of my glass with the rim of his. "*Budem zdorovy*—remain healthy," he said, draining his glass. I did the same. The glasses were refilled. "*Do dna*—bottoms up, Dickie Marcinko," shouted Vynkenski, draining his tumbler of vodka. "A bullet shouldn't pass between the first and second toasts!"

Andrei gave the huge *byk* a look that made him cringe. Then he turned toward me, and his head inclined slightly in the direction of the huge, sloppy Ivan next to him. "Here," he explained, smiling, "is my old friend Viktor Grinkov. He works for the Ministry of the Interior." A pause. He sipped his champagne delicately. "And here"—he indicated past his wife's tit—"is another old friend, Werner Lantos, visiting from Paris, looking for new business."

I saluted them both with my glass. "To the dead—isn't that the proper third toast here in Moscow?" I paused long enough to get a good look at Viktor Grinkov's pudgy face, grimy collared shirt and baggy, Khrushchev-style brown suit. The slovenly picture was meant to put people off—disarm them. But Grinkov's eyes told another story—the guy was sharp. I wasn't fooled by Andrei Yudin's understatement, either. "Works for the Ministry of the Interior" indeed. Viktor Grinkov was an old-style hardliner who currently *ran* the fucking Ministry of the Interior. The goddamn OMON colonel with his new gold Rolex President worked for Viktor Grinkov. Now the empty dacha made perfect sense.

What burned me was that it was all so fucking open and out-front here, and nobody gave a goddamn. None of that behind-the-scenes shit like almost everywhere else in the world. Graft, corruption, murder—here in Russia it was all an ongoing part of everyday life.

Meanwhile, Werner Lantos's soft gray eyes tried to get past my own—but I wasn't about to let him do that. With the door shut, he tried his considerable charm. *Enchanté*, Captain Marcinko," he oozed. "I hope you've had a pleasant four days here," Lantos said, saluting my Bombay with his Evian water.

"They've been busy," I said noncommittally. I sipped my Bombay and returned my attention to Andrei. His English had been remarkably fluent, and I told him so.

"I learned my English—" he began to shout over *Zorba*. Abruptly, he halted, swiveled in his chair, looked at the two musicians, and drew a finger across his throat. They stopped in midcrescendo, as abruptly as if they'd been unplugged.

He turned back toward me, his guttural voice cotton-ball soft in the sudden silence. "I learned my English in New York. Two years," he continued. "I drove cab. Seven days week, fifty-two weeks year. Took orders from rich bitches from Fifth Avenue and Sutton Place. Go here. Go there. Sit. Wait." He smiled coldly. "Now, *I* own flats on Fifth Avenue and Sutton Place." He flicked the nipple of his wife's aroused tit with the back of a tiny index finger. "I have my own rich bitches."

He paused to gauge my reaction. When I gave him none he

sipped at his champagne and regarded me coolly. "I understand you have been looking for me."

That was an understatement. "A friend of mine was killed—his whole family murdered."

He nodded, the smug little face downturning into a Cheshire frown. "Ah, yes—I heard about that," he said innocently. "From embassy, yes? The military attaché and his wife, yes? I am told reliably they were attacked by brigands." He translated what he'd just said for the rest of the table's benefit. He sipped his champagne as they all laughed. "There is a lot of crime in Russia today. Too much crime if you ask me." He laid the coupe back on the table and called for silence. "It is a great pity what happened."

I was losing patience with this performance. I once-overed Andrei and his champagne, Werner Lantos, who was sipping his Evian, and Viktor Grinkov slurping from the King Kong shot glass. "It was a pity for whoever did it. The little boy was my godchild— my *first* godchild. I'm told that you Georgians are very family oriented, so you understand the significance of that."

Andrei's eyes showed some surprise but he managed to maintain a neutral expression. The flash in Grinkov's was the giveaway that he was not only sharp, he understood exactly what I was saying. Werner Lantos was shocked, too—you could see he hadn't anticipated any personal connection between Paul and me. Andrei, however, missed the dangerous look altogether. "You have my condolences, Captain," he continued, his voice low.

I'll bet I did. "I don't want condolences. I want whoever killed my friend and my godchild."

He picked up his coupe and drained it. Immediately, the glass was refilled. "That has nothing to do with me, Captain Marcinko. I am simply a businessman trying to make a dollar or two." He gestured expansively left and right. "Like tonight. As you see, I have put together old friends. If they form a successful venture, they pay me a small finder's fee. But if I can help you in any way, then I would be happy."

I realized right then that this absurd verbal tennis could go on all night if I didn't put a stop to it right away. And so I made a command decision to use a technique I'd developed over the years after watching some of the world's best journalists and most talented intelligence officers practice their trades.

Oh, yeah—just in case you didn't know it, the practice of journalism is very similar to the practice of intelligence.

I see you out there—you're dubious. Well, Mr. Dubious—come on into the tent and let me lay out the basics to you.

Both journalism and intelligence are based upon the timely exploitation of sources. In journalism, you try to get some poor asshole to betray his (or her) company or his (or her) boss or his (or her—and, by the way, are you getting enough of this ironically employed EEO shit yet?) country so you can put that information into a magazine or a newspaper or onto a TV news show. In intelligence work, you try to get some poor asshole to betray his (or her) company or his (or her) boss or his (or her) country so you can use that information to promote your own national interest.

In journalism, you are genteel. You call said A^2— Aforementioned Asshole—a source. In intelligence work, which is slightly less genteel, the A^2 is known as an asset. (Known as an asset, incidentally, because you SET said source's ASS on the street to dig up info.) In both cases, when intelligence officers or reporters are in private, their A^2s are more accurately described. In private, sources and assets are both referred to as "snitches."

Having laid out the general philosophical framework, let's get down to specifics. Interrogation, for example. The interrogation techniques employed by intelligence officers and journalists are remarkably similar. No, torture is not a realistic option in either field. Most editors and reporters are liberals and hate violence. The same, incidentally, goes for career intelligence officers. More of *them* are liberals than you might imagine.

Besides, in 99 percent of all cases you get more information by using your brain than your fists (or a twelve-volt battery or a pair of pliers). And both journalism and intelligence work employ false flag recruitments—which, as I explained before, is when the reporter or officer makes you think he represents one country (or business) when in fact he represents another. And both use the gambit I like to call the PIP, or Partial Information Ploy.

The very best journalists will make their sources believe that they know far more than they do. Sometimes, if they have only an inkling, they'll lay a scenario out and hope it's close enough to being right to jar the subject and coax him to talk. Sources love to correct reporters' perceived misconceptions—and the scenario approach lures them into doing exactly that.

Sometimes the scenario elicits an HTF, or, "How the fuck did you know that?" response. That's when you say bingo to yourself while never showing your cards. In other instances, you use buzz words, code phrases, and other mumbo jumbo to convince your sources that they might as well spill the whole kettle of beans because you, the journalist or intel officer, know the whole story anyhow, so they're not giving up any information you didn't already have.

Tonight, I'd use PIP on Andrei. So I drained my Bombay, slammed the glass back on the table, and gave the Georgian my best Nasty Rogue Look.

"You're nothing but a fucking liar, you *moodyuck* cockbreath," I said, calling him an asshole in Russian.

The way his eyes screwed up behind the glasses, I thought he was going to shit—or sic his *byki* on me. But I didn't give him a chance to do either. "Paul knew you were tied into the dual-use smuggling—the stuff that's going to the Middle East through your 'old friend' Werner Lantos, here—and a bunch of other stuff you're moving courtesy of your other 'old friend,' Viktor Grinkov. So you had him killed before he could do anything to upset your action. It was nothing personal. It was a simple business decision on your part—*zapodlo.*" I used the Russian underworld idiom that translates as "illegal commerce." It was a word Avi had used earlier in the day to describe Andrei's activities.

Since I knew my rapid-fire English was supposed to be flying past Viktor Grinkov's head untranslated, I concentrated on Werner Lantos's face as I spoke. It was hard to discern any change in his expression. He sat there, immutable as a statue. Except that he didn't have the degree of muscle control he might have desired. Just below his right ear, his neck was throbbing like a fucking tom-tom. His carotid artery was going crazy and there was nothing he could do to stop the pulsing. That told me Werner Lantos was exercised. Exercised, hell—Werner Lantos was homicidally furious.

I poured another Bombay, picked up the glass, drained it all at once in the Russian style, and slapped it back onto the table belligerently, as if to say Fuck You. As I did, Lantos leaned toward Andrei and started to say something in Russian. But I wasn't about to let anybody break the mood, so I interrupted. "It's that fundamental, Andrei, so don't try to shit me."

Andrei did an HTF. How did I *know* he HTF'd? Because the sonofabitch didn't have me killed on the spot. He didn't call me names—didn't tell me I was full of shit. He didn't even try to deny what I'd just accused him of. He only tried to parry it.

"You have no proof," he said, his eyes moving in tight little circles, his eyelids fluttering in those micromomentary tremors psychologists will tell you indicate mendacity. "Only what Vassily told you—and he is a known liar."

Here is what I did not say: *Oh, I see you know I spent some quality time with your U₂ goon Vassily Chichkov, whose information sent me to your dacha. But guess what, asshole—even though the dacha was empty, I managed to find one shard of evidence on the premises. Yeah, the Air France waybill you left behind. And the Israelis have a lot more in their files.* Now, to be perfectly honest, you know as well as I do that until right now, I'd been working with evidence that was almost completely circumstantial. But the look on Andrei's face, the micromomentary eyelid fluctuations, and his lying response added up to Guilty As Charged.

However, this was not the time to pass sentence. That would come later—in a one-on-one—and in a place more private. Right now, there were more immediate things to do. Like get my behind out of this place.

I pushed my chair back from the table and stood up. I nodded in Ministry of the Interior's direction. "Nice to meet you, Viktor," I said. I bowed slightly at Werner Lantos. "A pleasure, monsieur," I lied.

Then I fixed Andrei in a murderous stare. "See you 'round, *Koresh*," I said, calling him pal. "We'll do some serious talking, you and I."

Vynkenski and Blynkenski bookended me as I rose. "They will take you back to your hotel," Andrei said between gritted teeth.

Like hell they would. "I'll find my own way."

"No—" He frowned. He obviously wasn't used to being contradicted by anyone. "They will take you. It is no problem."

I bet it wasn't. I looked up at Vynkenski and Blynkenski. They had the kind of open, unsophisticated, guileless faces that spoke volumes if you know how to interpret the pages on which they're writ. Dear friends, I am the Evelyn Fucking Wood of face reading. Right at this moment, for example, these two *byki* were trying to sort out exactly where in the Moscow River they were going to dump my body after they'd finished with me.

Now, as we're all making our way out and you start thinking that I'm being reckless, let me explain a few elements of my SpecWarrior strategy.

First, I knew—and they obviously didn't—that I had four very aggressive shipmates watching everything that was going on. Second, I had no idea where Andrei was holed up but I still wanted to talk. There was the matter of Paul Mahon and his family, which had to be cleared up. And there was the cozy relationship between Andrei, Werner Lantos, and the head of the Ministry of the Interior, which had to be explored.

I mean, friends, the nasty possibilities are endless. The Ministry of the Interior controlled all exports of dual-use technology. It also had jurisdiction over Russia's nuclear materials industry and domestic arms production. And it was the Ministry of the Interior's troops who controlled the borders, as well as maintained counter-terrorism units like OMON. Come to think of it, many of the old KGB's functions were now under the direction of the Ministry of the Interior. Kind of makes you nervous to know that the man who ran that ministry is an old friend of a *vor*, doesn't it?

Well, at least one thing was clear. Now I realized how the dacha operation had been compromised. In fact, it occurred to me right then that the dacha might have been a trap, set for Boris, the still-honest cop, or for one or two of the OMON shooters who perhaps refused to take bribes and become part of the system—or a trap set for me. You say that sounds far-fetched? Perhaps you are right. But in my line of work, the alternatives are endless, and you take nothing for granted. As the old Rogue's SpecWar Commandment reads, "Thou shalt never assume." So I wasn't about to assume anything.

Now, perhaps in all honesty the cops on the organized crime squad and the intel weenies from the Ministry of the Interior had no idea where Andrei Yudin could be found, on a day-to-day basis, even though it hadn't taken me very long to learn that he hung out at the Dynamo. It was vaguely conceivable. After all, Moscow is a confusing city. Not to mention the fact that they've changed hundreds of street names since the fall of communism—and not all of the new, more democratic-sounding ones are on the maps yet. There are also huge numbers of anonymous, unnumbered apartment blocks, unheard-of warehouses, and other sundry obscure structures scattered throughout the city.

It was also possible, if somewhat unlikely, that Andrei, by playing the old Yasser Arafat shell game of residence switching, had managed to "elude" the authorities. It was much more likely that since his old friend ran the ministry that was ostensibly in charge of taking him down, Andrei simply stayed one step ahead of the few honest cops left in Moscow.

But tonight, things were different. Tonight, I knew exactly where he'd be staying. Well, I didn't actually know it yet. But I was being presented with impeccable sources: my two huge bookends. Vynkenski and Blynkenski knew exactly where Andrei was going to rest his well-coiffed little head tonight.

Moreover, Andrei knew they'd be late getting home—because they'd have to dispose of my large, muscular, and hard-to-conceal corpse. So he wouldn't worry if they were a little late showing up.

And third, it is always advantageous to allow your enemies to believe they are overrunning your position, when in fact, you are simply drawing them into a trap. That maneuver, incidentally, is a tactical homily first mentioned by Sun Tzu more than two thousand years ago. It was preached during the French and Indian wars by Major Robert Rogers, the CO of Rogers's Rangers and founding father of American SpecWar, and brought into the twentieth-century Navy lexicon by Roy Boehm, the legendary maverick mustang who is the major heir of Major Rogers's philosophical legacy as well as the godfather of all SEALs.

"Okay, you guys," I said. I punched Blynkenski on the upper right bicep hard enough so that even in his well-fortified, feel-no-pain condition he winced. "Let's move it, boychik."

They tried to steer me through the crowd, but there was no way I was going to allow them to put their hands on me. So we played touchie-feelie-slappie-slappie all the way out the door. As I passed the jam-packed bar I caught Wonder and Doc in my peripheral vision but made no attempt at eye contact—no telling who might have been watching—and continued toward the exit. Besides, contact was unnecessary. My guys are operators. They'd know exactly how to play it.

The Ivans pushing close right behind me, we walked past the bouncer onto the sidewalk. They wobbled slightly as they tried to veer me starboard. Blynkenski pointed toward a dark Mercedes sedan that sat in a cusp of street light half a block away. "We take my car," he said.

No fucking way. I stopped short, swiveled, and headed the opposite direction. *"Nyet*—we'll walk *this* way," I said, pointing in the direction my men and I had arrived from.

Vynkenski looked at Blynkenski, Blynkenski looked at Vynkenski, and the two of them shrugged conspiratorially, as if I was nowhere to be seen. "Okey-dokey, Dickie Mar*chin*ko," he said, "we go the long way. More interesting maybe if we walk."

I let them bookend me as we marched back past the well-lit hard-currency stores, slaloming past tightly packed Mercedes and Beemers. "So, Ivan," I said, slapping Blynkenski's back, "do you know Vassily Chichkov?"

"No Ivan. Not Ivan—me *Volodya*," he said, underlining each and every syllable. He chewed my question for a few seconds before digesting it. "Vassily," he said, a smile spreading across his face as he obviously remembered something they'd shared. "Is very good man. Old-time friend."

"You know he was wearing my friend's Naval Academy ring," I said.

"Naval? No—Vassily not naval. He was with me in army," Blynkenski said, simultaneously misreading my question and signing his own death warrant so far as I was concerned. After all, I only needed one of them for information.

We turned the corner. The lights were dimmer here, the block of nineteenth-century apartments a shadow on the opposite side of the street. To my left stood a low wall, which marked the border of the small, neglected cemetery.

Blynkenski stopped and peered into the deserted graveyard. I could see his mental gears trying to shift. It was like his lips were moving, it was all so obvious. He winked at Vynkenski and said, "Hold it all up, please."

We held it all up, thank you.

"Having to take big leak," Blynkenski pronounced. He stepped over the decaying, three-foot stone wall that set the graveyard off from the street, then turned toward me. "What about you, Dickie?"

"Hey, Volodya, right on—nothing like draining the old liz-ard," I said.

"Liz-ard?" Blynkenski looked back, confused.

"Shakin' the snake, bub—uncoiling the old pocket anaconda and lettin' it breathe."

Behind me, Vynkenski laughed. It was somewhere between a belch and a guffaw. He moved close, as if to help me over the wall. "I got it," I said, elbowing him hard enough in the gut to make him keep his distance. Once over the wall I stayed well ahead of him—out of reach of those size twelve paws of his. Vynkenski might be drunk, and stupid. But he was still big, and potentially dangerous.

And he was ready for action, *now*. I knew that because despite the chill he was sweating. He was also breathing deeply. Those are two of perhaps half a dozen overt signs that the body is preparing for combat. The Warrior works hard to keep such signs to himself. These assholes weren't Warriors. Bullies. Muscle. Goons. I wouldn't trade one of my SEALs for a hundred of 'em.

Now, speaking of SEALs, I knew that my guys were close by. They'd have shadowed us from the moment we left the Dynamo. Which is why I'd taken this route. Wonder had done his homework well—the cemetery was a fitting place to take these two assholes down. But I wasn't about to call for any backup. I'd decided to deal with these two pigs myself. Especially since they were pals of Vassily's. Maybe they'd been there, too. Helped Vassily and Andrei to kill my shipmate. And his wife. And their firstborn—my godson.

We moved away from the cemetery wall, walking nonchalantly past the ragged rows of headstones, clustered sarcophagi, and small mausoleums. Oh, yes, it was appropriate that we were here in this place of death together; this burial ground, where I'd begin to take revenge for what they'd done to my extended family.

Blynkenski stopped next to a large, ornate mausoleum, sidled up to the wall, unbuttoned the fly on his trousers, and began to take his leak.

He sighed the way so many do as the lizard's draining, then turned his head vaguely in my direction. "Hey, Dickie Marchinko—I *zamochit*—piss on this guy's grave. Maybe some day I *zamochit* on yours, too, huh?"

"Highly unlikely, cockbreath." In the darkness my hand had slipped under my jacket and retrieved the P7 from its holster in the small of my back. It takes fourteen pounds of pressure to cock the squeeze safety on the pistol's grip, but only a pound and a half to keep it cocked. I cocked the weapon, holding the safety pressed down. My trigger finger indexed along the trigger guard, just below the frame. I held the gun next to my right leg, where it was invisible in the shadows.

My major concern was sound, so I decided to take him out with a contract shot—not as quiet as a suppressed weapon, of course, but Blynkenski's clothes and his body would absorb some of the gun's report.

I moved up toward the mausoleum wall as if I was going to take a piss, too. Blynkenski sensed me approach, but was in the middle of shaking his wanker off, so he was somewhat distracted. I got directly behind him as he faced the mausoleum stones, his cock in his hand, his gaze directed downward. I brought my right arm up, jammed my pistol's muzzle tight against the base of his neck, using the suitcoat he wore as insulation, and squeezed off two rapid shots—*ba-boom, ba-boom!*

They were louder than I wanted, but not as bad as they could have been. And they were the last sounds that fucking Blynkenski ever heard. The sonofabitch sprayed bone, brains, and blood all over the mausoleum wall as he dropped like a fucking stone.

I stepped back far enough to admire my handiwork. Now there was an example of an asshole who'd literally pissed his life away.

For the first half-second or so, Vynkenski was too surprised to move. Maybe it was the alcohol he'd consumed that slowed his reactions—I didn't know, and I didn't care. I just wanted to deal with the motherfucker. I wasn't going to kill him—not yet at least. I needed information.

Of course, he didn't know that. He moved in my direction. I stepped away from Blynkenski's corpse, and as Vynkenski advanced, his hand digging frantically in his saggy trouser pocket for the pistol I knew was there, I charged his ass.

Can we stop here long enough for me to give you all a piece of sound advice? Good. It is this: if you carry a pistol, use a holster. Do not stick the sonofabitch in your pocket. If you store a revolver in your pocket, it is likely that the hammer will snag as you withdraw it. Even if you carry a bobbed-hammer weapon, it will not withdraw easily. Autoloaders are even worse. If they are of the Glock persuasion, and you are carrying the pistol locked and loaded, there is a good chance that in your excitement you will shoot yourself in the groin or thigh. Other autoloaders, even the hammerless kind like P7s, are hard to draw from a pocket. Anything with a hammer is nigh on impossible. And don't even think about shooting through your pocket—you are much more likely to kill yourself, than wax the opposition.

Okay—back to real time. I came on him from his unprotected side and slapped him hard across the face—*whap-whap*—with the barrel of my pistol, cutting him deeply with the front sight. That got his fucking attention. His free hand went to his face and came away bloody.

Drunken panic showed in his eyes as he saw the expression on my face. I was the fucking god of war and I was about to sacrifice him the same way I'd just sacrificed his buddy. He backed away, a scream choking in his throat. I advanced—kept pushing. Slapped him again with the P7. Never give up ground. Always advance into the vacuum left by your adversary. War is the act of taking turf from your opponent—and this was fucking war. I hit him again—a hard shot to the throat. He tripped, stumbling backward over a grave marker, lurched to his feet, and tried to get away.

Impossible. I was all over him. I hit him with the pistol again, knocked him on his ass. He rolled away from me. I jumped his bones. He tried to wriggle out from my grasp. Never happen. No need to use the steel on him now—didn't want to. I jammed the gun in my waistband, straddled Vynkenski, and beat a tattoo on his face with my fists. This was one of the assholes who'd killed my godchild—murdered the youngster I'd dreamed would follow in my own warrior's footsteps. And I was taking my revenge here and now. With every blow came a name. *This* for Paul. *This* for Becky. *This* for Adam. *This* for Louise. I grabbed a fistful of hair and began slamming his ugly head onto the ground in a steady syncopation— *wham,* Paul, *wham,* Adam, *wham-wham-wham-wham–*

Hands reached out to grab me but I fought them off. Slapped them away. Doc Tremblay grabbed me around the throat and gently, but forcefully, eased me off Vynkenski's limp, bloodied body.

"He's had enough, Skipper—let us take him, now."

I was shaking all over. Vibrating from the rage. Had to calm down. Get control again.

I raised my arms to force some air into my lungs. "I'm okay, I'm okay," I wheezed. "Just let me grab a breath or two."

Duck Foot and Wonder pulled me to my feet. I was goddamn lightheaded—woozy, almost. Doc was checking Vynkenski's swollen eyes with his pencil light. "You came real close to killing this one," he said.

"Too fuckin' bad." I wasn't feeling very much sympathy for the s.o.b.

No time to waste, either: there was work to be done. "Wonder— get the fuckin' keys out of the dead Ivan's pocket. He has a Mercedes stashed near the club—end of the block under a streetlight. We'll need it tonight."

He didn't have to be asked twice. "Roger-roger, Skipper."

"Rodent—you and Doc get this one ready to move."

Doc's corpsman expression told me he'd rather work on Vynkenski here and now. "C'mon, Doc—you can practice healing arts
later, when we've cut ourselves a little slack."

He looked at me as if he didn't quite trust what I was saying.

"Hey, I'm totally serious. I want him patched up." I did, too—I
had two or three questions I needed to ask him before he left us for
good.

Chapter

6

WE ARRIVED SEPARATELY—AND VERY QUIETLY—AT OUR RENDEZVOUS point, a deserted, secluded side street two blocks from Dostoev-sky's house, just after 0315. Yeah, it's the same place *Crime and Punishment* was written. I found that fact appropriate: after all, I was planning to perform both in a few minutes. Furthermore, I believed I'd be able to do my work without interruption, because tonight I wasn't taking any chances with our OPSEC.

We'd worked out what I believed was a passable operation, given the time constraints and lack of intelligence we were faced with. Let me take a minute here to talk about what the folks who design SpecWar ops for the Pentagon often refer to as "mission planning." To achieve success, all special operations require what the doctrine writers at the Special Operations Command at MacDill Air Force Base in Tampa like to call "the dynamic of relative superiority," or more simply, RS.

RS takes place when a small, unconventional force wins out over a larger, but more conventional force. You want an example or two? Okay. How about Entebbe, when Israeli commandos rescued a planeload of hostages from a force of terrorists who were protected by two companies of Ugandan regulars. Closer to home, there was the time not so very long ago when I led seven shooters against a large, well-armed force of tangos in the northwestern mountains of Afghanistan.

Now, the core of the principle of relative superiority lies in the dynamic, the gestalt, the very heart, of special operations itself. I see you waving at me out there, accusing me of falling back into Navyspeak bureaucratic gibberish. You're saying, "What the hell are you talking about, Mr. Rogue?"

Okay—I'm saying that all the elements—intelligence, communications, and training are some of the most critical—must combine to allow you to act decisively in SpecWar, otherwise you will lose the advantage. The longer you take to achieve your mission goals—the more steps there are in the mission, for example, or the older the intelligence—the more chances there are that you will fuck up and get you and your men killed. An example? Eagle Claw—Tehran, 1980. My old friend Charlie Beckwith was saddled with a bad ops plan that had too many steps and too many stages and not enough decisive aggressive actions. That series of complexities, defective intel, and flawed training is what led to the fiasco at Desert One.

Tonight, we had to achieve a dynamic, decisive victory even though we had crude and incomplete operational intelligence, numerical inferiority, and lack of time to plan for contingencies.

What's all that ruckus I hear? What? Oh, you're accusing me of being contradictory. No, I'm not. Despite all the doctrine, and all the case studies, there are times in SpecWar when you simply have to ACT—*now;* times when you simply have to GO and to DO—and hope for the best. This was one of them.

We'd packed, locked, and loaded, then left the hotel as covertly as possible. I went out first, carrying a radio. I circled the block checking for surveillance and discovered none I could discern. So I hit the transmit button twice, which was the signal to move. Wonder, Doc, and Rodent slipped past the snoozing desk clerk, one by one. Duck Foot and Gator, ever the impatient leprechauns, had already exfiltrated their own way—they'd gone out the window, shinnied down the back drainpipe, and slipped out via the courtyard. Wonder and Doc drove the weapons to our assembly point near Dostoevsky's house using Blynkenski's car. The rest of us dispersed and traveled there by foot—a forty-plus-minute slog through the nasty Russian night that did nothing to improve my mood.

Still, we had made it cleanly: traversed the city passing as few as possible *stakans*, the round, glass-encased metal booths manned twenty-four hours a day by traffic police—and intelligence spotters—to keep an eye on things. More significant to our OPSEC preservation was the fact that, as we were moving at night, it was less likely that we'd be spotted by the passive monitors of the venerable but still fully operational KGB *visir* system.

You say you haven't heard about *visirs* before? That's not surprising—very few people have. So let me clue you in. During the height of the Cold War, the KGB set up a highly classified system of surveillance devices atop (and inside) many of the buildings that line Moscow's main avenues and boulevards. The system worked so well because it was so KISS—Keep It Simple, Stupid. It had no technogoodies or fancy bells and whistles. Instead, it was assembled out of old-fashioned telescopic devices— an altogether inconspicuous yet highly accurate way of observing what was going on inside the automobiles that drove along the street.

You see, back then, there weren't very many cars in Moscow. Most autos, in fact, were driven either by privileged Party members, high-ranking government officials, or foreign diplomats—and all of those categories were designated as official targets of KGB kuriosity. To satisfy that kuriosity *sans* attracting undue attention, the KGB developed *visir.*

The system employed exceptionally stable, high-powered, re-motely controlled telescopic devices that were fitted with panning heads and zoom lenses. Using a system of prisms, the images from the telescopes were projected onto matte screens much the same way a college professor projects his notes onto a screen in an auditorium. It was practical, simple, and efficient. It was also kept very secret.

The *visir* stations were run by Line Q, sub-line VT, of the Sixteenth Chief Directorate. Just in case you've forgotten, that directorate was a self-contained subsection of the KGB's internal counterintelligence division, which remained hidden from Western intelligence sources well into the late seventies. There was no outward evidence that the Sixteenth Directorate or its Line Q, sub-line VT, even existed, hence no way to learn about *visir.*

Moreover, the *visir* locations were interconnected by a Mark-1, Mod Zero communications system that relied on telephones and underground cables instead of more technologically advanced UHF or VHF radio transmissions. The *visirs* had been built like that not because the Sovs were smart, but simply because the Soviets didn't have any more advanced technology at the time.

But their KISS design meant that it was impossible to detect the network even after NRO—remember, the initials stand for the National Reconnaissance Office, a spooky agency run out of the Pentagon and headquartered in a huge, modern, luxurious office complex near Dulles International Airport. NRO is responsible for operating all our satellite programs. In that capacity, the agency began regular SIGINT and ELINT (SIGnals and ELectronic INTelligence) satellite overflights of the Moscow region with a dedicated KH-9 (Keyhole-9) reconnaissance bird from the National Security Agency's first BYEMAN orbiting collection program. The project was code-named IVY CHARM, and it began early in August of 1974. But it never picked up *visir*. Billions of your tax dollars spent, and still we didn't have a fucking clue.

In fact, our friends at Christians In Action did not (as usual) know fuck-all about *visir* until a Sixteenth Directorate officer defected in the late seventies and told them both about it, and the rest of the Sixteenth Directorate's Line Q, sub-line VT covert programs.[5]

And, while there may not be a KGB anymore, I can assure you that *visir* is still in place—and it is monitored, moreover, by minions of Viktor Grinkov's Ministry of the Interior. I know all of this because I have scoped it (heh, heh) out myself. And so we took our time getting to our assembly point, especially as, in addition to our diplomatic passports, we were carrying the sorts of weapons and other lethal devices that neither the Moscow police, nor the

---

[5] The officer, Sergei Motorin, was a KGB captain who defected in place (that is to say, while on duty in Moscow), in 1977. He ingeniously contrived to make his first contact with the Americans by staging a fender bender with a U.S. diplomat in one of the *visir* system's blind spots and passing a note about his intentions that scheduled a subsequent rendezvous. It was he who first divulged information about *visir* to the CIA. In 1980, Motorin, then a KGB major, was posted to Washington to gather technological intelligence for Line X of the First Chief Directorate. Once in the United States, he worked for the FBI, passing on crucial information about Soviet spy activities directed at American defense technology. Motorin's story, however, does not have a happy ending. Late in 1985, he was abruptly recalled to Moscow, imprisoned, and executed, one of the more than fifty U.S. agents whose identities were turned over to the KGB by Aldrich Hazen Ames, the American traitor.

Ministry of the Interior, nor anybody else for that matter, generally approves of.

Our target was a six-story block of flats that sat in an isolated, dilapidated cul-de-sac one street to our west. Godfather Andrei was staying the night on the top floor, in what our unwilling but finally compliant source, Vynkenski, had described as a three-room flat shortly before he departed for destinations unknown. Translation into English: it had three bedrooms. The information he provided allowed me to make a rough, sketched floor plan of the apartment, as well as a map of the neighborhood.

To reach Andrei, we had to make our way through the locked courtyard doors, crack the locks of the inner doors, sneak up the stairway, and penetrate the flat—all without waking any of the neighbors. And we had to do it all before 0500, which is when greater metropolitan Moscow starts to yawn, wake up, and take its morning piss.

0325. We moved out. I took point. We stayed close to the buildings as we moved toward the cul-de-sac, taking advantage of the shadows. One point in our favor was the lack of street lighting. There was one working street lamp half a block away. Six others were down for the count—shot out, judging from the shattered lenses.

I moved as cautiously as I would going down a jungle trail. I didn't expect trip wires or land mines, but I didn't want to announce my presence by stepping on a piece of broken glass or any other brittle garbage, either.

I put my fist in the air at shoulder level to silent-signal a halt as we came up to the corner. From the pocket of my black BDU shirt I extracted a night-vision monocular. Then, I dropped to the ground and very, very carefully, peered around the corner at our target.

Why did I suck concrete? The answer is because I didn't want to create a nasty silhouette. At night, you will remember, you don't see things directly. You see them peripherally. So if I were to stick my big Slovak nose around the corner at a height of six feet, it would be easily discerned by anybody halfway alert—because the line of the building wall would change—and I would stand out. It's similar to the way you spot a deer when you're hunting. You almost never see the whole deer—but the motion of its haunch, or ears, or tail, draws your attention, because something is moving where something shouldn't be moving.

97

Same principle here. By sticking close to the ground, I was making sure that I was presenting the smallest, least noticeable profile to whomever was standing guard.

And there was somebody standing guard. Well, he was sitting guard. An Ivan, alone in a BMW seven thousand series—that's a quarter of a billion, with a *b*, rubles, more or less—worth of car. The Beemer's motor was purring, no doubt to keep the heater running—and its amber parking lights were on. I could make out the Ivan's face. It was actually too bright for the night-vision monocular because he had the dash lights on, too. He was looking down—maybe reading, maybe nodding off. Whichever, it didn't matter, because the sound of our approach was going to be muffled by the idling engine. I slid the NV back into my pocket and signaled back to the others that there was a single target ahead.

He was parked dead center in front of the courtyard entrance, a pair of heavy, paneled wood and wrought iron doors set into a sturdy steel frame. The right-hand door panel, which measured about six feet wide by eight feet high, contained a small entry door. That way, if a single person was coming into the apartment house, they wouldn't have to open both courtyard gates in order to get in.

Once we cracked the building's outer shell, we'd split into working groups. Duck Foot, who liked heights, and the Gator, who didn't, would shinny the drainpipe that the late and unlamented Vynkenski promised ran up the side of the apartment house from the courtyard. They'd slip over the roof, lower themselves by rope, and come through Andrei's bedroom window at the same time that the rest of us were coming through the door.

But first things first. I silent-signaled my intentions, then moved out, keeping low as I crept around the corner. The rule here is to keep it slow and steady, so as not to attract attention. The key word is slow. We are talking about inches-at-a-time progress, friends. Indeed, all that sneak-and-peek stuff you see in action movies by Steve and Chuck and Bruce and the rest of 'em is crapola. They move so fast and loud that even a wannabe would notice 'em in real life.

I got about three-quarters of the way down the cul-de-sac— about sixty-five or seventy yards from the corner—and was about to work my way around a raised window well set into the wall along which I was crawling, when Mr. Murphy decided I was lonely out there and that he'd join me.

The Ivan in the Beemer stretched and peered out through the

windshield. I froze in midcreep, outlined against the dirty gray stone of the window well.

He yawned wide, cracked his knuckles and stretched again. Then he switched off the BMW's ignition, opened the car door, and pulled himself outside. He stood for a second, silhouetted by the car's interior lights. Obviously, he had no sense of tradecraft. I could hear the jingle of the keys as he dropped them into his trouser pocket. He reached into his jacket and pulled out a package of cigarettes, shook one out of the pack, and inserted it between his lips. Then he found a lighter and applied it to the end of the cigarette. He took a couple of deep drags, exhaling smoke from his nose and mouth simultaneously.

I stayed frozen. And I mean frozen—I didn't even breathe. Don't forget, it was cold—and when it's cold, your breath comes out like smoke, and it picks up any ambient light. Even though he probably had no night vision, given the fact that the car's interior lights had gone on when he'd opened the door, I wasn't about to take any chances.

He zipped the leather jacket he was wearing up to his throat. As he did, he turned slightly. And as he turned, despite the cigarette, despite the night blindness—despite everything—his peripheral vision caught me.

The knowledge that he'd seen me hit me like, well, it's ineffable. I can't really describe it, but you know it when it happens. And it wasn't even that he saw *me*. It was that he saw *something*. And that something made him suspicious. He froze for an instant. Then his arm started north, the preliminary step to tossing away his cigarette, unzipping his jacket, and reaching for whatever he had concealed inside.

In a case like this, there is only one thing to do—and I did it. I charged. Put my head down, used the window well as a starting block, and ran like a motherfucking bull toward him.

He was still working at the zipper when I got there. He dropped his hand and feinted left, then right, as I came up on him like the proverbial Mack truck.

Feint, schmeint—I went barreling into him the way a fucking cornerback goes after a wide receiver. I took him down onto the pavement—the momentum carried us three or four yards beyond the car—and we scrambled for position. He rolled on top of me and brought his knee up into my balls. Ooh, it took my breath away. But not before I slammed him upside the head with my fist.

We rolled around some more, our hands, arms, and legs grappling for advantage.

The training regimen for Alpha Teams, the most elite of both Soviet and post-Soviet special forces, divides hand-to-hand combat training into two parts: combat for capture, and combat for killing. This Ivan was trying to use Part Two on me. And from the way he was simultaneously chopping at my throat, elbowing at my face, and trying to remove my eyeballs, he had obviously gone to Spetsnaz school. What they teach there is rapidity—that is to say, they want their students to be able to deliver more than two hundred blows a minute. This guy was trying—really trying—to do a lot better than that.

But speed ain't everything, folks. Accuracy counts, too. So he chopped, and he punched, and he gouged, and smacked, smashed, and swatted. And he was pretty good at it, too—powerful in the resilient, supple way that thin, wiry guys are strong.

But I outweighed him by fifty pounds at least. And I am a big, solid, strong sonofabitch who presses 400 pounds, 154 reps, every morning at 0545 on the outdoor weight pile at Rogue Manor. Rain or shine. Snow or sleet. Hung over or hung out. So 200 blows a minute or not, when *pousser* comes to *bousculer*, as they say in Paris when you're roughing and tumbling, I was able to muscle him more than he could muscle me. I threw him the same way rodeo riders toss a heifer, rolled him over onto his stomach, straddled him, contained his flailing arms with my legs, grabbed him under the mandible—that's the jawbone in medical school—and turned his head about 270 degrees to the right, which did downright nasty things to all those small cervical vertebrae in his neck.

You could hear the bones go *ka-pop-pop-pop*. I chopped him a downward blow just above the shoulder blades with my elbow to make sure he'd stay down for good, then rolled off his body, exhausted.

The whole episode, from the time he'd seen me until now hadn't taken more than twenty-five seconds. But they were a tough twenty-five seconds, believe me.

I lay on the pavement with my eyes closed, sweating, hyperventilating, and feeling sore in every single one of my muscle groups. Finally, I looked up to see Doc Tremblay's handlebar mustache twitching nervously above me.

He knelt, reached down, and plucked my left arm from the ground, held it and lightly pressed two fingers across my wrist.

"You're getting old, you broken-down asshole," he whispered. "Two years ago, your heart wouldn't have broken a hundred dealing with him—" He gently shoved the corpse with the toe of his boot. "Now your pulse is about one forty, one forty-five."

"Yeah, but this is the second time in one night for me," I croaked. "And besides—he's still dead and I'm still alive." I wiped the sweat from my face, rolled over, went to my knees and began searching the corpse. I extracted a locked, loaded suppressed Tokorev auto-loader and a spare magazine holding eight rounds of jacketed hollowpoint ammunition from his shoulder holster. The rest of him gave up the cigarettes and lighter, a thin, cheap wallet, a crumpled handkerchief, and the car keys, which were on a stainless steel band that held more than a dozen others as well. I checked the wallet. There was a photo identity card—military or paramilitary from the look of it. I tried to make out the Cyrillic lettering, but it was impossible. Was he a cop, or a soldier? I knew that a lot of both worked for the mafiya as bodyguards and security types, so either was altogether possible.

I handed the key ring to Wonder, who'd moved up with the others. "See if any of these fit in the door."

Then I pulled myself to my feet. "Let's get Ivan back where he belongs so we can get to work."

Gator reached inside the Beemer and switched off the dome light. Then Doc took Ivan's feet, I held him under the arms, and we schlepped.

None of the keys worked the gate lock or the gate doorway. That set off my danger Klaxon, which sits positioned between the pussy detector and the bullshit meter in the lower-right quadrant of my brain, right behind the cerebellum. I sent Rodent and Gator to do a quick sneak and peek. Their fast recon uncovered nothing amiss. It was still all quiet on the Eastern front.

Why did the fact that the dead Ivan's keys didn't fit any locks trouble me? Because, friends, from experience I know that sentries usually have the keys for the gates of the houses they are protecting—especially if they're posted outside and there is no security in the inner courtyard.

Yeah, yeah, I know that on the one hand, we hadn't checked that last element yet. But on the other hand, no one had come out to check on the noise we'd made—there hadn't been a lot, but there'd been some.

0331. We stacked outside the right gate single door. Wonder picked the rudimentary lock in less than ten seconds, then eased behind the door, which opened outward, and pulled it wide, allowing us to make entry.

Have I spoken to you before about the military discipline of what we were doing here? No—okay, while we're getting into position, let me explain. These kinds of moves are what I call R^2D^2s—that is, Ritualistic, Rehearsed, Disciplined Drills. At units like Delta Force or SEAL Team Six we practice them thousands of times under all kinds of physical situations and conditions. That way, when we do it for real, we don't have to think about which of our shipmates is doing what, and how we go about accomplishing the rudiments— all of that has been so thoroughly inculcated deeply inside us that we JDI—Just Do It.

Hallways, doorways, and gates; ships' passageways and super- structures; fire escapes, ladders, stairwells, and foyers—all of 'em get rehearsed, over and over and over. We practice at all hours, too. I've been known to stage a call-out for a live-fire room-entry exercise at 0345, about seventy-five minutes after my guys have sacked out, exhausted after a long evening of pussy chasing and beer swilling at a series of user-friendly saloons. They just love it when I do that. But I have always believed in the SpecWar doctrine that I first saw on a hand-lettered sign tacked up over the doorway of UDT-21's quarterdeck at the Little Creek, Virginia, Amphibious base. It read, THE MORE YOU SWEAT IN TRAINING, THE LESS YOU'LL BLEED IN BATTLE. That sign, as you can probably guess, was the source for one of the Ten Commandments of SpecWar.

It was also a credo much taken to heart by the chiefs who trained me. Chiefs like Grose, Red Coyle, Hoot Andrews, Mugs Sullivan, and of course my favorite sea-daddy, Everett Emerson Barrett, Chief Gunner's Mate/Guns for whom I worked at UDT-21, never let us young Frogs slack off. Under their dedicated and inventive tutelage, we learned to polish both the tops and the soles of our boots. They found ingenious ways in which to keep our minds and bodies busy, too. When we trained in Puerto Rico, for example, they made us construct neat little walkways bordered by sand-filled empty beer cans outside our tents. And when we visited the Virgin Islands (where we never found a single virgin, either), Ev Barrett once sent us scampering up palm trees to find tender fronds from which to make straw hats.

Palm fronds? Straw hats? Yeah—it toughened our feet, and

sharpened our climbing skills, although Ev never bothered to explain himself to us at the time.

Of course, he didn't have to explain—he was the platoon Chief. That word is spelled G-O-D. His every wish was my command. And despite the fact that most of us were younger than he by a couple of decades, and we thought of ourselves as *t-o-u-g-h* motherfuckers he could (and did) regularly plant his size nine-and-a-half, double-E, spit-shined boondocker toe firmly six inches upside our recalcitrant bungholes whenever he felt the situation demanded it.

Another momentary digression here. I grew up in the tail end of a Navy culture in which discipline in the ranks was enforced by chiefs, not officers. They called it Rocks and Shoals back then. And it meant that every once in a while, a chief would beat the bejeezus out of you for making some dumbass mistake. There were no memos, no notes, no written reports. Nothing would ever appear on your record. You would fuck up. The chief would simply flatten you, right there, on the spot. Lesson learned. End of story.

Well, today, there is no longer Rocks and Shoals. There is the 967-page Uniform Code of Military Justice, which is enforced not by chiefs, but by officers. In fact, under the UCMJ, any chief who lays hands on a sailor gets himself court-martialed. And since there are so many rules and regulations in that big fat book, a lot of sailors get written up for a lot of infractions by a lot of officers. But discipline in the Navy is, in a word, lousy. The officers aren't leading—they are, in effect, writing traffic tickets. And chiefs aren't teaching. No—they are worried about protecting their own butts from the officers. And the men aren't learning—by example, or any other way. If you ask me, we could benefit the system by returning to Rocks and Shoals. Of course, nobody's asked me.

Anyway, the point of all of this nostalgia is to explain that, coming out of the Ev Barrett, Red Coyle, Mugs Sullivan, Hoot Andrews tradition, I push my guys harder than most COs do. I also lose fewer men in battle than most COs do. In fact, after more than three decades of the Warrior's life, I can still count my losses on the fingers of one hand. So you R^2D^2. Over and over. And when you think you've got it all down absofuckinglutely perfectly, and there's nothing more you can learn, you train some more—and you learn some more.

No matter what the situation, the principles remain the same: you go through the entryway, moving quickly so as to get the greatest number of shooters inside without hanging up in the choke point, where you are vulnerable. As you go in, you scan for the nearest threat. If there is a threat, you move toward it and you neutralize it. You never stop moving. Let me repeat that, because it is important. You never stop moving. Never, ever.

Where was I? Oh yeah—we'd just stacked. Wonder stood next to the unlocked door. He nodded, letting me know that he was ready. Even though I couldn't see it happen, I knew that Rodent was giving Gator's left shoulder a squeeze to tell him he was ready. Then Gator would do the same to Duck Foot, who would do the same to Doc, who—yup—squeezed my left shoulder firmly. That told me we were all ready to go.

I nodded my head up-down once. Smoothly, Wonder pulled the door toward him. I went through the opening and advanced immediately to my right, my back parallel to the wall, my eyes scanning. Now, if you are a devotee of all those quote realistic unquote Hollywood movies about SWAT and SEALs and SpecWar, you'll remember how they do this—the guys go in from opposite sides of the doorway, pistols and SMGs pointed up toward the ceiling, fingers on the triggers, moving and stopping, moving and stopping in jerky, macho choreography.

Well, friends, there is a SEAL technical term for that stuff. It is: bullshit. What it is, is Hollywood horse puckey. Pure fantasy. You go into a real-life situation like that and two things are definitely gonna happen. First, you're going to shoot your swim buddy when you trip on the doorsill. Why? Because your finger is on the fucking trigger, and he is standing directly across from you, and Mr. Murphy has his hand firmly in the small of your back. That's why we always stack on the same side of the doorway—so we know where we all are and we don't shoot one another.

Second, if you manage not to shoot your buddy when you trip, you're going to shoot the ceiling. Why? Because that's where your gun is pointed. I am a big believer in what is known in the Warrior biz as the laser rule. Simply stated, the laser rule is that you never point a gun where you aren't going to shoot it. You say you don't want to shoot at the ceiling? Okay—don't point your gun at it. The P7 in my hands was in what the folks at H&K call the low ready— that is to say, it was held close to my chest, my finger indexed on the frame next to the trigger guard, in the revolutionary and effective strong left-hand, modified Weaver grip pioneered by the Mid- South Institute's pistoleer John Shaw. The gun's position was more or less horizontal—the barrel was pointed slightly downward, so that my eyes could sight-align instantaneously but not remain locked on the front sight. If your eyes lock on the front sight, they will not scan left right, left right. If you do not scan, you will not perceive threats. If you do not perceive threats, you will get dead.

Okay. So I'm through the doorway. Moving. Scanning. Breathing. Whoops—have I said anything about breathing? No? Well, you gotta remember to *b-r-e-a-t-h-e* during these types of maneuvers, because if you don't, you will actually seize up and fuck up. You will not move, or scan correctly, because your body will become oxygen-deprived, and hence not be working at 110 percent. Moreover, you will almost immediately begin to hyperventilate, which is a Bad Thing during an entry, where your heart rate is going to be pumping somewhere in the 160 range under normal (!) circumstances.

Okay, let's try this one more time. Through the doorway. Move. Scan. Breathe. Doc right on my tail, going left as I go right. Gator, Duck Foot, and Rodent behind him. Wonder, with the suppressed MP5, brings up the rear. Scan. No threats. Breathe. No threats. Move. No threats.

We worked our way all around the courtyard—it was deceptively large, perhaps seventy by seventy—exploring quickly and efficiently. It was empty—and it was clear. I silent-signaled Rodent to pull the gate door closed and remain behind as rear security until we'd made entry. Then he could join us. He answered me with a rueful, single-fingered salute.

I pointed toward the drainpipe and gestured "up." Duck Foot, the lead climber, nodded once. He stowed his weapon and double-secured it in its holster, using both the thumb break, which snaps closed, and a Velcro strap that rides over the top of the thumb break and secures it. Many is the time that a pistol has worked itself loose during a climb, only to drop five or six stories and leave its unfortunate owner with no more than his own limp dick to threaten the bad guys with. Pistol secured, Duck Foot checked the coil of soft nylon rope slung across his shoulder, then started up. When he was ten feet above the ground, Gator, who'd been securing his own weapon and equipment, gave me a dirty look and followed him.

Now it was up to Doc, Wonder, and me. Vynkenski had said there were four wooden doors leading from the courtyard to a series of stairwells. Each of the stairwells led to six pairs of apartments—two per floor. I picked up that quartet of stairwell doors. But just to be certain, I slid my night vision out of my jacket pocket and scanned. Guess what—there were four *more* doorways, two on each side of a narrow, garbage-strewn passageway that separated the two wings of the building.

Great. Exactly what we needed right now: bad directions. Which fucking door was the one we needed to go through to get up to Andrei's private landing? Vynkenski had sworn it was the second door on the left-hand side of the courtyard. But there were now *two* second doors on the left-hand side of the courtyard. Which one was ours?

The answer was, we had to pick each lock, and then go exploring. Which is exactly what Wonder did. And, true to Mr. Murphy's law, the first lock took him more than his accustomed ten seconds. He worked on it for a minute and a half. And if you don't think that's a long time when you're hanging out all exposed in the middle of an operation, just try counting to ninety right now—no, do it *slowly*.

Wonder was either cursing or praying in six or seven languages by the time he'd convinced his fingers and his brain to read off the same sheet of music and act in tandem. You could see his sweaty lips silently reciting whichever form of catechism it was he'd chosen.

Finally, through gritted teeth, he whispered, "Okay," opened the door, and slid his picks back into his pocket. He started to head toward the second door. I silent-signaled for him to stop. No use disturbing any more doors than necessary.

I put my night vision to my eye and I went through the door into the blackness. I saw a light switch at the base of the stairs. The French call these auto-timer light switches *minuteries,* because when you *allumer la minuterie* (figure it out yourself—it's pretty basic French), they stay allumed for about a minute, then automatically switch off, having allowed you to scamper up the stairs in light.

I peered up the stairwell. It was empty. Andrei was in apartment fifty-two. There would be a number on the door. I knew the information was good because Vynkenski had been in considerable discomfort when he'd given it to me.

I made my way to the first landing. The doors were numberless. I climbed another floor to find another pair of unmarked doors. I went up another flight of stairs. More doors *sans* numbers. I knew that this was the wrong stairwell. But I had to make the fucking climb anyway—because Thou Shall Never Assume anything. So I humped myself to the top landing, checked the doorways, saw no numbers, and quietly descended to the ground floor.

Wonder's quizzical face greeted me at the bottom of the stairs. I turned my thumb down, then hooked it toward the other doorway. He rolled his eyes to tell me I'd wasted his time by keeping him waiting, retrieved his lock picks, and shuffled into the passageway, slaloming his way around the frozen garbage.

Wonder breezed through the second lock without an ambient scrape, scratch, or graze. Night vision to my eye, I took point and slipped inside. I hugged the wall, and scanned the floor to make sure there weren't any trip wires, marbles, tin cans, or other makeshift alarms set out. The floor was dirty, but clear.

I moved toward the stairwell and inspected each tread leading to the first-floor landing. All clear. Now I angled my neck and panned slowly up the stairwell itself. Nothing. I made my way up until I could see a door. There was a number on it: 11.

0336. I returned to the main doorway and brought the team inside. We stacked against the stairwell wall and began our climb. In case you hadn't figured it out already, operating in total blackness is tough, stress-producing, uncomfortable work. The dark makes most people claustrophobic. You're moving against an unknown, unseen enemy. Where he is, you have no idea. What he's done to make your infiltration a goatfuck is equally unknown. And then there is Mr. Murphy, who has positioned himself in the stack where he can make the most noise and do the most damage. Have I made my point sufficiently enough? I have? Good. Then I can get back to work.

Here is how our "train," which is what they call the single-file stack when it moves, was lined up. I had the point—and all my energies were going to be devoted to getting us up to Andrei's doorway without attracting any attention. Yeah, I had my pistol out, but it was Doc Tremblay, who rode my shoulder, who'd take out any threat with the suppressed Tokorev. Doc has a kind of Zen ability to shoot blind and hit what he can't even see. It's as if he comes with radar. Behind Doc came the Rodent. Stevie Wonder and his suppressed MP5 brought up the rear.

I took the ascent one step at a time, my toes exploring the marble for loose treads. The pace was excruciatingly slow. It had to be—there was no other way to maintain noise discipline. And so we moved more like SNAILS (Slow, Nerdy Assholes In Ludicrous

Shoes), than SEALs, which as you all know stands for Sleep, Eat, And Live-it-ups.

On the second floor I called a halt—there was light coming from under the door on the left side of the landing. That was potentially Bad Juju—I didn't need to be seen by some insomniac checking the landing. We cut the pace in half and continued.

0351. Andrei's landing. His doorway was on the left side—the number 52 in brass. No sentry outside. In fact, we hadn't seen any sentries since we'd made entry. Did that still make me nervous? Well, kinda. But to be honest, it was nice to be able to take "yes" for an answer just this once. Tonight, Relative Superiority was going to be easy to achieve.

0352. We stacked in the usual sequence. Wonder borrowed my night vision and examined the door lock. I stood opposite him. Behind me came Doc and Rodent. Wonder signaled he was ready to perform his "open sesame" act. I turned the radio's on/off switch to "on," hit the transmit button three times to let Duck Foot and Gator know we were ready and stacked, and then turned the damn thing off again. I've been there, Charlie, and I didn't want Mr. Murphy transmitting during times of radio silence. Carefully, Wonder took his lock picks in one hand. Then he turned the doorknob with the other to test for latch tension.

The fucking door latch clicked open with an ungodly loud *click*. It was unlocked.

I hesitated. Yes, I know that hesitation is a Bad Thing during entry. But this was not a normal entry. I took my night vision back from Wonder. The door swung wide open now.

Fuck. There was only one thing to do—go. I went into the vestibule. I didn't like it but I did it. I swung the monocular left/right/left. Nothing. I kept moving. Down a narrow hallway toward the living room. The night vision picked up something on the floor ahead of me. A body, lying in a pool of dark green. I checked it. Corpse. I peered down at the face through my glass. I knew him—it was Nodyev.

I heard Duck Foot and Gator as they cracked through the living-room windows. *Keep to the ops plan, Dickie.* I cut to the right, into the kitchen. My night vision picked up three more bodies—sitting in chairs, collapsed on the kitchen table. I checked them quickly. They'd been head shot in tight groups, which indicated the kinds of double taps we call hammers, because you shoot tap-tap, tap-tap, real fast. It's a technique unique to spec-ops shooters. I shook my head to clear it. What the fuck—this place was a real goddamn abattoir.

Two more corpses in the dining room. I cut back and left down a long corridor to my primary target—the master bedroom.

The Yudins were there all right—but they were corpses. He had been shot through the head twice, from the rear, at the base of the neck, in much the same way the KGB used to execute its prisoners. Her body had similar bullet wounds. But I could tell from the bloodstains on the bedclothes—not to mention the attitude of the corpse—that she'd been turned over and searched after she was dead. Her left arm was twisted grotesquely—wrist askew, fingers broken. It didn't make sense until I realized that her rings were missing.

Chapter

7

0357. WE SECURED—AS BEST WE COULD. FIRST, WE COVERED THE windows. Then we turned on just enough lights to let us examine the place. The verdict didn't take very long, either: this had been one fucking professional job. Better than most Phoenix ops in Vietnam. As clean as the Israeli hit on Abu Jihad in Tunis. There was no sign of forced entry. No indication of defensive counter-measures. The place had been taken down by the numbers, and everyone in it had been executed.

The bodies were still warm. We'd missed the killers by a matter of minutes. Now the fucking sentry in the Beemer made sense. Now I understood why his keys hadn't fit the front gate door lock. He wasn't Andrei's guy—he was one of the killers' lookouts. Had the bad guys been behind the light on the second-floor landing and let us go by so they could make their escape?

Why had Andrei been waxed? A lot of reasons occurred to me— but only one of them made any sense: Andrei was the most direct link to Paul Mahon's murder. His goon Vassily Chichkov stole Paul's Academy ring. His guys Vynkenski and Blynkenski had been in on the hit. And killing Andrei wasn't the same as, say, wasting John Gotti. In America, there are only a few Godfathers—killing one always makes news. Here, there were hundreds of *vors*, and their deaths hardly caused a ripple anymore.

I hear you—you're asking about Andrei's connections to Viktor Grinkov at the Ministry of the Interior, and to Werner Lantos. In point of fact, any service Andrei provided to either of them could be replaced in hours by one of the dozens of Georgian, Chechen, Armenian, or Russian gangs that controlled huge chunks of this sprawling city. No—he'd been killed to silence him.

We split up and went through the flat looking for evidence. There was lots of booty—art, icons, silver, TV sets, electronics, all piled haphazardly in closets and in the bedrooms. But evidence—whatever it might have been—was not to be found.

I pulled Andrei's clothes from the chair where they'd been piled and went through his pockets. Empty. I checked under the bed. Nothing. I ran my hands between the mattress and box spring. I felt a lump, pulled it out, and extracted Andrei's wallet. I dropped it into my blouse pocket and shoved my arm deeper. My fingers touched the edge of something firm. I extracted it. It was a folder containing three sheets of paper covered with sloppily handwritten notations in Cyrillic. I folded the sheets and slipped them into my pocket, then replaced the folder. Since I was wearing gloves (we all were) I wasn't concerned about leaving any fingerprints. I took a look inside Andrei's wallet, which had a number of business cards that had notations in Cyrillic on them, two laminated photo IDs, and a few Russian banknotes. The wallet went back into my blouse pocket. I took the business cards and slipped them down my thick sock, well below my left boot top.

Wonder spent his time slitting open all the sealed cartons. He came up dry. Doc and Gator searched for caches—hidden drawers, and other hiding places. Nada. Duck Foot and Rodent checked behind the picture frames, lifted the mattresses, tilted the fridge, and checked under the stove. They, too, found nothing.

0429. I was getting nervous. It was time to move already.

We killed the lights. Duck Foot headed toward the window.

"Skipper—" I knew what he wanted us to do—which is exfiltrate down his rope.

I waved him off and pointed toward the hallway and vestibule. With six of us moving at once, it was more efficient and faster to go out the front door, slip down the stairs, and disappear.

0431. We extinguished all lights, waited until our eyes grew accustomed to the darkness, then went out the door. I waited until we all gathered on the landing, then signaled Wonder, our rear guard, to ease it shut, which he did without any sound whatsoever.

I almost started to descend the stairs. Instinct made me pause. I stopped, and silent-signaled to Doc to be absolutely quiet and pass the command down the line. Then, for fifteen to twenty seconds, I listened—really listened—my ears as sensitive as any other watchdog's on that quiet landing.

I heard only silence. Nothing else. That was bad.

Bad? You ask. Yes—bad. At night, even in an apartment house, there are always myriad ambient sounds. Creaks. Vibrations. Other noises that can be technically explained as "stuff." From my earliest days as a tadpole, I'd been taught to set my ambushes as far in advance as possible—so that the normal sounds of the jungle (or the mountains, or the city) would resume around me and my men. Once that happens, once the crickets chirp, and the mosquitoes buzz, and the birds beat their wings, and the alley cats screech, your ambushee will not realize that he is being stalked, and he will proceed toward his own annihilation unprepared.

This silence was unnatural. It was just too quiet; too hushed. My verdict: it was we who were being stalked. I cupped my hand to my ear—silent-signaling for them to stop and listen. Once again, Doc passed the signal on. Then I thumbs-downed—the signal for "enemy suspected."

But we couldn't remain stationary forever. So, without a sound, we began to file down the stairs. We moved quickly but silently in the same order we'd ascended. Behind me, Doc had the Tokorev pointed over my shoulder, searching for targets. Behind him, Duck Foot and Gator moved like shadows. Rodent and Wonder, antennas up, were rear guard.

Halfway to the second-floor landing—the landing where I'd seen light behind a door as we ascended—I called a halt. The SEAL train stopped, stealth-silent, while I proceeded on. Tread by tread I made my way down to the suspect door. The light had been extinguished. Now, moving in increments of centimeters, I eased up to the heavy wood, put my ear to the half-inch of air between, and listened.

There was breathing on the other side of the door. It was unmistakable. Human breathing. Long, deep breaths.

They were behind the door, waiting for us—whoever *they* were. I knew what they were up to because I've done the same thing myself. You let the opposition go by, then sandwich 'em between your forces—catch 'em from two directions at once in a deadly crossfire.

Not tonight. Tonight these assholes were going to be on the

receiving end of any deadly crossfire. It took me almost a minute to make my way back and, with my hands in that dim, dim light, explain what I wanted my men to do.

Plan set. Now, all we had to do was execute. Wonder went up the stairs to Andrei's flat. He opened the door, then closed it again—this time, with an audible "click." As he began to come down the stairs, Duck Foot and Gator took the lead. Rodent and Wonder followed quickly behind them. They went past the occupied doorway, moving quietly and efficiently, but not without making enough noise to get noticed.

Doc and I remained on the landing, our backs pressed against the wall, positioned right up against the door frame. I'd traded my P7 for a Gerber boot knife. Doc's suppressed Tokorev rested steady in his hand.

We waited in total silence. No breathing. No movement at all. I wanted those assholes behind the door to hear the team's progress—not ours.

The silence was absofuckinglutely deafening.

I could hear my decoys as they hit the first-floor landing. And that was when the door next to my left ear cracked open.

There were three of them—a pair of shooters in ninja black, complete with balaclavas, body armor, and stubby Bizon submachine guns, followed by an officer. I knew he was an officer because even though he wore the same balaclava and knit assault cap as his men, he carried only a pistol in his gloved hand.

They crept onto the landing. The shooters were so focused on my decoys, and so intent on maintaining complete silence, that they missed us. The officer, better trained than his compadres, bothered to check in both directions as he came out the door.

Doc jammed the barrel of the Tokorev in his ear. His eyes went wide with shock. Before he could react, I snatched the pistol out of his hand, and slapped my palm across his mouth. The gun went clattering to the ground—so much for noise discipline—and the ossifer tried to wrestle my hand away, pulling at my wrist with his own gloved paw. Hey—there was metal on his wrist. Familiar metal. I couldn't see this asshole's face obscured behind the balaclava. But I recognized that brand-new gold Rolex President and whispered a friendly greeting. *"Yob tvouy mat*—Fuck you, Colonel Rolex!"

And that was when the *minuterie* light came on and an amplified Russian voice from below ordered us to do something. It was the kind of staccato, universal phrase that needs no translation, because whether it's shouted in English, French, Italian, German, Hebrew, Arabic, Portuguese, Urdu, or Russian, it sounds exactly the same.

How do the words actually translate? That's unimportant. What is important is the gist. And no matter what language it's shouted in, said gist is the same. It goes, "Freeze, motherfuckers, or name your beneficiaries."

Only tonight, I had some gist of my own. My gist went, "Doom on you, Russkies."

I blinked in the light, and focused down the stairwell toward the threat. The OMON colonel started to fidget, and I slipped the point of my Gerber under his chin, nicking him just above the Adam's apple. "Play nice, boychik," I said.

The light had caught the pair of Russian ninja shooters on the landing just below us. The rearmost one was swiveled in our direction. His gun was in the CQB mode—up and ready. The AK-style safety was in the full-fire mode. I could see his finger on the trigger—in fact, I could see the Ivan taking up the tension on the trigger as he started slowly up the stairs, moving steadily in our direction.

Behind me, Doc Tremblay took no chances. He dropped the ninja with a single shot in the middle of the temple. No sound—just *whaap* cut him a third eye right through the balaclava. The Ivan slid down the wall leaving a bloody smear on the tile where the back of his head had disintegrated, plopped into a sitting position, rolled over, and collapsed on top of his subgun.

The movement was enough to make ninja Two swivel away from his position focused on what was below him and check on his buddy. There was a micromomentary freeze—the Ivan saw his comrade down and realized he was in trouble, too. So he didn't take any more time to evaluate or analyze—he simply let loose a fat, panicked burst of automatic fire that was sprayed more or less in our direction. There is an accurate technical term for our Ivan's indiscriminate shooting method, friends. The term was first used by that old and respected pistoleer Colonel Jeff Cooper. He calls it, "Spray and pray."

It is amazing the number of things that occur to you when some Ivan asshole with an automatic weapon is trying to wax your ass. For example, right now, I was thinking that in training we almost always wear ear protection, while in battle we do not, and it never fails to amaze me how fucking loud automatic gunfire is, when it's encountered within tightly confined locations—like this goddamn tile-lined, marble-treaded stairwell. I was thinking that I felt like fucking Quasimodo in the fucking Notre Dame bell tower. I was thinking that we were in the middle of an F³—that's a Full Fucking Faulkner—by which I mean there was as much fury as there was sound.

Damn—I flinched involuntarily as the rounds stitched the stairwell and jagged, sharp tile fragments spewed like cluster bomblets all around us. Sit-rep: I took a quick look and saw that no one was hit. Colonel Rolex was okay, although he was hyperventilating. Why? Because as I'd flinched, I'd unwittingly stuck him about a quarter inch deep with the tip of my knife and his throat was bloody. Fuck him—he'd survive. But just to make the sonofabitch feel better I changed the blade's position, laying it flat against his neck. With my left hand I picked a long shard of tile out of my upper thigh, and plucked another pair of splinters from my face—I was probably going to need a stitch or two on my right cheek by the time the night's festivities ended.

Doc was going to need stitches, too. His face had that "death by a thousand cuts" look to it—nasty razor lines all over that big New Englander's puss of his.

Now, the frame for all of the above perceptions and observations wasn't more than a second or so—time does fly by when you are having the kind of fun I like to have—and, despite the aura of slo-motion, things were actually taking place in real time. By which I mean, that the Ivan had loosed a volley of autofire at us, we'd ducked, and now (nice to see Mr. Murphy visit somebody else for a change) it would appear that fucking Ivan's magazine had jammed on him.

Whoops—back to slo-mo again: he fumbled, but ejected the bad mag. *I thrust Colonel Rolex over at Doc, who stuck the Tokorev in his ear.* Feverishly, the Ivan racked the Bizon's bolt. *He was three, maybe four yards away.* He was trying to clear the chamber. *I launched myself toward him.* He realized the chamber was too fucked to clear, realized he was in real trouble, let go the Bizon, and started to reach for his backup weapon. *I caught him with the Gerber in midreach, the tip of my blade finding the two-inch gap between the shoulder pad and rib-plate of his bullet-proof vest.*

The knife caught him just in front of the scapula; I twisted it down and in—using it as a lever to slap the sonofabitch up against the wall. I used the wall—snapped Ivan *craaack* up against it hard. Extracted the knife from his ribs and drove the point into his neck just below his ear, where I cut forward, which severed his carotid artery. His eyes caught mine for an instant. Then they clouded. I kept away from the blood, which was puddling rapidly now, let his body drop, wiped the Gerber on his uniform, and holstered it securely on my belt.

I took three steps and rolled the corpse Doc had shot, plucked the Bizon SMG from the steps, cycled the bolt to make sure the gun was functional, pulled a second helical cylinder magazine from the tactical sheath on the dead Ivan's belt and stuffed it into my pocket, then retreated back up the stairs to where Doc and Colonel Rolex were waiting.

"Everything okay, Skipper?" That was Rodent's squeak from below.

"Two Ivans down. Got us an ossifer. Sit-rep by you?"

"Big fucking welcoming committee out front, boss—we're holding tight until you get here."

"Okay—gimme a minute and we'll be down." I traded Doc the colonel for the submachine gun and spare mags, took the Russian by the throat, and backed him up against the wall. "Doc—watch."

Doc kept the colonel company with the muzzle of his Tokorev while I relieved him of his balaclava, and performed a rapid frisk and inventory.

Top blouse pockets were empty. Back of the neck? Clean. Duty belt—handcuffs, folding knife, and two Tokorev magazines. BDU rear trouser pockets: one wallet, filled with U.S. currency. A laminated ID card—just like the one I'd removed from the Ivan in the Beemer. That explained a lot. Front slash pocket: nasty pocket handkerchief. But just to be sure (and since I was wearing gloves) I shook it open and discovered a pair of diamond rings remarkably similar to the eight-carat marquise solitaire and platinum wedding band I'd last seen on Mrs. Yudin's well-manicured ring finger. I slipped the rings into my own pocket—I'd turn them over to the embassy.

The greedy asshole started to say something. What—didn't he like the fact that I'd found his souvenirs? I gave him a roguish smile and backhanded him hard enough to bring blood to the side of his mouth. "Fuck you, cockbreath."

His right thigh bellows pocket held a Motorola cellular phone. I flipped it open to make sure it was working, listened until I heard the dial tone, shut it, then continued my frisk.

The rest of him was clean. Let me rephrase that. The rest of him did not conceal anything that might have been potentially lethal to me and my men. Once finished, I took the colonel's handcuffs and ratcheted them tight around his wrists. Tight. Did I scratch his new Rolex? Aww, golly.

I stage-whispered down the stairwell, "Rodent—"

From below: "Yo."

"We're coming down."

"Roger that."

I put the colonel in front of me and held him firmly by the bicep. Doc covered our six with the Bizon. We stepped over the pair of corpses and made our way down to the ground-floor landing.

It didn't take long to discover they were a small force, and they had us bottled up—at least they thought they did. I did a quick recon—made my way back up to the apartment that Colonel Rolex and his ninjas had used, and peeked out the window. OMON had done this operation in a pretty basic fashion. There were no searchlights, no barriers, and no Moscow cops to keep the street clear. All I saw were four vehicles spread out like a fan in the big courtyard, their lights shining toward the apartment house. The gate where the Beemer had been was now wide open, and the Beemer was missing. Behind the cars, I counted eight, nine, ten— eleven OMON shooters in black. I played the monocular up on the opposite roofline and picked out three snipers. *There was something wrong here*—the old Rogue saw something pogue.

I lowered the glass, focused, and examined the opposition a second time. The practiced eye will tell you a lot. First, I saw that none of the Ivans were carrying climbing gear—not a single rappelling harness, coil of rope, or carabiner in the bunch. That meant they weren't going to try to climb to the roof and make their way down through the stairwell behind us. No way to run an urban op.

Second, all the cars were private. Okay, I'm no authority, but I'd seen enough of Russia and its officials to know that when I see two white Beemers, an ivory Mercedes, and a goddamn silver Chevrolet Caprice, we're not talking POG—property of the government. Moreover, there was no SWAT truck with its equipment and backup. There was no command and control vehicle, coordinating communications and keeping civilians out of the shooters' hair.

Ah—I see your hand waving, gentle reader. Yes, Colonel Rolex had all that ancillary stuff supporting him when he'd hit the dacha two nights ago—including the goddamn climbing equipment, even though his men didn't need it. But he sure as hell didn't have any of it tonight. Verdict: these assholes were operating on their own.

I double-timed back to the ground floor, plucked the cellular phone from Wonder's hand, and punched zero, nine, five, two, five, two, two, four, five, one into it.

Bring-bring. Bring-bring. Bring-bring. You get the idea. It went on like that for about thirty seconds. Then, finally, a sleepy, surly, Russian-accented voice answered, "American Embassy. Can I help you please?"

"This is Captain Richard Marcinko, commander of the United States Navy Naval Security Mobile Training Team," I said. "This is an emergency. Put me through immediately to the deputy chief of mission's quarters."

Chapter

8

OUR FRIENDLY DEPUTY CHIEF OF MISSION (AND ACTING AMBASSADOR plenipotentiary and extraordinary) Bartlett Austin Wyeth the BAW arrived on-scene sixty-eight minutes later, in an embassy limo, driven by the RSO—State's Regional Security Officer—and sandwiched between a pair of Silverado war wagons—huge, Chevy four-by-fours—holding half a dozen DSS gumshoes armed to the teeth. All the vehicles flew the Stars and Bars from their fenders, and all arrived with their red-and-blue flasher lights working. Just after the Americans pulled into the illuminated courtyard, three more cars arrived: first, a huge black stretch Zil limo sporting half a dozen different kinds of antennas pulled into the courtyard. It was driven by a black-bereted OMON driver who, I saw, kept a 410-gauge, automatic, AK-47 shotgun bolted muzzle-up next to him, and half a dozen of AK's big box magazines strewn on the bench seat. The Zil was followed by two small black Zhigulis, stuffed so full of humongous hoodskis that they looked like those tiny circus cars filled with clowns. It occurred to me—one of the more pleasant thoughts I'd had tonight—that my analogy wasn't too far from the truth.

The DSS agents emerged from their war wagons, MP5s and cut-down Benelli M1 entry shotguns ready, and surrounded the

119

Caddie, facing outward. Then Bart climbed out. He'd taken the time to dress for the occasion: double-breasted diplomatic blue pinstripe suit, white shirt, polka-dot tie. Polished cap-toes. But you could almost sense the sleep in his eyes, and his body language gave away the stress he was under. The RSO instructed his men to give Bart some room, and they expanded the cordon sanitaire around the Caddie by three yards on each side. Bart began to parade like a cell-bound prisoner next to the car door—three paces, then an abrupt, soldierly about-face, three more paces, and another abrupt reverse.

Now it was the Russians' turn. Viktor Grinkov rode alone in the Zil—I knew that because he had the interior light on and I could see his slovenly profile. He waited until four of the hoodskis in the ugly Zhigulis disembarked, surrounded his car, and opened the rear door for him. He emerged, holding a black leather portfolio, shot his cuffs, and sniffed the air like the old, mean Russian bear he was.

Then he nodded imperceptibly, the hoodskis surrounded him, and walked him in the diamond over to Bart's car. The diamond, in case you're not familiar with such shorthand, is the shape of the protective shell favored by Secret Service agents when surrounding POTUS. And, just like the Russkies have copied everything from our weapons systems to our TV studios (and not paid a penny in licensing fees for 'em), they've appropriated our executive protection techniques as well.

Now, the first of the Russian bodyguards drew nose to nose with one of Bart Wyeth's DSS agents. The Ivan pressed ahead, as if to move him aside. But the DSS man didn't budge. The Ivan stopped, then, inexplicably, he backed up, causing the diamond to collapse inward.

Bad move. You never, ever give up ground. The DSS agent simply took two steps forward, and occupied the vacuum left by the Russian. Now the Russian hoodski was really confused. He turned, as if to ask his boss, Grinkov, a question. Instead of an answer, he received a resounding slap across the face. Chalk up the first points for the Americans.

Then, having made its point, the solid wall of armed Americans parted, and Viktor Grinkov—alone—was allowed to proceed to the DCM, who received him with a single, formal handshake.

I descended from my observation point on the second floor and peered through the cracked front door to get a ground-level view of the negotiations. The two of them were looking over a thick sheaf of papers in Grinkov's folder.

The Russian was growling. Bart obviously answered him in kind, because he stuck his nose in the DCM's face and said something to which Bart obviously took offense.

Bart's shoulders hunched, and his arms flapped wide, palms upward, as if to say, Well, what the hell can I do about it? The Russian didn't like what he'd heard—he shook his head vigorously—but Bart wasn't having any of it. His arms crossed, he shook his head in the negatory fashion, and told Grinkov, *"Nyet."*

The Russian didn't take it well. He slammed the folder on the roof of the Caddie, stuck his finger under Bart's nose, and mouthed off. Bart uncrossed his arms and pouted. The Russian sneered, turned on his heel, grabbed his folder, and strode back toward his Zil limo, proceeding down a gauntlet of Russian and American bodyguards.

Bart followed him, entreating as he walked. The Russian was not happy. Then Grinkov stopped in his tracks.

He asked Bart a question. Bart answered. The Russian nodded in agreement, and began to follow the DCM back up the gauntlet toward the Caddie.

Bart took Grinkov's right elbow with his left hand. They walked, their heads inclined together, whispering.

They stopped. Bart stuck his free hand in Grinkov's direction, and the Russian took it. They nodded at each other.

God, how I love to see true diplomacy at work.

Obviously, it hadn't been easy. You see, I'd made things tough for both of them. The Russkies and I were in what they call in France, "Le Mexican standoff." I had Colonel Rolex. He—his men actually—had me and my guys bottled up.

Now, I knew damn well that neither the United States nor the Russkies wanted any publicity about this here incident. It was an embarrassment to both of 'em. Which is why I'd told Bart the BAW that if he didn't get his diplomatic butt out of bed and deal with it, I'd call ABC, CBS, NBC, CNN—and any other news organization I could think of, and invite them to come down here with their cameras rolling and sort out the good guys from the bad guys.

Talk about your nasty wake-up calls.

Oh, Bart had bitched and Bart had moaned. But he'd pleaded

with me not to do anything rash—"No publicity at all—none—"—and promised that if I kept silent he'd have the matter solved within the hour. From the look of things, he'd been almost as good as his word.

Now, obviously the problem had been compounded because this stalemate had occurred while both Colonel Rolex and I were engaged in slightly, ah, irregular activities. But that is where all similarity stopped. Colonel Rolex and his men had been at Andrei's because they'd been ordered to neutralize him. He'd become a liability to a business venture that was making a lot of money for somebody. Andrei's execution was what they call *zapodlo* in Russian—seemple beeziness.

I, on the other hand, had been protecting my country's interests when this-all happened. Sure, it may have been something of a rogue operation, but I hadn't been out playing games, or because I wanted glory, or more medals; I hadn't been at Andrei's just because I like to shoot & loot & sneak & peek & hop & pop, I happened to have the evening free, and there was no convenient Russkie pusskie at hand.

I was at Andrei's because I had perceived what I considered to be a palpable, credible, genuine threat against the United States of America, and against the Republic for which it stands. It has always been my job, as I understand it, to uncover and then promptly neutralize threats to our nation. It is a diplomat's job to make talk. It is a warrior's job to make war. I was doing my fucking job.

Bart and Viktor Grinkov were walking back to the Caddie like old friends. I didn't like that at all.

"I'm going to see WTF," I said to Wonder, handing him the cellular phone. "You guys keep an eye on the colonel."

I cracked the door open. "Bart," I called, "I'm coming out for a sit-rep."

The look on his face told me that he didn't like that idea at all. He tried to wave me off. I ignored him. I strode toward the limo. One of Grinkov's hoodskis got in my way. I took him by the throat—my right thumb and forefinger pinched his windpipe until his eye popped—and moved him aside. The roguish expression on my face dissuaded him from any further protest. The DSS agents let me pass through their line without incident—I even got a friendly wink from one of 'em.

I didn't bother with formalities. "What's the score?" I asked Bart.

He looked at me with the sort of expression that maharajas reserve for untouchables. "You have caused a great embarrassment to the Government of the United States," Bart began. He turned away from me, and spoke in rapid Russian to Viktor Grinkov.

The Ivan grunted, then opened the thick leather portfolio while Bart extracted his three-hundred-dollar bureaucrat's fountain pen from an inside pocket so he could sign the thick wad of papers that sat inside.

I put my hand on the DCM's shoulder.

He turned, and actually lifted my fingers off his bespoke-clad shoulder. "What *is* it?" he snapped.

"I want to know what the fuck is going on."

"Minister Grinkov and I have negotiated an agreement acceptable to both of our governments," Bart said slowly, as if talking to an idiot. "You and your men are being PNG'd—which is to say the six of you are being declared personae non grata by the Government of the Russian Federation."

"That's horse shit."

"Perhaps. But it is a fact," the DCM said. "It has been further agreed that you and your men will be expelled from the Russian Federation directly."

"But I still have work to—"

He cut me off. "You have no say in this, Captain. It is a diplomatic matter, not a military affair. I have already been in touch with your superiors in Washington—Rear Admiral Prescott to be precise. He has assured me that whatever I choose to do, he will support. Now, if you please . . ."

Bart turned his back to me, slipped on a pair of tortoise shell-framed half glasses and examined the fistful of Cyrillic pages, which had embossed seals and ribbons and other diplomatic garbage attached to them. He read each document in the wad with painstaking concentration, signed and/or initialed where indicated, then handed them back page by page to the Grinkov as soon as he'd finished his autographing.

The Ivan examined each signature closely, wrinkling his nose as if the ink smelled like sour manure. When Bart had finished, he countersigned three of the papers, and handed them back to Bart. The rest were stored in the leather folder, which Grinkov snapped shut with a flourish. The Russian held his left hand out. The Zil's driver produced a worn, brown leather briefcase, which he handed to the Internal Affairs minister. The folder was slipped inside and returned to the chauffeur, who stashed it on the limo's backseat.

Grinkov turned toward me. He did not look happy. "You have caused me great problems," he said in English. "I will not forget."

"It's been nice meeting you, too," I said.

The Ivan put two fat fingers into his mouth and whistled, as if he were calling a cab. The OMON shooters stood down. I ran my night-vision monocular over the roofline. The snipers had disappeared.

I turned toward the doorway where Wonder and Gator had Colonel Rolex by the collar.

"Let him go," I said. "And let's get the fuck outta here—despite what these assholes say, we still have some work to do."

Viktor Grinkov and his hoodskis escorted us back to the embassy. We surprised them when I had the Silverado in which I was riding stop by our hotel, so we could grab our luggage and pick up our steel lockbox.

When Viktor saw the box, he went bananas, screaming at Bart that it was obviously evidence that belonged to the Russian Federation, and he wanted it—*now*. Frankly, if it hadn't been for the regional security officer and the DSS shooters, I think Bart would have tried to force me to hand the fucking thing over (fat chance of that, friends). But the RSO protested—loudly—to Viktor that, as anyone could see, the box had been sealed with a pair of stamped lead POGUS—that's Property of the Government of the United States—security seals, and that it was, therefore, official U.S. government property, and that any attempt to appropriate it would result in physical, not diplomatic action.

That hurdle passed, we continued on to the embassy gates. Once there, the Zil and the Zhigulis stopped well short of the entrance. I turned just in time to see Viktor's tinted window slide down and, a dour expression on his face, watch as our American convoy drove safely inside.

Safe, of course, is a relative term. We pulled up in front of the main chancery entryway. I climbed out of the Silverado and headed for the doors, watching Viktor and his ugly Zhiguli crew watch me. Bart jumped out of his Caddie and actually sprinted, so he'd get to the doorway before me. But his hand brushed me as he passed, and he screeched to a stop, then recoiled physically as if he'd touched a leper.

He turned to look me in the eye. The expression on his face was absolutely absolute in its portrayal of aristocratic loathing and repugnance. "You and your men will wait in my anteroom. I will deal with you in half an hour—and you will regret causing me this extensive trouble and embarrassment with our host government," he snapped.

Dearest gentle reader, as you can probably imagine I was feeling neither particularly amiable, genial, nor benign right then, so I responded with the sort of established and habitual roguish response favored by most SEALs in similar situations, "Why don't you go bugger yourself, you numb-nutted, pencil-dicked asshole," I stage-whispered, smiling all the while just in case there were security cameras rolling.

Gee whiz and golly, video rangers, for some reason that really set the cocksucker off. He began jumping around like a fucking organ grinder's monkey, flecks of spittle flying indiscriminately past my ear as he waved a bony index finger under my nose and promised the end of my career and the demise of my unit and all sorts of other dire fulminations.

Y'know, Bart's behavior upset me. I am, after all, an O-6, which is a captain, in the United States Navy. I am the commander of a tactical unit. Let's talk about those factoids for a minute. A commanding officer's responsibilities are, by Naval custom, tradition, and doctrine, categorical. He is entirely, utterly, wholly, completely answerable for the safety of his ship, and the welfare of his men. And while he may be a part of a chain of command—a *Navy* or at the least a *military* chain of command, let me emphasize—his authority (and the utter responsibility thereby attached) as a CO is unequivocally nonetheless absolute. Simple declarative sentence. COs run their units. Period. Full stop. End of story.

Now, my tactical unit may not have been the largest, or the most influential tactical unit in the U.S. Navy. But it was *mine* to command, and to field. And, from my perspective, Bart—no matter what his rank, his stature, or his bloated self-image might have been—was not an element within my unit's chain of command. I answered to Rear Admiral Kenny Ross, back in Washington, and ultimately to the chief of naval operations, the Chairman of the

Joint Chiefs of Staff, the secretary of defense, and the president—not to the Department of State or its duly appointed representatives.

Or, to put it into the sort of fundamental, UDT/SEAL language you probably realize I like to use most of the time, I didn't have to take this kind of shit from him, nohow.

And I wasn't about to make Bart's tactical error, either—that is, jumping around and spewing invective, not to mention saliva, in front of my men, or his men. You may not know this, but I was once a diplomat myself—I spent a year wearing not pin but tiger stripes (SEALs don't wear any other kind) as the naval attaché in Phnom Penh, Cambodia. And I learned early in my diplomatic career that when you want to say something to one of your fellow diplomats that might embarrass, chastise, or otherwise unsettle him, you should do it in private, and not in full view of any governmental representatives of your host country. Now, perhaps Bart had forgotten this elemental facet of diplomatic conduct. But I hadn't. The Russkies were still watching and I didn't want to give them any more satisfaction than they'd already had this morning. Therefore, whatever I had to say, I'd say it inside—in private.

I took hold of Bart by his upper arm, spun him around, and began walking him inside the embassy, so that it looked from the rear—that is to say, from beyond the embassy fence—as if we were deep in serious conversation. Have I told you that I press four hundred plus pounds on a regular basis? I have? Good. Have I reminded you that I do thrice-a-week exercises to strengthen my delts, brachs, biceps, triceps, pronators, and palmars? No? Well, I do. Which means, when I want to hold on to something, I can fucking well grip it *h-a-r-d.*

The DCM's eyes went saucerwide; he looked over at me and whimpered, "Wha-wha-wha—" You see, I had Bart by the back of the delts, which are in the back of the arm, halfway between the elbow and shoulder. I'd lifted slightly, so he had to walk on tippy-toes. I can tell you that he didn't work out at all, because there was no trace of muscle where I was grasping him tightly enough to leave fingerprints. None at all. And from the way he was breathing, I knew it must have been very painful for him as I marched him lockstep and double time through the door, past the security checkpoint, and up to the elevator doors.

I released him and he stepped away from me, rubbing his arm. "Geezus—what the hell are you trying to—"

I was in no mood for this. "Look, Bart, give it a rest until we've had a chance to—"

"Dammit"—he started to sputter again—"I *told* you—I *ordered* you—"

"You don't order me, Bart. Full stop. End of story." The look I gave him told him I'd break his arm the next time I took hold of it. He stopped babbling long enough to let me get a few more words in. "Additionally, if we're going to discuss this any further, we'd better do it in the bubble, because what I've got here"—I tapped the steel lockbox that Doc and Wonder had carried into the chancery—"is code-word stuff."

That brought him up short. I think he actually thought I'd been out there playing fucking games.

The bubble, as it is commonly known, is on the eighth floor of the old embassy building. Actually, it takes up so much of the seventh, eighth, and ninth floors that if you want to pass from one wing of the eighth floor to the other (the embassy has two wings and the bubble sits more or less equidistant between them), you have to go either up to ten, or down to six to do it. The bubble was built in the late seventies by a joint team from the National Security Agency, the CIA, the State Department's Bureau of Diplomatic Security, and the U.S. Army Corps of Engineers. It is probably the only place inside the U.S. Embassy compound in Moscow that is absolutely secure from eavesdropping. The room itself is small, perhaps sixteen or seventeen feet wide and twenty-three or twenty-four feet long. There is an unpretentious, wooden conference table, and two dozen uncomfortable, cheap, molded white plastic porch chairs, which are usually left stacked in three rows against the wall. The reason for using those specific chairs is so that nothing can be concealed inside them. On the table sit a secure fax and a pair of scrambler phones. There is no video monitor. There is no computer. The less equipment in the bubble, the less they have to worry about being compromised or bugged.

When you are inside the bubble, you always, somehow, feel claustrophobic. The reason that you do so is that you are actually inside a room within a room, within yet another room, which in turn has been suspended inside still another huge, secure, cube-shaped framework.

Now, what I'm about to tell you is secret, so please don't pass it along to anybody, okay? In fact, when you're finished reading this section, you might consider ripping the pages out of the book and shredding them, then burning them. Okay—each of the more than a dozen security layers comprising the bubble has a different type of baffle system to defeat the various forms of surveillance and TECHINT, ELINT, and SIGINT devices that the KGB used (and the Foreign Intelligence Service currently uses) against American diplomats.

You want specifics? Okay. Against UHF and VHF radio waves, the engineers suspended honeycomb-shaped metallic foil barriers. Against the microwave and X-ray bombardments common in the eighties, they installed a series of lead shields. To block ultrasonic penetration—that's where you read the sound waves that vibrate off walls, windows, doors, and so on—there are two vapor-locked, hermetically sealed barriers through which separate waves of white sound (each has its own unique vibrating tone) are continually pumped. Moreover, the walls were all constructed so as to absorb, not reflect, any stray morsel of sound. Finally, the interior conference room itself is actually floating inside a bath of thick liquid— much the same way the yolk of an egg is suspended by the white inside the shell. The doors (there are two of them, separated by a dead space into which sound is pumped) are eight inches thick, and they resemble hatches on a nuclear sub more than they do doors at an embassy.

Bart and I, accompanied by Gator, Duck Foot, and the lockbox, all took the elevator to the eighth floor, turned left, walked down a short corridor, and went through a set of double doors outside of which stood a single CIA or DipSec security man who either pumped iron thrice a day, or wore an MP5 submachine gun in a shoulder holster under his well-tailored sport coat, or both. From there, we maneuvered the steel chest through the cumbersome, two-step, air lock door system and into the bubble.

The boys set the chest on the table, saluted me in an offhanded way with a "There you go, Skipper," and exeunted upstage.

Bart lifted a molded plastic chair off the pile next to the wall, looked it over, then took a handkerchief from his trouser pocket and wiped its seat off. Satisfied it was now worthy of receiving his SFS—Senior Foreign Service—butt, he positioned the chair at the head of the table (I knew it was the head because it was where the phones were), then plunked himself down, his arms crossed and his expression dubious. He looked at me. "Well?"

I reached down and extracted the small Gerber blade from the sheath on my belt. Bart saw that the knife had blood on it, started to say something, then thought better of it. I cut through the wire on the lockbox. Then I unlaced my right boot and removed it, pulled my sock off, and retrieved the small, flat key that I'd taped to the sole of my foot with a Band-Aid. I used it to unlock the small but effective padlock that secured the hasp on the lockbox, dropped the lock on the table, opened the box, took Paul's files and the materials Avi'd given me, and removed them from their folders.

Bart's arm extended toward the thick sheaf of papers, notes, and photographs in my hand. "All right, let's see them."

"I think it would be better if I laid it all out to you," I said.

He gave me a bemused look but dropped his arm back into its crossed, RIP position, and sat there, Waiting with a capital *W*.

For the first time, I examined Bartlett Austin Wyeth closely—I mean *real* closely. He had, I realized, a certain otherworldly, vampiric quality to him. Which made sense—he was, after all, a diplomatic bloodsucker of the Olde School. But I'm talking deeper than that. I mean that, come to think of it, sitting there with his folded arms, with the slicked hair, the natty, bespoke pinstriped suit, the pristine starched white shirt with its long-pointed, wide-spread English collar, and the burnished bench-made cap-toes, the sallow little motherfucker looked like he'd just climbed out of a box of his native soil. Yeah—all he needed was the cape and the gloves.

I wondered whether or not one could see his reflection in a mirror. I wondered how he'd react if I suddenly made my index fingers into the sign of the cross. I wondered whether—and then he broke into my reverie. "Okay, Dick, it's your show," he said, his thin lips drawing back to reveal pointy little teeth in an ironic half-smile. "I'm all ears."

Y'know, there is an affliction common to many high-ranking diplomats and flag-rank military officers. It is called HICS, or head-in-cement syndrome. Its most conspicuous symptom is an unshakable, pig-headed reluctance to change one's opinion. Once anyone affected with HICS has a preconception, no matter what you say, no matter what facts you can marshal, you cannot overcome it. What I'm getting at is that despite two hours of monologue in the bubble, I was as stymied at the end as I had been at the beginning. Bart's sardonic expression never changed. Neither did his opinion of what I told him.

What was that opinion? Why don't you hear it for yourself

directly from him. "I explained this to Paul Mahon, and now I'm telling it to you," he intoned pedantically. "Yes, there is a problem with smuggling of dual-use materials, former Soviet military equipment and weaponry, and other forms of contraband. And yes, the so-called Russian Mafiya, as well as various entities within the Russian government, may very well be involved in those activities. I don't dispute either of those assertions. But the embassy is on top of it. Moreover, there is a separation of duties within an embassy, Dick. And at the highest levels, it has been determined that these problems do not fall under the military's purview. They are political concerns, and we at State are dealing with them on the proper diplomatic level."

Do you hear that? The sonofabitch was trying to blow me off. Well, I wasn't about to let him do that. "Don't give me any doublespeak, okay. Paul Mahon was killed because he was investigating the connections between the Russian Mafiya and the smuggling of dual-use materials. Andrei Yudin was killed because he was the connection between the crooks in charge, and Paul's murder."

"Perhaps. I will grant that your suppositions are not inconceivable. But even if they were proved beyond a reasonable doubt—which is far from the case—there are a number of your actions that simply cannot be excused."

Geezus. "Such as?"

"Such as trying to investigate matters that are far removed from your purview. Such as creating the sort of diplomatic incident that I have had to deal with this morning. Such as the killing of Russian nationals. You have singlehandedly upset the Russian-American relationship to a degree that I cannot fathom."

Whose side was this guy on? "Everything I have done," I said, "I have done to identify and neutralize the murderers of a U.S. Navy officer who was killed while in the performance of his official duties."

"Yes," Bart snapped, "that is true. But you have done it by acting as prosecutor, judge, jury, and executioner." His face grew tight. "Captain, even here we have rules of evidence that have to be followed."

Rules of evidence? WTF. We were talking about a situation that had caused the murder of a United States Navy flag rank officer, and this asshole was talking about rules of evidence.

I rubbed at my beard and my 0820 shadow with the back of my

hand. This was like trying to talk to a fucking wall. No, this was more difficult. But I kept going.

I went down the list: the NATO break-ins, the DITSA memos, and the probes of the Paris embassy, and the Customs intercept in Virginia.

Unrelated, said the DCM—and by the way, how the hell do you know what's being discussed in internal, eyes-only, Department of State memoranda?

I brought up the meeting at the Dynamo—Werner Lantos, Andrei Yudin, and Viktor Grinkov, all at the same table, and all hours before Andrei Yudin was murdered in his bed. The Russian Mafiya, I was told, was vastly overrated—scare tactics from American conservatives. Andrei Yudin might be an enterprising guy—a cut-the-corners entrepreneur. A criminal? Sure, it was very possible—it certainly would help to explain Andrei's unfortunate demise. But Bart insisted he'd never heard the name Yudin mentioned by any of the embassy staff involved with Russian organized crime.

And what about the cozy relationship between Werner Lantos and the Russkies, and his current involvement with the shipment of dual-use materials.

Let me give you that response verbatim from Bartlett Austin Wyeth's own lips. "Werner Lantos has been a friend of the United States—and of this particular embassy—for more decades than I can remember. Specifically, he has been of invaluable help in furthering American diplomacy, through four administrations and six ambassadors."

Yes, I showed him the Air France waybill, as well as the materials I'd received from Avi Ben Gal. The only things I didn't show him were the papers I'd taken from Andrei's—simply because I had no idea what significance they might have had, and besides, I didn't know what was in 'em. They probably wouldn't have mattered anyway, because Bart explained my evidence away by saying that if there had been anything suspicious about the transaction, the French would have stopped the shipment in the first place. Since there were French Customs stamps on the paperwork, then everything was kosher.

And why had the waybill been discovered at a dacha owned by a criminal who was known to be smuggling dual-use materials to the Middle East? A criminal who had just been assassinated—an execution most likely carried out by a corrupt police unit.

The question itself was hypothesis, not fact, insisted the DCM. "There is reasonable doubt about your conclusion."

Reasonable doubt? What was this—the fucking OJ trial?

"I do not appreciate your sarcasm," Bart said.

Yes, I felt like reaching across the table and throttling the sonofabitch. But killing him would have done me no good—what I had to do was harder. What I had to do was convince him that the Russians were up to something that jeopardized our national security. I stopped and gathered my thoughts. What about the fact, I argued, that the Israeli embassy's agricultural attaché, my old friend Avi Ben Gal, had told me that Andrei Yudin was moving dual-use technology to countries cited in the State Department's yearly publication *Patterns of Global Terrorism?* And what about the documents Avi had turned over to me?

And what, the DCM wanted to know, gave an Israeli agricultural attaché named Avi Ben Gal the credentials to know so much about dual-use smuggling, and waybills, and Russian criminal activities?

I told the DCM what gave Avi Ben Gal those credentials. But nothing I said did anything to change his opinion. In fact, the DCM's only reaction was to unsheathe the three-hundred-dollar fountain pen that was probably twice the size of his dick and commence making notes on the legal pad that sat directly in front of him on the table. "So what you are telling me," he said as he scribbled, "is that you met one-on-one with a foreign intelligence official, but you didn't report the contact through the proper channels here."

"Proper channels?"

"Yes, 'proper channels,' " he said, ice tinging his voice. "You did not clear your meeting through the DISCO." He looked up at me. "Well, I am correct, am I not, Captain Marcinko?"

He was getting so formal all of a sudden. I sighed the sigh of the uncomprehending and the innocent. Yes, he was correct, was he not. And what the fuck was a DISCO, anyway.

"DISCO stands for Diplomatic Intelligence and Security Coordination Officer," Bart prattled. "And"—he shuffled the paperwork in the black leather binder he habitually carried—"I see no indication here that you observed the regulations."

"Well, technically not, I guess. But—"

" 'Technically not, you guess.' " He looked up at me with that triumphant sort of bitchy expression bureaucrats have when they realize that they have launched a successful ambush in the Paper

Wars. "And you know that such a meeting, when unreported, is a security violation, Captain Marcinko?"

Well, actually, I knew it—but hadn't given the matter a flying F-word. So far as I was concerned, I'd been meeting with an old friend and comrade in arms. A man with whom I'd operated on the battlefield. A man who'd saved my life, and whose life I'd saved. So far as I am concerned, Avi Ben Gal is my shipmate—with all the touchie-feelie shit that word connotes. And that, friends, is exactly what I told the deputy chief of mission.

Of course, my explanation didn't matter. In fact, I could almost see my words entering his left ear, shooting straight through his skull, exiting the right ear, and being sucked up by the soundproof baffles of the wall six feet away. Because Bart wasn't listening to me. That was obvious. No—he was already drafting his cable back to Washington.

As he wrote, I packed—I slid the papers back inside their folders, then tucked the folder inside the steel box. Maybe I'd find somebody back in Washington who'd listen to reason.

Bart's eyebrows flicked to attention. "Hold on, Captain," he said. "You can't do that. Those documents have to stay with me. They are embassy property now."

I locked the box securely and peered across the table at him. "Listen up, *Bart*, because I'm only going to say it once. This box and everything in it is the property of the United States Navy," I said. "Moreover, this box contains explosive devices and weaponry. And by Naval regulation, I am allowed to protect explosive devices and weaponry by using lethal force." I picked the box up by its handles. It was goddamn heavy, but I was angry enough to carry it. In fact, I wanted the DCM to see that I could carry it—unaided.

I fixed him in my sights malevolently. "Pretty please, Bart, old man," I said. "Pretty please—give me an excuse to use lethal force."

Chapter

9

WASHINGTON WAS UNSEASONABLY WARM BUT SEASONABLY WET THE afternoon we arrived. So, between the sweat and the thundershower I was soaked to the skin by the time I found my van in the satellite lot. I toweled off with a greasy shop rag then drove back to the arrivals area. The guys stowed the lockbox, and, after a long detour through Old Town Alexandria, I headed west and south through Prince William county to Rogue Manor, my two hundred acres of lakes and snakes that kind of but not quite backs up onto the Marine base at Quantico.

It had not been an easy or a pleasant flight home. We'd been flown to Paris in steerage class on an Air France A-340-300. You ask why that is significant. It is significant because A-340-300s have 47 rows of steerage seats, 208 in all, instead of the 139 economy-class seats in an A-300 or an A-310. It is significant because if you are a 46 extralong slash extramuscular like I am, you get a case of terminal leg cramping if you spend more than an hour in the tiny steerage-class seats, which are only eighteen inches apart, seatback-to-seatback, and which do not tilt. Let me add that the flight from Moscow to Paris lasts roughly four hours. No, let me phrase it differently. The flight from Moscow to Paris lasts four rough hours.

You're asking why we didn't take Northwest, or Delta. It is

because PNGs from the Russian Federation don't have the luxury of waiting for their own flag carriers. They get bused to Sheremetevo ASAP and shipped out on the first available aircraft. Frankly, I didn't know who wanted us out of the country more—the Ivans, or Bart Wyeth.

Our problems didn't stop with cramped seating. Once on the ground, we played games with the French *douaniers* (those are the kepi-sporting customs agents) at De Gaulle Two over our lockbox of lethal goodies. See, because we'd flown Air France out of Moscow, we had to switch terminals, and I insisted that we hand-carry the box with us. Now, French Customs may not have blinked an *oeil* at Werner Lantos's hot-freon tanks transshipping through Paris to the Middle East via Mustique, but they busted an *intestin* when they heard about our fully declared and POGUS (Property of the Government of the United States) MP5 submachine guns and pistols.

Three obscene phone calls to the defense attaché's office at the American Embassy later, we had solved everyone's problems and we transited (yeah—that's how they call it) the mile and a half to De Gaulle One. Then we cleared security. (That act, incidentally, took two and a half hours of wrangling and another phone call to the embassy, since the customs agents at De Gaulle One obviously do not speak to the customs agents at De Gaulle Two.)

Exhausted and palavered out, we finally made our way to the concourse, found the only open restaurant, and ate an expensive lunch of *sandwich jambon avec la moutarde sur pain Poilane.* That's a ham sandwich with mustard on brown country bread that is crusty, for those of you whose French has gone rusty, accompanied by two dozen or so eighth-liter, twist-top bottles of cheap, generic red wine. We six accomplished this lunch, incidentally, while crammed in a booth built for four, whose previous occupants had managed to spill mayonnaise all over the Naugahyde banquette.

After our repast and the antacid cocktails that followed, I paid my respects at the duty-free shop, where I bought a liter of Bombay gin that turned out to be twice as expensive as what I pay at Fort Belvoir's Class IV package store. I also dumped two kilos of French coins into a pay phone and called Avi Ben Gal to tell him I wasn't going to make our rendezvous. No luck. I gave my name, got switched to his office, and was told he was out of the building for a few minutes. Then the line went dead. Nothing devious or furtive, friends—only the vagaries of international telecommunications at work.

Then, my duties completed, we space-availabled on the first available U.S. carrier back to Dulles, and things began to look up. First, we got upgraded to business class. Then, by the time we were over Greenland, Wonder and Gator had wangled assignations with two of the flight attendants, and Doc, Duck Foot, and Rodent were huddled together like Wobblies, plotting an anarchic recon of Old Town in search of cold beer and warm pussy.

Ah, the eternal optimism of youth. Oh—you want to know about me? Well, I'd considered heading straight to the Pentagon to see Ken Ross and tell him what I'd found in Moscow. But that was when we were clearing Nova Scotia and I could see the water thirty-nine thousand feet below. Then the headwinds increased and the weather changed. By the time we hit our second nasty front of squalls over New Jersey, we were already half an hour behind schedule. Then we circled over western Maryland (or was it southern Pennsylvania?) for just over sixty-five minutes. By the time we wheels-downed at Dulles, it was already just past 1800, and the lockbox and I didn't clear customs until 1946. That's almost eight o'clock at night in cake-eating, civilian time.

Almost no one in the Pentagon works late anymore. If you work late you don't have the time to sell real estate on the side, or manage your portfolio of mutual funds, or engage in any of the other money-making schemes in which officers and gentlemen (not to mention enlisted pukes) are engaged these days, instead of spending their time figuring how to make war. Now, Ken Ross didn't strike me as a nine-to-fiver. But I doubted that even he'd still be on the job at 2200 or so. Therefore, I dropped the guys in Old Town, then worked my way south on I-95 toward Quantico, turned west, then took back roads to the Manor. Yeah, I'd have preferred an evening of beer and pussy, and not necessarily in that order. But I had the box to look after, and some planning to do.

And so, instead of soaking my aching muscle between warm thighs, I did an hour on Rogue Manor's outdoor weight pile, followed by a hot sauna and a cold whirlpool. And the only red meat I got to see was nineteen ounces of USDA choice sirloin, cooked Pittsburgh—that's black-and-blue for the uninitiated among you.

Then I laid out every piece of paper, every record, every photograph, clipping, and memo from Paul's file, and each sheet of

Avi's paperwork, as well as my own sparse notes, like the pieces of the puzzle that they were, on the tile floor of my basement rec room.

I arranged them. I rearranged them. I stacked, piled, aligned, sorted, and catalogued. I itemized and tallied. I positioned and prioritized. Then, like a deck of cards, I shuffled the fucking pile and began all over again to see if the results came up the same.

When they did come up exactly the way they had, I started making notes.

Oh—you want to know what I'd discovered.

Okay, I'll tell you. I'll tell you, because a good epiphany—an event as full of ecstasy, rapture, and bliss as any orgasm—is, just like orgasm, an experience that should be shared with a friend, not performed alone.

- The signs, as I read them, pointed toward a broad conspiracy. Russian bears were prowling and growling: probing Western facilities; making off with Western technology; recruiting Western assets. But this time, they'd added a new wrinkle. The Russkies were using their mafiya as part of the intelligence-gathering equation.

How did I know this? I knew it because there was no other reason for Paul Mahon to have spent so much time taking pictures of Russian mafiyosi, and tracking their organizations and movements. I knew it because the Israelis, who still run a lean, mean intel machine, had detailed one of their best military intelligence officers—a man, I will remind you, who was an expert on the Soviet military and its procedures—to Moscow, to do precisely the same thing I'd discovered Paul had been doing: track Werner Lantos, the Russian Mafiya, and the connections between them and the Russian military.

But most of all, I knew it because it made keep-it-simple-stupid sense. Who better to sluice supplies from East to West than a criminal culture that had been stealing goods for decades under the noses of the Commies? Who better to smuggle weapons and dual-use technologies than the same people who'd been bringing everything from Scotch to drugs into the old Soviet Union? Who better to recruit new agents—remember when I told you how the old KGB used honey-traps to snare Western businessmen and diplomats—than the same pimps and other no-goodniks who'd been running whores for years? In fact, as Avi had said, every Russian hooker, whether she worked in Moscow, Paris, Tel Aviv, or New York, worked for a mafiya *vor*.

- What was in it for the mafiya? That was easy. Money—lots of money. Billions, even tens of billions of dollars. And access—tacit government support for their illicit activities.
- What was in it for the Russkies? That was easy, too. Powerful political elements within the Russian government—Viktor Grinkov was a prime example—were trying to move the country back toward communism. One of communism's goals was the destabilization of the West—specifically the United States. By creating new intelligence networks to harass the West, and by slipping weapons of mass destruction to some of the old Soviet client states, these hard-liners hoped to foster rapid destabilization. Their goal was to keep the United States off-balance while Russia reconstituted itself as a super-power.
- Now, where did Werner Lantos fit in this equation? He was the linchpin of the whole plan.

I see you out there, including Mr. Editor. You're all yelling, "Whoa, Dickie—that's too big a step right now."

No, it is not. Let me explain. When I ran black programs out of the Pentagon—and I ran a lot of 'em, believe me—the one thing that I needed most of all was a banker. See, finding the men to staff a covert unit is easy. Equipping it, keeping it supplied, and moving it around is hard. Hard, hell—it's almost impossible.

Why? Because despite all those stories about six-hundred-dollar toilet seats and eight-hundred-dollar wrenches, the government actually likes to know where its money goes. It does not hand a suitcase of greenbacks to a unit commander and say, "Go forth and spend ye the cash." There is paperwork. There are requisition forms. There are purchase orders.

Now, when the unit you command is covert, your problems are increased geometrically. Every penny you spend has to come from somewhere legitimate and accountable, then those pennies have to get lost, and—mirabile dictu—reappear again, freshly laundered and completely untraceable. Depending on the size of the unit, you sometimes have to move huge—and I'm talking tens of millions, friends—even humongous sums of money all over the world, without stuffing hundred-dollar bills into a suitcase and schlepping it from capital to capital. The answer is: you need a bank, and a friendly banker who can bend the rules to launder your funds, and get 'em where you need 'em, and do it all without attracting a lot of unwelcome attention from the banking authorities, foreign governments (not to mention your own), the press, and those other nasty folks known as The Opposition.

How did I do that when I ran black units? I found a small, shady investment banker in Italy I'll call Schultz, because he looked like the chubby Cherman guard in the old *Hogan's Heroes* TV series. Schultz had connections all over the world—the kind of juice that allowed him to play the shell game called international finance. He also had a rep as a quick-and-dirty money man who handled a lot of money for a dozen Saudi princes as well as a bunch of less pleasant types based in various South American countries. In other words, he handled a lot of cash-intensive transactions for dictators, thugs, and probably worse, and he didn't ask a whole lot of questions about where the bucks came from. Was he a nice guy? No. Was he ultimately indicted for bank fraud, and is he currently serving twenty-five years in a European prison? Yes. But when he worked for me, he got my funds precisely where I had to have 'em, exactly when they had to be there—and no one was ever the wiser.

- Item: Lantos & Cie were investment bankers. Werner Lantos knew all the shell-game techniques of moving money around.
- Item: Werner Lantos had been doing business in Moscow for more than two decades. He knew how to move, who to pay off, and most of all, he kept his mouth shut.

Ah, but Master Marcinko-san, there are a lot of other banks doing business in Moscow.

True, tadpole. But Werner Lantos was the only banker in Paul Mahon's notes. He was the only banker Paul had a photograph of. His name was on the waybill that I discovered in Andrei Yudin's dacha, and I met him in the company of Andrei Yudin and Viktor Grinkov. And the Israelis had been on the scent for years—in fact, the Israelis had assigned one of their top intel officers to keep track of him. One plus one plus one plus one equals four.

Ah, Master Marcinko-san, you are guilty of chop-logic. You give only one side of the equation. Your own diplomat in Moscow, Bart Wyeth, deputy chief of mission, told you in no uncertain terms that Werner Lantos was a Good Guy.

You are correct, tadpole. But guess what? I've decided to discount Bart Wyeth's input.

Why, Master Marcinko-san?

Because, tadpole, I have decided that Bart is part of the problem, not part of the solution.

Now you have completely lost me, Master Marcinko-san. You have just made a huge jump—and I cannot follow.

Listen and learn, tadpole. In his second-century treatise on strategy, the master Wu Ch'i talks of defeat through contempt. "Falsely convince the enemy to despise you," he writes, "and you will overcome him."

That is precisely what Bart had done with me. From the very first day we'd set foot in Moscow, he had worked—hard, I might add— to make my life difficult. My reaction was, I am sorry to say, not unconventional at all. I'd spent a lot of time and energy thinking of ways to get around Bart's strictures. Mostly what I did was stay away from the embassy—which I realized now was exactly what Bart had wanted to achieve in the first place.

There was another thing, too: I instinctually disliked Bart Wyeth in an active, visceral way that doesn't happen too often. Over the years, I have learned to trust my instincts. They have kept me alive. Now, deep in the marrow of my bones, I had the hunch that Bart was part of the problem. Could I prove it? No, not yet. But right now, just feeling that he was hinky was enough for me.

At 0835 the next morning I showed up in proper uniform and French braid outside Rear Admiral (Lower Half) Kenneth Patrick Ross's office on the fourth-floor E-ring lugging a huge black leather satchel—the suitcase-size kind pilots use to carry their charts and books. The senior chief yeoman behind the desk pointed her thumb vaguely toward the doorway, and hit the electronic lock release. I turned the polished handle downward and pushed the heavy paneled wood door inward. The director of operations, plans, and politico-military affairs was sitting scrunched in his high-backed leather judge's chair, a pair of half-glasses perched just above his eyebrows, concentrating on whatever was on the huge Sony computer screen that sat on the port side of his Executive Group One desktop.

He waved me inside but kept me standing while he punched keys and did all those wonky, computer geek kinds of things that byte-size dipdunks do to save their documents and close their programs and mash their modems or WTF. As you know, computers and I are not friends.

Then, finished with his wonk-work, he pushed the drawer that held keyboard and mouse pad under his desk until we both heard a satisfying *thwock* that told him it was STOWED. That's when he pointed toward the well-worn wood-framed leather armchair that faced his desk and indicated that the satchel and I were to Park It There. No, he wasn't smiling, either.

Nor was his greeting very friendly. "Dick, has anybody ever told you that you have a world-class talent for pissing people off?"

Oh, yeah—I've heard all hundred-plus choruses of that song before. It goes on longer than "Ninety-Nine Bottles of Beer on the Wall." "Fuck, Admiral, I may not have the best bedside manner in the world, but I'm a hell of a brain surgeon."

Now, there are admirals to whom you can say the dreaded F-word, and there are admirals to whom you cannot say the dreaded F-word. Ken Ross, whose own supply of profanities seldom progresses beyond "darn," surprisingly falls into the first category. Even so, he looked over his desk at me in the understated, I Am Not Amused expression with which nuclear submariners discipline their troops. "You may call yourself a brain surgeon, Dick, but I'm beginning to think you work with a jackhammer instead of a scalpel." He rapped a thick file on his desk with the back of his knuckles. "This stuff is serious. What the heck did you and your guys do over there—gang-bang the ambassador's wife?"

"Look—"

"Hey, Dick, *you* look. Our friend Paul and his family get dead. I pull a huge load of strings to send you over to do a little covert recon—precisely the sort of thing you, as a SEAL, are supposed to be good at. And what happens? Chongjin harbor all over again. Remember Chongjin? You and your Red Cell were supposed to sneak and peek and that was all. Instead, you blew up a gol-darn North Korean ship, and my butt almost got fried over it. Now instead of sneaking and peeking, you get yourself PNG'd. You'll never be allowed back to Moscow, y'know? And that's not the

Russians talking—it's *our* embassy. And guess what else? The French don't like you very much, either. It seems as if you can't even pass through an airport without causing a diplomatic incident."

I shrugged. I had better things to talk about. "Big effing deal."

His face told me it was a big effing deal so far as he was concerned. But he paused to let me speak. Instead, I retrieved the three sheets of paper I'd taken from Andrei Yudin's flat and slid them across his desk. "I need these translated ASAP," I said.

"What are they?"

"Don't know—but I found them in a dead mafiosi's apartment the night I got PNG'd, so I'd like to know."

The admiral looked at me, plucked his phone up, and dialed a number. "I need a Russian translation done—now," he barked. "Here. My office. Right." He looked at me and sighed with the resignation of a pissed-off but devoted parent. "Okay—it'll be done in the next hour. But I don't think there's anything you could discover that will improve your current situation."

"Look, Admiral—I'm a SEAL. I'm used to all sorts of maritime situations. That includes hot water."

He didn't appreciate my attempt at humor. "Hey, if you don't think this is serious, guess again. It's gone to Pinky Prescott's desk, and he's gotten himself involved already. Meetings all day yesterday. Late into the night, too."

"What about?"

The submariner drummed his finger pads on the desk in a silent arpeggio. "I don't know. He shut me out. All I've been told is that he wants your behind in his office in—" Kenny Ross glanced at his watch. "Twelve minutes—zero nine hundred. And just in case you didn't know, he isn't very fond of you."

Pinky—shit. Now I realized why Ken Ross was so upset. It was doom-on-Dickie time—which meant I was about to get fucked in Vietnamese (and every other language I could think of).

Okay, a few words of literary digression are probably in order here. If you have read the previous trio of *Rogue Warrior* novels, then you know all about my long-standing and ongoing relationship with Pinckney Prescott III, Rear Admiral (Upper Half), United States Navy, and you can skip the next few paragraphs. If you haven't, then go out and buy the fucking books—now. You should also pay attention, because I might very well spring a little quizzie on you later.

Pinckney Prescott III, or Pinky the Turd, as I prefer to call him, is the son and grandson of admirals. Like them, he went to Annapolis. And like them, he has spent his entire Navy career in a series of landlocked staff jobs. The one disparity with his daddy and granddaddy is that Pinky the Turd somehow made it through BUD/S and ended up in Naval Special Warfare. Now, let me stipulate for the record that Pinky has never seen combat, or led men in battle, or engaged in any actual SpecWar operations whatsoever. He has, however, perfected the art of PAPWAR— paper warfare. Give the man a sheet of twenty-pound bond, a word processor, and a laser printer and he can slice you up good. In fact, Pinky is the goddamn Miyamoto Musashi of memo writing.

Ever since I can remember, he has used this singular talent to maul, bawl, and keelhaul me. It began when he was the commodore in charge of NAVSPECWARGRU Two, which is the mouth-filling acronym for NAVal SPECial WARfare GRoUp Two, and I ran SEAL Team Six. Pinky tried to have me disciplined for buying too many shoelaces. No, I am not kidding, so pick your jaw up off the floor. That's the kind of guy Pinky is. And to show you what kind of guy I am, I have evaded, stymied, and just plain fucked with him ever since the shoelace incident.

Now, on the one hand, Pinky has always appeared to hold certain strategic advantages over me. For example, he's always outranked me. I'm a captain. I wear eagles on my collar. He wears stars on his—currently two of 'em and going on three if you believed the RUMINT—that's RUMor INTelligence—on the fourth-floor E-ring. But on the other hand, I have always managed to maintain a slim tactical advantage or two over him. A few years back, for example, I was able to get my hairy paws on a certain Naval Investigative Service report focusing on Pinky's extracurricular extramarital activities and blackmail him with it. Yes, I realize blackmail is not a nice thing to do. But in Pinky's case, it was justified. Come to think of it, in Pinky's case, murder would be justified.

These days, however, I'm a bit shaky in the tactical advantage department for a couple of reasons. First, the NIS report, which was hidden in a cache below the kitchen floorboards at Rogue Manor, was turned into mush about five months ago. While I was in California chasing down an asshole named LC Strawhouse, a goddamn pipe running in a channel under the kitchen floor burst. I came back to find my floor ruined and, more significantly, Pinky's file destroyed.

Second, in the past I have generally had a rabbi—like CNO Arleigh Secrest, for example—who could shield me from Pinky's wrath. See, the way things work in the Navy these days, if you have a protector who wears four stars, you can fuck with one- or two-star officers and suffer only minor dings. But I didn't have any rabbis these days.

In fact, it had been so long since I had a rabbi to go to, I was beginning to feel like an out-of-work Shabbas goy. The only star I could count on was Ken Ross's—and not only was he junior to Pinky, he reported to the sonofabitch. Currently, you see, Pinky was assistant to the deputy chief of naval operations for plans, policy, and operations. He was at the top of the food chain, Kenny Ross was somewhere in the middle, and I was the fucking dog meat.

How Pinky'd wangled the job I do not know. Probably, through one of his Annapolis classmates—notably a one-star named Don Layton, who was the executive assistant to the acting chief of naval operations. Point was, Kenny Ross was in no position to protect my hairy Slovak ass from Pinky's wrath.

As you know from experience, I have a constant and ongoing relationship with pain. I hurt, therefore I am. This morning, however, I'd have preferred the birch tree from Chapter 1 to what I was about to experience. Still, as our dweeb editor is so fond of misstating, "no pain . . . no pain." And so, hurting and therefore existing, I marched the three hundred feet from Kenny Ross's office down the hall, turned right, then left, then right again, until I came to the warren that was Pinky's suite.

Now, friends, let me add a couple of things here about Pinky's character. First, he is a bully—and like all classic bully personalities, he acts aggressively only when he senses his victim is weaker than he. Second, his idea of unconventional warfare in interpersonal relationships is to spring something at the very last moment and hope that the person affected will not have time to react to it. Now, if one knows about these facets of his personality, one can react accordingly.

This SEAL do know, and this SEAL do-do. Or, as Roy Henry Boehm, the godfather of all SEALs, likes to put it, I was about to go out and fuck the fucking fucker.

He kept me in the anteroom, cooling my fins for seventy-five minutes. I knew what he was doing inside. He was watching *Live with Regis and Kathie Lee,* or whatever other morning trash was on the TV. I could fucking hear the muffled commercials and the banter right through the door. But the prissy yeoman behind the Executive Group Three, Bureau of Prisons-manufactured, genuine imitation walnut desk kept looking at me, and repeating the same goddamn mantra, as if it was that fucking recorded voice mail shit you get on the phone these days: "The admiral is quite overwhelmed this morning with urgent matters but he wants to see you and he will be with you shortly."

It was like, "Press 'One' to leave a message; press 'Two' to press 'One.'" After three-quarters of an hour, shortly had stretched to longly. I sat, meditating, my eyes focused on a small crack in the wall just above and to the left of the yeoman's perfectly cut hair.

Meditating? Yes. You see, friends, you cannot allow assholes like Pinky to disturb your equilibrium.

That is their whole strategy—to knock you off balance and thus defeat you. But being in balance—with yourself, with your situation, and with the world around you—is a lot of what being a Warrior is all about. You see, Warriordom is more than the ability to jump out of a plane, or take down a building, or board a ship under way, or neutralize a fortified position with a flanking maneuver. Warriordom is also a mental state that incorporates a high, even spiritual degree of awareness.

Yes, I said spiritual. No, I am not about to enter the realm of touchie-feelie. I am about to give you a no-shitter, a wisp of the ethereal, metaphysical gestalt that surrounds the making of a Warrior.

Sure the Warrior can do anything that he has to in order to fulfill his mission. And the Warrior is always ready to die. As the seventeenth-century Japanese master swordsman and poet Fudo wrote: "The Warrior knows there is nothing to be won or lost, except that which is to be won or lost. Everything becomes everything, and death follows naturally."

What Fudo is saying is that the Warrior must always be ready to accept death—death, after all, is the natural result of his art and his craft. And the soul's acceptance of death is one important and fundamental element of the Warrior's makeup.

But there is another essential principle as well. The thought was perhaps stated most effectively by Huang T'ai Kung, the famous strategist of the Han dynasty in China almost two thousand years ago. It was T'ai Kung who wrote: "Before the Warrior can face the enemy, the Warrior must face himself."

What this means is that the Warrior must have a sort of spiritual and moral gyroscope; an internal mechanism that keeps his soul operating on an even and constant high plane, no matter how adverse the conditions under which he must operate.

It is this gyro that makes it possible to endure. You endure, because you know you are a better man than your opponent— purer, more consecrated, and sanctified. You have been blessed by the God of War. You can suffer, tolerate, or undergo *anything*.

It is my unshakable belief that when these two intrinsic values— the total acceptance of death as a natural condition of life, and the total acceptance of an absolute moral code—are combined, the Warrior becomes invincible.

We Navy SEALs begin the long inculcation of Warrior values during BUD/S by exposing our tadpoles to formidable doses of physical pain and mental strain during the fifth week of their training—a time that has come to be known as Hell Week.[6] Now, the challenge is overtly physical during Hell Week—lots of cold, and sleep deprivation, and exhausting exercise in the surf and the mud. But physical transmogrifies to mental, when, after Hell Week, those tadpoles who made it through realize that they can do about 1,000 percent more than they thought they could. They are beginning to think like Warriors.

But that is only the beginning. One begins the real training—the mental work—later. It is the mental edge that keeps a SEAL prepared to fight, and kill, even though he may never have to do so during his entire career. There are times—and I've been there— when you train for months on a single, exhausting mission element only to be stood down at the last moment because the diplomats have found a political solution. Or when you hone yourself to a razor's edge, and train, and train—but never get the call to go to

---

[6]Significantly, under orders from the Clinton administration in the midnineties, the Army introduced what it called "Stress Cards." These pocket-size, yellow, laminated plastic cards are distributed to recruits just after they arrive for their basic training and indoctrination. If the training becomes too much to bear, or if the trainee believes he is being unfairly singled out by his drill sergeant for punishment, he can hold up his stress card and declare, "Time out." The sergeant must then back off, and leave the trainee alone for half an hour, so the soldier can compose himself. It is the kind of touchie-feelie, feel-good, pointy-headed liberal pseudothinking that will get men killed in battle. Are things too tough in Bosnia, Somalia, or elsewhere? Just hold up a yellow (yellow for coward—just like the cowardly president who instituted it) fucking card and the enemy sniper will let you alone for half an hour. Right. Sure.

war. That is when the Warrior's spiritual gyro becomes most important. When it sustains you and keeps you at your mental and physical peak—even though you may never be used in the ways you thought you would be used.

And so I sat and I meditated until my consciousness was invaded by the prissy yeoman's prissy voice, the door opened, and I was admitted to the Royal presence. You'll be pleased to know that Pinky looked terrible. He reacts badly to stress, and from the look of him, he was really stressed out. His hair, which has a tendency toward cowlickery, was in full Dagwood Bumstead. His skin was gray-yellow, his cheeks sallow. He'd tried to hide the fucking slimline TV remote control under a pile of papers. But it stuck out like the sore pencil-dick Pinky is. He followed my line of sight, saw that I saw what I saw, and tried—without success—to nudge the remote farther under cover.

"You called?" I didn't see any sense in using his first name yet.

Pinky picked up a curly sheet of fax paper from a thick pile of faxes, messages, and other documents, and shook it at me as if it were a shaman's rattle. "This c-c-cable is a c-c-c-complete outrage," he stuttered.

I wasn't about to make things easy for him—and he didn't know that the NIS file in my possession had turned to mush. So I asked, "What is, P-pinky?"

"G-g-goddammit, don't do that. Don't mock me." He sat up as straight as he was able. "And that's 'What is—*sir?*' " he intoned. He pointed to the stripes on his sleeve. "What are those? Chicken liver?"

"No, sir," I said, enunciating the *c* and the *u* so he could hear them plainly, "they are chicken something else."

"D-don't talk to me like that, Dick," he said, trying his best to sound authoritative. "I'm a goddamn admiral. I am about to be appointed to a job at the White House."

Oh, sure. And I was about to be made CNO.

Pinky closed his eyes and took a series of deep breaths—no doubt to bring his blood pressure down a hundred points or so. Then he laid the fax sheet back onto his desk, smoothed it out, and pointed at the pile it lay atop with a bony index finger. "It has come to my attention," he said, accenting the syllables with finger taps on the fax sheet, "that you exceeded your directives in Moscow."

"I did what I thought I had to do."

"Precisely." He smiled up at me in the supercilious way all

147

bureaucrats smile when they have discovered that an *i* isn't dotted or a *t* isn't crossed. " 'Did what you thought you had to do.' But you exceeded your directives. They were plainly spelled out in your mission order. I have them here in front of me and I have highlighted the relevant section. You and your men were to—and here I quote: 'Advise and train U.S. Navy personnel assigned to AMEMB Moscow in security procedures, urban survival skills, and counterterrorism.' Full stop. End of assignment. But not for you. No—*you* created a diplomatic incident. *You* were declared persona non grata and deported. And as if that weren't enough, *you* caused our Naval attaché in Paris—an old and dear friend and a classmate of mine at the Academy, I may add—great personal embarrassment."

"What's your point?" I asked. I didn't have time for this bureaucratic crapola. I had to get my men together, come up with a workable plan, and go hunting. There were bad guys prowling and growling, and I was stuck in a fucking office, wasting time with this arrogant asshole.

"My point," Pinky said, an edge creeping into his voice, "is that I have disbanded your unit."

"What?" It was absurd. He couldn't have.

He was plainly elated by the expression on my face. "Oh, yes. Dismantled. Dissolved. Dispersed. *Disassembled.*" He clapped his hands together like a child with a new toy. "Scattered to the winds."

Like I said, it was impossible. He couldn't have moved so fast, and I told him so.

"It's amazing what BUPERS—that's our Navy's BUReau of PERSonnel you'll recall—can do when you light a fire under them," Pinky said.

It had been a bad, bad error on my part to assume that no one at the Pentagon works late anymore. Obviously, Pinky had been working lots of overtime on this little move of his.

I also realized that Pinky wasn't stuttering anymore. That, I understood in the very pit of my gut, was an exceptionally, exceedingly, extremely sinister omen.

"Your SEALs have been sent back to their original units," he said *sans* repeating a single excess vowel. "Their transfers are irrevocable. There is nothing you can do."

Oh, yeah? Listen, I still had friends—at BUPERS, and elsewhere in the Navy. There was Karen, the new, young secretary in the

SpecWar detailer's office—she worked for my old friend Marguerite—who'd reassign a SEAL every now and then in return for a night of B&B and B&B, which as we all know stands for Benedictine & brandy, and blow jobs & back rubs. There were all those chiefs in my old Safety Network. There were a few young SEAL officers who I'd trained in my image who'd be willing to make a wave or two if necessary. "We'll see about that."

Pinky leaned back in his huge leather chair and grinned up at me. "Oh, this isn't me talking, Dick. If it were only me, you'd find a way around. I know you. After all, I've been saddled with you for years. No—this is the *system* talking, not me. And the system works best for me these days—not for you. Moreover, the acting chief of naval operations himself has given his blessing to this new arrangement. It's he who wants your unit disbanded—now that I've shown him some of these unfortunate messages. CNO doesn't want any more humiliating embarrassments. CNO doesn't want any more diplomatic incidents."

"There was only one incident, Pinky. One."

"In this Navy," Pinky proclaimed oratorically, "CNO believes that is one too many. We tolerate zero incidents these days. Zero defects these days. Zero. None. No mistakes allowed. No social errors. No harassment. No sexism. No racism. No intolerance of any kind—implied or otherwise. And certainly, no diplomatic incidents. They are severe embarrassments, and severe embarrassments will not ever, ever be condoned. Let me be clear on this: four-star admirals have been fired for a single, ungentlemanly misstatement. Captains like you have been retired for lesser offenses than you have committed." He riffled noisily through the papers on his desk. "The fact that you are still in the Navy— haven't been relieved of duty and forcibly retired—mystifies me. But for some reason, you are being allowed to continue your service—continue . . . *for the present.*"

Oh, that was gratifying. But Pinky didn't give me a chance to be ironic. "In fact, as of this morning," he continued, "you have been named deputy assistant to the assistant coordinator of security for the acting chief of naval operations' office at the Navy Yard." He paused. "It is a position with no staff, no travel, and very little budget. It is—obviously—based here in Washington, at the Navy Yard. You will report to the acting chief's assistant, Rear Admiral Layton, at precisely thirteen hundred." The Turd ostentatiously checked the heavy gold Rolex, a watch that had once belonged to his father, Pinky Two, and now hung on his own scrawny wrist. "That's two hours and twenty-seven minutes from now."

He flicked the back of his hand vaguely in my direction. "That is all. You may go."

I just stood there. My friends, for once in my life I have to admit I was absofuckinglutely speechless.

Which you could see just pleased the hell out of Pinky the Turd. He grinned up at me with those bad teeth of his showing. "Dismissed," he said, looking as happy as I've ever seen him. "Oh, yes, you are indeed dismissed, Dick." I could hear him chortling as the door closed behind me.

Chapter

10

I DOUBLE-TIMED BACK TO KEN ROSS'S OFFICE, SNATCHED THE FIRST phone I came to, and called down to my Naval Security Mobile Training Team office on the third-floor B-ring. There was no answer at NSMTT—not even the voice mail message I'd recorded. I called the Pentagon locator and asked for myself. The operator told me I didn't exist. I dialed the apartment Gator Shepard shared with the Rodent and Duck Foot Dewey. No answer. I tried Duck Foot's pager. The pager number didn't respond. I tried Gator's pager, then Rodent. Ditto. I called Doc Tremblay's bungalow off Route 1 near Fort Belvoir and let the phone ring two dozen times. Nada. I tried his pager. It, too, had been disconnected. Now I was really unnerved. I punched the number for Wonder's rented English basement in Old Town and got a message that the phone had been disconnected and there was no new number. This was fucking crazy.

Ken Ross stuck his head through his office door. "Yo, Dick— what'd he say? How'd it go?"

I guess the expression on my face told him how it had gone. He waved me toward his office, his own expression grim but determined. "C'mon in. Let's see what we can do."

For a submariner—for most submariners, I remind you, if it's not on the checklist, it doesn't exist—Ken Ross had a wonderfully

151

independent and aggressive attitude toward my situation, something I appreciated a lot right then.

Because the fact is, friends, I was not about to accept Pinky's verdict—or the system's. First, there was Paul's death. That ship's cruise log was still open and would remain so until I exacted vengeance on all his killers. Second, there was something big and dangerous afoot—and I wasn't going to stop until I'd discovered what it was. And last, even though you may think it unimportant, I believe there are serious problems with the concept of a zero-incident, zero-defect, or ZD, Navy. I believe the concept must be challenged if the Navy is to survive.

Oh, ZD is the politically correct solution to a series of convoluted, complex, and often knotty problems. Politicians love ZD because it takes care of all those nasty media-whipped events like Tailhook. Everything is neat. Tidy. Shipshape. I'll give you all that.

But my friends, the military is not a social club, or a university, or a corporation. It is a huge and sometimes unwieldy structure that exists for one reason only: to fight wars. Many politicians forget this basic mandate and try to use the military for other objectives. Now, so far as I am concerned, the instant you give the military other missions—being cops, or social workers, the way they were in places like Haiti or Somalia, for example—you are going to see failure. And the instant that you try to make the military into just another civilian-type organization with zero-defect social rules and regulations and mores, you will doom it to failure as well.

Even at the most basic levels, the military is different. You civilians out there have a president. I don't. I have a commander in chief. You have civil rights. I don't. I fall under the Uniform Code of Military Justice, which denies me many of the Constitutional rights that I am willing to die to protect.

So we are different. Moreover, the minute you try to make everyone in the military equal in every way, you are going to fail, too. Sure, all soldiers are OD—olive drab. Yes, all Marines are green, and all sailors are blue. Race, religion, social background, should not and do not count diddly-squat so far as I am concerned. Like I say, I am an EEO kind of guy. Which means—as the Roguish SpecWar Commandment says—I treat everyone alike. Which is (let's all repeat this together, shall we): *just . . . like . . . shit.* I will not tolerate any less.

Now, having said that, there are certain jobs—being a SEAL or a

Ranger are two of 'em that come to mind—that are not conducive to EEOdom. In fact, they are not jobs conducive to 99.9 percent of any kind of "dom."

Since I'm a Navy fella, let's examine the personality type who becomes a SEAL. He must tolerate pain and discomfort well. He must become part of a team but know how to think for himself. He must be willing to look an enemy in the face and pull the trigger without hesitation—whether that enemy be man, woman, or child. Yes, child. An eleven-year-old girl with an AK-47 is just as potentially lethal as a twenty-five-year-old man with an AK-47. You have to be willing to shoot her. Does that shock you? Well, let me remind you that SEALs were created by Roy Boehm as killers first and foremost. In fact, Roy used to tell me that he preferred his men straight from the brig—because that way he knew they had a little felony and larceny (ofttimes it was a lot of felony and larceny) in 'em. He was being serious, too.

Roy also used to tell me that if he had to choose between his family and his SEAL team shipmates, he would unhesitatingly choose his teammates. "You can always get yourself another family," Roy growled. "But you can't get another team."

Fact: when you combine the personalities, the edge-of-the-envelope missions and the closeness of a group of testosterone-prone males who have been forged on an anvil of pain, steel, and blood, you are going to get sparks every now and then in units like SEAL boat crews, Green Beret A-Teams, and Marine Recon platoons. And that is a Good Thing. As a SEAL CO, you shouldn't want to lead a bunch of men whose idea of a good time is an evening of tiddlywinks and cocoa. You should prefer a beer-drinking, pussy-chasing, bar-brawling group of shooters.

But guess what? In today's Navy, a SEAL who receives a DUI from a Virginia Beach cop loses his security clearance. No security clearance means he's booted from the Teams. Brawling? One strike and you're *O-U-T*. Even a speeding ticket can get you cut from the Teams. Pussy chasing? Forget about it. As a matter of fact, if you're socked with a sexual harassment charge even though you can prove you haven't done anything wrong, it can mean the end of your career. That's what happened to Captain Ev Greene—he was found innocent of sexual harassment charges by a court-martial board, and yet the politically correct SECNAV still denied Ev his rightful promotion to rear admiral.

My friends, that is wrong. You cannot take a man, teach him how to jump out of planes at thirty-five thousand feet, swim miles in cold water lugging sixty pounds of combat gear, clamber up ice-coated oil rigs, egg-fry hot steel bridges, and humongous dams; inculcate him in the deadly arts of flattening buildings with explosives, rigging lethal ambushes, and silent take-downs—and not expect him to blow off some steam every now and then.

Fact, bub: you cannot take a man and train him to kill efficiently, and then expect him to act like a wimp when it's Miller time. Train hard, work hard, play hard, is my credo. But that principle is DOA in today's Navy.

In today's Navy the most talented SEALs—the real shoot-and-looters—are retiring early. Why? Because they have too many demerits next to their names—and their officers, afraid of not receiving the next promotion, won't back 'em up. Back 'em up, hell—the officers are the ones writing out the charges, because in today's politically correct, wimp-driven Navy, it is the C²CO— that's can't cunt commanding officer for anyone who's forgotten— who's gonna make flag rank. And so, the Navy is losing its best men o' warsmen. The danger exists that there may never be another generation of real killers—SpecWarriors in Roy Boehm's image— or mine.

Well, friends, that also is just plain wrong. The nasty but nevertheless irrefutable fact is that this nation needs killers. Not often—at least not as often as I'd like to see it. But when the time comes, we've got to have 'em—men willing to do any nasty, hostile thing they have to do to accomplish their missions. Men who'll win at all costs. Roy Boehm, the godfather of all SEALs, calls 'em men o' warsmen.

And that, friends, is why I fight so fucking hard to stay around as long as I can. I don't need money—these books have made a fucking dump truckful of cash, believe me. And I don't want glory—I have all the medals I can use. And I know I'll never make admiral—they don't promote brawlers like me to flag rank. Well, friends, guess what? None of the above matters to me. Not a whit. My reason for staying where I am and fighting the Pinky Prescotts and the rest of the C²COs is a very elemental component of my character. Simply put, I will use every particle of my energy, every atom of my being, to fight the status quo in order to continue to train and lead warriors in my image, so that when the SEALs of war *are* unleashed, *we will not fail.*

Despite those sentiments, there was nothing we could do about reassembling my unit. Not, at least, at the present time. I phoned Karen, my kuddly kontact at BUPERS, and engaged in a little aural sex. Ten minutes later she called back to give me the bad news. Duck Foot Dewey had been assigned to BUD/S as an instructor. He was due in Coronado twenty-two hours from now. My pair of animals, Gator and Rodent, had been transferred henceforth and forthwith to the Special Boat Unit at SPECWARGRU Two, down at Virginia Beach. I called the amphibious base at Little Creek, talked to a lieutenant commander who didn't mind helping an untouchable, and found out they were due in by COB—close of business.

Doc Tremblay was impossible to track. Until, that is, I called Rogue Manor and cleared my answering machine. Message number one was Doc's depressed voice, growling that he was calling from an Amtrack train phone, already on his way to the submarine medical unit at Groton, Connecticut, and WTF could I do to get him the hell out of there ASAP. Messages two, three, and four were from the rest of my guys—with similar gist. Do? I hung up the receiver knowing that there was nothing I could do.

The only survivor was Wonder, who wasn't a SEAL, and who had never officially been transferred out of his classified job at the Navy Yard into my NSMTT. Kenny Ross did some quick checking and discovered that, so far as he could tell, Pinky'd never even discovered that Wonder existed. Count that as a small but significant victory for the good guys. But what about the message I'd gotten—the one that said his phone had been disconnected? I dialed Wonder's home number again, punching each keypad distinctly. This time, I got his growly message that the lights were on but no one was home. I'd simply misdialed the fucking number in my crazed state. I left a short sit-rep and warned him to keep his head down and his pecker up.

But the fact that Wonder was all right didn't solve my own dilemma. Pinky had boxed me in very neatly. I couldn't go around him—because there was no one to go around *to.* My entire fucking chain of command, from CNO down, was in Pinky's camp.

Ken Ross settled back in his chair and dropped his shoes atop the desk pad. "We're overlooking something," he said. "Oh, and by the way, I got your papers back." He pointed at an envelope under the heel of his right shoe.

I retrieved them, opened the envelope, and stared at a list of gibberish. A list, detailing such items as vacuum furnaces, centrifuges, pumps, gas purification equipment—they made no sense to me.

Ken Ross held his hand out. "Let me see what you have there."

He looked. He read. He said, "Holy shit."

"WTF, Admiral?"

"Dick, this is basically a list of the equipment you need to take uranium and enrich it into weapons-grade plutonium."

I didn't quite understand. But Ken Ross did. "You take uranium and heat it in a vacuum furnace until it becomes a gas. Then you spin it in a centrifuge. The U-238 atoms are spun off because they're heavier. The U-235 atoms—that's the stuff we make weapons out of—falls to the bottom. It is collected, then centrifuged again and again—hundreds or even thousands of times—until you get pure U-235."

"It sounds like making moonshine."

"Basically it's the same kind of principle. You take your mash— the uranium—and 'distil' it down until you come up with a two-hundred proof, head-splitting atomic cocktail. The major difference is that there's no real distillation involved in the atomic version. You superheat, then you supercool, then you centrifuge and purify. Once you complete that process, you have your weapons-grade plutonium."

"Do you need a big plant to do this?"

"It depends on how big a device you want to build. Iraq tried to construct a series of atomic weapons—nuclear warheads and artillery shells. But if you wanted a portable device, you wouldn't need more than a few ounces of enriched plutonium." He thought about it. "Conceivably, it could be produced on a reasonably small scale."

"Admiral," I said, feeling comfortable enough to use his first name, "I realize what the reaction was in Moscow, but with what you just said—the list I found at Andrei's, I believe this material is absolute dynamite. So do the Israelis—they assigned one of their top people to Moscow to work a course that was just about parallel with what Paul was doing. And I believe we're looking at a potential disaster—not to mention the fact that Paul died collecting this stuff—if we don't act on it. And I can't act on it if I'm the fucking assistant to the assistant asshole over at the Navy Yard." I paused. "Look—if I got an opportunity to show my materials to somebody with half a fucking brain, I know I could convince them I was on to something."

Kenny Ross pulled his glasses off, put his arms behind his head, and frowned in my direction. "Convince *me*, Dick," he said. "I'm listening."

So I opened up the case, piled all the papers on his desk where I could get to them in the proper order, and gave the admiral the same briefing I'd given Bart Wyeth two days previously.

My monologue was complex, but not convoluted. Let me give you a few of the most basic elements.

- Paul's basic research indicated that the Russian government, or an element within it, was using the mafiya to steal everything from nuclear weapons to dual-use equipment. Why? First, because by using the mafiya, the Russian government had absolute deniability. Second, because, by using the mafiya, the operation paid for itself. It was organized crime that bore the costs—and skimmed the profits afterward.
- Many of those weapons and much of the nuclear-manufacturing equipment were being sent overseas to former Soviet client states that were still strongly anti-Western in their outlook. Why? The answer was obvious to me: to help them destabilize the West.
- The financing for doing all of this was being run through Lantos & Cie in Paris. As the enterprise's banker, Werner Lantos got a cut of the action. And he also served as the banker for those Russian government officials who were covertly running the scheme.
- The papers from Andrei's seemed to confirm that his mafiya organization had been able to supply Werner Lantos with a lot of the dual-use equipment necessary to set up a nuclear weapons-manufacturing facility. How many other mafiya *vors* had sold Lantos the remaining pieces of the puzzle?
- Today's revelation tied right to Mossad's claim—that a small thermonuclear device, manufactured with plutonium purified by dual-use equipment smuggled from Russia, was close to being completed at a location in Syria. If the bomb

was built, it would devastate the Middle East peace process and throw the region into another cycle of war.

Ken Ross interrupted. "Mossad claims there's a bomb being built in Syria?"

I thought about it. "No—they don't claim it as a fact. So far as I can tell, they've only been hinting at it, because CIA doesn't have any definite information."

"Let's start from the top again. Go slow, Dick, and try to be as accurate as you can." With that premonition, he pulled a yellow legal pad from his desk drawer and nodded for me to begin. This time, he made notes as I spoke. By the time I'd finished speaking, a dozen pages of his compact, penmanshipshape handwriting were stacked in front of him.

Then he asked to see Paul's materials, as well as Avi's and mine too. I moved the piles around to where he could see them. He went over each sheet of notes, looked at every photograph, and examined every one of the documents I'd brought back.

He paused at the Air France waybill. "Hot freon," he said. "Remember when I explained the process of bootlegging nuclear material?"

"Yes."

"Well, hot freon is part of the purification process that comes in the final stages of manufacturing. If they need this stuff, they're well under way." He lapsed into silence, wheeled his big leather chair back from the desk, tilted it, and set his feet up again. He made a temple roof of his hands and gazed at the ceiling of his office. He sat like that for five or six minutes. I didn't interrupt, because I knew what he was doing: he was thinking.

And then, having thought, he brought his feet back onto the rug, began collecting the evidence I'd brought, and sorted it into orderly stacks.

"What's up, Admiral?"

I watched as he picked up the phone on his desk and punched a number. "It's Kenny Ross," he said to whomever answered. The admiral covered the receiver mouthpiece with his hand and looked at me impatiently. "What the heck are you waiting for? Get this stuff organized and packed."

As I began reaching for the piles of paper, he nodded. "Yes, yes, I can." He waited, drumming his fingers silently on the desk's surface, looking at my efforts impatiently. "Uh-huh. Right. Ask if he can see me on an urgent matter." He paused. "Five minutes."

Kenny Ross looked in my direction and saw that I was not moving at flank speed. "Dick," he said quietly, "get the fucking paperwork packed up—in proper order—right now!"

When he used language like that I knew it had to be serious.

Eight minutes later we were sitting in the secure, river-view, hideaway office of General Thomas E. Crocker, a former West Point wide receiver who for the past two years has been deputy chairman of the Joint Chiefs of Staff. Two months ago, the chairman, a Marine four-star named A. G. "Gunny" Barrett, unexpectedly resigned for what the office of the chairman of the Joint Chiefs of Staff press release stated were reasons of health.[7] Within eight hours of Gunny's retirement, General Crocker, a career armor officer whose previous assignments included service as the deputy NATO commander in Brussels, and a short stint as the CINC of U.S. Army, Europe (USAREUR), was appointed to the job.

Unlike his predecessor, Tom Crocker didn't jog or play golf with the president. He didn't spend much time in the Oval Office. Neither did he court the press, nor anyone else, for that matter. As CINCUSAREUR, he'd been known to take off his blouse and tie, cover his stars with a sweater, and visit the troops anonymously, *sans* aides and retinue, listening to their gripes in mess halls, enlisted men's clubs, and commissaries, then acting to fix those gripes quickly.

He was what they call a soldier's soldier. He was not a manager who wanted to go on to greater things in the corporate or political worlds; he was a leader who knew he'd already reached the apex of his career when he was put in charge of his men. He'd been appointed, according to the conventional wisdom, exactly for that reason: he was the apolitical choice, the man who'd get the job done without complaining.

From the way they greeted each other, you could see they had what's called in Spanish a *cuate* relationship. That translates literally as "twin," and in the idiomatic, it means being an asshole buddy. Now, frankly, gentle reader, I had no idea how a one-star

---

[7]If you want to learn more about the real reasons behind General A. G. "Gunny" Barrett's sudden resignation, you can do so by reading *Rogue Warrior: Task Force Blue*. Frankly, there's no time to explain things now.

submariner and the four-star CJCS got to be such close friends until the Chairman explained that they'd both been detailed to the National Security Council during the Bush administration. "Long hours make for unexpected relationships," is how General Crocker put it. "After six weeks of eighteen-hour days, which is what we put in during the Gulf War, even the Army and the Navy saw eye-to-eye on a *few* matters."

The Chairman looked at me curiously. "Don't I know you from somewhere, Captain?" he asked, the hint of a twinkle in his eye. "I never forget a French braid."

I explained that we'd met very quickly in Gunny Barrett's office about half a year back. He nodded but didn't ask for any further explanation. Instead, he sat down in a well-used leather wing chair, raised his knees by putting his shoes on a low ottoman, and balanced a legal notepad in a black leather binder with four gold stars emblazoned on it on his lap. He held his right thumb and index finger, as if they were a .45-caliber pistol, then pointed his hand in Ken Ross's direction. "Fire away, Kenny," said General Crocker.

Kenny Ross looked as confident as if he had an Ivan boomer in his sights, the torpedo-firing sequence programmed into his computers, the twin firing keys firmly in their locks, and his hands on the "launch" buttons. "Aye-aye, sir," he said. "Dick—report what you told me to Chairman Crocker."

Two hours and fifteen minutes later, I knew my rabbi problem had been solved for the immediate future. First, General Crocker asked us to leave his office so that he could place a secure call. I started to say something, but the look on Ken Ross's face told me it was way above my pay grade to ask who the Chairman was dialing up. So we exeunted, left, into the office of General Crocker's confidential assistant, while said CA, a ministerial straight-leg colonel wearing a telephone headset whose wires were connected to a red scrambler phone, took shorthand with a series of old-fashioned yellow Ticonderoga pencils as the Chairman and whomever he was speaking to palavered. Eight minutes later, when the conversation was over, the notes were slipped into an orange-bordered Top Secret folder. The folder was placed reverently in the CA's safe, which was then locked. The process finished, we were readmitted to JCS Valhalla.

"This is now officially a 'go,'" the Chairman said as we resumed our seats. Two minutes later, with a single cordial yet tough phone call to the acting CNO, the Chairman had me detailed to his office, to engage in what he described as a sensitive special project of an ongoing nature. In requesting my services, he reminded CNO that jointness—which is the current fancy and bureaucratic way of defining interservice cooperation during mission planning and execution—was very much on Congress's mind these days, and that my services to the JCS would be favorably remembered when it was time to testify at appropriations hearings, and the Navy's funds were being threatened with even more severe cuts than ever before. Because of CNO's help in this matter, the Navy, Chairman Crocker promised, could count on at least one Army four-star's unqualified support at budget time.

That settled, he and the acting chief of naval operations worked out a chain of command for me. The Chairman got what he wanted there, too. He had Kenny Ross removed from under Pinky Prescott's jurisdiction and detailed to the Joint Chiefs of Staff J-2—its intelligence staff. Then the Chairman called the three-star who ran the JCS's J-2 operation. He explained that Kenny was reporting tomorrow morning to handle a compartmented program that was being run out of the Chairman's office, and that Ken was to be given full cooperation.

General Crocker aimed his index finger at my nose. "Dick, you will report directly to Rear Admiral Ross." He looked over at Kenny. "And you, Ken, will report directly to me." He cracked a half grin. "We're going to 'keep it simple, stupid.' That way maybe we'll actually get something done."

I asked for my men back. That was the one big disappointment of the session. The Chairman insisted that reassembling my unit would be impossible. Doing so would cause too many waves within the system—and perhaps even alert someone to what was going on. I was, Chairman Crocker said, on my own—at least for now.

His decision disheartened me. SEALs do not ordinarily operate alone. From the very first days of training, you learn to act as a part of a team. From swim buddies, to boat crews, to SEAL platoons, everything is done in a way to promote unit integrity and interdependence among shipmates. So sending me out solo made me tactically less efficient than I would have been with a small unit.

On a more personal note, I believed that allowing Pinky's decision to stand sent the wrong signal to my men—that signal being, that they were being punished because of me. I considered that specious reasoning on his part. I have always believed that an officer's foremost duty is to his men. *He* may be punished for his poor decisions—or decisions that make too many waves—but *they* shouldn't suffer for 'em. Obviously, Pinky the Turd didn't think the same way I did—and now my men were suffering because of it. Worst of all, there was nothing I could do about it—for the present.

It may have hurt, but there was no time for ruminations now. There was a mission to be fulfilled—and for the moment, at least, I was going to have to do it alone. And, in some ways, the results of the past few hours were gratifying—they meant that once again, I could work around Pinky Prescott and the Navy's cumbersome bureaucracy with relative (and I stress that word) impunity.

But manipulating the system, as personally satisfying as it might be, was not what this particular little exercise was all about. It was much more serious than that. The people who'd set in motion the chain of events that had ended with the death of Paul Mahon and his family were still out there, and untouched.

The Russians were up to something new and dangerous, and my country was in jeopardy.

It was time for me to go to work.

Part
Two

TRUST BUT VERIFY

Chapter

11

I HEADED BACK TO ROGUE MANOR AT 1330. FRANKLY, I PREFER working at the Manor, and since it didn't make any difference to General Crocker (as you can see I was now on a first-name basis with the Chairman of the Joint Chiefs of Staff), I drove the sixty-five miles south and west to my two-hundred-plus acres, three beer coolers, four cases of Bombay gin, and five hundred thousand rounds of ammo. I like working at home because the exercise equipment, the sauna, and the outdoor Jacuzzi are all handy. So is a twenty-foot long, copper-topped bar in the basement rec room that would do credit to most Old Town saloons.

But more to the point, the old Pentagon office for Naval Security Mobile Training Teams (even if I'd wanted to use it for my current assignment) was totally unsuitable. The NSMTT office is located in a byway off a back corridor that runs off the third-floor B-ring. It's little more than a three-room suite with desks, chairs, three phones, and a fax. But I'm not griping about location or decor. The real problem was that there was no access to information there. No computer. No admission to the classified Intelink system, and hence no way of learning about your enemies.

Why was that? Well, according to a memo on the subject Pinky Prescott wrote roughly six weeks ago, NSMTTs aren't supposed to think—they are simply supposed to . . . train. Like automatons, I guess. But you cannot train sailors to counteract terrorists unless they know who they are up against, what the stakes are, when the whole problem began, where the tangos are most likely to strike, and why they are fighting in the first place. Then it's possible to teach how to stop the tangos if they try to kill or kidnap you, and how to stay alive if you are captured.

Those sorts of EEIs—the acronym stands for essential elements of information—are obviously crucial to any training mission. But Pinky had denied them to us, and we had gone to Moscow essentially blind.

Now, things had changed. I guess that with the juice of the CJCS behind me I could have obtained an office in the Pentagon, requisitioned the proper computers, and gone to work. But as you are most certainly well aware, I tend to attract attention—most of it unwanted—at the Pentagon. And since attention was something Chairman Crocker had been emphatic about my *not* attracting, it was better and more efficient—not to mention a lot more comfortable—for Wonder and me to work at home.

How emphatic had the Chairman been, you ask? Well, friends, he'd been quite specific about my mission's ROEs, or Rules of Engagement.

He wanted results—he wanted Paul Mahon's murderers put away. He wanted to know what the Russkies were up to, so we could take whatever steps necessary to thwart what he called, "that damn project in Syria. If it is what you say it is, I want the effing thing neutralized." But he wanted all those steps done quietly. *Sans* diplomatic incidents. *Sans* waves.

He'd looked at me intensely over the top of his big desk. "Remember how SEALs operated in Vietnam?" he asked. He didn't wait for me to respond, but told me what he wanted to hear. "I do. I was there. They operated SBD—silent but deadly. Go into a village at night, snatch one man, and do it without waking anybody up." The Chairman paused. Put his elbows on the desk and leaned toward me. "That's how I want you to do this one, Dick. When it's all over, I want results—but no newspaper stories. I do not want to have to appear in front of some goddamn congressional committee to wring my hands and perform all kinds of public somersaults and whine mea culpas about some action that you and I know was tactically sound and strategically imperative to preserve our national security, but was neither politically acceptable nor lint free."

"I'm going to eyes-only this arrangement to SECDEF," General Crocker had said. When he saw my eyes widen, he continued quickly. "Dick, we can't operate without his consent—there has to be a National Security Finding. After all, this has to be legal. So he'll get it, believe me, even if I have to wring it out of him."

He'd paused, noting my concern. "Don't worry—I'll take all the political heat. Besides, on this one, SECDEF will back us. The Russians and the Chinese are getting tight all of a sudden, and he's begun to see that all these budget cuts are really hurting us—cutting muscle, not fat. We can't fight two wars anymore, Dick—and SECDEF knows it. So, he's in our corner these days. You just get the job done. You succeed. I'll protect you."

I'd looked over at Kenny Ross, whose face told me that what Tom Crocker said, Tom Crocker meant.

Even so, I got it in writing. Not that I didn't trust the Chairman of the JCS, or SECDEF. But I've BTDT, and the scars on my beat-up Slovak body are ample evidence of the times I've sealed bad deals with a handshake. So I remembered what Ronald Reagan told Mikhail Gorbachev—*noviry v proviry*—we trust but we also verify, and at my request, the Chairman wrote a memo to Ken Ross outlining my mission, signed it, and gave us each a copy.

Froggishly happy with paper in hand, I headed south, toward moisture—in this case all that Coors Light in the beer coolers. Wonder and I were about to set up shop in my basement.

Our first priority would be research. In the past, most of my research has come from clipping newspapers and magazines. Those clips, filed by topic and date, still repose crammed inside the dozen or so legal-size file cabinets that line the corridor between the basement guest room and the furnace room.

Today, however, I am considered a Luddite. An analog asshole in an age of digital sphincters. What can I tell you? I remember typewriters with some fondness—manual ones, too, Royals, and Underwoods, and—big sigh, big creeem—Smith Coronas. Shit, I even was nostalgic over IBM Model Bs—the same ones Christians in Action liked so much because of their one-time self-destructing carbon ribbons. In fact, until about ten years ago, we SEALs still used manual typewriters. Then, our budgets got expanded, and we were dragged—bitching and moaning, most of us—into the Information Age.

Anyway, just so that I can keep up with the times (not to mention the glut of factoids and infobits), Stevie Wonder has taken pity on me and assumed the job of what he likes to refer to as my Director of Research for Electronic Killing, or DREK. He does this work on the Internet, and he has formed some very interesting, nay—fascinating, even—relationships out in cyberspace, wherever the fuck that may be.

Moi, I still prefer things I can pigeonhole and retrieve. So I have file cabinets for the UNCLAS (unclassified) papers. All materials that carry security classification designations are secured in a pair of twelve hundred pound, fireproof safes that were originally bought by the National Security Agency for Soviet intercept tapes. The safes are lag-bolted into concrete and sit in the furnace room behind the wood pile. Of course, the most important and sensitive stuff around is what I keep in my head. Yeah—I have a long and detailed memory.

As I turned off the half-mile gravel road into the long, curved driveway I saw Stevie Wonder's gray VW bug parked on the macadam apron in front of the garage and heard gunfire from way behind the house—double taps coming in the rapid *ba-bang, ba-bang* sequence known as "hammers." That meant he was down at the range. I built a hundred-yard combat range down in the back forty a few years ago. Yes, I know that I am a convicted felon and that therefore I cannot possess firearms. But Boy Wonder and the rest of my merry, marauding leprechauns all have current and legal Virginia concealed carry weapons permits. Moreover, when I am on a military assignment, I can—indeed, I must—carry whatever weaponry is necessary to do the job. It's part of the mission.

So, to make sure that I stay both current and deadly, I built the range, where the guys can sharpen their lethal talents, and—careful always to use only approved military weapons—I can sharpen mine. Shooting, after all, is a frangible skill. At SEAL Team Six we shot daily. I think I've told you all before that when I ran SEAL Team Six, I insisted that my seventy-two SEALs put more rounds through our targets on an annual basis than the entire U.S. Marine Corps' 174,000 leathernecks put through theirs. We did, too—because Pinky Prescott complained long and loud that my ammo budget was bigger than the USMC's. Pinky doesn't believe in shooting skills. That's because he's never been shot at.

I peeled off the uniform and changed into jeans and a T-shirt that extolled Dirty Deeds Done Dirt Cheap. I checked the answering machine—there were a string of messages from the guys, asking WTF and pleading with papa-san to fixee-fixee. I'd already vowed to fixee-fixee, but getting back to them would have to wait a while. There were more urgent things to do right now.

Then I pulled on my sandals, jumped into one of the two six-wheel ATVs parked next to the weight pile, careened around the two-acre pond's six-yard-high berm, sped over Pork Chop Hill, and tore through the woods. No, I wasn't going to grandma's house. I was going to the fucking range.

I wheelied the ATV so it just caressed the muddy one Wonder'd driven, jumped out, and waved. Wonder waved back with his left hand. His right held a small—and I mean small—pistol. I got closer and saw that it was his latest toy—the Glock 27 he'd carried in Moscow. Wonder has always preferred Browning High Power nine millimeters to any other autoloader. He says he likes their classic style—and the fact that he can hit a dime at twenty five yards with one that has been properly tuned. But they are bulky and they are heavy to carry when out on assignment, especially when you're traveling as light as we do. So he has recently switched to the Glock, which fits very nicely, thank you very much, in either a small-of-the-back holster, or one of those small, fluorescent lime green Uncle Mike's fanny packs that make you look like a dumb tourist.

He replaced the Glock in his fanny pack and looked at me from behind his mirrored wraparound shooting glasses. "What's up?"

His response, when I gave him a sit-rep was, "Holy shit." He does have a way with words, Wonder does. His reaction was to jump into the ATV and shower me and my clean jeans with mud as he wheelied, spun out, and charged toward the house and his beloved computer. There was work to do—and Wonder is the anxious type. I followed, shouting imprecations at his driving.

While he played with his keyboard and mouse, I scribbled notes to myself on a legal pad. Three hours later, he and his computer and me and my legal pad had all come to the same conclusion: we had two immediate choices. The first was New York, where the late but unlamented Andrei Yudin owned a minimum of two apartments, and a bunch of Russian Mafiya goons was operating fast and loose. Upside: it was close and the food is good—especially deli food. Downside: there was no real promise of finding anything there, and no targets in New York had been hit recently. The second—and more target-rich environment for me—was Paris, where Lantos & Cie was based, and the embassy had been broken into twice.

"New Yawk's closer," Wonder said encouragingly, regressing into the thick Queens accent of his childhood. "And the corned beef's better."

He had a point. But I'd already settled on Paris. A choice that was reinforced by the intelligence monitor in my little home office.

You are asking WTF is an intelligence monitor? Well, friends, I keep a TV set on at the Manor twenty-four hours a day when I'm in residence. I keep it tuned to CNN. That way I learn what's going on in the world as quickly as I would if I were sitting in the fucking CIA op center seventy miles away at Langley, in the War Room at the Pentagon, or the Sit Room in the basement of the White House's West Wing. Why? Because CNN is what they're watching there, too.

The on-screen graphic told me this was breaking news. There was a live shot—a lot of smoke in the background, lots of police and rescue workers on-scene, and a trench-coated correspondent in the foreground talking breathlessly into a handheld microphone. I turned up the volume.

". . . it appears that the attack against the two diplomatic locations was coordinated, because each of the explosions went off within just a few minutes of the others . . ."

I peered at the screen—French cops and soldiers were running back and forth chaotically. White-coated medical personnel were rolling stretchers with bodies strapped onto them. The lights on the police cars and security vehicles blinked crazily, and in the background I could hear the unique, electronic hee-haw, hee-haw of European sirens. Hey—I *knew* that street, and the building, too—it was the U.S. Mission to the Organization for Economic Cooperation and Development, known as USOECD. It was in Paris, on the Rue de Franqueville, just a block or so away from the Bois de Boulogne.

But I didn't know USOECD because I follow economic policy. I knew the place because it was also the cover location for the Defense Intelligence Agency's intelligence-gathering operations for France, and—as I've mentioned earlier—the Pentagon's Paris counterterrorism operations center. It was also one of the probe targets Paul Mahon had in his collection of sensitive State Department memos.

Now the picture switched. Another correspondent stood at a

police roadblock on a broad avenue. A block or so behind her, you could see the devastation from what had to have been a car bomb. "... the six casualties appear to be French and Israeli employees of the Israeli cultural center here on Avenue Marceau just a few blocks from the Arc de Triomphe ..."

She was interrupted by my telephone. I hit the "mute" button on the TV remote control and snatched the phone up. "Marcinko—"

"It's Ken Ross. Have you seen—"

"Yeah, yeah—I have CNN on now." The on-screen picture shifted back to the first correspondent, standing in front of the smoldering USOECD building.

"Well, turn it off and get moving. You-know-who wants your butt in Paris ASAP."

"What's the story?"

"Hey, *c'mon*, Dick, this is a nonsecure line."

"Gist, Admiral. Give me gist."

Kenny Ross hesitated. You could hear him thinking—his mind checking off alternatives the way submariners are trained to do. Finally, he spoke. "You hadn't been cleared to know this before, but there was some research being done by a few of the folks at the USOECD—folks now deceased—that paralleled Paul's work as well as your own recent inquiries."

That was gist enough to make things clear. "Gotcha. I'm on my way." I rang off, then punched the number of Avi Ben Gal's apartment in Moscow. It took six tries to get through, but he finally answered.

"Yo, Avi—Washington calling."

"I was worried. You disappeared off the face of the earth."

"I was PNG'd by the fucking Russkies. Didn't you get my message? I called your office on the way home."

A pause. He seemed distracted. "No—no messages." I heard him cup his hand over the receiver and say something in muffled Hebrew to someone.

Then he must have pressed the "hold" button because there was total silence on the other end of the line. "Avi?"

More silence. Then a click: *"Rak rayga*, Dick—wait a second." Fifteen seconds more of nothing, then his voice came back on-line. "Dick," he said, "sorry, but I really have to go—something important's come up."

I looked at the pictures on the silent television screen across the room. "Paris, right, Avi? Paris."

Avi went as mute as my TV. "Yes," he finally said. "I've got to go to Paris."

"I'm headed there, too."

"That makes sense." I could hear his breathing on the line. His tone was cold and professional. "Let's stay in touch from time to time, okay? B'bye, Dick, b'bye." I could hear his voice fade as he started to put the receiver down.

I shouted, *"Avi, Avi, Avi*—hang on!"

He must have clapped the receiver to his ear again, because his voice came back strong and exasperated. He wanted to *move* and I was holding him up. "Mazzeh—what *is* it, Dick?"

"I'm coming by myself. You're going by yourself. Let's play it the same way we did a few years ago."

"Hold on." The phone went silent for some seconds. Then his voice came back strong. "Done and done," Avi said.

"Where do I contact you?"

He thought about that. "Do you still have the number you used to call me at home? Home-home, not here."

"Hold on." I ran down the hall, up the stairs, grabbed my briefcase, dumped its contents on the bed and pawed through the pile until I found my aged, dog-eared address book. I unwrapped the rubber band that held it together and thumbed through the ragged pages until I found Avi's unlisted phone number in Herzlyia, Israel.

I galumphed back down to the phone in the basement, trophy in hand. "Got it!"

"Good—but don't repeat it over the phone."

"Gotcha."

"Now take down the following numbers: two hundred and six, and one hundred and thirteen."

"Got 'em."

"Good—now subtract the first number from the first three figures of my number, and add the second number to the second three figures of my home number."

I did as he asked. "Got it."

"Add the right country code and city code, and you'll have my location in Paris."

"Okay—done. I'll see you there tomorrow."

He didn't waste any time on pleasantries. "B'bye, b'bye." The line went dead.

I hung up the receiver, picked it up again, then dialed the number

I'd come up with using Avi's formula. I got a busy signal. I waited thirty seconds and tried again. Busy. I hate it when it does that. On the fifth try, the phone brooha-broohaed three times. Then a Gallic male voice answered, *"Cercle National des Armées, bon soir."* It was the fucking Army Club of Paris—which was located right under a big French nose.

No, there isn't a statue of de Gaulle out front. But the *Cercle*, as it's known, is right next door to one of the op centers for France's largest clandestine intelligence organization, *le Service de Documentation Extérieure et de Contre-Espionnage,* which as you can probably already figure out translates as the External Documentation and Counterespionage Service, more commonly called SDECE—le Frog equivalent of the CIA.

Avi was going to hide in plain sight. Well, if he could, so could I.

Meanwhile, Wonder, grousing loudly—some might even say obnoxiously—because he was being left behind for the present, spent all his time in front of the computer, extracting bits and bytes out of cyberspace. As Avi had told me in Moscow, there was very little material on our quarry. So the public access material on Werner Lantos, and Lantos & Cie, was very sparse—at least in English. But then there is FBIS. What is FBIS? It is the Foreign Broadcast Information Service, an unclassified subsidiary of the CIA. Every day, it translates and then puts out a selection of foreign-language broadcasts and newspaper articles made by countries around the world. The FBIS files are available at many college libraries—and many of them have put the information in the Internet. Wonder sorted through two years of FBIS records. He printed out his findings, highlighted what he thought significant, and handed them to me without further comment.

I looked. I read. According to radio broadcasts and official government statements, Werner Lantos's investment bank had made cash-rich investment deals in the following countries within the past twenty-four months: Syria, Iraq, and North Yemen; Angola, Sudan, and Ethiopia; Poland, Estonia, and Latvia.

Does anything about that list strike you as strange or significant, gentle reader? There were two elements that struck me. First, I realized that Lantos & Cie was doing a hell of a lot of business in former Soviet client states and former Soviet stooge states. Was Lantos & Cie financing covert ops in those places? It wasn't out of the question. You are dubious, I see.

Well, friends, let's turn the tables. What would you have thought in the seventies and eighties if you'd discovered that a single small investment bank based in Europe was handling billions of dollars worth of cash-rich investment deals in El Salvador, Honduras, Panama, Pakistan, Italy, Morocco, Jordan, Israel, Egypt, South Yemen, and Abu Dhabi? If you surmised that said bank was a front, moving cash around the world for the CIA's covert operations, you'd be absolutely correct.

Wonder assembled other open source materials, too. He obtained counterterrorism information from the Israeli Government Information Service. He tracked down World Bank and International Monetary Fund information on Werner Lantos's deals. He pulled information on Russian Mafiya activities in Paris. When he collated everything, variegated patterns began to take shape. Seemingly unrelated events transmogrified into recognizable structure.

Have you ever seen those comic-book visual puzzles? They look like a jumbled maze of color and shape on the page. Then you hold the frame in front of your nose, and you stare at it. Really stare— sometimes for a minute or more. And then, all of a sudden, the picture comes alive—it turns three-dimensional. And you say to yourself, Why the fuck didn't I see this before? Same thing here.

While Wonder sleuthed at the Manor, I took a look at the classified stuff—and *décroche le pompon,* as they say when they hit real paydirt in Paris. From the secure Intelink terminal in Kenny Ross's new office in the Joint Chiefs intelligence staff in the second-floor E-ring, I was able to obtain a file of documents, pictures, and studies ample enough to give me one leg over the rail of this ship under way named Lantos. I also learned that Avi Ben Gal hadn't been totally up-front with me when he'd claimed Mossad didn't have a lot of material on Werner Lantos. Why? Because Intelink showed me that NSA had dozens of Mossad intercepts mentioning the asshole's name.

The CIA also had a shitload of files on Werner Lantos. I could tell *that* from the way Intelink kept asking me for more and more code-word clearances every time I typed his name into the terminal. Kenny Ross and I tried using the Chairman's clearance code. Not high enough, responded the system. We tried to sneak in the back door using a DIA password Kenny knew. We were turned away.

I used the secure phone in Ken Ross's office to put my pal Tony Mercaldi on the case. An hour later, he called back to say the system had shut him out, too. After six hours, I realized that unless I was the CIA's fucking DDO—that's the Deputy Director of

Operations, better known as the Head Spook—I wasn't going to access any Christians in Action material on Werner Lantos.

Why not? The reason was apparent from the little bit of raw material I was able to see: Werner Lantos was obviously a CIA agent, and the Agency was going to do everything it could do to protect his nasty wrinkled asset.

Now before you start screaming WTF about how can he be a CIA agent when he's the financial linchpin of an operation that is probably putting the United States in jeopardy, let me splain you about CIA agents. CIA agents are not the same as CIA officers. CIA officers are U.S. government employees—and they are forbidden by oath from acting in ways that will harm the national interest or security.

CIA *agents* are not U.S. government employees. Most often they are non-Americans—FNs, which stands for foreign nationals, although I tend to think of them as Fucking No-goodniks—who have been recruited by and are run by our intelligence service to provide information, or influence, or services, or all three. They are paid for their work—sometimes they are very well paid indeed.

Often, those who choose to become agents are not society's most favored personages. Pond scum would be one way of describing them, but I don't want to dwell on their most positive aspects. Typically, the types who are recruited include traitors, self-styled visionaries, corrupt government officials, and greedy petty bureaucrats. But murderers are accepted, too, if they work for an intelligence organization that CIA would like to penetrate. That's how Manny Noriega got recruited. Other felonious types find their way into the fold as well: rapists, child molesters, torturers, and others with equally delicate occupations have been recruited from various countries' secret police organizations, paramilitary units, and security forces. Which is why one CIA agent, according to a recent secret congressional report, was able to kill an American citizen residing in a Central American country, tell the station chief about it—and still remain on the CIA's payroll for years afterward.

Y'know, come to think of it, the CIA's policy on its agents' activities is very much the same as the Clinton administration's policy on homosexual buggery and other same-sex activity in the military. Because it, too, can be summed up with the phrase "Don't ask—don't tell," or DADT.

Anyway, if you will remember what I have been preaching about intelligence gathering for the past three books, intelligence is sometimes what you don't learn, as much as it is what you do learn. And so, working my way up the chain of Intelink reports, I realized that, given the sourcing and the methods used in the reporting, Christians In Action had obviously been paying Werner Lantos your tax dollars to keep the folks at Langley updated on the activities of the Russian Mafiya, and the internal workings of the Russian government. And, what about Werner's making money by selling weapons and dual-use materials to potential adversaries? That was DADT.

I learned something else, too. The more I read, the more I realized my instincts had been correct: Avi Ben Gal had held back on me in Moscow. Well, that was to be expected. Avi and I are professionals. And while we trust each other, we also operate within certain tradecraft parameters—which is a polite way of saying we keep our professional secrets secret unless it becomes operationally necessary to share 'em.

I've never told Avi, for example, about the 1987 operation I ran just outside the Lebanese town of An Nabi Shit, even though I first visited An Nabi Shit in his company. I'm not going to go into details right here—all you have to know now is that I staged a terrific counterterrorism op, waxed a lot of nasty tangos—and the Israelis got blamed for it.

Anyway, among the infobits Avi hadn't passed on—and had to have known—was that, as of late 1995, Lantos's Number Two was a retired Mossad heavyweight named Ehud Golan. That's pronounced A-hood. Which is altogether fitting, because Ehud is a hood. Indisputably.

Yeah—I knew the name and some of the history that went along with it. And I remembered the face, too—ruggedly handsome, yet completely unemotional and dangerously vacant-eyed. The face of a homicidal sociopath. Despite his repeated failures in the field, Ehud Golan had been one of Mossad's fair-haired boys. In the seventies, as a young member of the well-documented Operation *Kidon Hagideon*—Sword of the Destroyer—he and six other officers had each commanded five-man teams that were assigned to track down and assassinate every one of the Black September terrorists who planned the 1972 Munich Olympics massacre.

The other teams succeeded in their missions without incident. But Ehud's flunked lunch. In Lillehammer, Norway, Ehud Golan shot and killed a Moroccan waiter as he walked to work. He believed the Moroccan was Ali Hassan Salameh, the head of the

Black September terror organization and the mastermind of Munich. But Ehud was wrong—he'd acted before he'd done enough homework. And worse, he got caught—he'd designed an absolute disaster of an exfiltration plan—and he spent twenty-two months in a Norwegian jail before he was released in a quiet deal that cost the Israeli government millions of dollars.

You'd think that fucking up like that would cost a man his career. But the Mossad is obviously less ZD—that's zero defect, remember?—tolerant than the current U.S. Navy. Because once Ehud Golan returned to the Mossad's headquarters, a complex of discreetly secure buildings that sits directly above the Gelilot interchange on the Tel Aviv-Haifa highway, right opposite the Tel Aviv Country Club, he was made the assistant to the deputy director of operations.

As such, he was largely responsible for Mossad's intelligence fiascoes during the 1982 Lebanon invasion. Fiascoes? Well, first of all they had no idea that the Palestinian forces were as well equipped, or as well trained, as they turned out to be. What the then-defense minister, Ariel Sharon, had envisioned as a two-week blitzkrieg turned into a year-and-a-half quagmire. Then came the matter of the Lebanese Forces, which is what Israel's Christian allies called their militia.

Army intelligence—Avi's pals at AMAN—argued that the Lebanese Forces were not an army, so much as they were a bunch of gangsters who'd cut and run when challenged. Mossad, which held sway over both the prime minister and the minister of defense at the time, disagreed, loudly. And it was Ehud Golan who'd done the arguing at those top secret sessions.

But Mossad was wrong. The Lebanese Forces turned out to be great throat slitters—*if* they're slitting women's and children's throats, the way they did at the Palestinian camps of Sabra and Shatila. But going up against well-motivated, armed men was something else again. When confronted, the Christians ran away.

Anyway, after that disaster, Ehud was farmed out to the boondocks as a Mossad *Katsa*, or station chief—first in Guatemala City, then Tegucigalpa, Honduras, San Salvador, and finally in Panama. The Israelis had finally retired him in the early nineties after he'd caused them a huge embarrassment by warning Manuel Noriega that the United States was coming after him. The earwigs at No Such Agency had picked up the call and played the tape for the head of Mossad. Less than two weeks later, Mossad brought Ehud the hood back to Gelilot, where they gave him a medal, a pension, and a kick in the ass out the door. Now, he turns up working for Werner Lantos, CIA asset.

Guatemala was where I'd first met him. He was "advising" the Guat military on security matters—interrogation techniques, to be precise, in the days when overt U.S. military aid had been cut off because of the Guats' extensive human rights violations. I was visiting the country clandestinely—fake official passport but Guatemalan military cooperation—to get a look at the supply trails along the Guat/Salvadorean border that were being used by the FMLN Marxist guerrillas to supply their camps in western El Salvador. Once I saw how the guerrillas moved, I could prescribe a solution to the Salvadoreans. Anyway, I stopped by the *Estado Major*—Guatemalan Army staff HQ—to see some of the officers I knew. Someone told me an Israeli was giving a class and invited me to observe.

And thus I got to watch as Ehud plied his inhuman trade on an unfortunate guerrilla who'd been captured and provided to the Israeli as the day's lab animal. Ehud's interrogation techniques ran to dental drills, twelve-volt batteries, and hot wires. They were not pleasant to watch—and downright lethal to undergo.

Now I am not one of your touchie-feelie types who condemns the use of torture out of hand. I have used it—when my men's lives depended on getting information that I could not obtain any other way. Let me repeat that: any other way. But you get more with a carrot than a stick, and I prefer to use other methods. It wasn't that way with Ehud Golan—you could see that he obviously enjoyed inflicting intense pain on another human being. I never forgot the look on his face that day as he worked—it was orgasmic. So the knowledge that he was working for Lantos & Cie set off the sensor system in the back of my brain. This guy was a pretty dangerous motherfucking person.

Chapter

12

I caught an Air France A-300 Airbus out of Dulles for Paris twenty-eight hours after I'd hung up with Avi. Yes, I know that as a government employee I was supposed to travel on a U.S. carrier. But I was a MILPER (that's a military personnel for anybody who wants to know) operating covertly. Which means it's healthier to stay away from flights where counterintelligence types may be taking pictures as you're deplaning. I also carried a passport, credit cards, and other personal ephemera. Of course, none of them were in my name. The authentic passport issued in my name and other matching IDs were in a hidden compartment in my suitcase. The ones in my pocket were real enough, though—they'd all been created at Documents 'R' Us, the little shop across the street from the State Department where my multiple personalities are conceived by the eccentric but brilliant Freddie the Forger. Freddie does his government work in a building that half a century ago belonged to the CIA. These days it masquerades as the Naval Health Services Command. Oops—did I reveal something I wasn't supposed to? Well, it was time for Freddie to change locations anyway.

Even though it had been a rush job and there hadn't been time to build me a new identity, Freddie'd still managed to supply me with a passport, a driver's license, two credit cards, and an assortment of miscellaneous goodies, including things like an AAA membership, a Blockbuster Video rental card, a voter's registration certificate, as well as a wallet for me to put them all in.

Let me wax eloquent for a second or two here. There cannot be too much attention lavished on the details when it comes to creating a cover. I have seen the screwups before. You spend half a million bucks training some poor asshole to operate overseas under NOC—that stands for Non-Official Cover—and then you send him out with a passport, a Social Security card, a driver's license, a credit card or two—and that is it. It is like putting a huge flashing sign that says SPY in visibility orange right over his head.

Why? Gentle reader, take out your wallet. Go ahead—do it. Open it up. C'mon, c'mon, don't waste my time. Lay everything out in a pile, and let's go through it all piece by piece to see what is in there.

Right: Ah-hah! There's the dentist's business card from two and a half months ago where the receptionist wrote down that you have a cleaning three and a half months from now. (You forgot to transfer that into your appointment book, didn't you?) Hey, there are the three business cards from those people you met at the trade show last month. You were supposed to call them, weren't you? Here's your health plan ID. Next, a gasoline company credit card that you don't use anymore—it expired last year but it's still taking up space. Then three check-cashing cards from your local supermarkets. Your ATM card is buried here, too. So is the membership from that fraternal order of whatever, and the card that gets you into your tennis, or golf, or swim club. Retired military? There's the laminated card that says so. Your auto registration and auto insurance certification cards are folded together—easier to find when you're stopped by a smokey out on the Interstate. And here's a card that says you gave blood at the Red Cross last year. Hmm— two old restaurant receipts. Guess you should have taken those lunches off last year's taxes. A checkout receipt from a department store you've been looking for for a week so you can return the skivvies that are one size too small. Oh—there's more in that hidden compartment, too. There's that lucky five-dollar bill—the one with the six fives you used to win all those liar's poker games back in school. And the cocktail napkin with what's-her-name's phone number—she was the one with the huge gazongas you met in a bar three months ago and never called. And finally, what is that in the bottom of the billfold? Yes, friends, that is genuine wallet crud—real nasty lint. Disgusting, isn't it?

Now, if you are a trained counterintelligence operative working the immigration control counter in Lower Slobovia, and you come upon a good man who says his name is Thomas Goodman from New York, New York, and all he's got to prove it is a passport, a driver's license, two brand-new credit cards, and one or two other items in his nice, clean wallet, you're gonna get suspicious. Because *you* know all too well what is generally contained inside people's wallets—which is, exactly the kind of stuff I've itemized above. And poor Goodman the NOC is gonna be *Issi-doombu*—which as we all know, means doomded in pidgin Zulu.

Ergo, when I go covert, Freddie supplies me with a full load of goodies—right down to the wallet crud. Lucky for me he can work fast. I was also carrying enough cash on me to last a few weeks. No, Freddie hadn't made my wad of hundreds. They'd come from the Chairman of the Joint Chiefs' slush fund, identified in the line-item Pentagon budget as "CHAIRMAN OF THE JOINT CHIEFS: MISCELLANEOUS ENTERTAINMENT AND TRAVEL EXPENSES."

But I was going out tremendously underequipped. Underequipped, hell—I was *non*equipped. I had no communications gear. No weapons. None of the specialized, painstakingly developed paraphernalia that SpecWar units normally travel with.

Now, some of these deficiencies would be corrected once I got to Paris. Weapons, for example, would come from the Israelis—I had no doubt Avi would help if I asked. But for the rest of my supplies, I'd have to improvise on-scene, which is a polite way of saying I'd beg, borrow, or steal whatever was needed. Well, friends, I've been there before. And I can tell you that living off the land isn't all that bad, or hard.

Even so, it had been a chaotic twenty-eight hours. I'd arranged the logistics for this little venture, pursued tactical intelligence, obtained operational funds, documentation, and other materials, and managed to accomplish it all without (let's all repeat this mantra together, shall we?) *attracting any attention to myself or my mission.*

I arrived at Charles de Gaulle Two thirty-five minutes early, grabbed my luggage from the *tapis roulant*—which is what they call the baggage conveyor belt at French airports—and caught the bus for Porte Maillot. I lost that thirty-five minutes (plus another three-quarters of an hour) on the *périphérique*—the elevated beltway that circles Paris's outer perimeter, where *le gridlock* is a permanent way of life.

When the bus finally docked at the Port Maillot Air France terminal, I unfolded myself from the narrow, cramped seats, slung my carry-on over my shoulder, hefted the suitcase, and threaded my way down three flights of stairs into the rush hour metro. I bought a *carnet*—book—of ten metro tickets, shouldered my way onto the first eastbound train, ran under the Champs-Élysées to Franklin D. Roosevelt, then switched to the Mairie de Montreuil line and rode three stops to St. Augustin.

I emerged up the stairs onto a crowded sidewalk. I moved to the curb, dropped my suitcase, and got my bearings. It had been some years since I'd been in Paris, and while I'd remembered the metro route, I wasn't absolutely sure which way to head now that I was on the bustling street.

It didn't take long to recall: I was standing on the Boulevard Haussmann, an old thoroughfare that runs more or less east-west through some of the best and most expensive real estate in Paris. I did a one-eighty—and there, straight ahead, was the Place Saint Augustin, a huge, irregularly shaped square from which more than half a dozen streets radiated in all directions, like uneven spokes from a cubist's wagon wheel hub.

Security was tight: scores of blue-uniformed and jack-booted national police, some carrying automatic weapons, patrolled the Place St. Augustin in pairs. Rubber truncheons and black leather gloves whose knuckles I knew were filled with lead shot hung off their belts. The closest pair eyeballed me as I stood. They slowed down, subtly spread out to give themselves separate fields of fire, and watched until I picked up my luggage and moved on.

I walked to the corner and peered to my right. There, across the street, stood the huge, columned portico of the *Cercle National des Armées,* which translates roughly as the French National Army Club. Beyond it was an adjoining gray stone structure with a restaurant on the ground floor which, behind its anonymous, ornate nineteenth-century facade, housed the SDECE's op center. The entire block was surrounded by a series of waist-high steel barricades, each four-foot section of steel held in place by cubic-meter chunks of concrete. The French, it was obvious, were worried.

Just in front of me, on the narrow spit of street corner stood a crowded coffee bar. It had the same name—Café Augustin—as the dark, old-fashioned, tin-ceilinged, *cafeton* I'd been going to for years. But the etched windows, crocheted curtains, brass fittings, murky oak panels, and tin ceiling were all gone. They'd been replaced by bleached wood beams, potted ivy, and double-pane glass. The fucking place looked like a damn California plastic-fern-and-blush-chablis bar.

I peered inside. Well, thank God some things never change. Behind the heavy wood bar, a harried little man with a Charlie Chaplin mustache, bedecked in white shirt, an apron tied under his armpits, and high-rise black trousers covering a tidy paunch, brewed tiny cups of frothy espresso and huge bowls of café au lait for the throng of waiting, thirsting Parisians. That was Monsieur Henri LeClerc, the overworked *patron*, or boss. And over there, way down at the end of the zinc-topped counter, was the large, red-faced woman he was married to, Madame Collette.

Just like Old Man and Mama Gussy, the rough-and-tumble couple who'd given me a job as a wet-behind-the-balls teenager, lived above their bar in New Brunswick, New Joyzey, the LeClercs lived in a huge, labyrinthine apartment on the floor above the Café Augustin. Like the Gussys, they'd kept their six bedrooms long after their five kids grew up and moved out. They put up with me— but they loved my men. Especially Stevie Wonder, whom they referred to as *"Monsieur prodige rouge"*—which means, more or less, Mr. amazing red (hair).

I spied on Madame Collette as she worked, occasionally wiping a bead of sweat from her brow with a forearm. In her strong right hand she held a huge knife with which she worked nonstop. With the nonchalant expertise that comes of constant practice, she slit crusty, fresh-baked *ficelles*, *baguettes*, and *petits-pains*, slathered each half with butter scraped from a brick-size block, then added slices of cheese, ham, sausage, or dollops of raspberry jam, or honey, slapped the two halves together, cut the sandwich in two equal pieces and slid the whole thing onto a plate—all in one sensual, fluid motion.

My friends, everything would have to wait. Werner Lantos would have to wait. So would the Russian Mafiya. So would Avi Ben Gal. This was *love*. Now, as you probably know, I have a weakness for sixtysomething women who run restaurants. I guess it started when I was a kid and I worked for the Gussys. Since then, everywhere I go, I seek 'em out—places like Mama Mascalzone's Casa Italia in Huntington Beach, California, and Germaine's Restaurant in Washington are two that come to mind right now. And here in front of my broken Slovak nose was yet another of Demo Dickie's favorite homes away from home—the Café Augustin.

So what if they'd redecorated—the LeClercs were still there, and *maman* still looked great. I nudged the glass door with my shoulder, pushed inside, dropped my luggage in front of the bar, and did what I thought was a passable Spike Lee. "Yo *Maman*."

No reaction. Perhaps a more Parisian approach would work. *"Alors, Madame Collette, salut—*what's happening?"

She looked at me without really looking, smiled the professional smile of all restaurateurs, and said, *"Bon jour, monsieur."* Then she looked again, saw to whom she was speaking, and double-took wide-eyed. *"Alors, c'est nos petit phoque, Dickee—*it's our little SEAL Dickie." She dropped the big knife on the cutting board, came waddling around the counter, grabbed me by my top cheeks, and planted four big, wet sloppy kisses on 'em, left-right, left-right. *"Petit Richard—bienvenue à Paris—*welcome back."

I swept her off her feet and hugged her tight. *"Merci, Maman—*it's great to be here again."

She waved at her husband down the bar. "Henri, Henri—*regarde qui est là—*look who's here."

Monsieur Henri's bloodhound eyes turned slowly in my direction. I've known Monsieur Henri LeClerc for almost twenty years now, and I've never known him to do anything quickly. So . . . he . . . turned, and . . . he . . . focused, and . . . he . . . saw.

You could watch the smile spread across his face—it was like watching a sunrise at sea on a perfectly clear morning. *"Mon cher Richard,"* he drawled, *"bien . . . venue."* He turned . . . and reached for . . . and took hold of . . . a big cup and started to make my customary Parisian breakfast beverage—a double espresso fortified with a splash of *calvados Valée d'Auge,* the pale, rich, aged apple brandy of Normandy.

Henri's coffee was the perfect eye-opener. Maman examined my jet-lagged expression. Then she slit two *ficelles,* buttered them with what looked like half a kilo of the farm butter she liked so much, and spooned a huge dollop of raspberry jam onto the bread.

"You look exhausted, *minou,"* she said to me as she simultaneously slid the plate under my nose and called me her pet. "This will give you some energy."

184

When you're in Paris, you do not watch your cholesterol. I devoured those two *ficelles* with every bit of butter and jam she'd served, downed three double espressos *avec calvados*, and accrued four more motherly pecks on each cheek as she inquired about her *prodige rouge*, frowned matriarchially, and wagged a big finger under my nose when she learned Boy Wonder wasn't traveling with me this trip.

Then, both fortified and loved, I strode across the street, slipped between the barricades, and pushed through the heavy glass doors of the Cercle. Check-in at the club was as simple as signing my name—Captain Herman Snerd, U.S. Army, Retired—and listing my home address and passport number on a postcard-size form, and running my credit card through the machine. But I knew that within hours, French intelligence—to be specific, a branch of the Ministry of the Interior known as the DST *(Direction de la Surveillance du Territoire*/Department of Territorial Surveillance),[8] would run a trace on the name, address, and passport I'd used.

Now, it wasn't just because I am a visiting retired military officer. In France, you see, all *étrangers*—foreigners—are required to fill out a similar form at each hotel where they stay. In the old days, these forms would be hand collected by *flics*—cops—and taken to a local police station, where they'd be bundled and shipped to Paris for examination. (In fact, poring over hotel registration cards was the device Freddie Forsyth's Frog cops used to track the assassin in that great book *The Day of the Jackal*.) These days, the examination process takes place over fax machines, computer modem lines, and the Minitel system, a French invention that combines the best elements of phone, fax, video, and data transmission in one desktop instrument slightly bigger than a standard telephone. The system reacts a hell of a lot faster than it used to, which means it forces guys like me *être alerte*—to be on our toes.

Now, I wasn't being paranoid here, I was just being prudent. The French have a very long history of keeping their eyes on visiting firemen. And I didn't need that kind of trouble.

---

[8]Interestingly, the late former director of French Intelligence, Alexandre de Marenches, in 1986 publicly referred to DST as *Direction de la* Sécurité *du Territoire*. That word change, if accurate, would broaden the DST's mission—making it much more akin to Britain's MI5, or the old Soviet KGB. Was Marenches's slip of the tongue rehearsed, or was it a Freudian slip? We'll never know, because he went to his grave without explaining it.

So I signed in, trying to remember whether or not I'd used my Captain Herman Snerd pseudonym in France when my boys and I tracked Call Me Ishmael Lord Brookfield and his tango pals to Beaulieu sur Mer, on the French Riviera, in *Green Team*. I'd forgotten to check this small but significant statistic before I'd left. If I'd signed the Snerd name anyplace, using another passport number, I'd be *pâtée*, which is how the French say dog meat, when they washed the alias through *les computers*.

My room wouldn't be ready until after noon. It was just past ten hundred hours now, which gave me some time to kill. I asked for messages and was handed an envelope with Avi's handwriting on it, even though the clerk said, "Colonel Ashcroft left this for you."

While my standard multiple personality is aptly named Herman Snerd, Avi's preferred alternate is Colonel Gordon Ashcroft, Royal Canadian Army (Ret). Now how the fuck he's used such a straight-upper-lip Brit-sounding name and survived going in and out of the Arab world for so long, I do not know. But it has worked for him for years. He travels most often on a Canadian passport with a Quebec address, he speaks nothing but French (which, of course, he does as perfectly as he does Arabic and Russian), and he never has had a problem.

I examined the envelope casually. The security seal Avi'd left behind on it—a single hair cunningly placed on the right edge of the rear flap—hadn't been tampered with. I slit the message open and unfolded a single sheet of heavy bond club letterhead. A brief note told me Avi had some urgent work to take care of—I interpreted that to mean that he had meetings with his AMAN people and that he also wanted to pick up our weapons and other supplies. It went on to suggest that we meet for a late lunch at La Petite Tour, a small, quiet restaurant he knew and liked on the Rue de la Tour, near Trocadero. If I had a problem with that, I could leave a message at the desk, as he'd be calling in during the late morning. Otherwise, Avi's neat writing continued, he'd be waiting for me at 1430. It all sounded good to me, because I had things to do, too.

Chapter

13

IT WAS COOL OUT—THE SORT OF BONE-CHILLING DAMP MORNING FOR which Paris is famous in the autumn. But Paris, even cold and wet, beats Moscow—or just about anyplace else. I may not care for Parisians, but the city itself is always wonderful. I dodged speeding traffic on Boulevard Malesherbes, dashed across the Place St. Augustin and headed west, up Haussmann, toward the Arc de Triomphe. Just to be on the safe side, I jumped onto the metro at Miromesnil, rode one stop, got off at the last instant, and waited as the train pulled out of the station. So far as I could discern, no one was following me. It was improbable that I was a target at this point. But, as I have said many times, there is no being too careful.

Especially here in Paris. Of all our Western allies, the French are the most alert, suspicious, and watchful about American operations on their soil. Now, they will tell you indignantly that *any* foreign ops—*l'Amérique inclusif*—are contemptible violations of the great French Republic's sovereignty, and up with zem zey wheel not *poot.*

Maybe. So far as I am concerned, however, the answer is more basic: old-fashioned Gallic paranoia about *les États-Unis*—which is what they call the U.S. of A. in case you didn't know.

You've probably heard it all before—the French insisting— loudly—that theirs is the finest culture, the best food and wine, the richest language, the most imaginative arts and letters; indeed, most French will even stipulate, in writing, that the best of everything is French.

But let me tell you a secret: deep down in their Frog souls, the French know they are inferior to the United States. Despite Renoir, Monet, or Toulouse-Lautrec; Racine, Molière, Voltaire, or Albert Camus; triple-crème, truffles, or Château Trotanoy, *they* are a third-rate power. And despite the Fox network, Chicken McNuggets, and plonk wine in boxes, *we* are a superpower. More evidence? Okay— *we* have not become a nation of Francophiles. When's the last time you had a Kronenbourg beer and a side of foie gras at the Horse Shoe Curve (or whatever the name of your local watering hole may be)? But in the last two decades, the French have become totally Americanized—from le Big Mac to les jeans Levi's to le Diet Coke, to le *bière* Budweiser, they have adopted our culture and lifestyle at the sacrifice of their own.

So far as I am concerned, that is a BFD (look it up). But to *les Françaises,* it is profoundly . . . galling. Bottom line? The French are saddled with a deeply rooted inferiority complex, which often makes them paranoid and unfriendly where Americans are concerned. Have you ever been to a restaurant in Paris where they absolutely refuse to speak English? Or stood in a bank on the Champs-Élysées while the teller, arms crossed, pretends that American Express traveler's checks are not valid in his country? Behavior like that is symptomatic of French inferiority.

Moreover, despite all their Gallic pride and snappy military uniforms, the French are all too well aware of their sorry history as warriors during the twentieth century. They fought badly during the 1914 to 1918 war. During World War II they collaborated with the Germans. Their leadership—the Vichy regime headed by Marshal Pétain—was cowardly and cozy with the Nazis. In the fifties, they lost their colonies in a series of humiliating wars and guerrilla actions.

Bottom line? The French, because they feel inferior, have set out to prove their greatness and their Frenchness on the world stage, often with disastrous results.

- They have "proved" it by using their special forces to sink the Greenpeace ship *Rainbow Warrior* at harbor in Auckland, New Zealand (they got caught in the act, too, and were badly embarrassed).

- They have tried to "prove" it by continued testing of nuclear weapons—a tactic that backfired and made them the object of international scorn.
- And they tried to "prove" it by snaring a quartet of CIA NOCs—officers operating with nonofficial cover—engaging in industrial espionage a few years back, to show *les États-Unis* that *les Frogs* were still good at something. (Actually, all *that* incident proved was that the CIA is as inept as the French in certain areas, industrial espionage being one of them . . . especially when a female NOC falls in love with her target and admits who she is and what she's doing. Kind of makes you wonder about the CIA's much-vaunted training program for operations officers, don't it?)

Néanmoins, which is how they say notwithstanding all of the above around here, Americans—especially military personnel, business travelers, and expatriates—are targets in France. All of the French security and intelligence agencies, paranoid about any perceived or imagined violation of *la sécurité de la République,* spotlight them.

Well, friends, paranoia is contagious. I may have known I wasn't being followed. But I still wanted to know I wasn't being followed. So, when the station was empty, I bounded up the stairs, sauntered down the street, and quick-marched once around the block. My six was clean.

I jumped the metro at Iéna and took it two stops to Rue de la Pompe, climbed off, walked through six blocks of imposing old Paris architecture that now housed a dozen or more embassies, and finally stood on Rue de Franqueville, in front of the U.S. Mission to the Organization for Economic Cooperation and Development, which as I've already explained, is better known as USOECD.

It didn't take long for me to see that they'd done the damage with a RPG—a Rocket-Propelled Grenade. Obviously, they hadn't been able to get close to the building, because of the steel antiterrorist barricade that had been erected in the driveway. But they'd been able to park across the street and fire the RPG from a car directly into the first-floor offices where the DIA officers who were concentrating their efforts on Russian Mafiya activities were located. None of the windows on the building had been fitted with the thick wire screen mesh that guards against RPG attacks. After all, this was Gay Paree, the City of Light.

After ten minutes I'd seen enough. I caught the metro back three stops to Alma Marceau, turned north and walked back past the Chinese embassy toward l'Étoile. Three blocks from the Arc de Triomphe, the wide street was cordoned off by barriers behind which stood submachine gun-toting soldiers in full battle gear. Beyond them I could see the forensics teams still at work picking through the rubble outside the entrance to the France-Israel cultural center, one of the targets that had been hit two and a half days ago.

There is a lot that you can learn by looking at the site of an explosion—if you know what to look for. I was able to see, for example, that the charge had been shaped. I knew that because, while the destruction to the building's facade was concave—it looked as if it had been scooped up and out by the explosion and dumped on the sidewalk—there was very little damage to the street directly in front of the building itself. There was no huge, gaping hole in the ground the way there is with car bombs. And, judging from the lack of repair trucks on the scene, there'd been very little apparent damage to the electric lines, water mains, or sewers that ran under the nine lanes of Avenue Marceau.

My quick verdict: someone had broken inside, planted a shaped charge on the ground floor, and then set it all off remotely. Had the Israeli site been the target of the same sort of probes as USOECD had? I bet myself a hundred francs that when I asked Avi, his answer would be in the affirmative.

From the barricade, I cut north to the Champs-Élysées, turned west, then walked to Rue Marbeuf and jogged left, turned up Rue Clément-Marot past a nice-looking bistro named Chez André, and crossed Avenue George Cinq onto the wide street named for King Peter the First of Serbia.

There, I hinked left, then jinked right, until I stood across two lanes of tightly parked cars and two lanes of traffic from one of three adjoining turn-of-the-century gray stone buildings each six stories in height, replete with ornate frieze work between each floor, wrought iron balconies, and eight-foot-high windows. On the fifth level of the one I faced, a series of small, beautifully pruned trees adorned the widest of the balconies. Below, flower boxes added splashes of color to the gray stone and black wrought iron. Set into the facade next to the doorway was a large rectangular, polished brass plaque on which were engraved the words LANTOS & CIE., DEUXIÈME ÉTAGE.

The entrance itself was spectacular, too: a gorgeous pair of tooled antique walnut double-width doors, into whose right-hand panel had been built a third, single entry door, in the same style that is common to courtyard buildings all over Europe (remember— Andrei Yudin's apartment house had a similar entry). The reason? Same as Moscow: the double doors allow cars in and out; the single door is for pedestrians. And positioned adjacent to the single door was an electronic keypad so that visitors could enter a code, and the automatically controlled lock on the single door would slip open.

It didn't used to be that way. Almost every apartment house in Paris had a concierge—the accepted typecasting was a crusty, blunt, middle-aged woman—who greeted visitors, took in the mail and packages, cleaned the public areas of the building, and knew every secret of every occupant. For their work, concierges got a small stipend, and a free apartment on the ground floor. But these days, concierges are an endangered species. Instead, there are the modern, efficient, and wholly impersonal keypads. No one takes messages, holds your mail and packages, and keeps track of your business. And God help you if you or a guest forget the keypad code—because there are no intercoms, and no one to let you in.

I walked past the building, doing a quick target assessment as I went. Target assessment is a completely natural act for me. After all, I see things differently from you. You see structure— architecture, detail, craftsmanship. I see those things, too—but I evaluate them in a slightly different light. I appraise them for their potential demolition value. You see windows and balconies. I see clandestine exits and entries. You see a beautiful antique walnut door. I want to know how thick it is, so that I'll know exactly how many feet of ribbon charge it will take me to destroy that door in a millisecond.

So, as I glanced up at the building that housed Werner Lantos's corporate headquarters, I wasn't admiring the friezes and hand-wrought ironwork. I was making mental notes about the four small, state-of-the-art television cameras that were suspended just below the second-floor balcony. It took me seven paces—just enough to see past a truck that was double-parked in front of the building—to determine that their field of vision encompassed the entire width of the building, as well as the sidewalk in front of it. In another six paces I learned that two cameras were on gimbals, which allowed them lateral and vertical movement, and that they had zoom lenses. Three paces later, I was certain that the other two were stationary—which meant they probably had wide-angle lenses.

A red and white placard next to the doorway proclaimed the fact that security at Lantos & Cie was provided by a company named SECOR. That was good news and bad news. The bad news was that Lantos's security monitoring was done by professionals. That would tend to make things difficult (but certainly not impossible) for the CIA or Mossad or Russian intelligence gumshoes who probably had tried to get inside Lantos & Cie to plant their various listening devices. It's a constant battle. You sweep the location weekly—or even daily—and the opposition keeps trying to bug your ass.

The good news was also that Lantos's security monitoring was done by professionals. You see, rent-a-cops don't get paid very much, a reality that tends to make them less than assiduous in the pursuit of their duties. So, while the security cameras might be state-of-the-art, the security folks who monitor them tend to be run-of-the-mill. It's a combination that makes life much easier for sneak-and-peekers like me.

I continued walking. To the left of the entry was a small bookstore. To the right was a store whose awning bore the legend *Le Petit Marché du Vin*—the little wine market—a small wine bar. Just to the right of the wine bar were the building's drainpipes— which could be climbed to gain entry to the starboard-most windows on each floor. The bookstore had a metal awning that also could be scaled. But the cameras would easily pick up anyone trying to make a vertical incursion.

I ambled down to the end of the block, turned the corner, took out a small notebook and a ballpoint pen, and made notes. Then I slipped paper and Montblanc back into a pocket, and wandered back the way I'd come. This time I took a good look at the street in front of the building. Almost directly opposite my target, three of the square manhole covers the French like so much sat in the middle of the roadway. I crossed over and examined them as I passed. One was a sewer cover. Below the other two were power and water lines. It was altogether possible that I could gain entry to the building through one of 'em.

I edged between the double-parked truck and tightly parked cars and walked in front of the building entrance, moving deliberately so as not to attract the attention of the gimbaled cameras, and concentrating on the keypad to the right of the doorway. It was an old Siemens electric unit with ten buttons and a—*shit*—I stopped short, one step before dropping into a fucking hole in the sidewalk.

I guess the French don't believe in red flags and flashing lights. At my feet was a mere six-inch-high barrier of steel—the rim around an elevator shaft. I peered down. Ten feet below me, two men were wrestling a large wooden barrel into the subterranean darkness.

I stepped back a foot and looked through the curtained window. They were setting up for lunch inside the small café. Suddenly, from behind me, a voice called my name. "Captain Marcinko—"

I turned to see Werner Lantos emerge from the rear of a black, four-door Citroën Xantia station wagon that had pulled in front of the double-parked wine-delivery truck. Lantos pushed ahead of the four bodyguards who were attempting to shield him inside the tried-and-true diamond pattern, stepped onto the curb, and headed toward me.

He had your regulation, political-issue SES (check the Glossary) on his face. In his left hand he carried a Nokia cellular phone. His right arm was extended; his hand anticipating a shake, was open. "Well, Captain, I hadn't expected to see you again so soon—especially in Paris."

Frankly, I hadn't expected to see him, either, although I didn't say so.

"Le Petit Marché du Vin—it's a good little restaurant," he said, his thin, aristocratic nose shifting vaguely in the direction of the wine bar's curtained window. "Simple, but nicely balanced menu. They serve a wonderful steak tartar, and a great plate of *andouillette.* They even bottle their own wines—bring them in from Burgundy by the barrel."

"Maybe I'll try it someday." My mind was racing. Of all the people I didn't want to run into right now, Werner Lantos topped the list. But here he was, and here I was, and there was nothing that could be done about it—except to exploit the situation to my advantage.

You see, one of the lessons I learned at the gnarled, webbed feet of my SEAL godfather, Roy Boehm, is that adversity is an unacceptable condition to a SpecWarrior. "When they try to wear you down by throwing half a dozen targets at you simultaneously," Roy used to growl at me, "the only question you should have is, 'Which one do I shoot down first?'"

Lantos strode up to me and pumped my hand up and down. His grip was firm. But his hand was soft—almost oily, as if he'd just rubbed moisturizer into it. He was as tall as I, and you could see from the way he fit into his European-style suit that he kept himself in good physical shape. He was probably one of those guys who played a lot of tennis or squash every day. His crimped white hair was slicked down along the sides of his head. His white eyebrows stood out against the deep tan skin of his high, creased forehead. He looked at me with a pseudoskeptical flicker of his cruel, gray eyes. "So, it is the food that brings you to Paris these days," he stated rhetorically.

He was playing with me. Or at least he was trying to.

But this wasn't the kind of game I care to play. So I didn't. "Actually, I'm here for the hunting," I said.

Werner Lantos stood facing me, his quartet of bodyguards spread out, enclosing the two of us within their defensive perimeter. "The hunting? The hunting?" he repeated to himself quizzically, stroking his chin with the antenna of the cell phone. "Isn't the season closed?"

"Not for the game I'm after."

He got the point. "Oh—the *hunting*," he said, finally. His expression remained unfazed. "Well, I hope you have an easier time of it here than you did in Moscow. You left under something of a cloud, I was told." He paused, as if expecting me to react.

When I didn't, he continued. "You know, I wish you'd come to me, first—"

Now that was interesting. "To you?"

"I could have smoothed the way for you. Getting results in Moscow isn't hard—*if* you know how to conduct business."

"We're talking about working a mafia murder investigation, Monsieur Lantos, not buying a truckload of *matryoshka* dolls."

He slipped his arm inside mine in the way that old-fashioned European gentlemen of a certain age like to do, grasped me by the elbow, and endeavored to walk me up the street. "Captain," he said, calling me by my first name, "in Moscow, there isn't always a lot of difference between the two."

There is nothing like being obvious when you have nothing to lose. So, I stopped in my tracks, turned, and pointed toward the wooden double doors of the building that housed Lantos & Cie. "Why don't we go up to your office and discuss the similarities?"

He stopped long enough to give me a truly frightening look. "Oh, I believe not." Then he tightened his grip on my elbow and started to walk again, trying to move me up the street. I allowed him to proceed, at which Lantos's mouth turned up into a reptilian smile that displayed his perfectly white probably capped teeth. "You see, Captain, I prefer to discuss business out in the open. There's much less of a chance that one gets . . . overheard."

Bien sûr—Right. And much less of a chance that this hairy SEAL would get a peek at his office's security arrangements and other vital factoids.

We discussed no business at all in the first two blocks. We actually spoke very little. He made small talk about the neighborhood, carried on about the quality of the Beaujolais at the wine bar, and—I'm serious here—he actually tried to frisk me. Well, it wasn't much of a frisk—more of a slap and pat. He ushered me between a pair of parked cars toward a crosswalk, and as he did so, he put his hand just above the small of my back, as if he was trying to keep me from tripping, and then twitched it up-down, side-side, as if to check whether I was wearing a pistol—or perhaps carrying a wire. I twisted out of his grip, elbowed his hand away, and gave him a look that warned him against trying that again.

We crossed a pair of wide streets, then turned up the Rue Bassano, all the while loosely encircled by Lantos's quartet of security men and trailed by the gleaming Citroën station wagon, which, incidentally, bristled with more antennas than the CIA director's car has.

At the Champs-Élysées we turned right and crossed the street, stopping in front of the broad, red and gold awning of Fouquet's. "Here," Lantos said, pointing toward the front door with his phone, as if it was a wand.

I should have known. Fouquet's is one of the most famous—and most expensive—cafés in France.

He cut past a barrier of white flowerpots, and slipped through the clumps of customers sitting in ranks of fragile-looking wicker chairs sipping their café crèmes and eating brioches or *petits–pains* topped with butter and jam, as they people-watched the shoppers and tourists who thronged the wide sidewalk, as well as the eight lanes of gridlocked midmorning traffic on the Champs. Fouquet's small round tables were all marble topped; the linens were starched and pressed.

From inside the doorway, the tuxedoed maître d' and white-coated headwaiter saw him approach and hustled toward us, bowing and scraping as if they were coming upon the sacred carcass of the goddamn pharaoh of Egypt. After a suitable period of ass kissing, Lantos allowed himself to be led toward a knot of five unoccupied tables that enjoyed an unobstructed view of the Champs all the way to the Arc de Triomphe. Three sat adjacent to the café's tinted plate glass windows. The other two were positioned one row closer to the sidewalk. Lantos dropped behind the center rear table, his back against the glass, the phone at his side. "This will do," he said, watching as his security detail split up and occupied one seat each at the other four.

"I will have my usual," Lantos told the headwaiter. He looked at me inquisitively. "Captain?"

I really didn't care what the hell I was served. "The same."

The headwaiter bowed once more and disappeared, backing away from the table like a goddamn geisha. Lantos's manicured fingernails played a series of mute chords on the cool marble tabletop.

It was time to get down to the business at hand. "You said there were similarities between investigating a murder and buying a truckload of souvenirs," I said. "I'd like to know what they are."

"You misinterpret what I said," Lantos said. "What I told you is that, in Moscow, the manner in which you do business is often just as important as the business itself."

He paused as two cups of coffee, two spoons, two napkins, and a bowl of paper-wrapped sugar cubes were placed in front of us. Immediately, the security man to our right picked up the bowl of sugar cubes and removed it from the table. "A competitor once paid a huge bribe to have a specially designed sugar cube placed in the bowl," Lantos explained. "The cube contained a microphone. I lost a very lucrative contract. Since then"—he extended his hand and the security man dropped two cubes onto the soft palm—"I have changed restaurants, and stopped allowing sugar bowls on the table. One should learn from one's mistakes, don't you think, Captain?"

He paused to allow me time to answer. When I didn't, he continued. "Now, back to your situation in Moscow—if, as I've said, you had come to me first, we might have been able to solve your problem without making as many waves as your visit produced."

"Solve my problem?"

"Close the books on the death of Rear Admiral Mahon."

"That, Monsieur Lantos, is for me to do. Not you, or anyone else."

"I think not," he said. "You see, I have a theory—and it is only a theory, Captain, not fact—that Admiral Mahon's death was not as simple as the Moscow police made it out to be."

"Perhaps you could explain your thinking to me," I said.

His gray eyes clouded over for an instant. "My theory," he said, "is that things are not always what they seem to be."

That, friends, is what G. Gordon Liddy likes to call Bravo Sierra, and we more plainspoken SEALs refer to it as bullshit. Things are usually exactly what they seem to be. Black is black. White is white. Two and two is four. And murder is murder—which is exactly what I said to Monsieur Werner Lantos.

"Either you are a naif, Captain, or you are playing the part of one."

I wasn't about to help this asshole one iota. "Think whatever you want to."

He inclined his head toward mine and spoke quietly. "Must I spell things out for you, Captain? All right, I will. There are forces at play here much larger and more consequential than the murder of an American naval flag officer—or, for that matter, the death of one, two—even ten Moscow gangsters. I am talking about the long-term strategic relationship between superpower nations. I am talking about the global balance of power."

"*Nations?* There's only one superpower left, Monsieur—and that's the United States. Which is exactly as it should be."

"There are, perhaps, too many people who think that way," Lantos said. "It shows a certain lack of sophistication. But there are those—and there are more of them than you might imagine—who believe that having just one superpower leaves the world unbalanced, and in great peril."

Peril? This guy was twisted. "They're wrong."

"That," he said, "may be your point of view. But you are not necessarily correct. There are others, both in your government, in Moscow, and elsewhere, who are convinced that the only way to achieve true long-term global harmony is to create—or re-create—another nation equal in power to the United States."

"In our government?" That was a surprise. I always thought the folks in our government had worked their butts raw for half a century to eradicate fascism, overturn communism, and promote democracy all over the globe. That's why I joined the Navy. That's why I serve my country—to promote those values.

"I don't mean to suggest anyone advocates a return to the old Cold War," Lantos said, his eyes narrowing. "That would be a disaster—for everyone. But many, and this includes high officials within your White House, your State Department, and your intelligence apparatus, realize that without another superpower on which to focus their attentions, American policy has become ambiguous, vague, and garbled."

Well, friends, as much as I hate to admit it, old Werner has a point. Our foreign policy *has* become ambiguous, vague, and garbled. But the reason wasn't the one he argued—i.e., because we lacked another superpower to offset us. The reason is that the current administration lacks focus in foreign affairs. We do not *lead* these days—we merely coast from crisis to crisis. And that vacuum of leadership is dangerous.

Lantos paused as the headwaiter slipped up to the table and deposited two plates of fried eggs, crisp bacon, sliced *ficelle,* and a jar of raspberry preserves in front of us. He arranged the plate in front of Werner Lantos carefully, placing it so that the eggs sat precisely at 0900 and the bacon at 1500, with the *ficelle* centered at the top of the plate, and a sprig of parsley garnish right in the center.

The vein on the right side of Lantos's neck started to throb—just the way I'd seen it pulsate in Moscow. He twisted his neck with the same sort of wild-eyed, jerky motion birds have when they turn their heads, and caught the headwaiter's eye with his own. Lantos's expression brought a look of abject terror onto the man's face. He snatched the plates up, begged Monsieur Lantos's forgiveness, and withdrew.

"I do not eat green," he said by way of explanation. "Nor will I tolerate green on my plate."

The throbbing vein in Werner Lantos's neck subsided. He took a sip of the strong, sweet coffee. "Look at how America struggles— everywhere from Europe, to the Adriatic, to the Middle East, to Asia and the Pacific rim, there is unease and unrest. America's old NATO allies are skeptical, anxious, even apprehensive about the way the United States will deal with them. During the height of the Cold War, no such doubts existed. Every nation knew where it fit in the strategic scheme of things."

"So, what are you advocating?"

Lantos shook his head. "I am not 'advocating' anything," he said. "It is not my position to advocate. I am a businessman who has been privileged to be able to help in some small way those who want a world that incorporates a symbiosis, a symmetry, a harmony, an *equilibrium*, between East and West. And I am proud to say that I am not alone." He paused. Then: "You, too, Captain, could aid that effort."

The sonofabitch was trying to recruit me. "You mean from my position in the Navy?"

"That might be feasible—if you decided that the larger objectives I have described to you are worth fighting for."

I played along with him. "That could be dangerous—working from within has its risks."

"Indeed it does. There are those who would call you a renegade—or worse." He showed me his teeth. "But then, Captain, you've already been called much worse by some of those with whom you work."

He was on the money there. I said nothing.

"Still," he continued, "you would be well compensated, if you chose that path. Very well compensated indeed. Not, of course, during your time of government service." He showed me his teeth and said, "That would be illegal." He waited for my reaction, then continued when there was none. "But afterward, you would find living very comfortable—there would be a large settlement after your retirement, when you would not have to enter the amount on your annual financial disclosure forms."

Something made me ask it. "Like the arrangement you have with Bart Wyeth?"

Werner Lantos said nothing. But the look on his face and the throbbing of his neck told me all I needed to know.

I continued. "And if I, ah, declined to work from within?"

"There could be a place for you at Lantos and Company should you choose early retirement, then come and work with us full-time."

Oh, he was smooth. He didn't quite ask me to commit treason. Oh, no—he'd leave that decision to me. The same way he'd probably left it to Bart Wyeth. And Bart, being a venal and greedy BAW, had jumped at the money. A notation went next to Bart's name in the little black book I carry in my head. I'd deal with the sonofabitch before this thing was finished.

Meanwhile, friends, it was about time to burst Werner's sicko bubble. First of all, I don't need any fucking money. These books are doing extremely well, thank you very much.

Second—and this is the important part because it has to do with patriotism. Now, patriotism is something we don't talk about much anymore. But we should talk about it, because it is a great quality. So, listen up. I took an oath when I joined the Navy. I raised my hand and swore to protect and to defend this country.

That oath is sacred to me. Sacred because it was (and is still being) written in the blood of all those who have died to protect our precious freedoms.

- It is written in the blood of Roy Boehm's shipmate, Dubiel, who was snatched from Roy's arms by a shark, thirteen hours after their destroyer, the USS *Duncan,* had been sunk during the Battle of Cape Esperance, back in 1942. Even today, Roy can still hear his shipmate's scream as the shark took him; even today he feels the pain of loss.
- It is written in the blood of the more than fifty-eight thousand American military men and women (including forty-nine SEALs and UDT frogmen) who died during Vietnam.
- It is written in the blood of the eight American military personnel whose charred corpses were desecrated by Iranian militants after the botched hostage rescue attempt at Desert One.
- It is written in the blood of those four brave SEALs from SEAL Team Six who drowned during the invasion of Grenada.
- It is written in the blood of those Americans who were killed during operations Desert Shield and Desert Storm.
- It is written in the blood of the tough Delta troopers and Army Rangers who gave their lives in Somalia so that Warrant Officer Michael Durant could live.

There is no fucking way I would ever betray the warriors who have given their lives to protect and defend the United States. Not by word, not by deed—not even by thought. Call it a profound sense of duty. Call it old-fashioned patriotism. Call it whatever you like—it is a motivating factor of my life.

So when I answered Werner, I was very direct. And by that, I mean very direct—even for me. "Help—how do you mean 'help,' cockbreath, by betraying my country? By dealing in dual-use systems? By selling nuclear technology to outlaw nations?"

The vein in his neck began to tremble again. "You do see everything in black and white, don't you?" he said. "Captain, for years, the United States and the old Soviet Union waged war on each other. They did it not by launching missiles at each other's capitals, but through the use of surrogates. Client states, who were supported by the superpowers."

I was getting pretty fed up with this argument. "What's your point?"

He paused. The headwaiter approached cautiously with two new plates of food, *sans* green garnish. Lantos waited until they had been placed in front of us. He took up his knife and fork, pierced the yolk of an egg, cut a piece of bacon, dipped it into the liquid, and raised the fork to his lips.

"My point," he said, after he'd chewed and swallowed, "is that the most progressive thinkers in Moscow and Washington want to re-create much of that old arrangement. You see, by reviving that balanced relationship, we will also revive the focus and direction that drove the foreign policy of both East and West for almost half a century. It will be a new world, one in which everyone will discover true purpose again—by which I mean a stable, long-term coalition from which all sides will benefit."

He broke a piece off the crusty *ficelle*, dipped the fragment of bread into the egg yolk, and ate it. "The superpowers will benefit from the increased stability of their balanced relationship. The client states—those old surrogates—will benefit from the renewed influx of military and commercial aid. It is what you Americans like to call a win-win situation."

My friends, Shakespeare had a phrase for the sort of dumbass reasoning Lantos was lobbing in my direction. He called it "chop-logic." I call it absofuckinglute craziness. "The world has changed," I said. "There's no way you can put things back the way they were."

"Don't be too sure," Werner Lantos said. "I am speaking to you of developments that have been sanctioned at the highest levels of your government. The very highest."

"Like who?" I wanted to know the names of the cocksuckers who were doing this. Not that he'd tell me, but I had to ask the question anyway.

He shook his head coyly. "Captain, you know I cannot reveal such a thing. But I can assure you that I have met with a very top-level representative of your government. This is not a trial balloon. This is policy."

That, friends, is impossible. Now, I can't vouch for what goes on in Moscow. But in Washington, every single element of American policy is scrutinized, investigated, and studied by two of the three branches of government. The administration may make policy, but that policy is paid for by money allocated by the legislative branch. Remember all of this from your social studies classes? It's called "checks and balances." And that is what I spelled out to Werner Lantos.

Lantos set his knife down and tapped a syncopation on the tabletop. "Technically you are right," he said, his fingers picking out the tune that must have been playing in his head. "But there is another branch of government as well, although very few choose to recognize it. That branch is comprised of the professional infra-structure." He retrieved the knife and resumed his breakfast.

"Politicians come and politicians go. But the system, Captain, remains in place. You tend to think of them as faceless bureaucrats—they work at the State Department, the CIA, the White House, the Department of Defense, and elsewhere in your government. But it is they who actually implement policy decisions that can profoundly influence what goes on. And I believe that some have chosen this path because it is in their interest—and they believe the country's as well—to do so."

"You are talking about a very broad conspiracy."

The knife came down hard on the table, splattering bits of egg yolk on the marble. "I am talking about nothing of the kind, Captain. This is not a conspiracy—it is policy that is being made at the highest levels of government. No, I am talking about a weltanschauung—a worldview—that is more enlightened, rational, and lucid than yours."

"You are talking about subversion," I said. "Full stop. End of story."

"As I have said, Captain, you tend to see things in absolute terms. But from my point of view—"

It was time for the kind of simple, declarative, monosyllabic sentence favored by UDT chiefs and Frogish mustangs like Roy Boehm and me. "Your point of view is fucked," I said. "Your 'theory'—as you put it—is that my friend Paul was murdered because some people have the crazy idea that the world is better off with two superpowers, not just one."

Lantos nodded. "You are oversimplifying, Captain, but yes, that is my theory. Now, let me add that the murder of your friend Rear Admiral Mahon was truly regrettable. But he—like you—managed to insinuate himself into the middle of a situation he did not understand. He, however, obviously did not enjoy the same level of operational experience that you have had. That deficiency, I believe, proved fatal."

"Paul was a warrior," I said. "Warriors die. But his family was murdered, too. My first godchild was killed."

Lantos nodded. "Truly a great tragedy," Lantos said, his reptilian face displaying a look of concern. "But that has been remedied, has it not?"

I didn't understand what he was getting at and told him so.

"It is simple," he explained. "With the death of the *vor v zakonye* Andrei Yudin, the book is finally closed. Andrei killed your friend and his family. Andrei was dealt with—and the death of your godchild was avenged."

So Lantos had ordered Andrei killed to placate me—perhaps ease me off the case. Well, he'd been mistaken. I put my War Face on. "You're wrong. The book is not closed at all."

"What?" The color drained from his face. His complete lack of expression told me the sonofabitch really was shocked.

Now that he was primed, it was time to give this asshole a SEAL wake-up call. "Andrei Yudin's death didn't bring closure," I said. "Oh, Andrei Yudin may have killed Paul and his family—murdered my godchild. But he—his people—only pulled the trigger. He was taking orders." I fixed Werner Lantos with my most Roguish War Face. *"My* book will be closed only when I work my way all the way up the fucking chain of command."

"But—but—" The vein on Lantos's neck began to pump overtime.

It occurred to me that maybe I could give the sonofabitch a heart attack right now. "Listen up, *cockbreath,"* I said, "I don't give a rusty fuck about your goddamn point of view, or your fucking theories. But let me accept them—just for the sake of argument. Okay. That means your fucking weltanschauung got my friend and his family killed. That makes you guilty."

"But my theory—" Lantos sputtered.

I put my nasty Slavic nose right up into his face. "Fuck your theory. We both know it's bullshit. You can talk all you want about 'harmony' and 'equilibrium.' But you and I know you're not *really* talking about harmony or equilibrium. That's a fucking smoke screen. You're talking about money—lots of money."

He started to protest. The goddamn neck vein started throbbing again. I cut him off. "Just like you said, you're a businessman. So it's all business—*zapodlo*—to you. Same thing I told Andrei back in Moscow, remember: it's all *zapodlo*."

I had things to do. It was time to say "Sayonara" to this pus-nutted, limp-dicked, no-load motherfucker. "See you in hell, Werner—which is where I'm going to put you."

Now, there are a couple of personality traits I should explain to you about people like Werner Lantos. Most assholes like Werner cannot stand two things. (That's not quite true—they can't stand a lot more than two. But these are significant, and can be used to provoke them.)

First, folks like Werner cannot stand being verbally assaulted. And second, they cannot tolerate having themselves befouled. Remember all those custard pies and other gooey goodies tossed at pompous swells in top hats in the old Laurel and Hardy movies? Well, there was a significant sociological point being made: he who wears a boiled shirt tends to take his appearance seriously. Me, I like a great food fight every now and then. But someone like Werner Lantos would rather get shot than soiled.

Ergo, I stood up as if to leave, picked up my plate of eggs, and turned it over directly onto Werner's four-hundred-dollar shirt, two-hundred-buck tie, and the bespoke Italian threads that cost more than most people make in two months. The bodyguard closest to us tried to intervene. Too late—I dropped him with an elbow to the side of his head. A second security man closed on me, his hand reaching inside his jacket pocket as he approached.

I stepped in close to take the offensive, grabbed the arm in question, pulled it in my direction, then took his wrist and folded it sharply forward, breaking it. I ignored his screaming, slipped my hand inside his jacket, extracted a blued Walther .32-caliber pistol from his shoulder holster and palmed it, pointing it vaguely in Werner Lantos's direction to forestall any further action by his goon detail.

There was murder in Lantos's eyes. He half-rose, my breakfast eggs dripping nicely down the front of his custom-made suit, and screamed unintelligible syllables at me.

I backed away, the pistol still pointed in his direction. The security detail was frozen in position. A table caught me in the thigh. I knocked it askew, stepped carefully over a rectangular white flower box, and backed onto the sidewalk.

My peripheral vision caught movement to my left. The driver of Lantos's Citroën coming at me. I ducked and whirled, catching him across the cheek with the side of the pistol, knocking him sprawling onto his hands and knees. Far down the Champs, I saw the blue flashing lights of a police car trying to fight its way through the traffic. I did a one-eighty, and saw a second black-and-white sedan heading in my general direction, siren hee-hawing and lights flashing.

How had *les flics* been summoned so fast? I didn't know and I didn't care—cops were trouble I didn't need. I started across the Champs, dodging and darting like a fucking broken-field runner as the traffic moved around me in fits and starts. As I ran, I dropped the magazine out of the Walther and let it fall to the ground. Once I'd made it to the opposite side of the broad avenue, I concealed the pistol in my big hand, worked the slide to eject the chambered shell (it, too, fell to the ground), then pulled the front of the trigger guard down and forced it to one side, which released the slide lock.

As I walked away from the sounds of sirens, I clandestinely fieldstripped the Walther, separating it into its component parts and wiping each one clean with my handkerchief to obliterate any trace of fingerprints. The slide assembly went into a trash container on the corner of Rue Washington. The spring got dropped into a mailbox outside the PTT next to the Chamber of Commerce just off the Rue Balzac. The frame was jettisoned into a storm drain on Avenue Friedland.

I kept moving north, and west, checking for anyone on my tail, until I reached the Parc de Monceau. There, I dropped onto a bench, caught my breath, and listened carefully for the sounds of pursuit. Five minutes later, I knew I was in the clear.

Chapter

14

My morning's encounter made me realize it was time for some form of self-defense supplies. Yes, I know Avi would probably provide me with weapons. But with Mr. Murphy around, I've learned never to take anything for granted—and besides, I hate to go around empty-handed. I wandered the side streets around the Avenue des Ternes until I found a small hardware store, walked inside, and browsed. It took me just a few minutes to find a six-inch screwdriver with a stout, hand-turned wood handle and a well-made, German stainless steel shaft. Then, I discovered where the *patron* kept the sharpening stones. As quietly as I could, I worked the tip of the blade against a medium stone until I'd given it a chisel edge.

I paid twenty-seven francs fifty centimes, declined the offer of a bag, slipped the screwdriver inside my coat, and left. On the street, I made some discreet adjustments. The screwdriver fit securely and imperceptibly, slid down inside the left side of my trouser waistband and held in place by my belt.

Armed and dangerous, I checked the address I'd written on a piece of scrap paper at the Cercle, and headed toward the restaurant.

Avi was late to lunch by almost an hour. I waited, content to nibble the half baguette in the bread basket down to the crumbs,

drink a nice, cellar-cooled carafe of Chenas down to the last eighth-
liter (and was just ordering a second), when he finally showed up,
apologetic, rumpled, and sweaty. His face reflected anxiety. I filled
his glass with the last of my wine. He waved it away, asked the
patron for a half-liter bottle of Evian water, and drained the whole
thing thirstily as soon as it was set on the table.

I waited until he'd drunk his fill, then asked him in French,
"Problèmes, Avi?"

He leaned forward and whispered conspiratorially. "I think I
picked up a tail," he said. "Outside the embassy. It's taken me the
better part of two hours to shake 'em—but I think I did—haven't
seen anything suspicious in half an hour." He shook his head in
disgust. "You'd think I'd know better than to go within half a
kilometer of the place."

"But you *do* know better."

"Yeah—but our asshole chief of station obviously doesn't. The
ben zona insisted on a meeting in his office. 'I command your
presence, blah-blah-blah. No place is more secure, blah-blah-blah,'
he tells me. Well, shit—no place may be more secure, so far as he's
concerned, but no place is more easily surveilled, either, so far as
I'm concerned."

Avi was right. The Israeli Embassy in Paris—I've been there and I
know—is located on Rue Rabelais, a narrow side street just off the
Champs-Élysées. The ornate, dingy gray six-story structure has
been totally isolated—even the office buildings and apartment
houses opposite the embassy have been evacuated. The street itself
has roadblocks at each end and is patrolled by squads of
submachine-gun toting police officers in combat fatigues. Their
weapons are always locked and loaded. Their trigger fingers are
always indexed—ready for action. Every car that passes through
the roadblock to park in the narrow strip in front of the embassy
building is searched. Not just cursorily, either. Trunks and hoods
get raised. Mirrors go underneath. Seats get pulled out. They are
serious about it.

The security is effective, too. There hasn't been a single incident
in the Rue Rabelais for more than a decade now. More than a dozen
potential tangos have been identified and snapped up before they
could act. Twice, someone managed to slip explosives underneath a
diplomat's car—but they discovered 'em in time and the pair of
potentially dangerous incidents were averted.

But all that isolation means that French intelligence has its work made easy when it comes to identifying Israeli intelligence person-nel and other interesting characters who may show up at the embassy from time to time. Cameras in the vacant buildings zoom in on every visitor and employee. Teams of watchers deploy nearby, ready to move. And those are the friendlies. Israel's adversaries are as well aware as the French of the embassy's tactical situation. And so all of the potential hostiles, too, gather nearby.

Don't just take my word for it, either—the next time you're in Paris, take a little walk and see for yourself. Follow a route that starts at the glitzy café at the corner where the Avenue Franklin D. Roosevelt and the Rue Jean Mermoz come together at the Rond Pont des Champs-Élysées.

Take a leisurely stroll up Rue Jean Mermoz to the Rue du Faubourg-St. Honoré. Take careful note of the customers in the trio of small restaurants that face the entrance to the Rue Rabelais. Then continue on, pausing at the intersection of the Faubourg to look back. Then turn right, go one block, turn right again on Avenue Matignon, pass the checkpoint, and continue to the Champs. Sit at the café, have a coffee or two, then do it all over again. You'll see 'em if you look hard enough—they're arrayed like birds on power lines. Two-, three-, and four-person teams. French countersurveil-lance units in unmarked cars. Algerians on motor scooters (the better for the thick Paris traffic). Flat-footed Russians. You'll see Egyptians, Libyans, Syrians, and Iraqis—even the occasional Brit or American team, scouting the opposition. It's like a fucking spooks' convention.

I signaled for more bread and wine. "So what did the asshole have for you?"

"Nothing I didn't know already—which makes me even more upset. He just wanted to bring me in to demonstrate that this is his turf and he's in charge, and nothing happens without his permis-sion."

From the sound of it, the Mossad's Paris chief of station had gone to the same operational schools as the big bad BAW from Moscow, Bart Wyeth. The prospect of which was truly frightening, given my morning encounter with Werner Lantos and the prospect that Bart the BAW was working for the opposition.

I gave Avi a full sit-rep of the morning's activities, recounting in detail my impromptu meeting with Werner Lantos.

He laughed when I told him about my breakfast on Werner

Lantos's chest. Then his face grew serious. "He's dangerous," Avi said.

"So am I."

"But you are also principled."

"Only when I deal with principled people. Believe me, Avi—I'll take this asshole down."

"He has a lot of *protekzia.*"

"More than you think." I told Avi about Lantos's CIA connection.

Avi's reaction was a long, low whistle. "It makes perfect sense," he said. "So, what do you want to do?"

"I want my lunch, and another bottle of wine," I said. "After all, I didn't get to finish my breakfast."

Avi cracked what was no doubt the first smile of the day for him. *"Ti Z'dayeen,"* he said, telling me to fuck myself in Hebrew. "First we'll eat. Then we'll plan."

So we ate, and we plotted—and I won a hundred francs from myself. The Israeli Cultural Center on Avenue Marceau was indeed the nerve center of AMAN's clandestine activities in Paris. More specifically it was also where the office of AMAN's three-man Russian-Mafiya working group—all were victims of the explosion—had been located. And guess what? There had been a series of attempted break-ins over the past three months.

Now, here is a piece of tactical information for you: if you can isolate the pattern of action being directed against you, you can then take steps to anticipate and counteract it.

Let's do just that. First, let's look at the current list of victims and see if we can discern a pattern. There was Paul Mahon, his family, and the Navy driver. Next came Andrei Yudin and several of his malevolent *byki.* Most recently, two American Army majors, two Israeli captains, and a lieutenant colonel became victims of violence. There have been other victims as well—French nationals at USOECD, and Israelis at the Cultural Center. But they had been what we call in the War business unintended collateral damage.

What did the real targets have in common? The first element was simple: they all had some connection to the Russians, and the Russian Mafiya. Now, what else did the pattern tell us? It indicated that all the nonmafiya victims were investigating mafiya connections, with the growth of Russian intelligence and military activities as part of their assignments.

So much for pattern. The next part of the equation, then, was anticipating the bad guys' next moves—and initiating counteraction.

Well, I have a theory about that, too. It is that you do not sit around and wait for something to happen. You must take the initiative—you must force events to happen. Indeed, as the sixteenth-century Samurai warrior Kojiro Okinaga taught his many students—among them, incidentally, was an ambitious thirteen-year-old named Miyamoto Musashi—"The Warrior provokes his adversaries into action before they are ready, because by doing so he will almost always gain the advantage over them."

I knew that the clock was ticking. The list of goodies I'd found at Andrei's apartment, which had been translated courtesy of Ken Ross, indicated that the Russians had managed to send a complete package of nuclear refining equipment to the Middle East. The Air France waybill from Andrei's dacha—the one for the hot freon tanks—told us that the processing site was virtually complete. And I knew that it wouldn't take much to make enough high-quality plutonium to construct a small but deadly weapon—something that could be contained in a suitcase-size package. Maybe given to a suicide bomber to set off in Tel Aviv.

You are asking me why the Russkies would risk a full-scale war in the Middle East.

The answer is that it would provide them with a huge opportunity to insinuate themselves back into the region—and virtually assure their reemergence as a superpower.

You are looking at me as if I am crazy. Okay, tadpole, I'm going to spell it out for you.

- Item: two of the most hard-line, confrontational states in the Middle East—Syria and Iraq—were former Soviet client states. In Iraq, the Soviets had provided weapons, spare parts, and money. In Syria, however, they'd built an elaborate military-intelligence infrastructure—an entire Soviet C^3I infrastructure—hidden inside the Syrian military system. You—and I—know that, because Avi and I had scoped it all out during our first joint mission back in the eighties.

So, it was time to see what Werner Lantos didn't want me to see in his office. And it was time to get on the phone to Ken Ross. I needed some technical support. To be specific, I needed to see whether or not one of our new FORTE—Fast On-board Recording of Transient Experiments—satellites could be reprogrammed to overfly Syria in the next twenty-four hours.

You haven't heard about FORTEs? Let me 'splain you, as Desi used to say. FORTE was developed during the Bush administration. It has a resolution that allows it to read a six-inch object from its 155-mile orbit height. But its main feature is a powerful nuclear sensing array that allows it to spot everything from chemical residue released during plutonium processing, to the heat signature of a nuke on ready alert. FORTE works through cloud cover, bad weather—and has a penetration capability of five meters. That means that even if an armed nuke is buried more than fifteen feet underground, it can sense its presence.

The problem is that we have only two of these birds. So they are used sparingly, and are always in demand. Now, I'm not supposed to know where the FORTEs are flying. But I still have friends in low places, so just between you and me, one bird was detailed over the Ukraine, checking on Chernobyl, while the other was somewhere in the mainland China AO—Area of Operations. I needed Kenny Ross to get one of 'em moved without making too many waves.

I took a copy of the list I'd taken from Andrei's apartment and slipped it across the table to Avi.

The Israeli read it, his eyes moving greedily down the pages.

When he looked up, I could tell that he thought things were as serious as I did.

"Viktor Grinkov is not only very powerful, he's getting very rich, I think," Avi said, folding the papers and slipping them into his pocket.

"How much money are we talking about here, Avi?"

"Well, my estimates—which are a lot more conservative than my bosses—project that Grinkov has collected somewhere in the area of twenty to thirty million bucks in payoffs in the last twelve months alone—and he's not at the top of the heap. Anyway, that money goes to Lantos. Lantos disburses it to numbered accounts in Switzerland, the Cayman Islands—wherever he can."

"And what about your old pal Ehud Golan?"

Avi's face flushed in anger. "He's not my friend, goddammit."

But it was me who was righteously pissed off. "You should have let me know about him, Avi."

He sighed. "You're right," he said. "I should have done. But it's complicated. Ehud is still working for Mossad. Now, nobody's told me that for a fact, but every time I bring his name up, I get told to lay off—there are ongoing operations that might be compromised, and so on and so forth. That is the usual Mossad mumbo jumbo bullshit, so I figure Ehud is still on the job. He's bad news—and they should have dumped him years ago. But you know how it is— the Agency's got its assholes, too."

"Like Lantos."

"Like Lantos. And for all I know Ehud's kept Gelilot up-to-date about all the dual-use equipment." Gelilot was Mossad shorthand for its headquarters, which, you'll recall, is located on a bluff just above the Gelilot junction of the Tel Aviv–Haifa highway.

"That doesn't mean he's on the side of the angels."

Avi's face went grim. "I've never known Ehud to be on the side of the angels," he said. "Ehud is on the side of Ehud."

To be honest, whether Ehud had an ongoing relationship with Mossad really didn't matter so far as I was concerned. We already knew that Werner Lantos had hitched himself to Christians in Action. So why shouldn't Lantos's number-one enforcer make a deal with his own old employer, Mossad?

Indeed, linking to an intelligence or law enforcement agency is actually a common ploy used by criminals these days. They make some kind of deal with an agency—maybe they promise to snitch on their money-laundering crime partners. Or they promise inside info from the Cali Cartel. Or perhaps it's intelligence about dual-use smuggling to countries on our SST—that's State-Sponsored Terrorism—list. Anyway, they volunteer to help. Then, when they're caught smuggling drugs, or laundering money, or waxing civilians, they protest—loudly, and often in the media—that they were only doing their nefarious deeds at the behest of the CIA, or Mossad, or FBI, the DEA, or whichever agency was dumbass enough to hire 'em in the first place.

The whole idea is so dishonest that it makes me sick. I drained the last of the Chenas. "C'mon," I said to Avi. "I have to make a phone call—see if we can get ourselves a little outside help. Then, if you would be so kind, allow me to give you the one-centime tour of Lantos et Compagnie. We'll see what we can find."

Chapter

15

IT WAS OBVIOUS AS WE EMERGED FROM THE RESTAURANT THAT ANY excursion to Werner Lantos's offices was going to have to wait. It was 1745. Dark—but not dark enough for them to hide. Two pairs of smokers sat in a dark sedan across the street. They were the ones we were supposed to notice—not too obvious, but *there* nonetheless. The ones we weren't were no doubt in two, or three, or perhaps even four additional cars and God-knows-how-many rice rockets—those low-slung Jap motorcycles that are favorites of the messengers who cut through Paris's gridlocked traffic.

The smokers' car sat on the corner directly opposite La Petite Tour's front door.

Had these guys been on Avi's six or mine? Avi said he'd shaken his tail. I hadn't noticed anybody on mine. But there was no time to debate the subject right now. I nudged Avi with my elbow. "We split up. See you back at the Cercle whenever."

He didn't bother to respond—just peeled off to the left, and walked up the Rue Gavarni against the traffic flow, and disappeared into the darkness. The sedan's rear doors opened and two hoods emerged from the darkened interiors with the easy synergy of a unit that's worked together for some time. (Good tradecraft there, friends. Always extinguish your interior car lights before opening doors when you're on a surveillance op. Remember the Ivan in the

Beemer in Moscow? Well, he was no pro—but these guys were.) They flung their cigarettes into the wet street, checked their own sixes, took opposite sides of the street, and started off after Avi, overcoated shoulders hunched against the chilled, wet Paris wind. It was like a scene out of a fifties French spy movie.

Were they French? Israelis? Arabs? Ivans? Fact was, it didn't matter right now who they were—what mattered was getting rid of 'em. That meant either shaking them, or disposing of them. So far as I was concerned, it didn't matter which way things went.

I cut right, and walked down the slight hill into the cold wind toward the Place Costa Rica. A shiny Mercedes cab slid to a stop in front of me—perfect timing for a getaway. I was reaching for the door handle when a tiny, birdlike woman with a croc Chanel reticule the size of a sixteen-pound sledgehammer ran up, cut me off, swung the cylindrical handbag into my chest hard enough to make me grunt, pushed me aside, climbed in, shut and locked the door, and began nattering at the driver in machine-gun French.

He shrugged at me—the classic Gallic palms up expression of helplessness—and drove off. I scanned 360 degrees. There were no more cabs—but a trio of hostiles was working its way down the street I'd just traveled. They were followed by a low-slung, dark Citroën Xantia—the same goddamn four-door station wagon with tinted glass windows and lots of cellular antennas that had accompanied Werner Lantos and me to breakfast earlier in the day—that was moving at a crawl.

I could take them all on right here, but there was no sense in doing that. Not now, anyway—not when I was in public, and at a tactical disadvantage. But I had to move—and fast. I crossed the crowded Place Costa Rica and dodged my way down Rue Rayounard to Charles Dickens Square. The main thoroughfares gave way to narrow, dark side streets.

The predicament was, no doubt, courtesy of the omnipresent Monsieur Murphy. Why? Because in situations like this one it's better to stay out in public. The more witnesses there are, the less chance that the opposition can act with impunity. I crossed the upper end of the square, striding rapidly to my left against the dwindling traffic flow, to the safety of a small, dimly lit café on the far side. A round *M* sign with an arrow posted on a street lamp pointed left, suggesting that I might want to head toward the Passy metro stop. BTDT—no way was I going to box myself in on any subway right now.

Instead, I kept moving, striding past the café. I glanced inside. Half a dozen regulars sat at the bar, drinking. The barman was polishing glassware. You might think I pondered going inside, finding a corner table, putting my back up against the wall, and forcing them to come after me. But I knew there was absolutely no advantage in my doing that.

You—yeah, *you* out there, the reader with your hand flapping like a fucking flag in the wind. You *what?* You want to know why there was no advantage to my planting myself inside that café and making the bad guys come after me. Simple. It's an old SWAT team lesson I learned from Dan Cusiter, a twenty-four-year veteran of the Los Angeles Sheriff's Department. You're chasing a suspect. He runs into a house—or runs into a room in a house—and slams the door in your face.

Do you follow him? You do not, says Dan the man. Why? Because maybe said malevolent miscreant has reinforcements in that house or that room, and you do not want to become a police statistic. So the rules change: the chase has now become a barricade situation, and you wait the sonofabitch out. Time is now on your side.

Well, same thing here. They could sit and wait all night if they had to. Call for reinforcements. Block off the whole fucking neighborhood. Sooner or later I'd have to come out of that café— either the front door or the back door. End of story. Time was on the pursuers' side, not mine.

Unless, of course, I could turn things around. But to do that I'd need wheels—and there were none available at the moment. I checked my six. The trio had turned into a quartet. Two pairs of two, working opposite sides of the square. They'd picked up another car, too—a second Citroën, this one a sedan. Both vehicles sat in the Rue Rayounard at the head of Charles Dickens Square, waiting to see what I'd do before committing one way or the other. Smart. These guys were smart.

They probably thought it was the best of times for them and the worst of times for me. I like it when my enemies get overconfident—that's when I strike back. So, as far as I was concerned, this was precisely the right time for great expectations. But first, I had to even the odds a little bit.

So I strode halfway down the square, noting that one team shadowed me on a parallel course while the other team moved to cut off my escape route. Good—that meant I had 'em right where I wanted 'em.

You, gentle reader, are asking WTF. Well, I will explain my optimistic outlook. Currently, the first pair of opposition gumshoes was now separated from me by the small park that sat in the middle of Charles Dickens Square. The park was similar to the kind of one-square-block parks one finds in London (and probably had been designed that way, given its moniker). A statue stood in its center—Dickens, no doubt. And the whole thing was bordered by a veddy English six-foot-high, spear-tipped picket fence of wrought iron—the kind of thing that would have done justice to Buckingham fucking Palace. There were four gates, one on each side of the square. And they were closed and—judging from the chains and padlocks I saw as I passed close by—secured.

So the bad guys, who were no doubt savoring the fact that I couldn't cross the park to escape, weren't going to be able to cross the square either—unless they were goddamn hurdlers. And even if they held Olympic gold medals, it was going to be nigh on impossible for them to jump six feet of wrought iron picket fence in their long, heavy—and currently extremely soggy—overcoats. So while Team One was physically close to me—close as the crow flies—it was in no position to do me any damage right now.

It also meant that the second team, which lurked on the Rue des Eaux, was currently isolated by a couple of hundred meters from any potential backup. Twenty to twenty-five seconds of running from the look of things and the physical appearance of Team One. That was plenty of time for me.

I cut back toward Team Two. As I passed through the shadow between streetlights I reached inside my coat. My right hand withdrew the screwdriver from my waistband.

I scanned the square. There weren't any people on the street besides the five of us players. Good. Time to move. I cut across the narrow street, moving toward my targets. My body attitude was shifting now from neutral to aggressive; the screwdriver sat tight in my right hand in a modified ninja grip—the shaft tucked tight against my wrist, pointed up my forearm. My left hand was balled in a fist. I had my War Face on.

What's that? You say you're dubious when I talk about a War Face? More macho bullshit psychobabble from the old Rogue, you say?

Listen and learn, tadpoles. A War Face is an important element of battle. The Marine Corps makes every fuzzy-scalped, stinking trainee develop one. We SEALs do, too. The War Face is the enemy's worst nightmare. It's the face you use when you charge, screaming, into his lines. It's the face you use when you work up close and personal, with knives, bayonets, and the other sundry hand tools of war. It's the man-to-man combat face that makes your enemy know, deep in his very soul, that you are going to kill him before he can kill you. It is the face that Means Business—the face whose very business is Meanness itself.

We were closing now like ships on a collision course—less than twenty yards apart; then ten, then five. They examined my expression and took note like the professionals they were. I did the same. I saw their narrow, dark eyes, expressionless, wind-creased faces, and the thick, brushy mustaches favored by Mediterranean types from Barcelona to Cairo; from Palermo to Tunis. But these two weren't Spanish, Italian, or Arabs. No. These two had the glacial, compassionless, indifferent look common to most of the fucking ugly Corsicans I've ever seen, so that's what I dubbed them—FUC One and FUC Two. FUC One was tall and thin, with a touch of gray in his thick 'stache. FUC Two was smaller and darker than FUC One. Uglier, too.

As I moved abreast of 'em, just below the empty, dark corner where the Rue Charles Dickens dead-ends at the Rue des Eaux, the opposition separated. A trio of antique store windows, each protected by its own roll-away metal grating, provided dim light. FUC One paused, as if to peruse a Louis Quinze divan with gilt frame and striped silk upholstery. FUC Two, five yards ahead, concentrated on a display of Empire chandeliers that hung above angled, polished wood furniture accented by bright metal.

You could see them both tense as I drew even with FUC One. He moved aside, simultaneously gesturing with his head, as if to let me see the goods displayed in the shop window more easily. *"Bon soir, m'sieur,"* he growled. He slipped to my right flank (and his left), all the while making sure that he kept the protection of the antique store's sturdy metal grating to his shoulder.

I appeared to peer—but I was watching his reflection in the window as he snuck silent and smooth, slightly behind me into the snooker position. Now the light was in his favor. But my peripheral vision still picked up all his movement.

And there *was* movement: I caught the hint of something dark in FUC One's gloved hand. A sap, a club, or a blackjack perhaps. His arm started to move—a short practiced, powerful swing that would catch me upside the head from the rear. FUC Two was moving up to my port side now, from two doors down, reaching into his pocket as he, too, edged within striking distance.

Up at the top of the square, the Xantia began to creep forward. I could see its parking lights moving down the street that ran parallel to where I stood. It was going to fishhook back—so they could snap me up. This had been designed as a snatch and grab. A cosh and carry. A hit and run. They didn't want me *dead*—they wanted *me*. Tie me up and ask me questions, maybe with the help of burning cigarettes, needle-nosed pliers, and a twelve-volt battery.

Did that make me nervous? Honest answer: a little. But if you're not on edge in a situation like this, if your heart isn't pumping and your pores aren't like antennas, sensing everything around you, then there is something wrong with you. Besides, the anticipation of blood and guts—especially my enemy's blood and guts—makes my adrenaline flow. Let me tell you something about me: tension makes me extremely dangerous.

Okay, where was I? Oh, yes—I was describing how the opposition had committed itself.

Well, I committed, too. I dealt with the most immediate threat first. I turned slightly to my right, reversed my grip on the screwdriver so that it pointed blade out, and—War Face kinetic energy mad as hell *Hoo Yaah*—stuck it completely through the wrist of FUC One.

From the pained look on his puss, I knew what I'd done to him must have smarted. I wasn't finished yet, either. I wrenched the screwdriver handle ninety degrees due north, ratcheting his arm up and around into a most unnatural position. From the timbre of the cracking sounds, I'd just dislocated it at the shoulder—or worse. FUC One screamed unintelligible imprecations, oaths, and other deleteful expletives in a language that I didn't understand, and then dropped to his knees in agony, pulling me and my screwdriver with him.

That wasn't very nice. After all, I needed the goddamn thing back, and FUC One—well, FUC One's arm anyway—was being recalcitrant about letting me have it. I stood over him, kneed him in the face thrice, simultaneously yanking hard on the screwdriver a couple of times, but the goddamn thing was as solidly embedded just above his wrist as King Arthur's fucking sword Excaliber had been locked in its medieval stone. I guess I'd put it right through FUC One's wrist bone. Oops.

A shadow fell over me as I struggled, and I whirled just in time to see FUC Two's fist slashing out at my head. He was holding something—a collapsible, spring metal baton. He whapped it in a short arc, punching the blow to give it extra power. Nasty things, spring batons. In fact, I wished I'd had mine right then. I pulled myself up, raised my arms into a defensive position, whirled, and sidestepped his powerhouse swing. But not fast enough. He'd anticipated my move, countered, and changed his angle of attack to uppercut me. So, as I raised my right arm to protect my face, the weighted metal knob on the end of the spring connected solidly with the tip of my elbow—and my whole fucking arm went numb.

Why the hell do they call that the funny bone? There is absofuckinglutely nothing funny about it at all.

Meanwhile, something actually went right: FUC Two's momentum carried him slightly past me. I used his weight to my advantage: numb elbow or no, I shoved him rudely in the direction he was already moving. My weight, combined with his motion, propelled him another five or six feet, and smacked him *whop* against the wall between two of the antique stores. He made contact with the rough stone fist first, face second.

Double smash, double ouch. The baton dropped onto *le trottoir*—which is how they refer to sidewalks here in La France. I scrambled to pick it up—but my fucking hand was still so numb I couldn't close my fingers around the goddamn shaft. I looked up just in time—he was coming off the wall to retrieve his weapon. If I couldn't have it, I was damned if he would. I slide-kicked it well beyond anybody's reach into the gutter and under a car, then rolled away from him.

FUC Two momentarily halted his activity to assess the situation, which gave me a chance to regain my feet, massage my sore elbow, and kick FUC One in the head to make sure he'd stay put. I moved clockwise, trying to pen FUC Two up close to the wall, where he wouldn't have much space to maneuver. FUC Two spat blood in my direction as if to ward me away, then growled, put his head down like a billy goat, and charged. Numb arm or not I caught him with a glancing blow on his thick neck. But he managed to grab me around the chest, pinion my arms, push me backward as if I were an unweighted tackling dummy, and sledded me—*slam*—up against a parked car. I listened as my back protested loudly. Hey, friends, I may love the sound of human vertebrae popping—but only when they're someone else's.

It was time to put the sonofabitch away. I took the initiative—

broke his grip, smacked him twice to set him off-balance, then grappling-hooked him up close by the lapels of his double-breasted overcoat so he couldn't get away, then head-butted him as hard as I could—and nearly knocked myself silly.

Oh, shit, oh, fuck, oh, doom on me. He was supposed to be out cold on the sidewalk, but I was the one seeing stars. Damn—was *that* ever a mistake. I'd misjudged our relative positions, or he'd moved and I hadn't compensated, or Mr. Murphy had interjected his miserable self between us and I hadn't noticed—whatever the case, the bottom line is that fights like these don't happen in a vacuum, and it's hard to get these things right when your opponent isn't standing still like people do during martial arts classes. So instead of stunning the sonofabitch, I'd smacked him right on top of his skull with my eyebrows, which did a lot more damage to me than it did to him.

As I woozed, he gut-punched me. When that didn't work—my gut, friends, is washboard tight and rock hard—he hugged me tight and whispered a sweet nothing in my ear as he tried to bite it off. What nothing? *"Kooz emeq,"* is what he told me. If I'd realized what he was saying and what language he was using I'd have answered him in kind. But I had no idea, except that it probably didn't translate as, "You are handsome and wise and your ear tastes good," so I told him to fuck himself in plain old Anglo-Saxon and tried to work my hands high enough to break his friggin' neck— except I couldn't get hold of him because there were currently three somewhat fuzzy FUC Twos—or at least that's the way it seemed in my somewhat headcombuttulated state.

From the way he kept p-p-p-pounding at me I knew that he knew I was fucking dizzy, while I knew he wasn't (this is a sentence, dear friends, that illustrates my woozy state through the literary means of construction, syntax, and irony). How'd I know? I knew that because I saw three nasty little FUC hands digging inside his coat pockets while three other FUC arms tried to keep me pinned up against the car. It was like trying to wrestle with one of those six-armed statues you see in Thailand. I stopped trying to choke him, grabbed the middle arm, and came up with air. Tried the next one and made contact just in time to see the surprise he had in his hand.

Doom on Dickie—it was a Syrette, which is one of those battlefield morphine self-injectors. They're built to penetrate through uniforms—even body armor. What the hell he had in it— ketamine, sodium Pentothal, or some other nasty love potion that would knock the shit out of me—I didn't want to know. Or experience, either. The needle guard came off and his fist started toward my upper thigh.

I grabbed his Syrette hand with both of mine and managed to clear it away about two inches before it would have pierced my trouser leg. He twisted, broke my grip, and brought his hand around once more as he worked the business end toward me for another try.

No way. I elbowed him across the face. That rocked him back a foot or so, which in turn gave me a little bit of working room. I slammed the base of my palm against the side of his nose. I must have broken it because he staggered backward, his free hand involuntarily letting go of my coat and moving toward the injury. But the Syrette was still too close. I mean, he didn't have to hit me in the arm as if he was a clinic doc giving me an injection. He could put the fucking thing anywhere and it would work. Leg, thigh, side, shoulder—it didn't matter. He wasn't worried about being gentle or accurate—I was simply a fucking pin cushion and he was TMWTP—the man with the pin.

But I'd hurt him—and he let me know it because he'd stopped pushing forward and started moving back to protect himself from me. Bad move. Retreat is something you don't do unless it is a tactical move to draw the enemy into an ambush—and this certainly wasn't the case here. So I moved in close enough to strike but far enough to keep away from the needle, faked right, dropped left, and roundhouse-kicked at his legs, sweeping them right out from under him. He hadn't expected that and he went down hard—which knocked the fucking Syrette out of his hand.

That was good—because I'd just used up eighteen or nineteen or even twenty seconds of the twenty-five I'd allotted myself to deal with these two ugly FUClings.

Time was short. I dropped on top of FUC Two, the full weight of my knee on his Adam's apple. He gurgled and went limp. The sonofabitch was *mine.*

Not an instant too soon, either. Because one of the Team One bad guys was huff/puffing in my direction from the top of the square. Good news: he must have been thirty kilos overweight, because he wasn't moving very fast. Bad news: he was waving something that appeared to be similar in size and shape to a suppressed small-caliber semiautomatic pistol.

I quick sit-repped to look around for the other bad guy from

Team One—and discovered him hung up on the picket fence on the far side of the square. No—I mean *literally* hung up. He'd caught his ankle between the iron spear points and was hanging upside down like a trapeze artist, trying vainly to extract his trapped leg from the pickets without breaking it.

Yeah—but there was the Citroën Xantia, too. While the sedan waited at the top of the square to block any potential escape, the Xantia was moving down the far side of the square, positioning itself to scoop me up as soon as I'd been disabled by the foot teams. I waited until the station wagon rounded the corner at the bottom and was fishhooking back on my side. When they were about sixty yards away, I shed my coat and vaulted the wrought iron fence in one motion, throwing my body over the top like a pole-vaulter goes over the bar. Listen, friends, once you've learned to pull yourself up an icy caving ladder to board a ship under way at twenty knots, a six-foot iron fence that ain't moving at all be child's play.

The sedan reacted—coming out of the intersection and beginning its pursuit. I stayed in the park, tacking back and forth, port to starboard. I could tell from the way the sedan was moving that the driver couldn't see me distinctly. Good—that gave me the opportunity to head toward a deserted taxi stand at the bottom end of the square.

Just beyond the phone booth—all Parisian cab stands have phone booths—perhaps a hundred meters from where I was currently running out of alternatives, I picked out a narrow street I hadn't seen before. Way down it, a blinking sign in orange, green, and white lights proclaimed a Neapolitan Pizzeria.

Time for a sit-rep. I turned and checked on my pursuers. By now, the station wagon had pulled abreast of the wounded FUCs. The driver, sensing he'd gone too far, stopped, threw the car into reverse, and began backing down the square, to cut me off at the bottom.

For once in my life, gentle reader, my constant traveling companion, Mr. Murphy, latched his miserable, rotten self to someone else. Just as the Citroën reversed course, a huge, white Mercedes sedan pulled out of the side street at the bottom of the square, made a left—and began flashing its lights and honking furiously when it came up upon the Xantia's rear bumper.

Now they couldn't back up to cut me off. But they didn't move right away, either: I watched as the front passenger door of the Citroën opened and a tall, silver-haired figure emerged, a pair of night-vision binoculars pressed against his forehead. Even at three hundred yards in dim light I realized who it was: Ehud Golan.

These FUCs weren't Corsicans—they were goddamn Israelis M²s—which as you can probably figure out, stands for Mossad Muscle. Avi assumed he'd shaken the tail set up by his own fucking COS—that's Chief of Station. Of all people, he should have remembered the old Rogue's Commandment, "Thou shalt never assume."

I threw the Hood a one-fingered *salut*, vaulted the fence at the bottom of the square, and jogged toward the pizzeria lights, the remaining armed asshole wheezing his way back to the Citroën sedan that sat some two hundred yards behind me.

Chapter

16

IN FRONT OF THE GAUDY ESTABLISHMENT SAT A LONE PEUGEOT TAXI. Its on-duty light was extinguished. I darted through the traffic, jogged up close, and saw the driver inside, a bulgy figure in a Disneyland baseball cap worn backward, hunched over a huge, steaming, sloppy calzone.

I knocked on the window. Without looking he waved me off and continued his munching. I knocked again. This time he looked up long enough to give me a dirty, chipmunk-cheeked look. Dirty, that is, until he saw my sweating face, my earnest expression—and the trio of two-hundred franc notes fanned in my hand.

The calzone was forgotten—that is to say he swallowed what he could (burning his mouth in the process from the look of it). He flashed a grateful smile behind his thick mustache and flicked the electronic door locks that would allow me to climb in the backseat.

Instead, I opened his door and shouldered him onto the opposite side of the front bench seat atop a pile of greasy pizza paper. He started to protest. I handed him the banknotes, turned the ignition, adjusted the mirrors, hit the lights, and edged into traffic, simultaneously explaining that I was in a hurry and that I preferred to drive myself. He started to complain again. I fixed him with my baby-blues and growled for him to S^2C: "Sit still, shut up, and count the

224

fucking money." I guess my friendly tone (not to mention the roguish War Face) dissuaded any further objection.

There are a couple of things about car chases that I should explain before we go much further into this action sequence, and I get too busy to talk. The first, is that unlike the car chases you see in Hollywood movies—*Bullitt* and *The French Connection* come to mind right now, as do a lot of the James Bond extravaganzas—the idea is not to wreck the car you're in.

Playing the sorts of fender-bender games you see in movies can be detrimental to your health in real life, where there are no stunt men, there is only one "take," the people chasing you really *do* want to wax your ass, and their ammo is all real. And as for the rest, such cinematic grist as demolishing fenders and doors against brick walls, scraping bumpers off on parked cars or highway barriers, jumping roadblocks like Evel Knievel, and other sundry forms of annihilation are bad Juju in the real world, because they mean you're going to lose your transportation and the bad guys will get their hands on you.

So much for real versus unreal. My second point can actually save your life in situations like the one I'm engaged in now, so pay attention. It is that in any vehicle chase, it is more important to concentrate on what is going on ahead of you than on what happens behind you. Do not give a rusty F-word about the assholes back there chasing you. Either they'll stay with you, or they won't. That is *their* problem. Now I am not saying that you should never pay attention to 'em. Of course you have to check your six—and more than every now and then, too. But if you spend all your time looking in your rearview mirror, your reaction time for dealing with what's in front of you will be severely cut back—and you'll probably end up in an accident.

Okay—back to real time. I swung out and hung a left, moving uphill slowly but steadily on Rue Le Nôtre as I rejoined the heavy, rush-hour traffic that was coursing off the Kennedy drive toward the big intersection at Trocadero. The driver had settled nicely into the passenger seat and resumed munching on his calzone. My eye caught his eye and he started to say something, then thought the better of it. I glanced quickly in the rearview mirror and caught a pair—nope, it was two pairs—of driving lights swerving crazily behind me. Ehud Golan's Citroën, no doubt—joined by a second chase car. Well, they were as stuck as I was, because no one was moving very fast right now.

I crept up the Rue Le Nôtre, turned right at the top and tried to make my way across three lanes of traffic on United Nations Avenue. If I could squeeze through, I'd have a shot at making my way north toward Étoile on a fast-moving thoroughfare.

Why Étoile? Because the six lanes revolving around the Arc de Triomphe combine the worst aspects of driving in a traffic circle *sans* stoplights or yield signs with a chaotic, aggressive traffic flow that combines the madness of Cairo, the machismo of Rome, the third-world fatalism of Tehran, and the belligerence of New York, all in one chaotic, uncontrolled intersection. If I made it as far as Étoile, I knew I could lose any pursuers.

But the French zey are an unforgiving race of drivers, and without physically altering the front end of the taxi, there was no way I could cross the lanes in time to hit the intersection I needed. So I cut a sharp right into the curb lane, and kept moving at a crawl, going east when I should have been going north. Behind me, the Citroën made the lane change—but now fell even farther behind. As we crawled along, I saw the reason: ahead was a bottleneck: a pair of flashing signs telling drivers to change lanes, due to construction in the road.

Well, friends, there are times when Mr. Murphy is helpful and times he is not. Right now, I was on the side of the bottleneck that was moving faster—and I must admit that I wasn't as courteous as I might have been when it came to easing from my lane into the through lane. That's a nice way of saying that I cut off three cars.

Just above the bottleneck, the road widened again—but there was now even more traffic—the flow from side streets—as I eased into the middle lane. Time to check my six. The Citroën was just pulling past the construction—he was perhaps fifteen car lengths behind me. It was adequate space for me to get creative.

A hundred yards ahead, the traffic light at the intersection began to change. You can tell when a light is going to change in Paris because, instead of going yellow as it does in the United States, the green light begins to blink. When that happens, you know you have about five seconds to stop—or run it. Now, it is a fact that Parisians love to jump stoplights. It always looks like the start of Le Mans when the light changes—and this evening was no different.

So, blinking light or not, no way was I about to stop. Not when I could artfully create an impenetrable barrier of *le traffic Française* between me and my pursuers. I rolled the window down, stuck my left arm out, and waved cars off as I nosed the cab through. Then I steered left, cut into an oncoming lane, and swerved around the cluster of cars between me and the intersection, and, grinning at my ingenuity, punched the accelerator. Demo Dick does it again—doom on you, bad guys.

Too much *Hybris,* the old Greek philosophers are fond of repeating, breeds *nemesis.* That is a fifty-dollar way of saying not to gloat too soon. Like now, when the taxi's tachometer needle climbed well into the red zone—but nothing else happened. I may have been running five thousand revs, but this fucking cab obviously had no more power than a goddamn Tinkertoy. The transmission was shot. Let me tell you how it was: both my hands were clenched on the wheel; my right leg was absofuckinglutely straight—I'd pushed the goddamn gas pedal two inches past the goddamn metal. I glanced to my right—it was like looking in a fucking mirror, because the driver was mimicking my every move, right down to the gritted teeth and the white fingers around his own imaginary steering wheel. His lips were moving. The motherfucker was praying. I hoped his pleas were directed at the gods of war, because I was too fucking busy to pray right now. I swerved left, then right, oozing through the fucking intersection at about twenty-two kilometers an hour—that's 13 point 75 miles an hour American, friends.

Shit—there were headlights to port. I slalomed, I fishtailed, and somehow they missed me. More cars coming—starboard—I swerved, spun out, and then the wheels found enough traction on the wet pavement to crawl straight ahead.

It was time to check my six again. Shit—both fucking cars had stayed with me. Just ahead, three streets curved away like the tines of a pitchfork. Directly opposite—the middle tine—was a wall of headlights. To my left, I could make out the low wall of the Passy cemetery. No good—that would take me back the way I'd just come. That left the right tine. There was no visible traffic, so I steered to starboard—until the driver started pulling on my arm, trying to reverse the steering wheel, all the while screaming, *"Pas la droite, pas la droite—sens unique, sens unique,"* and pounding on the dashboard with his free fist.

You know how it is with foreign languages—if you're not absolutely bilingual, you *think* in your native tongue, then you translate, and finally, you speak. That was precisely what was happening here. I'd learned the idiom *sens unique* during my language training as a young SEAL lieutenant commander. *Sens* is

French for *sense*—as in *avoir le sens de l'orientation,* to have a good sense of direction (which, obviously, I do). But *sens* can also mean direction, or way, as in (this is coming back to me now) *sens unique*—one-way traffic.

Message translated and understood. Now, friends, the essence of SpecWar is converting apparent disaster into victory. Like right now. I mean, I'd had enough of Mr. Murphy for the moment. Moment, hell—I'd had enough of the sucker for a lifetime. So instead of turning away, I headed straight for the "tine" the driver had just warned me about. Now I *did* check in my rearview mirror. The two chase cars were following. Good. I had 'em precisely where I wanted 'em.

Straight ahead was a wall of oncoming traffic. I downshifted into first, floored the Peugeot, and got maybe twenty-eight or twenty-nine miles an hour out of it. Not what I needed, but it would have to do—and I'd be helped by the slick, wet pavement.

Closing distance between me and the oncoming traffic was now about two hundred meters, and there was a lot of honking coming and flashing of headlights directed at me. Time to get moving: I reached down and yanked the emergency brake as hard as I could. The taxi's rear wheels locked. The driver crossed himself, rolled backwards over the front seat, and went full fetal just as the vehicle began to skid forward. I turned the steering wheel slightly to the left. Now the taxi was being carried along by a momentum that is roughly equal to the Rogue Warrior's Second Law of Physics, which reads, "If you grasp firmly by the short hairs and pull, the rest of the body will follow." In this case, the weight of the taxi and its momentum combined with the controlled skid to turn the vehicle 180 degrees in just about twice its own length. When we hit 180, I straightened the wheel, released the emergency brake, and floored the accelerator just as the mass of oncoming traffic caught up with me.

What I'd performed is called a bootlegger's turn. It is effective and efficient if you've practiced the technique enough to be able to do it without hesitation. Starting in the days when I commanded Red Cell, I made a regular habit of taking my men out to BSR— that's Bill Scott Raceway—in West Virginia for ten days at a time, thrice a year, running the tires off Bill's cars as we practiced J-turns, bootlegger's turns, high-speed chase maneuvers, and running roadblocks. I was delighted to see that I hadn't lost the edge that saturation training gives operators.

As we drove off, the driver's big nose and fingers came over the top of the front seat making him resemble a Gallic Kilroy. He saw we were alive. He patted my shoulder and said, "I'm happy, monsieur," and then he fainted dead away.

I was even happier than he—because I'd finally fucked the fucking fuckers who'd been chasing me. They were caught unprepared by a tidal wave of nasty Parisian traffic. I caught the crest of that wave—and my creeping-crawling taxi surfed merrily past Ehud the Hood and his pals. No way could they follow me now. I left them—and Monsieur Murphy, too, I hoped—in my wake.

There was a message for Captain H. Snerd, USA, Ret., at the front desk. I slit the envelope open. Inside was one of the Cercle des Armées note cards they provide at the writing desks in the foyer, with English notation in clumsy block letters. "Come directly across the street, Dickhead," is what it said.

The only directly across the street I could think of was the Café Augustin. Which is where I went. Directly.

Monsieur Henri was working the bar. He bid me a warm but s-l-o-w welcome, then pointed me toward the narrow stairway between the kitchen and the pantry that led up to the LeClercs' first-floor apartment.

As I climbed the creaky steps I heard him on the intercom announcing my arrival. Madame Colette greeted me at the top, an etched crystal glass of what had to be Bombay Sapphire on the rocks in her hand. "Welcome, Petit Richard," she said, beaming like a Jewish mother at her only son's med school graduation. "We've been waiting for you."

Oh, have we, now? I took a peck on each cheek, returned the favor, clasped the glass in my paw, and followed her into the salon, which is how they refer to the living room in France. Avi Ben Gal, legs crossed, was settled comfortably in the overstuffed sofa, a cup of coffee balanced on his knee. And sitting next to him, his red hair all askew from travel, his jug ears sticking out like mug handles, a frosty bottle of Heineken in his ugly fist, sat the ex-Marine I call Stevie Wonder, even though his real name resembles neither.

Wonder set the beer down and pulled himself to his size elevens. *"Bone swar, mon-sewer* Dickhead," he said, proving one more once that language isn't his forte but great timing is.

"Fuck you, you worthless cockbreath," I said, wrapping him around the shoulders in as tight a bear hug as I could muster. I can tell you honestly, gentle readers, that I probably have never been so happy to see anyone in my life.

"Nobody knows I'm here," Wonder explained, resuming his seat and taking a long pull on the beer. "I had fifteen days of leave coming, so I took 'em. Anything to get out of studying for the damn chief's exam."

I'd forgotten he was supposed to take the chief petty officer's written exam—and about fucking time. He'd been a first class too damn long. Today's Navy needs chiefs like Wonder—old-fashioned Warrior chiefs—even though today's Navy doesn't always know it.

"So anyway," Wonder continued, "I decided to bag the studying. I knew where you were. I *have* a fuckin' passport, and a credit card y'know—and . . ."

I knew. I knew. And despite the fact that I chewed the *prodige rouge* out for missing the chance to make chief this cycle, having him here was like being handed back my life. As you already know, friends, I had not been entirely happy about making this trip by myself. I am a Team guy—always have been. I like my team close by. Not necessarily physically close all the time—but around. I work better that way.

Yes, Avi and I had agreed to work together—as you already know we'd worked well together in the past. And it wasn't that I didn't trust Avi. But while he and I may have had similar missions, and a symbiotic operational relationship, we were working for hugely different national interests and organizations. Wonder's presence meant that I had someone whose whole raison d'être was the same as mine—he was U.S. Navy all the way. Not to mention he was an asshole with whom I'd operated for so long that we almost never had to verbalize during times of, ah, stress. I knew where he'd be. He knew the same about me. It makes things a helluva lot easier when the *merde* hits the old *ventilateur*.

"I know you two lovebirds have a lot to talk about," Avi Ben Gal interrupted Wonder's monologue and my musing, "but we have a situation here that has to be dealt with before it turns more nasty than it already is." He set his coffee cup on the adjacent table. "Those *b'nai zonim* on our tails were Mossad gumshoes—I caught a glimpse of one pair before I lost 'em and I knew them both. One is a Soviet-affairs type from headquarters. The other was Ehud Golan's deputy when Ehud ran networks in Lebanon. Which means the fucking chief of station here set me up. Obviously, he's got some kind of operation going on, and he thinks I'm going to horn in."

It struck me that for an experienced operator, Avi was being naive. Well, maybe that's to be expected: it's hard to think of your own people as potential bad guys. "Maybe he has," I said. "But I can't discount the possibility that he's dirty and he's doing this because he's being paid. It's happened before."

"Oh, c'mon, Dick—this is a chief of station we're talking about, not some damn asset with his hand in your pocket."

It was time for a wake-up call. I've read the fucking NSA intercepts and I know Mossad has had its problems. "Hey, fuck you, Avi. I love you, but get real. Remember that Mossad asshole in Belgium? He stole fifty thousand dollars worth of gold Krugerrands the agency had earmarked to pay its NOCs—nonofficial cover officers. What about the COS in Washington—the one operating under the nom de guerre of Cohen. He was yanked back last year because he fudged what, thirty, maybe forty grand in expenses. And that's just the penny-ante cook-the-books stuff. In ninety-one, ninety-two, they discovered three KGB moles buried at headquarters. And Lantos has real money to spend. So whether the guy's dirty, or whether he's just stupid, it doesn't matter. What does matter is that we have to move—and fast. The fucking clock's ticking, Avi. There's no time for navel-gazing right now."

The look on his face told me he realized I was right. Still, I knew how much the sorts of dishonesty I'd brought up offended Avi. He was one of those guys who spend their own money on the job, and then take a second or third loan from the bank to pay their mortgages.

My tone softened. "Hey, hey—not everybody's a Boy Scout like you."

He looked over at me as if he'd just remembered something important. "Hey, you know who calls me that?"

"Calls you what?"

"Boy Scout. Ehud does. Always has. Like it's an insult." Avi paused. His eyes lit up. "And I forgot," he said.

"Forgot what?"

"I was over on Avenue Marceau, checking things out at the cultural center. One of the tourist staff told me Ehud had come by a couple of times in the past week. Shown up out of the blue. Some coincidence, right?"

Oh, yeah. You people know how much I believe in coincidences when they are job related.

"Avi, whatever Mossad is doing right now is suspect, so far as I'm concerned. But it's not because the chief of station is having you tailed. It's because Ehud Golan is really behind this op—you know it and I know it."

"How do you know it?"

"He was the sonofabitch running the crew on *my* six tonight— and in my case they weren't just watching, either. Old Ehud wanted to haul my ass in for questioning." I sipped my Bombay and set the glass down. "I've seen his interrogations, Avi. No fun."

My friends, before we progress any further, it is probably time for a little recapitulation. Does anything about Avi's and my most recent escapade sound familiar to you?

You say you're thinking? Okay—concentrate. Think back to the time in Moscow when Bart Wyeth summoned me to the embassy first thing in the morning. Remember? He left all those messages the night I was out banging myself up at Andrei Yudin's dacha. So, the next morning, bright and early, I showed up at the embassy.

And guess what? As I left AMEMB Moscow, I was picked up and shadowed by that lamentable trio of Ivans, Vynkenski, Blynkenski, and Nodyev, who ran my ass ragged all over Moscow before I shook 'em off.

Now, it has never occurred to me until this moment to ask how the hell Vynkenski, Blynkenski, and Nodyev knew precisely where I would be at 0700 in the morning. Obviously, somebody had clued 'em as to my whereabouts. And who might have done that?

Well, frankly, the name Bart Wyeth, deputy chief of mission, comes to mind.

And how did the information get passed from Bart to Andrei's goons? Well, Bart's old pal Werner Lantos sure sits somewhere near the top of my list of suspects.

Now, here we are in gay Paree. Avi Ben Gal gets a call from the embassy's chief spook to show up. When he does, he's followed by a bunch of Israeli hoods, including Ehud Golan, as soon as he leaves the embassy.

- Item: In Moscow, Werner Lantos gets information about me from the U.S. Embassy.

- Item: In Paris, Ehud Golan gets information about Avi from the Israeli Embassy.
- Item: Werner works for Christians In Action.
- Item: Ehud is a Mossad boy.

Happenstance? Coincidence? Well, it all looks as parallel as goddamn Lionel train tracks to me, friends. What do you think?

Precisely. You think it's time to stop talking and start acting. I do, too.

First, I got on the horn to Ken Ross. No, I didn't call the Pentagon. Those numbers are all in the computer-programmed surveillance equipment on the B-4 level at NSA headquarters at Fort Meade, Maryland.

Instead, I called Rogue Manor. The phone rang six times. Then Brud's West Virginia drawl answered, "Manor."

Brud's the ex-Camp David Marine who does security work at Rogue Manor three days a week. The other two he commutes to a classified facility in the Blue Ridge.

"Yo—it's me. No names." I wasted no time telling Brud what I needed in oblique terms. It didn't have to be explained twice. I gave him the LeClercs' number and hung up.

Six minutes later, he was back on-line. So was Kenny Ross. Why? Because Brud had initiated a conference call.

In direct but coded language I told the admiral what I needed. He whistled. "Tough," he said.

"But possible?"

"Can do. The boss will take care of it."

"Timetable?"

"Well, I'll get on it now and get a message to you as soon as I can." There was a pause on the line. "How's it going over there?"

"It's getting very complicated. Too many layers, too many players." I hoped that he understood what I was saying.

"Well, just keep your head down."

"Oh, sure—and FYVM, too." I rang off.

Next, Avi and I each phoned the Cercle to let them know we were sending a messenger with a note to pick up something from our rooms. The LeClercs sent their aged busboy, Paulo, with two rolled-up shopping bags under his arm and a list in his pocket, shuffling off to the Cercle to make the collection. Item by item,

Paulo pulled enough clothes and sundries from our rooms to allow us a couple of days without having to go back, stuffed everything in the bags, and then, as directed, plodded the long way around the Place St. Augustin—twice, which must have done wonders for his lumbago—while Avi, Wonder, and I scanned the street from behind the LeClercs' draped and curtained windows, aided by a trio of powerful field glasses selected from among Monsieur Henri's dozen pair of bird-watching binoculars.

From our vantage point we were able to sweep the whole *Place*, back and forth, up and down, side to side, as efficiently as any KGB *visir* station or *stakan* observer in Moscow ever had. And we all came to the same conclusion: no one had followed Paulo, or had him under surveillance.

Tools of the trade came next. Weapons were a no-go. Avi didn't want to alert his people—and given the experience of the past few hours I had to agree with him. Wonder, traveling commercially and having to subject himself to the state-of-the-art airport security at Dulles International Airport, and the possibility of a customs inspection at De Gaulle, had come *sans* weapons or lethal implements. Except, of course, for the Mad Dog MiniFreq composite knife he wore around his neck under his shirt. And the set of titanium lock picks that sat directly behind the American Express card in his nylon wallet. And the small, triangular-blade dagger that masquerades as his belt buckle. And the SAS survival saw (it can double handily as a garotte) with which Wonder lines his belt.

The rest of our equipment we pulled from Henri and Colette. Actually, there wasn't much we needed. We borrowed the LeClercs' camera with its macrozoom lens, one roll of black-and-white film, three pairs of compact field glasses, three pairs of well-broken-in leather-palmed work gloves, a roll of tape that was as close to duct tape as one can get in Paris, *un tournevis* (as you recall I'd managed to lose my own screwdriver earlier), and a ten-meter length of half-inch rope. It was hemp, unfortunately. I hate hemp because it has splinters, which makes it hell to climb. I was hoping we wouldn't have to use it.

2145 hours—a quarter to ten on the big civilian clock that hung suspended across the square above a store window. We planned our route, using one of the street maps that Monsieur Henri keeps behind the bar to help tourists find their way around the city.

As we plotted, six liters of deep, fruity Chiroubles from one of the twenty-five-liter barrels in the coolest part of the cellar found their way to the table where we worked, accompanied by Norman-dy cheese and country *ficelles.* Madame Colette wasn't about to let us go out underfed or unfortified—and she let me know it as she fluttered around her small, efficient kitchen preparing a late supper. A two-kilo chicken was stuffed with a lemon and a bouquet of fresh herbs and tossed into a hot oven. I could hear it sizzling as it roasted. A kettleful of new, white, waxy-skinned potatoes from the root cellar bubbled as they boiled. Monsieur Henri chopped garlic to scatter over the huge bowl of baby greens he'd fetched from the café.

2325. We grabbed combat naps. Right. Funny thing about a three-thousand-calorie supper—it's hard to stay awake afterward.

0114. Up betimes, as olde Sam Pepys was fond of notating in his *Diary.* Showered and dressed, and ready to go within the hour.

0205. Down the stairs and out the back door, which put us on the north side of Place St. Augustin, on the Rue de la Pépinière. I took point, Wonder played rear guard fifty yards back, with Avi floating between us. I wasn't especially sanguine about tonight's little jaunt—my record of sneak & peeks in this book hasn't been very good, so far. I mean—Andrei Yudin's dacha had been cleaned out, and by the time we reached the Yudin apartment in Moscow, Andrei himself had been disposed of.

But that's the way it is in real life. In real life, unlike movies, Mr. Murphy is always around to keep you on your often-stepped-on toes. And just because you have struck out before doesn't mean you won't strike out again.

0252. We worked our way across Peter the First of Serbia Avenue, turned left, then right, and then worked our way along the street directly behind Werner Lantos's offices.

What I'd seen during my target assessment was going to make our lives as cat burglars a lot easier. You will remember that Werner Lantos's offices were located on the third level (the *deuxième étage,* or second floor) of a turn-of-the-century stone building—the easternmost of three adjoining buildings, all of which sat on the quiet, mostly residential street. The building housing Lantos & Cie had a security system—television cameras scanned the street and the entryway. The other two had no such devices. What they did share in common was a series of wrought iron balconies on each of the upper floors.

If you will remember my notes, two of the cameras were on gimbals.

And what might the significance of gimbals be, Master Marcinko-san?

Well, tadpole, gimbals mean the cameras can pan and zoom. Which in turn tells me they are remote controlled. Which in turn means that there's someone operating 'em. The question was whether that camera operator was on duty at Lantos & Cie, or whether he was at a security operation in another part of the city. No use guessing—we'd find out soon enough.

I parked Wonder and Avi in a dark cul-de-sac one street away from our target, then, following Chief Gunner's Mate/Guns Everett Emerson Barrett's advice of never assuming (because, as he told me so often, "It makes an *ass* of *u* and *me*"), I figure-eighted the two blocks on each side of Lantos & Compagnie by myself to scope the area out and make sure we were going to be able to operate safely.

As usual, Ev's advice was right on the old *argent,* which is how they refer to money in these parts. There were a few potential problems that I hadn't noticed before.

The first was that the Egyptian Embassy sat two blocks away—and from the number of blue-uniformed French security forces cordoned around the building the Egyptians were receiving Threatcon Charlie-level protection.[9] That meant if we were discovered, there were lots of cops available to chase us. Second, I saw that the streetlights on our target block were all working. Under normal OPCONs—OPerational CONditions—streetlights are never a problem. We always carry a small sack of ball bearings and a slingshot as part of our assault gear. But not tonight. Not when our "assault gear" was improvised. Tonight we'd have to move quickly and hope not to attract any attention.

0311. My plan was simple and direct. We'd go up the thick, cast-iron drainpipe to the fourth level (the third floor, or *troisième étage*) of the adjacent building, work our way along the balcony, then drop down one floor when we got to the Lantos & Cie location. There, we'd recon to make sure there were no security guards inside. Once we'd ascertained it was all clear (I didn't even want to

---

[9]You will recall (this was first explained in *Rogue Warrior: Green Team*) that there are four Joint Chiefs of Staff terrorist Threat Conditions, or Threatcons: Alpha, Bravo, Charlie, and Delta. Alpha is the least demanding—it is in effect at most overseas installations on an ongoing basis. Threatcon Charlie applies, according to the secret/sensitive JCS memo quoted in the book, "when an incident occurs or when intelligence is received indicating that some form of terrorist action against installations and personnel is imminent."

think about the possibility that it wasn't), then Wonder would shimmy the window, and we'd be in like the proverbial Flynn.

0312. Mr. Murphy decided that we needed company so he showed up. I sidled up to the drainpipe, felt around the back, reached up, straddled it with my knees, hugged with my thighs, and pulled my weight skyward.

The fucking thing *gave*. I tried again. No—it was definitely loose. No way was I going to try to get up that sucker.

On to drainpipe number two. Same drill. I waved Wonder over, and he gave me a boost. I took hold of the pipe, wrapped my legs as tight as I could, and pulled myself up. I was ten feet from the sidewalk when the pipe started to shake—there was this awful fucking ominous rumble, and the goddamn thing twisted three inches to port, then back to starboard. I came down like a fucking fireman on his way to a three-alarmer. As I stepped away from the wall, a rusty bolt hit me on the back of the neck.

The first climbable pipe was two buildings away—the very last house. That meant we'd be sneaking along forty-five to fifty yards of balconies instead of ten to fifteen. Which raised the possibility that we'd be spotted, unless we moved very carefully, and very quietly. Fuck—our six-minute entry was about to take half an hour.

I tested the pipe. It was solid. I shook it back and forth. It didn't move. So I made sure that everything in my pockets was stowed correctly, checked the coil of rope that sat athwart my shoulders, pulled Monsieur Henri's work gloves back on, and began my climb. Clambering up a six-inch cast iron drainpipe is harder than it looks. Belay that. It even looks hard—actually *doing* it is sheer torture. Especially when you are no longer a spry twenty-five-year-old, with buns (and abs, and dick) of steel. I pulled myself up the pipe half foot by half foot, my arm muscles burning, my thighs on fire. At least I was comforted by the knowledge that all those reps on my weight pile were getting me through this current ordeal. Yeah, right. Sure.

It was twenty feet to the first balcony, give or take a groan or two. From there, things were easy—well, relatively easy. I stood on the rail, reached up, grasped the floor of the balcony above, fingertip pull-upped onto the lip, found another four inches of finger purchase, raised myself high enough to get a leg up, pulled myself onto the outside of the railing, then slung myself over the rail— keeping low and quiet so as not to create any telltale silhouettes or embarrassing noises just in case there was somebody sleeping inside the room whose balcony I was on—rolled over onto the balcony, crawled away from the window to the outer edge of the balcony, then stood up, climbed onto the railing, reached up to the balcony above, and repeated the process all over again.

And where did I first learn to climb buildings, you ask. At Red Cell, I respond. After all, we SpecWarriors have been coming through the back door for years—that's what effective shoot-and-looting is all about, isn't it? Unconventional warfare means coming from where they least expect you.

So, ever after, as I commanded my unit of tango killers, it made perfect sense to me that if we were to kill terrorists the way terrorists should be killed—i.e., *stone cold dead*—we should do it the way they did: by making our approach from a direction no one was guarding. At one tango camp in Libya, we worked our way through the minefields—they never thought to defend those approaches. Who'd be crazy enough to come that way? At another—this one was in Sudan—we slithered through drainage pipes. In the Philippines, we crawled through mud flats and floated down the rivers. In France we swam in. In Panama, our quarry was tucked in an impenetrable high-rise with guards and locked doors and secure elevators. So at zero dark hundred we simply scaled the fucking building from the outside and took him down that way. It's not surprising to learn that almost no one locks a fifteenth-floor window.

We would practice these assaults whenever we were on the road—which was often. I made a rule of reserving our rooms on the top (or second-from-the-top) floors of hotels, then ordering my guys to get to them by going up the outside of the building. We used to make a race of it—two-man teams clambering up the outside, with a case of beer as the stakes.

We got damn good at it, too. So good that Duck Foot Dewey (God, I do miss the conniving, mischievous little sonofabitch) started coming and going from his own South Arlington apartment by the window instead of the door. Shocked the hell out of the neighbors he'd wave at on the way up or down—not to mention the shoppers in the Safeway parking lot across Lee Highway who'd watch, transfixed as he did his Spider-man act.

I halted on the third level above the street and beckoned for Avi to follow. What the fuck was he waiting for? He took a deep breath—like a kid about to make his first climb onto the sliding pond—and followed. Well, let me not overstate things. Avi tried to follow. But Avi is an intel operator—not a SEAL. What does that mean? It means he doesn't have the same kind of upper-body strength we do. In point of fact, he has what I'd call normal upper-body strength, which means he doesn't have very much at all. A deficiency that makes climbing such things as drainpipes impossible. He'd huff and puff himself six or seven feet off the ground, then slowly slide back groundward.

The situation was quickly passing directly from SNAFU to FUBAR. That was no good at all. I mean, we'd been fucking lucky so far. We were exposed here, but the street had remained deserted: no vehicular traffic, and no pedestrians—yet. But I couldn't count on that forever.

After three abortive attempts by Avi, I descended to the second level, lowered the rope I was carrying, and with Wonder pushing and me pulling, we managed to haul him up to the first-floor balcony. I climbed back up one more floor, lowered the rope, and we repeated the exercise. Then we did it again. Seventeen minutes later, Avi, sweating clear through all his clothes and feeling the cold, stood on the fourth-level balcony.

I looked at the diminutive Israeli. "I see you don't mind heights," I whispered.

He smiled gamely but I could see from the way he held the rail that he was your basic white-knuckle pipe climber and balcony walker. Well, that was all right. By making the climb at all, Avi had just gone through a kind of SpecWar bar mitzvah. Today (tonight, actually) he'd become a Rogue Warrior. He'd even learned a new Commandment: that he didn't have to like it—he just had to do it.

Chapter

17

0331. WE BEGAN OUR SLOW, DELIBERATE CREEP. I WORKED AROUND flowerpots and window boxes, slithered underneath a cracked-open window, cursing silently as puddled water was sponged up by my jeans. At the end of the first balcony, there was a gap of perhaps two feet between the railings.

We all crossed easily. The second balcony was smooth: no plants, potted trees, or other obstacles. We traversed the ten or so yards in virtually no time. That was when we hit our first real hurdle. I mean, a literal hurdle: a four, maybe four-and-a-half-foot gap between the balcony we were on, and the one we had to get to.

I straddled the rail, then brought my trailing foot over and onto the outer lip, paused, then sprang, catching the outer lip of the balcony with my toes as my fingers closed around the wrought iron. As I sprang, there was an overwhelming sense of déjà vu. It was the same sensation I had when I used to run the Dirty Name, which is what we called the obstacle course at the Little Creek, Virginia, amphibious base.

The Dirty Name was a series of stumps, logs, and telephone pole sections of various heights and diameters that had been planted in the ground. The objective was to make your way from one to the other without tripping, falling, or busting your head. But the enterprising gremlins—which is a fifteen-dollar way of saying the

UDT chiefs—who'd designed the Dirty Name long before I even joined the Navy had been devilishly ingenious. The wood was placed so that if you could make the jump from point A to point B easily, the height differential would make it virtually impossible without a lot of extra effort. When the height differential was easy, the space between poles was just enough to make your jump, well, challenging. If you misjudged, you'd either jump short—and crack your chin or face on the log, or you'd overshoot, go long—and catch one of the long splinters that felt oh, so good in your arms and legs as you tried to scramble back before you toppled to the sand below.

Now, you are probably asking why the fuck did the chiefs do this to us. To be honest, friends, I remember asking that very same question—although not phrased quite so gently—many times during my training cycle. Well, as you're probably well aware, the reasoning behind their crude, rude inculcation has become obvious in the real world.

So, taking a lesson from the old chiefs, I built my own Dirty Name at Rogue Manor. Each and every one of my men works out on it regularly—as do I. Now, every time I have a gap to jump, my body knows how to react, and what to anticipate. I have done it all before—and often. I do not, therefore, stutter-step, or falter. I do not hesitate, fumble, flounder, or vacillate. I move decisively. Unambiguously. Forcefully.

So, springing like the roguish panther I've taught myself to be, the ball of my right foot caught the balcony lip. Ditto my left. Then both my hands grasped the rail lip. Which separated at the corner seam.

Have you ever taken hold of something—a stair railing or deck post, perhaps—that suddenly gives way and catches you off balance? If you have, then you know that the common reaction at such time is to grip tighter and pull the errant object toward your body.

Big mistake. Do that and you will take the goddamn thing with you as you fall.

I let go of the railing before its weight moved my center of gravity irretrievably off center, simultaneously leaned forward—*in*, toward the collapsing rail, and toe-sprang, somersaulting over it. I flipped in midair, then landed shoulder first in a tuck-and-roll. It wasn't graceful, fluid, or smooth. But it kept me from falling backward, ripping the railing, and making a lot of fucking noise as it (and I) clattered onto the sidewalk some thirty-five feet below.

I lay on my back and caught my breath, waiting to hear if anything I'd done had attracted undue attention. After fifteen seconds of silence I rolled over onto my hands and knees, and crawled to examine the damaged railing. The wrought iron was rotted through—although it had about twelve fucking coats of enamel on it—all that had been holding the corner joint together was paint. I looked and saw where it had separated. I seesawed the railing back and forth, watched the play, scanned the four feet between balconies, and realized that Avi Ben Gal wasn't going to like that which he was about to do. Nope. Not at all.

Of course, Avi is a trooper—so he didn't complain as Wonder rigged the rope under his armpits and tossed me the other end. I took it and secured it around my own waist with a bowline. Avi didn't weigh more than 135, maybe 140 pounds. I am a bulky sonofabitch—a hair under 220 pounds—and most of it is muscle meat. Avi knew I'd play the role of sea anchor well.

Even so, he looked at me with inquisitive puppy eyes as Boy Wonder rigged him for action.

"Don't worry," I stage-whispered. "This is gonna be easy."

His expression told me that he wasn't as sure as I was about that.

I took up some tension of the rope as if I was ready to help Avi across, then nodded imperceptibly to Wonder, who had eased up directly behind him. As you can probably guess, Wonder and I have performed this little maneuver before.

Wonder simply picked the Israeli up by the belt and the yoke of his shirt, and—before he had any time to react—tossed him across the opening to me as if he were a sack of concrete. I dropped the rope (never any need for it anyway) in time to appreciate the look of incontrovertible, pure terror on Avi's face as he was in flight (for all of a second and a half). That expression, which combined consternation, shock, and horror was alone worth the price of his whomping, flailing impact on my chest as he came in for a landing. I caught him, wrapped him up, and brought him gently to the ground.

He lay there, hyperventilating, for some seconds. "I really wish, Dick—" he began.

I cut him off. "Listen, asshole, any flight you walk away from is a good flight. Besides, you're about to get all kinds of bonus miles on that one, so take yes for an answer, brush yourself off, and let's get the fuck to work."

0336. We formed up single file, and I moved out front by a couple of body lengths to begin a slow recon of this next ten or so yards of territory. I'd progressed five or six of them along the balcony when, directly in front of me, a light came on through the window.

I stopped and pressed myself up against the wall to hide any possible silhouette. I waited. The light stayed on.

At times like these, all you can think about are the possible goatfuck factors. I mean, all I needed now was somebody who couldn't get back to sleep, threw open their window to get a breath of fresh air, saw us creepy-crawling on their balcony, and screamed.

Or a dog. The French love dogs. There are probably more dogs per capita in Paris than any other city in Europe. All I needed was for some light-snoozing pup to sniff-sniff us three intruders outside and go bark-bark-barking to tell the master.

Or—well, you get the idea. There are a lot of things that can go wrong at times like this one—and I must admit, I thought about most of 'em.

I gandered the Timex on my left wrist. It had been six minutes and the fucking light was still on. If this was a nighttime piss break—*un piss soir* in French—it was a goddamn long one. I edged closer to the window, moving in inch-by-inch increments. Pressed my nose against the casing and slowly, slowly, swiveled so that I could just peer inside through the sheer curtain.

From the sofa, overstuffed chairs and the big coffee table, I could tell I was looking into someone's living room. The light was coming from a floor lamp that sat, incongruously, in the dead center of the room. My eyes followed the electrical cord, which had been augmented with an extension cord, which in turn led to an outlet that had been equipped with—eureka!—a timer. These folks were out of town. One less thing to worry about. I dropped low, signaled Avi and Wonder to move up, and continued my crawl.

0344. We positioned ourselves on the balcony directly above Lantos & Cie's French windows. The next move was going to be tricky. As you should remember, there are television cameras suspended from the Lantos balcony. If we made too much of a commotion, those cameras would jiggle—and whoever was watching the screen would, if he was even half awake, realize that something was awry. So we had to be *v-e-r-y* careful lowering ourselves these last eight feet.

I went first. Over the rail. Drop one leg. Drop the other. Hands on balcony lip. Slip down and then, oh-so-gently, let myself descend inch by inch until my feet touch the balcony railing, kick inside and drop another twelve inches (my fingers really straining now, burning with the pain of a hundred pull-ups) inch by fucking inch until (oh, God, that feels good) my Reeboks hit solid balcony floor.

I looked up and signaled for Wonder to lower Avi. There was no response. I stage-whispered a WTF. Finally, Avi's legs appeared above me. They came over, and descended toward me. I grabbed him around the knees and eased them inside the rail. He dropped slowly, caught himself, and pirouetted onto the balcony. He wasn't wearing the safety rope.

He shrugged as Wonder let himself down with the skill of a trapeze artist. "Time I learned how to do these things for myself," the Israeli mouthed. "Don't want to be a burden, y'know."

0348. We examined the tall, narrow-paned French-door windows. There were three pairs of them. Each ran from the balcony floor to a height of seven feet or so. Each held a double-pane of glass. There was no sign of electromagnetic tape or other obvious entry devices attached. You could see inside to Lantos's office. In front of the window was a desk on which, I could make out in the dim light, a laptop computer sat. The windows were simply secured from the inside by an old-fashioned cremorne bolt: a single knob mechanism that controls a pair of vertical rods. When the knob is turned, the rods jam up and down like deadbolts into the head and sill, securing the windows shut.

That was the obvious stuff. Avi Ben Gal examined the left-most window—the one closest to the wall—carefully. After fifteen seconds or so he waved me over. "Look—in the corner," he whispered. "But don't touch the glass."

I scrunched my neck and followed his instructions. By executing a bodily contortion worthy of a circus performer, I saw what Avi was getting at: the telltale red light of a laser security system had been installed just below the window frame. Step inside, break the beam, and the cavalry is automatically summoned.

Wonder was paying close attention to the double windowpanes. "I think we have some kind of gas inside," he said. "They're sealed in a way I've never seen before." He pointed his nose at the bottom of the pane closest to him. "See that greenish stuff in the joint?"

I looked. I saw.

"Seems to me I read about that. If you cut the window, the gas between the panes reacts to air and sets off an alarm."

"What about the locks?"

He shrugged. "No prob with them—they've gotta be fifty years old." He retrieved a wide-bladed pick from the nylon sheaf in his back pocket. "Five seconds—no more, and we're in."

That was good to know. And puzzling.

I mean—there was a laser alarm system in place, and the old windows had been replaced with double-glazed, inert gas-filled panes. And here are the door locks—locks that haven't been changed in fifty years.

If I were a suspicious type, my friends, I would guess that Monsieur Werner Lantos had created conditions that encourage me to come through the door locks. Why? Because Mon-sewer Lantos (as Wonder might aptly call him) has created a natural funnel. He has made my decisions for me.

It is a tactic as old as warfare itself. And it is effective.

Wonder had the pick in his hand. I tapped his wrist, and silent-signaled, Put that away.

He gestured wide-armed at me as if to say, Huh?

I used my hands to say, We're going back. This is a fucking trap.

Back up to the *troisième étage*. I lifted Avi high enough so that he got good purchase on the balcony above, and he hoisted himself easily onto it. Wonder followed, and I brought up the rear.

The timer light had switched off as we crept up to the vacant apartment's window. Softly, I tapped the single pane of glass in the French door and wiggled my index finger in Wonder's direction. Oh, doorman . . .

0359. Inside. We crept around the furniture, and moved into the foyer. The front door lay directly ahead of us. I went to it, and put my ear up against it. No sounds from the other side. Gently, I turned the knob and pulled. Nothing happened.

Wonder tiptoed up to the door. He played with the knob, then examined the locking apparatus as best he could in the darkness, running his hands over the metal as if it were braille. "Dead bolts," he mouthed. "Nonsequential, seven-pin, back-sprung, reverse-tumbled German dead bolts." He extracted his nylon pick-lock wallet. "Youse guys take a load off." He sighed. "This may take some time, because the fuckin' springs on these things are killers—especially in the dark."

Avi crawled up behind Wonder on his hands and knees, and nudged him aside. He kneeled next to the door, extracted a penlight from his inside pocket, and rotated the rear ferrule. A narrow shaft of red light illuminated the lock apparatus.

The Israeli gave the light to Wonder and plucked three of the lock picks from his hand. "You hold—I'll work. I'm probably more current on these than you are," he said. "Besides—it's about time I started earning my keep around here."

0402. The corridor was as dark as the apartment. We used Avi's red penlight to locate the *minuterie*—the timed light switch that sits at every landing. But we didn't use it. Instead, I started down the narrow stairway, moving cautiously, step by step. The stairway was dark—but not, fortunately, blacked out.

We descended to the *deuxième étage sans* incident. The Lantos & Cie offices would be to our right. As I approached the landing, the hair on my neck stood up. Don't fucking ask me why it stood up—it just did. I froze. My right hand balled into a fist and went level with my shoulder, then cupped and went to my right ear—the silent signal for "freeze and listen."

We froze and we listened. The first sense that got tickled was smell. The earthy, deep, rich afterscent of French tobacco wafted down the corridor. Then another of our senses kicked in: from somewhere in the darkness we heard someone breathing. I mean, in that dead-zone silence, it actually seemed loud.

I silent-signaled that I was going to take a look. First, I handed off my equipment. Then I raised my hands to my neck and made a choking motion. Wonder gave me a thumbs-up. He started to slip the SAS cable saw into my gloved hand. I shook my head. I have no qualms about killing, but I want to make sure I kill japs—which is what I call bad guys—not some fucking rent-a-cop night watchman who's being paid fifteen francs an hour to sit in front of a door. How do I know he's a night watchman and not a jap? I don't—not 100 percent. But the chances are good. First of all, if you recall, there is that security placard next to the front door. The one that reads PROTECTED BY SECOR, LTD if you know how to read French. The sign hinted that the surveillance cameras weren't being monitored on the premises, but at a central station. Second, he was the only security we'd encountered tonight. Lack of personnel is another giveaway that it's not bad guys. Bad guys like Werner Lantos or Andrei Yudin don't mind providing lots of cannon fodder for people like me because they don't give a shit about human life.

Okay, so I dropped low, then made the turn off the landing. Hugged the wall. Moved a few inches. Halted and listened. Moved. Halted. At times like this, you try to breathe so discreetly that you make no noise at all. I was having trouble doing that—all I could hear was the surflike sound of rushing air passing my ears, into my nose, and throat. I sensed each pumping thrust of blood in my neck and wrists and wondered why the hell the asshole sitting in the darkness didn't hear those tom-tom sounds, too.

I drew closer—eight or nine feet. I knew that because I could smell the sonofabitch. Don't laugh—we SEALs know from experience that, in the field, it is best to eat and drink the same foods as your enemy does, and follow the same sanitary habits as well because if you don't, he's gonna smell you out there. A gringo who eats MREs, slaps Aqua Velva on his puss after shaving, showers with Dial, and sprays the Sure under his arms, is gonna stick out like your proverbial sore dick in the boonies, where the opposition eats rice and *nuoc mam* fish sauce, or *frijoles*, or couscous, seldom shaves (and if he does, uses nothing more than cold water), and hasn't seen a bar of Ivory or any other soaplike material in a month. Matter of fact, the opposition is gonna smell you half a mile away. Roy Boehm, the godfather of all SEALs, learned that lesson back in Vietnam—and he taught it to all his pups so they wouldn't make mistakes and come back dead.

Now, this particular opposition wasn't gonna sniff me. He'd put out too much effluvium himself. First of all, he needed a shower— did he ever. His unique, even piquant bouquet included a remarkable mix of sweat, b.o., garlic, unlaundered clothes, and grunge foot. That was another indication he was a rent-a-cop, so far as I was concerned. Y'see, rent-a-cops make minimum wage. So, there's not a lot of cash to spend on dry cleaning.

I slipped closer until I could pick him out clearly. He was sitting in a wood chair, its two front legs tilted back, its top rail leaning up against the wall. His ankles were wrapped around the front chair legs.

Goddammit, be quiet out there. No, no—*you* shut the fuck up, I'm trying to work.

Sorry for the interruption, gentle reader, but it's that dweeb of an editor again making a bloody racket. He *what?* He wants to know how I can make the fellow in the corridor out so clearly when the corridor is dark.

A good point—and so, I'll take the time to explain. The fact of the matter is that the human eye is a remarkable, and highly adaptable instrument. You put it into total darkness (we're talking relative, here—not absolute), and the retina will open up sufficiently to allow you to make out shapes. Try it yourselves. Sit in a darkened room for half an hour, and after a while you'll be able to pick out all the furniture, the very configuration of the room itself—even somebody sitting in the chair across from you.

Same principle applied here. My night vision was at its peak, and thus I could make him out. And I liked what I perceived: there was no discernable movement, except for the gentle rise and fall of his chest. His breathing was so regular that I guessed the asshole had dozed off. I moved to within a yard or so of striking distance.

That was when he gave a start. I froze as he shook his head and snorted like a fucking ox, then settled down again. I waited, not even daring to breathe as his head lolled back against the wall, and his chest rose and fell, his breathing steady again.

Even better, he now began to snore—loudly. It took half a dozen snores until I'd finally edged to where I felt I had to be to get the job done.

I pounced. My left hand came up and caught his mouth to choke off any scream (or other sundry alarum, as Shakespeare liked to write). He tried to twist away from me but I was having none of that—I gut-punched him to take his breath away, then moved round in back of him, swiveling my body and his, so that the crook of my right arm trapped his neck just above his Adam's apple. Then I flexed my arm, an action that shut off all the air to his windpipe. This highly effective choke-hold maneuver, incidentally, is known as an LAPD caress. Almost immediately, he went limp—it didn't take more than nine or ten seconds.

I relaxed my grip and let his body slouch back into the chair. Then I taped his mouth, ankles, and knees with the roll of ductlike tape I carried in my pocket. I rolled him onto his stomach, and bound his arms behind him. Then I retrieved the penlight and played it over him. He wore a blue security uniform that bore a SECOR patch on the right shoulder. He was unarmed—except for a long chain clipped to his belt. Attached to the end of the chain was a ring of keys the size of a medieval mace head. In his pockets, he carried the normal assortment of gear—wallet, two house keys, pocket change, cigarettes, and a cheap butane lighter. I unfastened the humongous ring of keys and handed them off to Wonder, who'd crept down the corridor.

"Light," he whispered.

I handed him the penlight. He played it on the single, dead bolt door lock on the double doors to Lantos's office, and then on the two dozen keys he held in his left hand. He began to sort the keys, mumbling to himself as he rejected one after the other. "I think we have a winner," he whispered after thirty seconds. He took the key he'd selected and quietly inserted it in the dead bolt. He nodded. "Fits." Slowly, Wonder twisted the key counterclockwise.

Nothing happened. "Sorry." He went back to perusing. A minute later, he tried again. This time the lock turned easily—and silently—one revolution, then another, then a third.

"We're in," he said.

I shook my head. "No," I said, "we're not in yet—you simply got the door open."

Wonder gave me a dirty look. "You're so fucking literal," he said.

0407. Wonder turned the handle and eased the door inward. I moved inside, creeping inch by inch.

The foyer was clear and unprotected. No lasers, no motion detectors—as far as I could tell. That made sense, too. It allowed the man standing watch to come inside if he wanted to. Once I'd determined that it was all right, we brought the inert rent-a-cop and his chair through the door and put them next to the wall.

The office was a lot smaller than I'd expected. I would have thought Werner Lantos's company would have appropriated the entire floor—or at least the entire front of the building. Instead, we discovered a modest, four-room suite. There was the foyer, which had one desk that looked as if it had been outfitted for a receptionist/secretary, with a three-line phone and a fax. There were two small, impersonal, windowless offices. Each had a desk with a minitower computer, a phone, a small credenza, a desk chair, and two chairs facing the desk. And then there was the master office—the one I'd seen from the balcony—which was, in fact, the only room facing the street.

Making sure to stay well clear of the laser alarm under the window, I examined Werner Lantos's office carefully. The surface of his desk was polished—it looked as if it had never been used. Atop it, dead center, sat the computer I'd seen from outside—a Toshiba laptop, just waiting to be opened and purloined of its files.

I reached toward the machine to flip up its cover.

"Dick—No!" It was Avi. "Don't go near it," he stage-whispered.

I backed off, my hand in midair. "What's the problem?"

"Your old pal Ehud Golan is the problem," Avi said. He took the penlight and shone it around the Toshiba. "Mossad's technical operations division built thirty-six explosive devices to go into Toshiba computers—same model as this one—on the prime minister's directions. It was about the same time they got permission to reconfigure a bunch of cellular phones."

"Oh?" It was obvious what he was talking about. But for any of you who haven't read the news lately, the Israelis are the masters of the fine art of booby-trapping such items as phones and computers, and slipping them into the offices or homes or cars of the folks who wage war against the civilians of the Jewish State. These days, they use Semtex-A$_3$, a Sabra mutation of the venerable Czech plastic explosive that cannot be detected even by the most sophisticated airport sensors. Indeed, once a bomb has been built, the deadly item can even be taken aboard a plane and flown to its final destination without fear of discovery.

There are various ways of setting the device off. The computer bomb generally explodes when the laptop is opened. The phone can be detonated either by voice (using a chip that has been programmed with the voice frequency of the target), or remote control, in which a radio-controlled firing button is pressed by an agent on-scene, or someone on the other end of the phone who transmits the "fire" order electronically. Either way, the phone goes *ka-boom* and blows the head off the unfortunate tango who's holding it.

"They were made up for operations against Hizballah and the Islamic Brotherhood," Avi explained, as if I needed to be told.

I try not to play with other folks' improvised explosive devices unless I absolutely have to. They are unfamiliar and dangerous. "Can you disarm it?"

"If this turns out to be one of our devices, sure I can. The computer demolitions were designed so that the explosive component could be installed or removed in a matter of seconds." The Israeli pulled the PCMCIA slot cover open, and focused his light on the double-width modem card inside. "This is one of ours," he said decisively.

He extracted the device and examined it critically. *"Biduke—*

absolutely." He held it up so I could see it in his penlight beam. "The explosive is sandwiched in here," he explained, pointing at what looked like normal circuitry. "That way they could be shipped, then passed to our undercover agents who don't have to do anything technical."

"How do you keep the computer from blowing before you want it to?"

"Oh—our people in Tel Aviv reconfigured the electronics inside the card to arm the device as the modem or flash memory card was inserted in its slot, and disarm it when it gets pulled out. That way I can use any computer, demonstrating to the target that it's safe, then close it, switch the cards—and when the bad guy turns it on, b'bye-b'bye. Gram for gram, it's a big charge—" Avi swept the office with his eyes. "More than enough to level this whole place. Hell—one of these devices brought down a whole villa in Lebanon."

Avi slipped the modem card into his pocket. Then he flipped the Toshiba's cover up and turned the machine's switch on. "See— ready to go. Just like every other computer."

Now the easy-to-crack window lock made perfect sense to me. Mon-sewer Lantos had created a natural entry—pointing me (or whoever broke in) directly toward the computer on his desk. The sequence was KISS: go through the window, set off the laser alarm, grab open the computer, it goes ka-boom, the office—maybe the whole fucking building—goes b'bye-b'bye. And the blame? Hell, blame the same fucking anonymous tangos who've been blowing targets all over Paris lately. End of story.

I, however, had a different denouement in mind—one that involved Werner Lantos's demise instead of mine. But there was no time to think about that now—there was work to be done. I examined the desk. The drawers were all unlocked. Now, newly wary of more booby traps, I was careful as I checked inside. There turned out to be no reason for concern: the drawers were empty except for a half-inch thick stack of monogrammed stationery, a few paper clips, two rubber bands, and half a dozen of his business cards. I inspected the credenza. It contained a box of plain white business envelopes. In the small closet adjacent to the door there were three wooden hangers—and nothing else. The tooled, high-backed leather desk chair bore virtually no sign of wear.

Does this sparseness and lack of data, files, correspondence, as well as the other ephemera that you always find in offices strike you as odd, friends? It sure struck me as odd. I mean, here are the offices of an investment bank that allegedly does millions—perhaps billions—of dollars' worth of business all over the world. And yet, the place had the feel of a third-rate mortgage broker somewhere in suburban Virginia who's just gone out of business.

Oh, he had his *"Moi"* wall—two dozen framed photographs of Werner Lantos and "friends," all of them warmly inscribed. I could recognize three prime ministers of Israel. In another trio of photographs, Mikhail Gorbachev, Leonid Brezhnev, and Boris Yeltsin all scowled into the lens, their arms wrapped around Lantos's shoulders. Deng Xiaoping and Werner Lantos grinned into the camera. So did the French presidents François Mitterrand and Jacques Chirac. Framed, ornate certificates in three languages attested to Werner Lantos's great humanity and generosity.

But, more to the point, there were no files—not even in the trio of custom-built file cabinets we found on the premises. Two empty folders and that was it. While I examined the floor and walls for secret compartments, Wonder and Avi turned the computers on and checked the hard disks. There, too, the lack of material was surprising. Nothing was encrypted. Each station held its own correspondence files and a word processing program. But there were no spreadsheets, no databases—nothing more than the most rudimentary software. No Windows 95. No game of solitaire or black jack. We're talking about a paltry two hundred megs of data on a 1.6 gigabyte hard drive.

Avi stuck his head into Lantos's office and watched as I replaced the last of the wall-to-wall carpet on its tacking. "Find anything?"

I shook my head. "Negatory. What about you?"

"*Bupkis*—Nothing," he said. "The place is clean."

He was right. In fact, that was it. It *was* clean—as clean as Andrei Yudin's dacha.

Let me run that by you again. *As clean as Andrei Yudin's dacha.* Of course—Werner Lantos had cleaned the place out after our little breakfast. He'd taken all the evidence and moved it elsewhere but left just enough to make it appear that he still worked here, then had Ehud the Hood booby-trap his laptop with an explosive device that would destroy the whole suite.

But remember what I said when I searched the dacha? I told you that no matter how the assholes try to sweep a place clean, there's always a shard or two of evidence left behind. Always. It's simply a matter of looking hard enough. At the dacha, it had been the Air France waybill. Here, it was the booby-trapped Toshiba.

"Let's get the hell out of here," I said. "But bring the damn laptop."

Chapter

18

LET ME TELL YOU A STORY ABOUT OLLIE NORTH. WHEN THE SCANDAL that came to be known as Iran-Contra was discovered, Lieutenant Colonel Oliver North[10] and some of the folks working for him went through all the files in his office and shredded a huge number of them. Those files were never recovered. Then they went into the White House computer system and erased scores—even hundreds—more potentially incriminating materials. Virtually all of the correspondence, all of the E-mail, all of the sensitive messages to and from the participants of what the Iran-Contra Committees referred to as "The Enterprise," were shredded electronically. The hard disks were emptied.

Except that, unlike paper files, shredded electronic files aren't really shredded. The hard disks were not automatically wiped clean just because Ollie and his folks told the computers to "del *.*"

You out there raising your hand—you want to know why. Okay,

---

[10]It was once said (by *60 Minutes* co-editor Mike Wallace) of Ollie and me that we are somewhat alike, in that the "powers that be" went after us because we pissed off too many important people. Let me say for the record that I disagree. I believe they went after Ollie because he shred paper—destroyed evidence. But they went after me for shredding *people*. Let me also add for the record that I had more fun doing my shredding than Ollie had doing his.

I'll let Stevie Wonder, who understands this shit, explain it to you. Stevie, give the folks some background.

"Sure, Dick. See, deleting a file simply changes the first character of its name in the File Allocation Table (known as the FAT). The new name begins with a character that the computer has been programmed not to show on-screen—so if you ask the computer to display that file, it won't. But the 'erased' file is still on the hard drive. What's more, even if the file is overwritten, there are ways to manipulate the FAT that will allow part or even all of the information to be resurrected. Some of the basic utility programs—like Norton Utilities—allow you to unerase files. Ever see how the erased file is missing the first character of its name? Well, basically what the utilities program does is allow you to restore that missing character, thus making the file 'visible' to the computer again."

Thanks, Wonder. Now, you should also know that, unless you completely reformat a hard disk by using a special security utility, or overwrite every single byte of data on your disk, there is going to be a trail of electronic fingerprints left behind. And even if you do all of that it's often possible to retrieve a small part of a file—at least enough of a fragment to give a canny investigator a general idea of what was there.

Who's that in the back of the room with your hand in the air? You want to know *what?* You want to know why, if I know this shit, how come Werner Lantos doesn't know it too?

Good point. You should think about becoming an editor. The answer is that most people don't bother to learn how computers work. They just use 'em. That is especially true for big-time executives. That's why, for example, my old adversary former Defense Secretary Grant Griffith left all the files that incriminated him on his laptop—without any encryption on 'em at all. It never occurred to him to protect the information. Hey, Ollie North and the folks working for him were pretty sophisticated, too—and they didn't realize how much data is left behind after you've "erased" it.

So, if one has on hand a pair of accomplished computer wonks (like Wonder and Avi), and you have a nice warm apartment to hide in—and we did, courtesy of the LeClercs—and you have a few hours in which to play (and they did), and the LeClercs are willing to let you use their 200 megahertz, two gigabyte hard drive computer and laser printer, *and* you can write your own debugging programs, which my wild and wicked wonks were perfectly capable of doing, then you can start to reassemble some of the data that had been erased.

Which is exactly what happened. Oh, the pair of them didn't come up with 100 percent of the goodies that had been stored on the booby-trapped computer's hard drive. Far from it. It was obvious (well, it was obvious to Avi and Wonder, who explained to me that the C-drive was absolutely empty because it had been wiped clean) that before *Mon Sewer* Lantos had Ehud the Hood arm the computer, he'd erased all his files. But after three hours of hunt-and-peck searching, there were enough reassembled bits and bytes so that my guys were able to provide me with a kind of patchy picture of what the hell was going on in the life of Werner Lantos.

And what was that, you ask?

Well, a couple of things. First, I'm no CPA. But from what I saw on the screen, it would seem that our pal Werner Lantos had been playing a Nicholas Leeson game of fast and loose with other people's money. He'd invested tens of millions of dollars in a series of margin accounts on the Hong Kong stock market—and he'd lost. The people whose money he was playing with were out scores of millions of dollars.

But which people? That was a problem. The accounts were numbered. But there had to be a key somewhere—even a fragment would help. I turned to Avi and Wonder. "C'mon, guys, dig it out."

Finding that file took them another couple of hours of computer programming that was punctuated by polyglottal obscenity that I must tell you even made me blush. But when they'd finished, my wily wonks had managed to sort out a rough match between names and account numbers. How did they do it, you ask? Y'know what— I don't care how the hell they did it. All that matters is that they got the job done.

I perused the screen.

- Werner's personal finances were in pretty bad shape. But from the look of things he still had a quarter of a million dollars in one Swiss account, another hundred thou in a bank that had to be in Bahrain from the telephone code, and a third sum (amount unknown) in another location—which neither Avi nor Wonder could decipher.

They did a lot better when it came to the spreadsheet files. In fact, they were able to piece together more than 90 percent of the information.

- One spreadsheet detailed a series of Russian weapons transfers to the Chinese—more than sixty million dollars had changed hands in the past eight months alone. That, friends, buys a lot of AK-47s and other small arms. I wondered what the hell the Chinese needed Russian weapons for when they were the world's fifth largest arms exporter.
- A second file held information about stolen nuclear materials. Viktor Grinkov and his pals were selling *verboten* technology to anyone who had hard currency. I perused the list. It included Pakistan, Iran, Iraq, Libya—and the Syrians.
- A third detailed Russian investments overseas. Through a series of blind corporations and other fronts, the Ivans were trying to make inroads in a dozen high-tech areas. That made sense—the Russkies had always run second best in the technological area. Now, they were using their hard currency to buy into Western companies that made everything from microprocessors to computer-encryption equipment. The only problem was that—from what I could see—Werner Lantos had skimmed twenty-five million bucks from the Ivans' operational account to cover his margin-investment losses.
- A fourth detailed deposits in a Cayman Island trust account, opened by Werner Lantos for one Bartlett Austin Wyeth, Jr. The file had been partially overwritten, but as of eight months ago, there had been just over half a million dollars in the account. That's a lot of pieces of silver for selling your country out.
- A fifth spreadsheet tracked Lantos's private investment accounts—the ones he handled for the Ivans' *baksheesh.*[11] Viktor Grinkov's name turned up right at the top of that list. The man who ran the Russian Ministry of the Interior

---

[11]*Baksheesh* is Arabic for bribe.

was, it seemed, heavily invested—in a margin account—
in a series of high-risk Hong Kong stocks. Stocks which,
according to the figures I was looking at, had lost close to
eight million smackers in the last six months.

And Viktor wasn't the only Russkie who was losing his tunic in
the Hong Kong market. There were half a dozen other margin
accounts in various Ivans' names, all controlled, so it would appear,
by Werner Lantos.

Avi's eyes went wide. "He's got an account for an I. Katavtsev—
that's Igor Katavtsev, the chairman of the Duma committee on
intelligence matters," Avi said. "And Sergei Pavlov." The Israeli
whistled, impressed. "Pavlov runs GRU." The acronym stands for
the Russian Army's chief intelligence directorate.

I looked over at Avi. "I wonder if any of them know about this in
Moscow?"

"I'd doubt it. These guys aren't edge-of-the-financial envelope
types. They want their assets invested in nice, safe Swiss or
Bahamian accounts. I think Lantos skimmed their cash when he
brought it out of the country."

"I wasn't talking about the private stuff. That's bad enough." I
tapped the sheet of paper on which Wonder had printed up the
Russkie operational account. "This is worse."

Was it ever. It was a KISS plan gone bad. Werner Lantos had
skimmed somewhere between eight and ten million dollars from
his Russian partners. He'd used the money to open up accounts
under their names on the Hang Sang market in Hong Kong. Those
accounts gave him roughly fifty million bucks' worth of buying
power. Then he'd invested everything on margin—that is, paying
a fraction of the cost when he bought his shares, with the balance
to be paid at a later time. His plan was to pay in full after the
stocks had appreciated in value, then sell everything off, and slip
the millions he'd skimmed back into the Russkies' accounts in
Geneva, or the Bahamas, or wherever. But the margin investments
had gone sour, the banks had called in their markers, and poor
Werner had been paying them off with more and more of the
Ivans' money.

"Bottom line—Viktor and the rest of the Russkies are out"—I
looked at the screen—"somewhere between fifteen and twenty mil

of their hard-stolen profits." I pulled at my mustache. "Maybe we should print up all of these spreadsheets, fax 'em to Moscow, and see how they deal with Werner."

A malevolent grin spread over Avi's face. "I can do that," he said. "I have all the ministry fax numbers in my phone book. It would be even more fun to make the damn things public, y'know—send 'em to the Interfax News Agency." He reached into his pocket for the modem card and was about to insert it in the Toshiba when he realized what the hell he was about to do at the same instant Wonder and I tackled him and wrestled the goddamn thing out of his hand.

"Besides, I have a better idea," said Wonder.

Oh, did he?

"We have the Ivans' account numbers and passwords in Hong Kong—that's the money Werner's lost." He skimmed the laptop's screen. "But we also have Russkie accounts in Bahrain, Singapore, Geneva, the Cayman Islands, and a couple of other places—a sizeable chunk of the Ivans' weapons money. I'm talking about real cash in the bank, too." He scrolled the screen. "Like about fifty, sixty million bucks."

"So . . ."

"So, I suggest we take control of it all—change the passwords on 'em. I mean—who're they gonna blame, us, or Werner?"

It was a depraved, rotten, nasty, dirty idea. It was wonderful. It was marvelous. "Can you do it?"

Wonder's head went into its full-tilt Stevie Wonder left/right/left, right/left/right mode. "Whaddya you think? Of course I can do it."

"Then do it—it's a great idea. But don't touch Lantos's accounts. Not yet, anyway. I don't want to spook him." Another thought occurred to me. "Avi, is there any way you can check to see where Werner and Ehud are—quietly?"

Avi thought about it for a few seconds. "I think so," he said. "There's a secretary at the cultural center I've known for years—she's the one who told me Ehud had been in. She keeps her ears open about certain things. And she doesn't particularly like the current, ah, regime or its priorities at all. I think it might be worth buying her a cup of coffee."

"Avi, do you mean a secretary, or a secret-tary?"

He winked at me. "I could tell you, Dick, but then I'd have to kill you."

* * *

0825. Brud called with a message. My friend, he told me, cryptically referring to Kenny Ross, had left something for me at what he called, "The Gardener." I was to get it, then call the following number, which he repeated twice to make sure I got it.

There is something mystifying about French spoken with a West Virginia accent, but being fluent in both frog and Frog, I realized that Brud was describing the Gare du Nord, the largest of Paris's six railroad stations.

"And what about picking up the package?" I asked.

"Double *D*," said Brud.

That would be a dead drop.

"Roger. Location?"

"There's a mailbox at the the northern end of the first of the streets in the city you're in, named after his first name. You're to look for a double chalk. What you need is taped underneath." Brud paused. "Your friend says you'd get this. I told him he's crazy."

"You were right." I put the receiver down. WTF? The first street named Kenneth. I am familiar enough with the city to know that there is no street named Kenneth in Paris.

Duh—like how dense could I be? Gentle reader, what is Kenny Ross's first name? Let's all repeat it together. His first name is, *Admiral*.

I pulled out Monsieur LeClerc's Paris street guide and looked under *amiral*, which is the French spelling of *admiral*. The first listing was for a Boulevard de l'Amiral Bruix. I checked the map. The street ran southwest to northeast, and the metro stop closest to the northern end was Porte Maillot.

I pulled on my jacket. "Hold tight," I said. "I'll be back in an hour."

Wonder pulled himself out of his chair. "You want backup?"

I shook my head. "I can handle this."

1042. I made the pickup at the Gare du Nord. I'd been careful about surveillance and I knew I wasn't being followed. When I opened the locker with the key that had been taped to the bottom of the yellow mailbox, I discovered a plastic Galeries Lafayette bag, in which was a secure telephone. Secure phones are big and heavy. They're about twice the size of commercial models—just about the same as one of those old ten-pound, Vietnam-era PRC-1 radio-telephones you see in military museums.

I took the bag, tucked it under my arm, and hustled down to the metro, where I played a game of jump on/jump off until I was certain that I was clean. I transferred onto the Porte d'Orléans line and rode to Boulevard St. Michel on the Left Bank. The "Boo Miche" station is always a madhouse—a condition that gave me the opportunity to use the crowds to hide in as I took the elevator to the street level.

Once above ground, I scampered through the throngs of tourists, students, street people, and itinerant musicians on the Rue des Arts, circled a narrow block of stores, cafés, and pizza joints, and came back on my track. No sign of surveillance.

I took my time, and walked along the Quai des Grands Augustins, surreptitiously checking my six as I browsed the book stalls and antique print dealers. Nada. I ambled across the Seine at the Pont Royal, and walked the long way back to the Café des Augustins, stopping at three friendly bars along the way to sample the coffee—and check for the opposition. I was alone.

1315. Avi still hadn't returned from his assignation, so Wonder and I examined the phone carefully to make sure it hadn't been doctored.

Was I being paranoid? I don't think so—do you?

Wonder pronounced it clean. So, I disconnected one of the LeClercs' phones, connected mine (it had already been outfitted for European wiring since it had been shipped to Paris), and punched the number Brud had given me.

Kenny Ross answered on the third ring. "Ross."

"Hi—it's me."

"So you got the unit. Good."

"What's up?"

"That's what you're supposed to tell me. I have a certain four-star here who's awful anxious to know what the heck is going on."

First things first. "How did you get the phone to me?" I was worried about being compromised.

"The Chairman had me make a direct call to someone at the embassy, and had them dead-drop it for you. You're in the clear."

"You didn't get it from anyone from Christians In Action, Admiral . . ."

He paused to decipher my meaning. Then: "No, no, Dick—we

made sure you got one of the Chairman's own phones—the ones that don't have those damn chips installed."

That was welcome news. Back in the very early eighties, the then-director of the National Security Agency, Vice Admiral Bobby Ray Inman, who didn't like the fact that he couldn't read everybody's mail, lobbied for and finally received permission to design and deploy a computer chip that was subsequently inserted into all of the CIA's secure communications gear. (In fact, because Inman had terrific political clout, he also got his NSA chip installed in the commo packages of all the other government agencies that use encrypted message traffic, including DOD, State, the Department of Energy—even WHCA, pronounced "WHACKA," and standing for the White House Communications Agency.)

That chip allowed No Such Agency to monitor even their most secure transmissions.[12] But in 1996, the Joint Chiefs of Staff contracted with Motorola for a fifth-generation secure unit that, despite NSA's screams of outrage, did not have the chip installed. The reason is that the Chairman of the Joint Chiefs, as well as the other service chiefs of staff, wanted their own private network, so they could talk to their CINCs—that's Commanders-IN-Chief—privately. And since the Joint Chiefs can exercise a certain amount of short-and-curly control over NSA's budget and resources, they threatened, strong-armed, blackmailed, and intimidated the agency until they got what they wanted.

So, I was able to sit-rep the admiral, leaving out nothing (with the single exception, of course, of Wonder's presence) and pausing and repeating as he took notes. I waited until I'd finished to ask what I really wanted to know about: the FORTE satellite I needed shifted. Without its capabilities, we'd be operating essentially blind.

---

[12]That chip is called DREC—for Digitally Reconnoiterable Electronic Component. DREC allows NSA to unscramble signals and also trace the transmission location. In the early nineties, NSA convinced Congress to allow it to install a DREC chip in every piece of secure communications equipment purchased by the government. The agency argued that it would prevent the equipment from being misused, and also aid in recovering stolen equipment because the signal's emanation location could be pinpointed. In reality, NSA simply wanted to be able to read everyone's secure comms—from the CIA's internal e-mail, to State's confidential cables, to White House and National Security Council memos, something that would give the huge agency additional political clout in these days of intelligence agency budgetary downsizing. Only the Joint Chiefs of Staff and its component service chiefs managed to escape NSA's wholesale eavesdropping scheme.

I heard the door open. Avi waved at me as he came down the hall. "Admiral—hold on a sec—"

I cupped my palm over the mouthpiece. So?"

"They're gone—pulled out. Chartered a plane out of Switzerland. Flight plan includes a five-hour stopover in Geneva, then an overnight in Cyprus, and a final destination of Beirut."

The fucking plan was in motion. Had to be. It made perfect sense to me that Lantos was going to pull money from his account in Switzerland, grab some muscle in Cyprus, and then head toward Damascus from Beirut. I needed that fucking FORTE bird—and I needed it *now*.

"Things are about to blow wide open," I told Kenny Ross. "There's no time to waste, Admiral."

"We're facing a lot of resistance here," Kenny Ross said. "The bird over China can't be moved—some code-word project for the White House. The Chairman's pushing hard to get the Ukraine bird shifted—but they're telling him it's going to be at least another twelve, maybe sixteen hours until we can pull it off—*if* we can pull it off at all. It's darn hard, Dick, since he can't be specific about why he needs it."

Didn't he understand timing was crucial? "What's the goddamn hold up?"

"The usual junk. The Agency is screaming that we're exceeding our mission parameters—whatever the heck those are. The DCI even called Chairman Crocker demanding to know why we want a FORTE all of a sudden. State is convinced we're about to dismantle two decades of careful diplomacy—even though nothing's ever been accomplished. And that ex-journalist sonofabitch they brought in to run the NSC is demanding to know why we want what we want, too. He's been trying to make steers out of the Joint Chiefs ever since he was appointed—I think he guesses the Chairman has something going, and he wants a piece of it, or of him, or both. Then there are the usual interservice rivalries—the Air Force wants a slice of this, even though they have no idea what we're doing. Oh—then there's politics. Not to mention the departmental budgets—which are allegedly due on the president's desk in less than a month."

His voice grew serious in tone. "Frankly, this op had better pan out, Dick, because the Chairman's kicked a lot of butt and called in a lot of markers on your behalf."

Had he? Well, frankly, friends, calling in political markers, wheeling and dealing budget items, and kicking interservice butt should be what being Chairman of the Joint Chiefs of Staff is all about. The sorry fact of the matter is that too few of the people wearing stars are willing to lay those stars on the line anymore when it comes to backing up those of us who are actually doing the dirty work in the trenches.

The sorry result of the sorry fact is that when the folks who wear stars don't lead, the people who wear scars—operators like me—get a little more hesitant about following 'em. And when that happens, the whole system begins to disintegrate. So, while I was gratified that the Chairman was kicking ass and taking names on my behalf, I hoped he realized that he wasn't doing anything more than his job.

But I held my temper in check. No use mouthing off at Kenny Ross. "Try to get the fucking thing shifted ASAP, okay, Admiral?"

"Will do. Meanwhile, what's the plan?"

"We're going to shift our AO eastward as soon as we can."

He paused. I could hear him scribbling something. "Is that wise?"

"Say what, Admiral?"

"Moving before we know anything specific?"

That was the nuclear submariner in him speaking. Boomer COs don't do it if it ain't on a checklist. And moving eastward before we had a location to go to was not a list-checkable item, even though I knew Werner and Ehud were on the move. But I wasn't about to divulge that nugget. Too many ways for the information to run amok. Too dangerous for Dickie—and the rest of us.

So I was noncommittal. "It gives me a jump on the situation."

I heard him scribbling again. I guess it made some sort of sense, because he responded by saying—somewhat tersely: "Check in with me in eight hours. Give me a sit-rep."

"Will this phone work from where we're going?"

"It should—but y'know, Dick, no one's ever tried it before." The phone in my ear went dead.

No one's ever tried it before. Right. Sounds like the story of my life, Admiral.

I cradled the receiver on my own phone.

I was about to make some smartass remark when I saw the look on Avi Ben Gal's face. "What's wrong?"

"Nothing."

Yeah. Right. "Avi—"

The Israeli balled his fists. "He's a damn traitor, Dick."

"Who?"

"Ehud. Has to be. He did the target assessment at the cultural center. No other reason for him to show up the way he did—the last time less than a day before the explosion." He looked at me. "But why?"

Why? Why had Buckshot Brannigan, Manny Tanto, and the rest of Grant Griffith's crew sold out? Why had Dawg Dawkins done the same thing? The answer was because when the *merde* hit the *ventilateur*, they turned out to be greedy, selfish, unprincipled turncoats who betrayed the uniform they'd worn and the flag under which they'd served—for money.

Avi had told me the same thing about Ehud earlier—he just hadn't paid attention to what he'd said.

So, I reminded him. "Avi—remember when I said that Ehud might not be on the side of the angels?"

"So?"

"So—what did you tell me?" Avi gave me a blank look. "What you told me," I said, "was, 'Ehud is on the side of Ehud.'"

The look on Avi's face told me he'd heard what I'd said—but that he was having a hard time digesting it. Avi's values are very strong—he loves his country. He believes strongly in what he does. I do, too. And so, I shared his anguish, his pain, and his need for revenge. But to achieve that final element, we had to go east.

"Listen up, fellow crusaders," I said. "It's time to sharpen the swords, pack the armor, and leave for the Holy Land."

Wonder's hands were on his hips. "And who the fuck are you all of a sudden, King Richard the Lionhearted?"

"What's so wrong with that—King Richard sounds pretty fucking good to me."

Wonder turned to Avi, who despite himself had cracked a smile. "I guess he wants to be da king." Then he turned back to me. "So, then I guess it's 'Oh, thank you, your royal pus-nutted highness,' and 'by your leave, your grand sphincter-faced panjandrumcy,'" he said, bowing and scraping like one of those unctuous factotums in the B movies that starred people like John Agar, Basil Rathbone, and Yvonne De Carlo, "Well, okay, your dumb-shitted majesty— you *can* be King Richard the Lionhearted. But only to strangers. To those of us who know you and love you, Skipper, you'll always be Lionheart the Dick."

Part
Three

MATRYOSHKA

Chapter

19

TEL AVIV WAS UNSEASONABLY HOT AND MUGGY—IT FELT MORE LIKE Barbados than Ben Gurion as we stepped through the hatch and onto the patterned steel treads of the mobile stairway. We'd flown on Air France from De Gaulle Two so as not to attract attention. Most seasoned travelers coming out of France prefer the Air France or El Al flights out of Orly, the older airport that lies due south of Paris. Orly is much closer to the city, and the flights are less crowded. But since Orly is the hub for most of the flights to Africa and the Middle East, it is also blanketed by the French, Israeli, Egyptian, Moroccan, Libyan, Syrian, Iranian, and Iraqi intelligence services. My guess is that 25 percent of the people working as ticket agents, security personnel, ground crews, and various airline employees are, in fact, intel weenies, secret agents, and/or covert operators.

So, we skipped Orly, took the bus to De Gaulle Two from Porte Maillot, braved the crowds of tourists in the terminal, drank overpriced beer, and flew on a jam-packed, indifferently staffed Air France A-300 Airbus that departed three and a half hours late, and arrived in Tel Aviv long after dark. Avi left Wonder and me to ride the shuttle bus to the terminal and fight the long lines at immigration. He was recognized as soon as he started down the mobile stairway to the tarmac, waved aside, welcomed warmly, and guided into a light-colored sedan that sped off in a direction directly opposite to the main terminal.

Wonder and I took the shuttle to the huge arrivals pavilion, waited on line until our passports were stamped by a uniformed NYL—that's nubile young lovely in case you forgot—then claimed our bags. We took the Green Lane past lounging customs inspectors, then wandered out of the air-conditioned terminal into the steamy night, working our way through the bustling throng of people milling outside, waiting to greet arriving friends and relatives. We fought our way to the curb, dropped our baggage, and looked for Avi.

He was nowhere to be seen. We stood there for five minutes or so, fighting off the cab and limo drivers who promised best fare meester, best fare meester, in Hebrew, English, Arabic, Russian, and Turkish. Then a small white sedan with black-and-white Army plates screeched to a halt in the no parking zone where we stood, and the headlights flashed rapidly half a dozen times.

I squinted through the windshield. It was Avi. He was waving. "Over here, over here," he called. "I got us a ride."

It had been some years since I'd been in Israel, and frankly, the place looked like a different country. Most people who haven't been here visualize Israel as either a land filled with bedouin tents, date palm trees, citrus groves, and camels—kind of a Disneyland Saudi Arabia, or they see it as an extension of the Lower East Side of Manhattan—not so much the land of milk and honey as the land of bagels, lox, and kosher pastrami.

Well, friends, wake up and smell the falafel: neither is the case. Israel is a modern, vibrant country. You may be in the Middle East, but Tel Aviv resembles Miami more than it does Damascus. These days, you leave the airport, and all of a sudden you're whipping into a high-speed merge lane that swings you out onto a superhighway that runs between Tel Aviv and Jerusalem. Yes, there are still citrus groves and dunam after dunam of cotton and soybeans that grow within sight of the highway as you climb toward Jerusalem past the Latrun salient. But go west, toward Tel Aviv's coastal plain, and you'll find yourself cruising at eighty miles an hour past kilometer after kilometer of glass-and-steel office complexes, shopping malls, and huge blocks of modernistic apartment houses.

In fact, I didn't remember much of the route to Herzlyia at all. In the years since I'd visited, a whole new highway system had been constructed. I remembered stop-and-go traffic. This was eight lanes of uninterrupted testosterone driving.

Have I mentioned that Israelis develop an Attitude when they get behind the wheel? No? Well, let me put it this way: do not think that because some Israeli drivers look like rabbis (or other clergy), they will turn the other cheek and let you pass them on an open road.

Turning the other cheek is a New Testament canon. The God of Israel, Yahweh—the unnameable name—is the God who brought Moses out of Egypt. Yahweh is God as SEALs see God: the tough, unyielding, Old Testament God of War—the "I will utterly blot out the remembrance of Amelek from under heaven" God.

Bottom line: you do not want to play "chicken" with that devout-looking bearded fellow in the Renault-2 over there, dressed in rabbinical black, wearing a knit *kippa* (skull cap), and sporting *peyot* (Orthodox side curls), because he's not gonna say a prayer for you—he's simply gonna run your butt into the barrier and wave *litrahot*—see ya later—as you roll over. Avi, whose behavior normally reflects his soft-spoken demeanor, was no less macho than your average rabbi. He hunched over the wheel, put kosher pedal to kosher metal, and we flew at 160 kilometers an hour north, skirting the Tel Aviv metropolitan area without a single traffic light, until we reached a huge interchange that I didn't recall at all. "Didn't this used to be berry fields?"

"Yup," said Avi through gritted teeth as he swung the car to the left and floored the accelerator again. We sped past Ramat Hasharon, where I'd spent many a night drinking Bombay with IAF (Israeli Air Force) officers who could go me one-for-one with the drink I call Jewish Booze—J&B Scotch—and proceeded due west, toward the sea.

Just past the huge tennis center on my left I saw the lights of the coastal highway, and all of a sudden we were at Gelilot junction. On our right just above the highway sat the low, curved silhouette of Mossad headquarters. Adjacent to Mossad, but in a different compound above a huge supermarket, sat another complex that contained many of AMAN's offices. Avi veered into the left lane, cut past a double tractor trailer, shot across a no-pass lane, and slalomed into the northbound Haifa highway traffic. "Almost home," he said triumphantly. "I may have beaten the old record."

He cut off a Volvo station wagon, performed a credible four-wheel drift, and sailed onto the exit ramp that bore the word *Beach*

271

in Hebrew and English. We turned left, drove under the highway, and—holy shit, straight into Beverly fucking Hills.

The last time I'd been to Avi's home—roughly six years ago—I'd found my way by driving along a pitted dirt road through an ugly, refuse-strewn industrial zone that surrounded the beach community of Herzlyia Pituach like a rusty belt.

Nothing of that zone remained. Instead, Avi cruised slowly down wide streets filled with pedestrians and lined with espresso bars and trendy Italian, French, and Oriental restaurants. I peered through the windshield. To my left, a long, curved boulevard flanked by Art Deco–style street lamps stretched toward the ocean. "What's that?" I asked Avi.

"The road to the new marina—they finished it last year. There are fifteen hundred boats moored there."

"Shit—I didn't think there were fifteen hundred boats in Israel."

"Things have changed, Dick."

I guess they had.

Avi turned left and drove past a tall wooden fence line, behind which stood perhaps half a dozen narrow two-story town house villas in various stages of construction. Avi pointed at the fence, on which was attached an artist's rendering showing a dozen or so villas. "Those places will sell for more than three-quarters of a million dollars apiece," he said. "Ten years ago, you could have bought most of the land on the block for that kind of money." He turned right on a narrow, divided road that ran parallel to the Mediterranean shoreline. I remembered garbage-strewn sand dunes and patches of sharp-bladed salt grass. Now I saw mani-cured walkways, lighted tennis courts, wine bars, and glassed-in restaurants that looked like the ones that sit on the most exclusive portions of the French Riviera.

He veered right onto a narrow side street that I remembered, drove another hundred yards, then pulled over in front of a pair of unfamiliar, heavy ornamental steel gates that sat athwart a stone driveway. Avi killed the engine and shut the lights off, pulled the ignition key, and handed it to me. "Suitcases."

We climbed out. I stretched—the Israelis still favor small cars. It is a throwback, I believe, to their frugal past (not to mention forty-plus years of Arab oil boycotts). I opened the trunk, Wonder and I retrieved the bags, and I slammed it shut.

The noise was answered with barking and growling from behind the gates. I heard the sound of paws scraping at the metal.

Avi dropped his suitcase in front of a tall, arched security gate set into the eight-foot-high stucco wall that was topped with shards of broken glass. It, like the wall and driveway gates, had been built since I'd last been here. The barks and growls shifted. "*Sheket, klavim*—shaddup, dogs," Avi growled back. The noise stopped. He extracted a key from his pocket, turned the lock on the gate, and cracked it open. Immediately, a pair of huge black hairy faces insinuated themselves into the opening. Avi used his knee to move the dogs backward. "*Shev*—sit," he commanded. Obviously, the dogs obeyed, because he pushed the gate open and beckoned for us to follow him. "C'mon, c'mon," he said.

We followed him through the gate into a courtyard lit by lanterns, just in time to watch as two of the biggest Bouviers I'd ever seen sprang from their "sit-stay" position, jumped Avi's bones, and sent him sprawling ass over teakettle on the patterned stone that lead to the front door.

"See how well trained they are?" he laughed between licks. He brushed the dogs off and sat up, his smiling face wet. You could see he was happy to be home.

The Bouvier closest to me turned and sniffed in my direction. "This is Bilbo," Avi said, by way of introduction. "The smaller one is Cleo."

Smaller? They looked the same size to me—large economy size. Bilbo approached cautiously. He sniffed my hand, my knee, and my crotch, did the same to Wonder, then walked back to where Avi had pulled himself to his feet and licked the Israeli's hand.

Cleo was more standoffish. She skirted me, approached Wonder and growled. "Cleo—" Avi spoke to the dog in rapid Hebrew. Immediately, there was a change in the animal's attitude. She sat directly in front of Wonder and offered him her paw.

Wonder took it, shook it, then ruffled the Bouvier behind the ears. "How do I tell her 'Good dog?'"

"To-*vah* kal-*bah*," Avi said, speaking slowly and distinctly.

Wonder stroked the dog and repeated the Hebrew. Cleo cocked her head and stared at him, then stood on her hind legs and licked his face.

I looked at Avi. "I think that's a match made in heaven," I said.

Behind Avi, lights were going on throughout the house. Then the portico lit up and the front door opened.

Miriam Ben Gal stood in silhouette, framed by the doorway. "Dick, *Ahlan W'asahlan*—welcome."

I gave her a warm hug. "Shalom, Mikki. It's been a while."

She looked over at Wonder and extended her hand. "I'm Mikki," she said. "You must be the one Avi calls Stevie Wonder." She pronounced it *Vundaire* and it had never sounded better. "Welcome to Israel."

She stood aside so that we could move inside. "It's been a long time, Dick."

"Too long," I said. I meant it, too. "I hope we're not intruding, Mikki."

"This is the Middle East," she said reproachfully. "In this part of the world we do things without reservations. Besides, the kids are long gone—Ori is married with his own children. They live in Ramat Aviv. Tamar's at Technion, working on a master's degree in economics. We're what you Americans call vatchamacallit empty-nestairs these days. Just looking for some company. So, when Avi called from the airport to say you were with him, I told him I'd add some water to the soup and dig out two extra towels."

After dinner, I attached the phone to a jack in the living room, got a dial tone, and punched the JCS number into the keypad. I got through to Kenny Ross immediately. The admiral had good news and bad news for me. The good news was that the Chairman had done his job: the FORTE satellite was in position. There'd been all sorts of hang-ups—lots of back and forth with the Agency. But in the end, Ken Ross said, Langley had quite unexpectedly withdrawn its objections and FORTE had been shifted.

It had made its first pass twenty minutes ago—and it had taken a perceptible reading. Shit—that meant the location was ripe for plucking. Excited as a motherplucker, I scribbled the coordinates down as Kenny read them off to me.

I waved at Avi and mouthed the word *map*. He slid one over to me. They'd set the fucking site up just southwest of Damascus, between the Lebanese border and the demilitarized zone—convenient for Hizballah tangos, hard for the United Nations to monitor, and close enough to Israel to allow the use of conventional artillery—even 155mm would do the job—tipped with nuclear shells.

Then came the bad news. My operation was to be put on hold mode until certain problems could be solved back in Washington and here in Jerusalem.

Screw hold mode—I wanted specifics. "They're so far above my pay grade," Kenny told me, "don't even bother to ask."

I asked anyway. After all, we were on a secure line and I had nothing to lose.

"It has something to do with the White House and Langley and the Israelis." Kenny Ross sighed. "I'm not privy to the details, but from what General Crocker tells me, the Israelis want something done a certain way, and at a certain time, and until it is, they won't cooperate. All I know is that General C is steamed. I mean, he's gol-darned hot."

"All the better to let me operate," I said. "Time is short, Admiral—I want these suckers."

"So do we—believe me. But let me be explicit here, Dick, because my behind is on the line, too. Your op is shut down until you hear from me, or from General Crocker. Full stop. End of story." There was a silence on the line. "Gotta go," Ken Ross's voice came back at me.

"Admiral—"

"What, Dick?" There was exasperation in his tone.

I waved frantically at Avi and mimed for him to get the laptop we'd taken from Lantos's office. "Admiral, can you connect your end to a computer?"

I could hear Ken Ross's muffled voice as he clapped his palm over the phone and asked one of his people the same question.

"They tell me we can, if you give us a minute or so, then hang up and redial." He paused. "What's the point?"

"Before there's any final decision," I said, "I want the general to look at something."

"There's already been a final decision," Ken Ross said.

"Admiral—"

I guess the tone of my voice was urgent enough to convince him, because his own tone softened. "Okay, Dick—you send me what you have within the next five minutes and I'll pass it on. But get your stuff here quick—he's in a meeting, he's already screaming for me, and I'm keeping him waiting because I'm talking to you."

"Roger, roger."

"Oh, and don't count on anything—the Chairman's up against it politically, and I don't think he's going to be able to make any changes right now."

"I try never to assume anything, Admiral." I rang off. "Avi—"

I explained what I wanted to do.

"It's a great idea," Avi said. "Except we have a slight problem."

"Which is?"

"Which is that the only modem in the house is made of high explosive."

He had a point. "Can't we use your desktop computer?" There was a big, boxy IBM on a table in Avi's den.

"Nope." He shook his head. "No modem." He thought for a second. "We can attach the laptop to the printer, we can print whatever you want, and fax your admiral. I have a fax machine."

"How quickly?"

"How much do you want to print up?"

"Everything."

Avi scratched at his chin. "Twenty, twenty-five minutes." He saw my incredulous look. "Hey, Dick, not everybody has a laser printer. I gave mine to Ori as a wedding present—all I have is my old wheel printer, which prints four minutes a page."

"You mean four pages a minute."

"No—I mean four minutes a page."

Doom on Dickie. I redialed Ken Ross and explained that the situation had gone to TARFU. He wasn't happy. (And that, gentle reader, is an understatement.)

But while he pissed and moaned, groaned, sighed, and threatened, Ken Ross stayed the course. "Just get me the gol-darn information," he said, obviously upset as heck at me. "I'll do what I can."

I set the receiver down and told Avi what I hoped would happen when Tom Crocker got the materials we'd taken from Lantos's computer. He immediately excused himself and went downstairs to his basement office. Seconds later, I heard the tap-tap-tapping of the aged printer as it ground out the faxes we'd have to send.

Three-quarters of an hour later I had ten pages of material to transmit. I sent the Chairman the weapons accounts, and a few pages from Lantos's other financial portfolios, including the trust account he'd set up for Bart Wyeth in the Cayman Islands.

By 2230, Mikki'd long ago gone to bed. Wonder and I sat in the living room, discussing our alternatives—there seemed to be precious few of them—and sipping red wine grown in Israeli vineyards that had been first planted with grapes long before B.C. turned into A.D. As we spoke, we could hear Avi, engaged in what sounded like a series of angry conversations in full auto Uzi submachine-gun Hebrew. When Wonder and I turned in at 0145, trudging upstairs to the second-floor guest room that we'd share, he was still there, on the phone, arguing.

Then, all of a sudden it was 0320, and I sensed the dogs moving. Well, to be accurate, I heard their toenails tapping impatiently on the stone floors as they scurried back and forth. I rolled out of bed and into a pair of shorts, and slipped downstairs. Avi was standing in the night-lighted foyer in shorts and sandals, shrugging into a T-shirt. Bilbo's and Cleo's eyes were bright and their behavior animated, in anticipation of doggy fun.

"It's the only time I can get away with it anymore—walking them on the beach," Avi explained as we stole out of the house, the two Bouviers bounding in tight circles around us, and strolled 150 yards to a long, steep stairway leading down from the street to the sea. "Used to be, everybody took their dogs down to the beach. Let 'em run and do their business. About five years ago the first condo went up—that one over there—" He pointed toward a ten-story, glass-and-brick tower 200 yards to his left. "They charged a quarter of a mil for a two-bedroom flat with a view of the Mediterranean—and they got it. There was even a waiting list," he said incredulously.

"A quarter million shekels?"

"Shekels, hell—a quarter of a million *dollars*. Cash money. Greenbacks. Anyway, then half a dozen other condos went up—and the prices went even higher, and now there are all sorts of regulations about what you can and you can't do—including letting dogs poop on all that nouveau-riche sand."

He turned north, his left shoulder facing the sea, and we trudged along the high water mark, the dogs running long circles around us. We walked side by side for some minutes in silence, our hands behind our backs, lost in thought the way you can get lost in thought on a quiet beach in the middle of the night, with the sounds of water, waves, and wind playing around you.

Finally, Avi said, "You know this isn't going to be easy if we proceed."

I punched my left palm with my right hand. "Hey, c'mon, Avi—what's life without a little challenge every now and then?"

"No—I mean it. I've been told in no uncertain terms that what you want to do is out of the question."

"Fine—you pull out if you have to. I'll go it alone."

He looked north and gave a short, low whistle, which brought the dogs romping back in our direction. "That's not the point. There's no question about my pulling out—we began this together, and it'll finish that way."

I liked the sentiment, but wondered why. There was no overt reason for Avi to back me to the point of losing his own career, and I told him so.

"You don't understand," he said. "There's a lot more at stake here than Ehud Golan—although I'm convinced he's a goddamn traitor—or Werner Lantos, or even all that smuggled dual-use equipment and Russian weapons. Sure, that's all important. But what I'm really fighting for—what I'm willing to put my career on the line for—is the very soul of the State of Israel, Dick."

I didn't understand what he was getting at, and told him so.

"The point," he said, "is that we've gotten ourselves in the middle of a complicated political situation. You started all of this with the blessing of your Chairman. I began with the blessings of my director. But things have changed."

"My Chairman still wants these cocksuckers done. He wants the site destroyed."

"So does my boss. Don't forget, before he ran AMAN he was an operator. He went to Tunis and personally pulled the trigger on Abu Jihad. He wants us to go and do what has to be done. But as you know we've recently had a change in governments here."

"So?"

"The emphasis has shifted. There's a lot of pressure being put on the United States to keep its nose out of the region and let our government handle things its own way."

"That's crazy, Avi—"

"You're right. It is crazy. But the fact of the matter is that there are a lot of people in Washington who'd like to see a shift in the way the U.S. does business in the Middle East. And our new government is making things easy for them. Now, as a soldier, I'm expected to carry out my orders and protect my country. No argument there. But as an Israeli—I was born here, too—I have a larger mission. That mission, as I've always seen it, is to make sure that my country doesn't become . . ."—he groped for the right word—". . . become immoral. Not immoral in the Sodom and Gomorrah sense, but in the political sense. I think there's a danger of that happening now—and I'm willing to put my career on the line to stop it, just as you are." He paused and peered over his shoulder. "The bottom line is that the political situation has shifted—here, and in Washington. Which is why your chairman has reneged."

"But he hasn't reneged—he's just put things on hold."

"Right. Sure." The irony in Avi's tone was evident. "Dick, face facts: it's become obvious to me over the past few hours that your Chairman is fighting a nasty ground campaign with the White House, the State Department, the CIA, and who knows who else."

I started to say something, but Avi kept going. "I know all of this because my boss at AMAN is fighting the same damn fight tonight with the ministers in Jerusalem. And you know what he's being told? 'Hands off the Russian Mafiya. Hands off Werner Lantos. Hands off everything.' I work for a terrific guy, just like you do. But right now the director of AMAN seems to be getting screwed, and I'm the one he's taking it out on." He bent down, picked a shell off the sand, and threw it out into the water. "Things have changed in Israel, Dick. It started with Rabin's assassination. And now—now, the state's whole gestalt has, has . . ." He searched for the right word. "Mutated." He looked at me, a pained, bemused smile on his face. "Oy, gestalt—has it ever mutated."

Avi balled both hands into fists. "Like tonight. Your op was shut down. Well, mine was, too. 'Break off. Do not cooperate with the American. Full stop.'"

"Is that what you want?"

"Of course not."

"So, let's fuck 'em. Screw the apparatchiks. Fuck the bureaucrats. We just keep going—attack, attack, attack. Let 'em pick up the fucking pieces after we're finished. In the meanwhile, we get to kick ass and take names and maybe even kill a few japs in the process."

"That's too glib an answer, Dick—it's the kind of bullshit you like to throw around to keep people off guard. You know very well we can't go off like a couple of cowboys. There's too much at stake."

He was right, of course. And, despite my rogue rhetoric, there was no way I'd risk putting my nation in jeopardy. "That's why it was so crucial to get that information to Ken Ross."

"You think it will change the Chairman's mind?"

"I don't think the Chairman's mind need changing—but he needs something to help him secure the kind of political backup that'll allow him to act. I believe we got it for him."

Avi sighed. "It's gotten all so fucking complicated," he said. He laughed bitterly. "Things were so much easier when it was just the two of us, sneaking around the Bekáa."

"With you making sure we always pronounced *tomato* correctly."

He smiled. "I hadn't thought about that in years." He paused. "Those fucking roadblocks—the tomato test. It was absolutely biblical."

I didn't understand, and told him so.

"The Lebanese weren't doing anything that wasn't already done in the Old Testament," he explained. "In the book of Judges, the Gileadites set up roadblocks in the passages of Jordan to catch the Ephraimites. They asked them to pronounce the word *shibboleth* which means a small stream in biblical Hebrew. But the Ephraimites couldn't pronounce the *sh* sound—they said the word as *sibboleth*. Which was their death sentence."

He turned to face me. The dogs, panting from their exercise, dropped at his feet. "So much for your Bible studies." He stopped and ruffled Bilbo behind the ears. Cleo scrunched closer to Avi's leg. He reached over and scratched her, too. "Okay—now you know why you won't be left on your own. But since I've just come clean, maybe you should, too."

"Should what?"

"Explain why this mission has become so important to you. I understand America's concern about what the Russians are doing. But you've gone way beyond that, Dick."

I stopped and looked out at the ocean, way out, to where the clear, star-filled sky met the sea. I listened to the sounds of the waves lapping up onto the sand. Watched the Mediterranean's ebb and the flow, felt the perpetual motion that is absolute in its absoluteness. There is truly something mystical about the ocean. It is transcendental, metaphysical—magic. Those oceanic qualities, in fact, are a large part of why I joined the Navy in the first place. They were also a factor in my choice to become a SEAL.

The sea is a place of solitude, seclusion, and introspection. At night a man can stand at the rail, or on the beach, and as he watches the water and the waves he can, if he wants, learn a lot about himself.

"You're right," I said. "The truth for me is that this goes way beyond politics or national interest. Now, don't get me wrong, Avi—I'm committed to act, no matter what they decide in Washington. I'm committed because tactical nuclear weapons in the hands of terrorists is something we can't react to—we have to prevent it. The politicians don't always understand that—and they end up getting innocent people killed because of their inaction. But there's more here, so far as I am concerned. It's become personal. These sons of bitches killed my friend, my shipmate." I paused to collect my thoughts. "Okay—Paul was an officer. His life was at risk, just like mine is at risk. That's the job. You understand that—you're the same way. But they killed his family, too. His wife. His kids. My godson." I scratched at the damp sand with my big toe. "If Adam had lived—who knows. Maybe he'd have gone to Annapolis, like his father—gone on to nuclear submarining. But just maybe he'd have decided to become a SEAL, like his godfather, me. A SpecWarrior—like his godfather." I turned away from Avi so he couldn't see the moisture beginning to form in the corners of my eyes, and did a passable Marlon Brando Vito Corleone. *"I'd have helped him decide, y'know—made the kid an offer he couldn't refuse."*

I walked out into the water a few yards. Felt its reassuring coolness; drew strength from its surging, kinetic power. Took a very deep breath. Faced the horizon. "But Adam didn't get the chance. Didn't get the chance to grow up. Didn't get the chance to go to Annapolis. Didn't get the chance to make his own choice to become a submariner or a SpecWarrior."

I turned back toward Avi. "So I don't give much of a rusty fuck whether it's gonna be hard, or it's gonna be easy. All I know is that I am planning to go balls to the wall until I bring these cocksuckers down. Down *hard.* Like I said before, this goes way beyond global politics—or anything else, Avi—this one's personal."

Chapter

20

"How much help do you think we can really get?" It was just past 0700. Mikki had gone off to her job running the Herzlyia Medical Center. Wonder and I sipped mugs of steaming coffee as we sat at an oval table in the huge kitchen, poring over a pilotage map that Avi had pulled from his files. Avi was standing at the counter, chopping tomatoes. He diced them finely and tossed them into a Duroc glass bowl, added a sprinkle of salt and pepper, a dollop of olive oil, the juice of half a lemon, and topped them with fresh oregano and thyme that he'd just pulled from the herb garden outside his living room.

"Good question." He picked up the bowl and set it down in front of us, careful to miss the map, then went to the oven, where he plucked half a dozen loaves of fresh pita bread out, juggled them to keep his hands from being burned, and dropped them, too, onto the table. Finally, he reached inside the fridge and brought out a smaller Duroc bowl of what looked like sour cream. "*Labbane,*" he explained. "Arab-styled yogurt cheese."

"Watch," he told Wonder. The Israeli took one of the *pitot,* and gingerly broke it in quarters. He used one of the quarters like a spoon, scooping some of the *labbane* onto the surface of the bread. Then he quickly dipped the labbane-coated bread into the tomatoes, twisted his wrist to catch a few, then popped the whole dripping thing into his mouth. *"Metsuyan,"* Avi proclaimed. "Excellent."

Wonder, whose idea of breakfast generally starts and ends with a supersize 7-Eleven coffee and powdered nondairy creamer, looked skeptically at the bowls in front of him. But he is a trooper when it comes to food. Like me, there is nothing he will not eat. And so, he mimicked Avi's moves, chewed, swallowed, and was delighted with the results. "That's good," he exclaimed. "Beats the shit outta bran flakes."

Avi straddled a chair and joined us. He sipped at his coffee, nodding in my direction. "I haven't forgotten your question," he said.

"So?"

"So, the answer is: none. I'm sure the powers that be are going to do everything they can to actively discourage us."

"Active? How active?" I didn't need a bunch of Shin Bet, the Israeli domestic secret service, watching my butt's every move. "Is Shin Bet gonna get into the act?"

Avi frowned. "Doubtful. Frankly, they have more important things to do—like keeping track of Islamic Jihad or Hizballah cells that are operating in the territories."

"So what's 'active?' "

"Well, first of all, you've already been denied permission to use Israel as a base of operations. So that cuts out all official contact. You can't check in at the Kyria"—Avi used Israeli slang for the huge IDF headquarters complex in the middle of Tel Aviv—"to get intelligence briefings, or receive technical help, like secure radios, global positioning devices, or weapons. And no tactical support— which means no transportation. It also means you can't go to the Boys—either officially, or under the table, for help."

Too bad. Frankly, the Israelis are first-rate SpecWarriors, and it would have been nice to have been able to operate with a squad from the Boys, officially designated as *Saye'eret Matkal,* which translates as the General Staff's Special Reconnaissance and Intelligence Unit. *Saye'eret Matkal,* which used to be known as Unit 269 (much the same as the Naval Special Warfare Development Group, or DEVGRP, used to be known as SEAL Team Six), has carried out scores of black ops. They have their own specialized transportation—stealth-equipped choppers and other aircraft, as well as spec ops–capable ships. They have good weapons, secure comms, and a complete array of the sorts of goodies that make operations less prone to untimely intrusions by Mr. Murphy.

My friends, I've been denied official help before, and while it makes my life difficult, it doesn't make it impossible. "What else?"

"Who knows. If the government puts pressure on your embassy, they could do anything—even help us deport you."

I've heard that song before, too. "So we move fast."

"Not as simple as it sounds," Avi said. "We still need equipment."

"Fuck—we improvise. We can buy almost everything we need commercially. The only problems will be weapons, explosives, and transportation."

Avi rapped the table with his knuckles. "I have weapons," he said. "Two AKs and an M-16."

"What about ammo?" asked Wonder.

"I've got about a thousand rounds I guess. I keep it all in the bomb shelter."

"Bomb shelter?" Wonder dipped a chunk of bread into the *labbane*. "You have a bomb shelter in the house?"

"Everybody has one," Avi explained. "They were built that way." He saw that Wonder didn't understand. "The 1949 armistice line," he explained.

"So—"

"From here to the border is only nine miles. I grew up in Herzlyia proper, which is three miles east of here. The Jordanians used to shell us. So every house was built with a bomb shelter. They still are, too, although these days most people use 'em for storage. I keep my weapons and ammo there—it's cool, and it's dry."

"Explosives," Wonder said. "We're gonna need explosives."

"That might be a problem. They tend to be careful about handing out C-4."

I thought for a while. "What about those units of yours?"

"Which ones?"

"The modem and flash memory cards."

"So?"

"Still have the one from Paris?"

"It's in my briefcase."

"Let's look at it."

Avi brought the modem card upstairs and laid it on the table. Wonder and I examined it closely. It had possibilities. "Yo, Avi, you got a magnifying glass, a pair of nonmagnetic tweezers, and a plastic knife?" Wonder asked.

Fifteen minutes later, Boy Wonder looked up from his labor, a wicked grin on his face. "Oh, I can make this work real good," he said. "All I need is three or four more like it."

Just before noon, Avi slipped out to his office so he could get in and out while most of the folks he worked with were at lunch. Meanwhile, Wonder and I hit the bank to change dollars into shekels, then took the bus into Tel Aviv and went shopping. At a sporting goods store on a big, wide avenue called Ibn Gevirol we bought lightweight boots, two dark blue rucksacks large enough to be used as assault packs, and three two-liter Camelbak units— flexible, plastic water containers that attach to a rucksack or can be carried on your back. We found an army surplus store near Allenby Street, where we bought two one-piece jumpsuits, wrist com- passes, a hundred feet of soft nylon climbing rope, two sets of well- used but strong "Y" combat suspenders, pistol belts, and belt pads. Then we found an assortment of Velcro-equipped sheaths that would attach to the belts—they'd hold everything from wire cutters to electrical crimpers—and finally selected two stout hunt- ing knives.

I walked down the street to an electronics store and bought a cheap autofocus camera, five rolls of ASA 200 color print film, and two Magellan Trailblazer MGRS—Military Grid Reference System—direction-finding devices. They're made for hikers who don't want to get lost in the vast stretches of the Negev desert or down in Sinai. Trailblazers are accurate within fifteen meters— they take their reading from a dozen GPS—global positioning satellites—and work day or night, in rain, fog, or snow. And best of all, they have backlit LCD screens, which would allow me to read the dial in midair. They're operated off a pair of double-A batteries (I bought ten of those—no use waiting for Mr. Murphy to show up and lose one or two). While I paid, Wonder walked two blocks farther, found a hardware store, and bought two heavy-duty wire cutters, three rolls of the Israeli equivalent of duct tape, plus another hundred dollars' worth of miscellaneous goodies.

The total came to less than fifteen hundred bucks. What? *What?* Sorry about the interruption, friends, it's the editor. He's asking why I'm not tapping into the $50 million slush fund we stole from the Russkies. He tells me that $50 mil buys a lot of equipment, and that using it would make this book a lot more exciting.

Well, it might make it exciting, but it wouldn't make it real. See, the best thing about SpecWar is that you can do it on the cheap. You don't need a lot of technogoodies to wage SpecWar. All you need is a small, dedicated, lethal group of men who are willing to go balls to the wall and kill the enemy by any means possible. So, we didn't have to go out and buy a plane, or a ship. As a matter of fact, buying stuff like that tends to attract a lot of attention. And attention is something I didn't want to attract right now.

So we bought low-tech (except for the Magellans) and we remained nicely anonymous. And the best news was that every-thing we bought fit in the rucksacks—with room to spare.

We were back at Avi's before he was. We laid everything out on the cool marble floor of his basement office.

"Something's bothering me," Wonder said as we sorted equip-ment.

"What's that?"

"I don't understand why the Israelis are acting like they are."

It bothered me, too. I'd been chewing on it all night. "It's almost as if they want the fucking nuclear site completed."

Wonder finished coiling his thirty meters of rope and stuffed it in the rucksack. "That makes no sense at all. Why the hell would the Israeli government want the Russkies and the Syrians to build a nuclear site right in their backyard?"

When he said it like that, the answer became so fucking obvious that I wondered why I hadn't seen it before. You get it, don't you?

You say you're a little hazy.

Okay, gentle reader, allow me to lay things out for you.

- Item: the Russkies, with the help of Werner Lantos and Ehud Golan, have been slipping equipment into Syria, to help the Syrians build a bomb.
- Item: Werner works for CIA and Ehud for Mossad.
- Item: the Israeli government has recently changed—it's become a lot more hard-line when it comes to the peace process and dealing with its Arab neighbors.
- Item: the Syrians are the biggest stumbling block in the current peace process.
- Item: the current Israeli government does not necessarily want to trade land for peace when it comes to giving up the

Golan Heights, because the Golan is a very important strategic piece of real estate.

Have you caught on yet?

No? Okay. Let us deal with all of the above items as a part of a single problem. The problem: how to make peace with Syria but not give up the Golan Heights.

The answer was crystal clear, at least so far as I was concerned: it was to make the Golan Heights irrelevant. And the best way to make the Golan irrelevant was by attacking Syria directly—beating the shit out of the Syrians so that when peace was negotiated, it would be a peace firmly in the favor of the Israelis.

And how to do that without being condemned by the rest of the world?

Israel has always claimed the right of preemptive attack if it discovers nuclear weapons in a neighboring state. Remember how Menachem Begin used the Israeli Air Force to strike at the Iraqi nuclear reactor at Ossirak, just outside Baghdad, in 1981.

Same principle here. Wait until the Syrians have almost completed the project, then hit 'em—hard. Destroy the site with smart bombs—and maybe hit a few other targets as well.

I see you out there—the asshole with your hand in the air. You want to know why the United States would condone an attack against Syria; an attack that would almost certainly result in a regionwide war, when they could solve this same problem quietly. By quietly, gentle reader, I mean by using yours truly.

Good question. I believe the answer is because there are those near and dear to the White House these days who think that quick-fix schemes are better than long-term solutions. Of precisely which near-and-dear ones am I thinking? The current national security adviser comes to mind. Our NSC chairman, Matt Thompson, is a former journalist and Harvard professor who fancies himself the world's new Metternich. Matt's college roommate at Yale (after the requisite Rhodes scholarship to Oxford, the MIT economics Piled higher and Deeper degree, and the stint at a slightly oozed to right-of-center Washington think tank) was recently confirmed as the new DCI—the Director of Central Intelligence. These two self-proclaimed solons have money, position, and as you can well imagine, lots of friends in high places—including one old pal for whom "Ruffles and Flourishes" and "Hail to the Chief" is played every time he enters a room on ceremonial occasions. The only thing these two sphincter-brained schlemiels don't have is smarts.

So one—i.e., *moi*—can just see 'em, sitting with their tasselled loafers up on their big walnut desks, coming up with this hare-brained scheme of how to teach a lesson in realpolitik to the Syrians, reshuffle the balance of power in the Middle East, and catapult the United States into the dominant and pivotal role of power broker/peacemaker. Except for one little problem: neither of these two J. Pressed assholes have the guts or the backbone to do it using American resources—after all, if they did, they'd have to go up to Capitol Hill, salute the flag—or at least the chairman of the Senate Select Committee on Intelligence—and stand behind what they were doing.

Now let's add another ingredient to this Metternichian mélange. Remember how Werner Lantos talked about surrogates back at Fouquet's? Remember how he hinted that all sorts of things were taking place at the highest levels of government?

Well, I think Werner had it partially right. What he didn't realize is that he was the one being used. How, you ask? Simple: let me postulate, gentle reader, that the CIA and Mossad have concocted this whole charade as a sting operation that will ultimately allow Israel to go to war against Syria.

How? By using the same principle as any martial arts *sensei* teaches his students on the very first day: always use your enemy's momentum to help you defeat him.

The Russians want to re-emerge as a superpower. They were using their mafiya, as well as their agents of influence—like Werner Lantos—to help them do that. But Werner's also a double agent for Langley. So, somewhere along the line, CIA and Mossad decided to use Werner, Ehud, the Russkies, and the Russian Mafiya to sell nuclear weapons materials to Syria—there's the sting part of it. And Haffez el-Assad, like the big-mouth basshole he is, swallowed the lure. But all along, CIA and Mossad knew exactly what was going on.

Now, what the hell does that have to do with me? I will tell you what it has to do with me. Remember the files I took from Paul Mahon's office in Moscow? Remember that there were one or two elements I couldn't figure out at the time? Like the Post-It note on which Paul had written that cryptic list of words. *Sting, Mafiya— cover, Agcy/Mos,* and *Call KR.*

Now, that scrap of paper made perfect sense. Sting was what Paul had discovered. It was an Agcy/Mos (Central Intelligence Agency/Mossad) sting. They'd used their agents of influence, used the Russian Mafiya as cover, and piggybacked it all on a Russian op to climb back on the world stage as a superpower. We'd always believed that Paul had been killed because he was unraveling the relationship between Russian military/intelligence ops and the mafiya. Now, it occurred to me that maybe he started to put the big picture together—and he'd been killed to keep him quiet before he could get hold of KR—Rear Admiral Kenneth Ross—and blow the op. Killed by whom? Fact is, whether Werner had pushed the buttons that set Paul's murder in motion, or Ehud had, it didn't matter. They were both condemned men, so far as I was concerned.

I plugged in the Chairman's secure phone and dialed Kenny Ross's number.

"Ross."

"It's me." Quickly, I summarized the stream-of-consciousness thoughts that had been running through my brain. "Did Paul ever call you about any of that?"

"No."

"But it makes sense, doesn't it?"

"You bet it does. Especially in light of what you've already passed on to the Chairman."

"Ken"—it was the first time I'd used his Christian name since we'd been on the USS *Humpback* together—"I gotta talk to the Chairman about this, right now."

"I think you do, too," Ken Ross answered, his voice grim.

Less than two minutes later, the Chairman of the Joint Chiefs was on the line. I didn't waste his time. Once more, I laid things out the way I saw 'em. The only sound I heard was the scratching of Kenny Ross's rollerball on paper.

I finished speaking, only to be answered a second time by silence. I waited until I found it impossible to wait any longer. "General?"

I heard him sigh. "You've gotta be right," he told me. "Given the way things are going at the White House—plus the way Langley, State, and the National Security Council are treating us—you're probably absolutely on the money." I could hear him breathing heavily. Under his breath, the Chairman said to no one in particular, "Those lying, cocksucking sons of bitches."

I broke in. "So?"

There was another pause. This one longer than the first. "I spoke to the secretary of defense after your last call to Ken," General Crocker said. "I took your faxed material over to his house and explained what is going on. SECDEF has made it clear to me that he cannot allow those naive idiots to screw things up any longer. Let me quote his words to you exactly, Dick, so there is no mistake about his feelings. 'These people are placing our national security in jeopardy,' is what he said. And when he saw your fax concerning that, that"—the Chairman struggled to find the right word— "diplomatic embarrassment who's currently the DCM in Moscow, that put him right over the edge. He called the White House and took everything to the president. Straight away. Saw him in the residence, alone."

That was good news. It has been a while since our civilian leadership did much leading. "What happened?"

The Chairman's voice was tinged with bemusement. "The president caved. You know how he is—he goes with the last piece of advice he's been given, and SECDEF made sure he was the only man in the room. He came back to the Pentagon with a goddamn handwritten National Security Finding in his hands."

There was a pause on the line. Then—it was quite incredible—I could almost see General Crocker's right thumb and index fingers pointing like a Colt .45 in my direction. "So, go to work, Dick," his voice came through loud and clear. "We're not gonna let this happen. It's wrong. Plain wrong—and immoral to boot. You go get 'em, Dick—*get* 'em. And don't fail. But do it quietly—stealth. No ripples, because we don't want to alert anybody at Langley or Foggy Bottom. And work fast, because by this time tomorrow when the matter of Bart Wyeth has been brought up at the cabinet meeting—which it will—the DCI, the national security adviser, and the secretary of state are all going to know that they've been outflanked, they'll pile on and the president'll probably reverse himself, and ask SECDEF for the finding back."

Avi returned at 1830. He'd managed to get two PCMCIA cards, and one of AMAN's explosive-packed telephones. "But don't we need detonators? We can't use the computers, can we?"

Wonder shook his head. "Nope." He scratched his red hair. "I can improvise a detonator out of a .223 cartridge. But we'd still need some kind of fusing material." He looked at Avi. "You know anyplace to get blasting caps or fuse?"

Avi's face was blank.

Lightbulb. "I do—" I punched Wonder's shoulder. "There's that construction site down the street—the town houses we passed on the way here."

Wonder's face lit up. "Let's go shopping," he said, reaching for his set of lock picks.

"Maybe we should wait until it's dark," I suggested.

By 2230, we had two pencil detonators, three blasting caps, and twenty feet of fast-burning fuse. While Wonder built IEDs in the kitchen, Avi and I checked the weapons, loaded magazines, and finished packing the equipment we'd be taking. It would take Wonder a bit of time to rig the plastic explosives. The phone was easier: it had an ingenious, multifaceted remote device. You could make the instrument ring—as if there were an incoming call—then set it off. That, Avi explained, was because many of the targets had learned to let their wives and kids answer their phones. So you'd call, wait until you heard the right voice on the other end, then blow the fucker's head off. Or, in basic mode you could just make the phone go boom by releasing the safety, then pressing the transmit button on the detonator.

Having the explosives obstacles solved left us only one small problem: our method of insertion. Frankly, I didn't think we had much of a choice. We didn't have documents to get us into Lebanon through Cyprus, and without military support, a wet approach— that is, a covert insertion by sea—was going to be hard. Besides, such tactics take time—and time was something we didn't have much of. I took one of Avi's huge pilotage maps from the file of them on his desk, and spread it out on the floor.

"We go by air," I said, my finger tracing what I thought might be an acceptable route.

"Huh?" Avi was confused.

"We drop in on 'em—do the job, and get out as best we can, using whatever we find." I turned the pilotage chart so he could see it. "Here's where we have to go. If we can come up with a plane that will take us to twelve thousand feet, we can jump here"—I pointed to a spot twenty-five kilometers west of the target—"and HAHO in."

"HAHO?" Avi shook his head. "Don't understand."

"High altitude, high opening—we use flat chutes and we parasail. We come down five, six kliks away, and go the rest of the way on foot."

"Dick—" Avi's face had a panicked look that I didn't like at all.

"What?"

"That HAHO part makes me very nervous."

"Why—you made it through jump school." I'd seen Avi in uniform. He wore silver jump wings above his ribbons.

"Five jumps," Avi said. "Five jumps get you your wings. All of them were *automat.*"

"*Automat?*"

"Where you hook your line inside the plane—"

"Static jumps."

"Static, yes." Avi swallowed hard. "And I hated each one more than the last."

He was actually sweating now. "Dick—they had to throw me out of the damn plane every time. I mean it. Somebody really picked me up and threw me out the door."

"The hatch."

"You can call it whatever you like—but no matter what you call it, I didn't go through it willingly."

I had to laugh. Here was a man who could talk his way through a roadblock of hostiles without losing his cool. Who could operate in half a dozen countries where, if they knew who he was, they'd literally skin him alive. And he'd conquered his fears enough to make those five jumps and wear his wings. And now he was nervous about HAHO.

Let me tell you something about human character, my friends. It is this: when I go into battle, I would rather have with me a man who knows he is afraid but goes on anyway, than a man who professes no fear at all. That's how I used to select my shooters. I didn't want the gazelles—the ones who'd breezed through training seemingly without breaking a sweat. I wanted those men who tried, almost failed—maybe even did fail—but came back again and again and again until they'd made it. Those are the men with heart. Those are the shooters who will go until the end. Those are the true Warriors, who will not stop until they have completed their mission.

"I'm not laughing at you, Avi—I'm laughing with you."

"That doesn't make me feel any better about doing something I've never done. Dammit, Dick, I've never even used a flat chute."

He had a point there. It's one thing to drop out of an aircraft at five thousand or seventy-five hundred feet in a static jump, and float into a nice, flat drop zone that's been scouted for wind conditions. It's a whole 'nother thing to go out of a plane at night into weather and wind currents you know nothing about, and drop into hostile territory. Moreover, things get compounded by the presence of Mr. Murphy when you're trying to parasail eight, nine, even ten miles.

"We could practice," Wonder interjected. He'd wandered downstairs and was looking at the map over my shoulder. "Are there any parachute clubs around?"

"Yes, but—"

I cut him off. I saw the look in Avi's eyes. There was no way he was going to learn the fine art of HAHO. And certainly not in the next twenty-four hours or so. Mr. Murphy had obviously joined us tonight.

Sometimes, gentle reader, the answer is so simple that you do not see it immediately. I slapped the map with the palm of my hand. "Let's keep it simple, stupid—Avi jumps with me."

The Israeli looked confused.

"If you have commercial jump schools in Israel, you have tandem chutes here, too. They have about half again as much surface as your normal chute, so they can take the extra weight." I grinned at him. "And frankly, you probably don't weigh much more than my combat pack, so maybe we only need a single chute for us to jump together."

"Don't make jokes, Dick."

"Avi, it's simple. We hook up—your harness gets attached to mine—we go out the plane, and I fly your ass in."

"But—"

"It beats walking."

"*Lech la-azalel*—go to hell." He rolled his eyes. He groaned. He sighed. He hyperventilated. But I knew Avi was gonna do it. And so did he.

"Okay, if we're really going to do this I'll call Koby."

"Who's Koby?"

"A sergeant I know. We were in the same unit some years ago. He has a farm near Zichron."

"So?" The significance of what Avi was saying escaped me.

"Zichron—*Zichron Yaakov*—in English it means Jacob's memorial. It was built in 1886 by the Baron de Rothschild. Just about twenty-five kilometers south of Haifa. They have a little flying school up there—and they sport jump. Zichron is high—on a mountain overlooking the sea. Koby's a pilot, too—he flies every chance he gets at the jump school at Binyamina."

Wonder repeated the word. "Binyamina?"

"The next town to the south from Zichron," Avi explained. "Originally, Koby was in the Air Force. He loved it, but they told him he didn't have the right disposition to be a fighter pilot, and they washed him out."

"What do you mean 'the right disposition'?"

"He was too aggressive—way off the charts on the Air Force personality tests. And he hated officers. Made a habit of beating the crap out of them. So he was transferred to the Army, and he became a commando—I met him in *Saye'eret Egoz*."

I liked Koby already—in fact, there were a few officers I would have liked to introduce him to—starting with one Pinckney Prescott the Turd. "Give him a call. Can you tell him what we need without being specific?" I didn't want to alert anyone who might be listening in.

"Can do. The only question is how soon you want to go?"

"Tonight—now."

"So soon? But—"

"Avi, we don't have time to waste. You know it, and I know it. My Chairman wants to move—*now*. Besides, sooner or later somebody in Jerusalem or Washington is going to guess what we're up to. So—we go before they have a chance to react. If we're successful, they'll find a way to make us look good. If we screw up—WTF, we're expendable, right?"

Avi shrugged. "You know, I never really wanted to make *tat-aluf*—brigadier general—anyway."

I laughed. "What's your point?" Avi and I were cut from the same cloth—the rough kind that doesn't look as good in stars as it does with scars. The day I took the oath to become an officer I knew I'd never make flag rank. In fact, that was a part of the deal I made with myself when I went to OCS. I became an officer to lead SEALs into battle—not to become CNO or command a fleet. "So?"

In response, he walked over to the telephone that sat on his small, teak desk, plucked the receiver, and dialed a number from memory. The only words I understood during the next four minutes were the first two—"Koby—hi." The rest was unintelligible. Avi hung up the receiver. He swiveled the desk chair and gave me a thumbs-up. "We're a go," he said.

0100. We pulled the car inside the gates so we could load up in private. Avi went upstairs for a few minutes. When he came down, he said, "Mikki says 'Shalom.'"

"I hope you told her the same," I said.

"Absolutely." He ruffled the dogs behind their ears. *"Tovim klavim*—good dogs." Using his knee, he kept them from coming through the front door. "They think it's time for their early morning walk," he said. He spoke to them again in Hebrew, and closed the door. "I told them—when I get back," he said. "C'mon, c'mon—*hava na moova*."

0154. We'd driven most of the way in silence. Traffic had been light—a few trucks and a sprinkling of cars on the main highway as we flew past Netanya. The road signs spelled out names I'd first learned from the nuns back at Saint Ladislaus Hungarian Catholic School: SHEHEM—114 KM. MEGGIDO—65 KM. NAZARETH—142 KM. Just south of Hadera, where an orangy blaze of sodium spotlights illuminated the twin smokestacks of a huge power plant that sat on the sea, Avi veered off onto a smaller, unlit highway. We sped past farms and small villages. At one point the interior of the car filled with the pungent aroma of fresh manure. "Duck farm," Avi said by way of explanation.

A few minutes later, he swerved off the highway onto an unmarked dirt road. The small car bounced along the ruts, scraping the muffler as we began a long, slow ascent up a series of S-curves that took us higher and higher. The air got much cooler. "Look—" Avi pointed. A small deer stood, transfixed by the headlights, thirty yards in front of us. "We're almost there," he said, gunning the engine and sending the deer scampering into the thorny underbrush.

0205. The road leveled off, bringing us onto a wide, flat plain. As the car's headlights swept the area in front of us, I realized that we'd driven onto one end of a basic rural landing strip. I could make out a series of large sheds whose sides bore huge Hebrew lettering some distance away. Two of them had lights on inside. A pickup truck was parked next to the smaller of the sheds. Avi drove up and parked beside the truck, switched off the ignition, climbed out, stretched and yawned.

Wonder and I did the same. "Where are we?"

"Just north of a little town called Binyamina. This is a private airstrip—mainly it's crop dusters that hire out to the farmers. But Koby flies out of here, too—he ferries jumpers for the jump school."

We walked into the shed, and I felt right at home. It was a rigger's loft—long tables for packing chutes at the near end, offices and supplies on the far side. A huge bear of a man in his fifties, his face as suntanned as stained oak, stood packing a sky blue, flat chute. He was dressed in an olive drab flight suit, its sleeves rolled past his muscular forearms. Cinched around his waist was a black nylon pistol belt. From the belt a tactical holster descended, attached to a thick thigh. I could make out the easily recognizable butt of a Browning High Power pistol protruding from the double-tied flap. The man looked up, and a big smile spread over his face. "Avi, *ahlan.*"

"Shalom, Koby."

I watched as the two grasped one another the way Warriors do after long separation. Avi led his shipmate[13] over to meet us.

"Koby, this is my friend Dick Marcinko—he's the *Amerikai* I worked with in Lebanon. Dick, this is Koby Shomron."

Koby's size twelve hand was as tough as alligator hide. His grip tightened around my own hand like a blacksmith's pincers. "Good to meet you, mister officer," he growled like the sergeant he was, his blue eyes meeting my own without blinking. "Avi says you're a good man—even though you don't wear stripes."

"I used to."

"Did you? Good—I hope you didn't forget what they mean."

"I try not to."

"Good." He hooked a calloused thumb in Avi's direction. "He never forgot. Matter of fact he still looks like a skinny marink corporal—I think maybe Mikki doesn't feed him enough—but he can still get places and do things, y'know, even with his officer's epaulettes." Koby ran a big hand through his thatch of thick, silver hair and looked over at Wonder, who stood behind my right shoulder. "And what about you, *gingi,* can you get places and do things?"

Wonder introduced himself warily. Koby looked him up and

---

[13]Yes, I know they'd probably never literally served in a ship together, but remember what I said earlier about shipmatedom—it can be a matter of shared risks and responsibilities rather than the actual oceangoing experience.

down. "I guess he looks as if he can handle himself," he said to no one in particular. "Besides—I like *gingis*. I have two myself." He looked over at Avi and broke out laughing.

"What the fuck's a *gingi?*" Wonder's face took on a petulant expression.

"It means a redhead," Avi explained. "We used to have a saying in the Army—that after a war, there are a lot of *gingi* kids born, because, you know—our peckers, they're rusty from being away from home."

"Yeah, well, in my family it comes natural," Wonder said. "We're Scottish, in case you didn't know."

"I like the Scots," Koby said. "They make good booze—Jewish booze—J&B."

"Yeah, well listen, bub—" Wonder started. He'd balled his fists and taken a step in Koby's direction.

Avi looked at Wonder. "He's pulling your leg," he said.

Wonder thought about it for three or four seconds. "I knew that," he said.

Koby pointed toward a storage locker behind him. "The chutes are in there," he said. "They're already packed, but I know that you'll want to make them again over yourselves." He paused. "All except Avi, of course." He clapped me on the shoulder, moving me forward about six inches. Believe me, the man was strong. "In case you didn't know, Avi doesn't like heights. I don't know what I did wrong to get stuck with him the first day of jumping school but I did. By the second day I realized I was in charge of making sure he made it through so he could wear paratrooper's wings."

He looked at Avi, whose face was noticeably reddening. "So, every jump, I threw him out of the plane." Koby started to giggle. "First, we were using an old Dakota with a removeable hatch cover. He left fingerprints on the molding he was squeezing it so tight." The Israeli's head tilted back and he began to laugh uncontrollably. "Every jump—I'd pick him up"—Koby mimed the process—"and toss"—his arms swung forward in a big arc—"and he'd scream all the way down 'You *ben zonaaaaaa!*'" He wiped tears with his fist. "Then, then when we got to the Hercules, y'know—with the ramp—I had to—"

"Koby—*shtock*—enough," Avi interrupted. "I told him all about it. He knows—he knows. So, stop already."

"Oh, but it was so funny—" The big non-com daubed at his eyes and waved his friend off, "The point is, if he's going to jump, you'd better make sure he goes first out the hatch, otherwise you're going to be on the ground by yourself and he'll be waving 'shalom, *litrahot*, have a nice trip' from the plane."

"I understand."

"So, okay, mister officer," he asked, "what's the plan?"

I explained how I wanted to insert.

The Israeli shook his head. "No way Avi can do that. He's not trained."

"I know. That's why he and I'll tandem down."

Koby roared with laughter. "*Shiga-on*—fantastic idea." He looked at me again, this time with a hint of grudging respect. "I think maybe you were a sergeant once."

0250. Wonder and I repacked the chutes we'd use, and went over the harnesses carefully. The chutes were old, but they'd been well cared for. The tandem was a big, nine-cell commercial Vector. I'd jumped the military version before, and liked the way it responded. We sat them next to the shed's door, then packed and repacked the rucksacks. I covered all the rifle muzzles with tape to prevent their getting filled with earth on landing. We loaded magazines and set them inside the pouches we'd bought, then taped the pouches shut. Wonder gave me half the explosives he'd rigged and half the detonators. You never want one man carrying all the explosives—if something happens to him, the only thing you can do when you get to your target is point at it and go "Boom."

Koby took me to see the plane we'd be using. It was an old Arava. The Israelis first built Aravas in the late sixties. They're STOL—Short TakeOff and Landing capable—aircraft. I saw a lot of 'em in Honduras and El Salvador in the eighties, when they were used to resupply Contra troops or Salvadoran special forces, landing on rutted eight-hundred-foot dirt runways bulldozed out of jungle only hours before. They can hold seventeen paratroopers, or, when configured as medevacs, twelve stretchers. They also make nice gunships, air-to-air tankers, and ASW—Anti-Submarine Warfare—aircraft. Best of all, they come with oxygen for the crew and jumpers—they have a ceiling of about twenty-five thousand feet.

Of course, our problem was that while the aircraft had oxygen, Avi wasn't at all sure about the condition of the four portable oxygen rigs at the jump school. They had 'em—so the neighborhood paratroopers and *Saye'eret* personnel could practice HALO jumps. But Koby had no idea how full the bottles were—or what condition they were in.

Sometimes, friends, you just have to go. This was one of 'em. Besides, we wouldn't be going out of the plane at any twenty-five thousand feet tonight. I'd figured a ten-mile parasail—and given the charts Koby showed me, as well as what he'd overheard on the shortwave weather report broadcast by the Israeli Air Force tower at Ramat David airfield, thirty miles away, we'd be able to exit the plane at sixteen thousand feet. That's just over a mile above what's normally considered the safety limit for jumps without oxygen.

Safety limits? Yeah—you see, at altitudes above ten thousand feet, the air temperature drops just over three and a half degrees Fahrenheit for every thousand feet of altitude. At ten thousand feet, the air temperature is about twenty-five degrees. At sixteen thousand feet, that temperature drops to just below zero. Then you figure in the windchill factor—the aircraft speed—as well as the ambient humidity, and you end up with what is known as BFC—Ball-Freezing Conditions.

If we were doing this the SEAL way, we'd be outfitted with insulated undergarments, balaclavas, insulated goggles, heavy gloves, and other extremity-protecting accoutrements. Tonight, we had our jumpsuits, some light Nomex gloves, and balaclavas, and commercial plastic helmets and goggles.

But I was worried about the oxygen. Hypoxia can be a real problem at altitudes over ten thousand feet. It manifests itself in many ways—but the most common is drowsiness, sluggish reaction time, loss of muscle control, blurred vision, and a confused, almost drunken thought process. Kind of the way Stevie Wonder feels after a night on the town.

So were the bottles full, or were they empty? How could I tell? There is an answer, friends—one that I learned at the webbed feet of Roy Henry Boehm, the godfather of all SEALs. "Pour warm water over the oxygen bottles," Roy once growled to his SEAL pups—including me. "The place on the bottle where you feel a change in temperature, is where the oxygen level is."

But Roy, what if you're somewhere where there ain't no hot water?

"Then," Godfather Roy quoth, "you improvise. Fuck—you use piss if you have to. Better a smelly O_2 bottle than a dead SEAL."

I looked at Koby. "You have any hot water around this place?" I was downright relieved when he nodded in the affirmative and pointed me toward the spigot.

Six minutes later I knew that the school's oxy bottles were two-thirds full—more than ample to get us where we wanted to go. We'd solved another of the major problems when we'd bought our two commercial Magellan global positioning system finders. Using a flight map, we could punch our destination into the keypads, and the Magellan would read our positions off of a NAVSTAR satellite, giving us up-to-date information about where we were in relation to our target, as well as keeping us on our flight path. Of course, reading a Magellan while you're descending in total darkness at a rate of about sixteen feet a second presents its own unique set of challenges. But we'd worry about such things later.

It was the flight path itself that was going to present the greatest challenge. We're kind of short on time here, but let me give you a nutshell sit-rep. Most of the airspace over Israel, Lebanon, Syria, and Jordan is restricted. There are narrow ATS—Air Traffic Service—routes that are clearly marked on all commercial air pilotage charts. There are also notices on those charts that emphasize that travel outside ATS routes is (and I am repeating the capital letters just as you can see them on the maps) STRICTLY PROHIBITED. IOW—in other words—fly outside commercial air lanes and you can get yourself shot down. No warnings. No "excuse me's."

Now let us go over the map. To our east, lay two of Israel's largest and most well-defended Air Force bases, Ramat David and Meggido. To our north was the dual-use, civilian/military field at Haifa. So our options were somewhat limited. And in any case, all the puddle-jumper tourist sightseeing, crop-dusting, and parachute-school flights from Binyamina were vectored in a narrow north/south corridor, which stretched from the foothills ten kilometers west of Ramat David, to a five-kilometer strip over the ocean. It was a rectangle twenty-five kilometers wide and twenty kilometers long, which ran from just north of Hadera, to just south of Nasholim, so that tourists could overfly the extensive Roman ruins at Caesarea, peek down at the fish-farming *kibbutzim* on the coast, and ogle the *hotti-hot*—which is Hebrew for POA, or pieces of ass—who lay sunning themselves on the miles of first-class shoreline.

Koby stuck a large index finger onto the map just west of Binyamina. "Best bet is here," he said. "We take off, fishhook south, drop down off the plateau, and fly low along the water, maybe nine, ten kilometers out. It's the route the Army normally takes to Lebanon, and with the signature the Arava gives off—and if we

300

maintain radio silence—maybe we'll be mistaken for a flight from Sde Dov."

Sde Dov, you'll remember, is the small airstrip just north of Tel Aviv from which most of Mossad's clandestine flights leave. They don't usually identify themselves to air controllers. Avi ran his finger along the route. His Hebrew sounded to me as if he was in agreement with Koby.

He turned to me. "He's right—we'll stay low—keep it right on the water until we're past Nabatiyeh, then swing inland, cut past the oil tanks near the pipeline at Nahr ez Zahni, then go up the valley, just like we did in '93."

They were talking gibberish so far as I was concerned. In '93, I was chasing stolen Tomahawk nuclear missiles in the Pacific with Red Cell. Avi saw the expression on my face and explained. "We had a bad tango problem back in the early nineties," he said. "The Syrians were allowing half a dozen cells of Hizballah to operate out of the demilitarized zone about twenty kliks from Qiryat Shemona—lots of Katyushas." I knew where Qiryat Shemona is— it's the northernmost town in the Israeli panhandle, and the one most likely to be on the receiving end of hostile rocket fire.

Koby picked up the story. "The UN had set up sensors all along the southern route to keep us out." He spat derisively. "The fucking UN has always been on their side anyway." Koby's finger traced a longer, more circuitous route. "So we came in from the north— here—the way they least expected us. Hooked in from the sea, came down the valley, and took 'em from behind."

I gave Koby a double thumbs-up. "Classic back-door op."

He grinned. "We killed every one of the furshtunken Hizballah—as well as their Syrian advisers and the Russian mercs keeping tabs on the Syrians. The border was quiet for another seven months. No kids spending the night in bomb shelters. No Katyushas. No terror." He thumped Avi's shoulder. "We called it TNT, right?"

Avi nodded.

Wonder grinned. "Because it was an explosive op, right?"

"No—" Koby shook his head. "It's a whatchamacallit—when all the letters mean something."

"An acronym."

"*Biduke*. Acronym. In Hebrew, TNT stands for *Terror Neget Terror*—terror against terror."

I liked the way this man did business. He played for keeps. "We'll do a little TNT tonight, too—although we'll be well north of your AO," I said. I punched the coordinates I'd received from Ken Ross into the Magellan, waited for a readout, and showed the screen to Koby.

The big Israeli made notes on a sheet of paper, took a straight edge, and started drawing lines on his pilotage chart. Moments later, he called me over to the rigging table. "*Nu*, mister officer, what do you think?"

It was so KISS that it had to work. Which is exactly what I told him.

"KISS—keep it simple, stupid," he repeated. "I like that. I like it. You know, in the Israeli Army we also have a saying that means much the same. It is, 'The best is most of times the enemy of good.'"

I knew exactly what he meant, too. You come up with a plan—and it is a good plan, given time restraints, tactical limits, and other operational blips. A workable plan—something that will achieve success. Then, someone way down the line with stars on his collar orders you to stand down and wait. Why? Because staff is working on a better scenario. Or logistics is just about to receive a more sophisticated piece of equipment. Or the intel weenies are almost positively assured of receiving an additional EEI—an essential element of information. And so you stand down. And you wait. And in the meanwhile, crucial opportunities are lost. Your operational edge is gone.

So, in the end, you may achieve that strategic superiority the staff says you will achieve—but tactically, you're fucked. The hostages will already be dead. And you may now have the advantage of the best state-of-the-art equipment—but it doesn't do you any good anymore—because there are no bad guys to use that equipment on. And you may have the most up-to-date information available—but you'll have blown the mission because you waited too long. Bottom line? Lives will have been lost because you sat on your butt waiting for "best," when you should have kicked ass and taken names with "good."

Tonight, we were going to keep it simple, stupid—we'd go with good. Shit—we'd go with mediocre if we had to. We'd use what we had, and we'd do what we'd have to. But we would also win at all costs.

Chapter

21

0323. TAKEOFF WAS SMOOTH. KOBY KILLED THE PLANE'S EXTERIOR lights as soon as we were wheels up, just skimming a dark patch that he told me were banana trees. He banked the Arava to port, and dimmed the instruments. I slid into the copilot's seat. He handed me the pilotage chart, and a red-lensed pencil light.

"Here," he said, a finger pointing at a patch of blue off the coast, "is where there will be a problem." The red light illuminated an irregular-shaped dark blue outline just beyond the hundred fathom mark. It started at Hadera, and ended just south of the Lebanese border. "Military zone," Koby explained. "We run regular sweeps of the area to keep an eye out for the terrorists who come by sea. The Navy drops passive sensors, and we also use naval commando patrols and some kinds of electromagnetic buoys out there."

"What's the solution?"

"I'm going to drop to fifty feet and stay just inside the sensor line, mister officer. One thing in our favor—the Army's more worried about craft coming east or south. The way we're heading—north— and the way we're flying—just the way our Boys might go if they were planning something tonight—maybe we won't get asked any questions." He banked starboard as we slid over the coastline.

"Feet wet, I think," Wonder called out, his nose pressed against one of the small, double-paned aft ports.

I studied the map. "What's our ETA on drop zone?"

"Good question." Koby grinned. "Tonight we're flying—how do you *Amerikai* say it—by the bottoms of our trousers. If I monitor the radio, I give off signals. If I transmit, I give off signals. So we fly quiet, and maybe the plane will tell me what I have to know by how it handles, and what the winds are like. And if not—*inshallah*— what happens will be God's will."

"So like I said, what's our ETA?"

"Just like all officers—you want to know everything." The Israeli laughed. "Okay, mister officer, I would say, fifty-five, sixty minutes at the most—depending on what we find. Look, Dick, by the bird's route, we're only going two hundred, maybe two hundred thirty kilometers. But the long way—maybe three thirty, three forty, something in there. We've been airborne for what—twenty, twenty-one minutes. We're cruising at two hundred sixty kilometers an hour—and we're going to move slower or faster depending on whatever we find. So, you're the one with gold on his shoulders, you do the arithmetic. I'm only the sergeant—I'll fly."

I peered out the windshield for a few minutes, then pulled myself out of the right-hand seat and squeezed my way back. It looked the way most flights do at this stage—the men were grabbing some rest on whatever surface they could lie on. Wonder was sacked out, his head resting on one of the rucksacks. Avi had stretched out on one of the two canvas benches that ran along the sides of the fuselage.

I tapped them with my toe. "Let's start the check," I said.

Wonder cocked an eye. "Killjoy." He rolled over and pulled himself to his feet. Avi did the same. "Okay, Skipper," he said, "what's the plan?"

Good question. I mean, we had a location. But that was about all that we had. How many hostiles were we going to face? Who knew. How would they be positioned? No idea. Was the positioned fortified? And if it was, by whom—Russkies? Syrians? Mercenaries?

All that sat in the negative column. But we had certain advantages, too. I mean, who the fuck would expect us to come a calling in the middle of the night? Not in the middle of fucking Syria. Not forty fucking miles outside Damascus.

Well, friends, let me tell you a story here while Avi, Wonder, and I go over each and every piece of our equipment to make sure that Mr. Murphy has not screwed with it since we checked it last.

Back in December of 1990, when my nasty, hairy Slovak butt was incarcerated down at the Petersburg, Virginia, federal bad boy's prison camp and mayoral blow-job facility, my old friend Colonel Anthony Vincent Mercaldi, he of DIA spookdom, came to visit. Over Diet Pepsi and Moon Pies—two of the more gastronomically sophisticated selections from the visiting room's haute cuisine vending machines—he asked whether or not I'd be interested in a two-week furlough from my lucrative, ninety-eight-cents-an-hour job at the prison's cable factory, where I worked making electrical harnesses for the Department of Defense. The time, he explained, would be spent training a small unit—no more than eight men—of volunteers. When we'd completed our training, we'd all climb on a C-141 StarLifter aircraft, and ship out to an undisclosed location in the Middle East. From there, I'd infiltrate my team into Baghdad, where we would perform the kind of mayhem SpecWarriors get to do only once or twice in their lives—and that's if they are very, very lucky. Those of us who survived our visit, Tony explained, would have to find their own way out.

Now, the panjandrums at SOC—the Special Operations Command—down in Tampa, had already come up with an ops plan for the mission. Their blueprint, which had been designed with the help of three or four dozen think-tank professors, eight levels of middle-management officers who'd never seen the business end of an MP5 in their lives, and a lot of C^2—that's can't cunt—colonels who wanted that brigadier general's star real bad, predicted that the unit's losses would run somewhere between 90 and 100 percent. Friends, so far as I am concerned, those are great odds if your mission includes being on the receiving end of a firing squad. I, however, had other ideas. I can count the men I have lost in battle on the fingers of one hand. The reason I have lost so few is that I don't allow others to make my plans for me. And I don't allow others to set my risks.

So I toasted Tony with my Diet Pepsi, wished him the best of luck—and said, "No, thanks."

Now, you may think that what we're about to do here has roughly the same chance of success that the Baghdad plan had back in 1990. But you are wrong.

Here, we enjoyed almost every one of the elements that make for a successful unconventional operation. We controlled the timing. We enjoyed the element of surprise. We had momentum on our side—and most important of all, we had a will to win that was unwavering. We could not fail. More to the point: we would not fail.

0348. The plane banked to starboard again, and began to climb. I made my way to the cockpit. "We're in the dead zone between Sidon and Barja," Koby said. I noticed that he'd pulled on a pair of night-vision goggles. "There's a Lebanese power station that gives off a tremendous amount of ambient radiation. We've used it before to shield our approach as we head east." He climbed steeply, and banked the plane roughly left, then right. "You guys better secure back there," he said. "It's about to get interesting."

I started aft. "On my way."

"Oh—" he called, his concentration never wavering from the windshield. "Fifteen minutes to your ETA."

"Roger."

I clambered back. Wonder and I got Avi into his harness first, double-checking the straps that held him across the chest, under the legs, and wrapped around his thighs. We attached a reserve chute to his chest—but I made sure to rig the trip cord so I, not he, would control it. I didn't want him yanking on the wanker and killing us both. Below the chute was the oxy bottle we'd use during our initial descent. On his back, two sets of specially designed carabiners would attach to the straps on my own chest, so that as we jumped, I'd ride atop him, which would allow me to guide the big flat chute. If things went wrong, I could cut Avi away, open his reserve for him, then worry about myself.

I pulled the straps tight around his thighs, waist, and chest. The fit seemed good. I attached myself to him to check the play of the nylon straps.

I showed Avi how I wanted him to position his body as we'd go out of the aircraft. "Is this good for you, too?" I asked as we scrunched together. I nestled closer to him and hugged. "Matter of fact, if you had tits on your back I'd marry you now."

He told me to perform an anatomically impossible feat first in Hebrew, then in Arabic, then in Russian, and then in English.

I laughed. "I didn't know you cared."

We disengaged, so we could help him attach his rucksack and his weapon. "Don't forget," I said. "I'll tell you when you cut the pack loose. You don't want to land on top of it."

Avi nodded.

"Got the phone?"

He patted the pocket on his left thigh and gave me an upturned thumb.

"Phone detonators?"

He checked and found them in his right breast pocket. He took one and handed it to me. "I can't use them both—you keep one."

"Good idea." I stowed it securely. I looked closely at Avi. His face was white. He was hyperventilating a little, now.

"You gonna be sick?" I asked.

"No—I'm fine."

I knew damn well he wasn't fine—wouldn't be fine until he had both of his size seven-and-a-half shoes on terra firma. But he'd have to live with it.

I ran a top-to-bottom check on Wonder. His chute was okay. His reserve was tight on his chest. His right wrist bore the big-dial altimeter. His AK and ammo mags were stowed, strapped, taped, and double-taped.

"Got the plastic?"

He tapped the pair of zippered compartments on his chest. "Safe and sound. You?"

I did the same. I shrugged into the big tandem flat chute, and the reserve. Wonder double-checked my web gear, and ran his hands over the rucksack that hung below my butt.

0358. Koby called me forward. He'd connected up one of the cockpit oxygen masks. "We're at five thousand meters and climbing," he said. He pointed to the readout ticking away on the Magellan dial. "Six minutes to release. Plug yourselves in and blow the hatch." I gave him a thumbs-up and headed aft.

Koby was a good special operations pilot—that means he'd stayed down at wave level, climbing to the release altitude of twelve thousand feet only when he absolutely had to.

But now we were climbing and it was time to plug in. I made sure everybody's masks were tightly strapped, and we ran the hose nozzles into the oxy tits. There was one element working in our favor. This was a commercial jump-school plane, not a military craft. Which meant, so far as I was concerned, that the owners would have probably taken good care of the internal oxygen system, since they didn't want a bunch of lawsuits from their students.

I breathed deep. It smelled like everyday O_2 to me.

I saw Koby's gloved hand waving. Three fingers—he'd put the plane into a slow arc now, changing our heading to due south, and into a gentle, gentle climb. Wonder and I went aft and unbolted the port-side hatch, which we stowed and tied down. I held on and leaned outside, the blast of freezing air feeling great on my face. It was still dark, although there was the barest hint of crepuscular light coming from the east, over where I knew Iraq lay more than three hundred miles away.

Time to move. I pulled Avi up, turned his back to me and attached us together. I looked back toward the cockpit.

Fuck—Koby'd obviously put the goddamn plane on autopilot, because he was moving aft toward us. He'd pulled on a chute and a reserve, strapped a combat pack to his ass, and slung an AK over his shoulder. His jump helmet was tight, his goggles covered his eyes, and he had an oxy mask plugged into the quart-size bottle that hung at belly level.

I gave him a "WTF" look. He tossed me the bird and yanked the mask off long enough to tell me that there was no way I was going to HAHO with Avi without him coming along to watch. "I've been waiting to see this for twenty years, mister officer," he said. "The plane's on autopilot—it'll make it back out over the ocean easily if somebody doesn't shoot it down first."

I pulled my mask. "I'll buy you another plane when we get back," I shouted over the wind noise. "It'll be my pleasure."

"Hein-hein—thank you so very much, mister officer." Koby's head inclined slightly in my direction. "Avi told me you'd come into money recently." He laughed. "But this is for pleasure, this jump—the pleasure of seeing Avi squirm. Besides—you could use an extra pair of hands I think."

There are times, friends, when even I am smart enough to take "yes" for an answer—and this was one of 'em. I answered him by giving him a thumbs-up, grabbing the hatch rail, and throwing Avi and me out into the darkness.

The turbulence caught us right away—blast of cold air—and twisted our bodies belly up—the wrong way if you want to HAHO. I tried to throw a hump—arch my back to flip us around, but Avi wasn't giving me any help. I pounded on his shoulders, trying to hint—in my subtle SEAL way—to let me do the fucking work, lay back, and enjoy the ride. Somehow, I don't think he was getting the message.

I slapped him on the back of the helmet hard enough to make him cringe—even in the air blast. That quieted him down enough so that I was able to roll, shift, and pull.

I heard the chute release go, felt the first tug, and then all of a sudden I was kicked in the balls by the biggest mule I'd ever felt. It's bad enough when I pull—I'm over 200 pounds, and the shock of the chute opening is considerable. Now, between my pack, weapons, ammo, and other miscellaneous goodies, plus Avi's weight and supplies, we were probably somewhere in the 500-pound area. Try focusing that kind of weight entirely on your testicles some dark night and see if you don't feel like singing soprano for a while.

There is a SEAL technical term for what I'd just experienced. It is called FUCKING PAIN.

But there was no time to think about pain right now—I was more concerned with the condition of the nine cells of the parachute. There was a sudden drop—about thirty feet—and I looked up to see the whole front edge of the chute folding under.

It was a motherfucking wind shear. Why they happen, who knows—and right now, who the fuck cares. All that mattered was that it had happened, and the cells were beginning to collapse on me.

Normal rate of descent is about sixteen feet a second. By the altimeter on my wrist and the pumping of my heart, I guesstimated that we were dropping at about thirty feet a second, which—lemme do some quick arithmetic here—works out to just under twenty-four miles an hour. For the record, let me say that hitting the ground at twenty-four miles an hour is not recommended under any circumstances.

I threw my body—and Avi's—to the left. No response. I pulled our combined weight up three feet or so on the starboard side risers and steering lines, then dropped abruptly. There was still no change in our velocity. I tried it on the port side—playing with the lines, twisting my body, shifting side to side, all the while screaming the kind of epithets that I hoped would encourage the big chute to fill properly—things like, "you motherfucking cocksucking shit-eating piece of crap—fill the fuck up."

Once in a great while, inanimate objects actually do take direction when it is positively offered. And, as I watched, the edge straightened, the last of the cells filled out, and our rate of descent slowed to a pace I'd call tolerable.

I slammed Avi in the back, and shouted in his ear through my mask that we were okay. He didn't reply except to hunch his shoulders even more than they'd been hunched. My guess was that he'd closed his eyes and he wasn't gonna open 'em until we were on the ground.

I checked the Magellan that was taped to my left forearm. We were more or less on course—even with the slight headwinds that I sensed we were facing into. Altimeter check. We were at eleven thousand feet—we'd jumped at about thirteen five, maybe fourteen—and we had an eight-mile sail ahead of us.

Us—time to check to see we were all still alive. I did a quick three-sixty to make sure that Wonder and Koby hadn't flamed out. If this had been a training mission, I could have made 'em out easily because in training we normally wear strobes on our helmets or taped to our ankles, so we can pick one another up in the dark. Now, all I saw were shadows. But I could, I believed, make out the distinctive, fluttering sound of chute foils nearby. They make a kind of throaty, ruffling noise that once you hear you'll never forget.

I checked the compass again. Had to keep a straight heading. The LZ I'd designated was a narrow—that's five miles or so—area just east of the demilitarized zone in the low foothills that eventually climbed to Mount Hermon, and just west of an old Palestinian refugee camp—more a small city than a camp—called Jdaidet Aartouz. In the old days—that is, during the days of the "hot" war between the Palestinians and the Israelis—the Fatah Provisional Command, a pro-Syrian Palestinian terrorist unit commanded by Colonel Sa'id Musa Mugragha (Abu Musa), maintained a clandestine base there. I knew the place—it was one of the locations Avi and I had recced back in the eighties—and I didn't much care for it. Jdaidet Aartouz was less than fifteen miles from the outskirts of Damascus. And Abu Musa had for a long time been a paid agent of the KGB.

0402. Eight thousand feet and descending. The ground was indistinct but I knew it was there all right—there were occasional lights in the tiny villages that dotted the foothills to our right—west of the glide path. At one point, directly below us, a bright white strobe flashed in an irregular pattern. I remembered from the map it was a smokestack just southeast of Sahl As Sahara.

0405. Five thousand two hundred feet according to the altimeter on one wrist, four-and-a-half miles from our drop zone according to the Magellan on the other. I tapped Avi on the back to let him know we were okay. As I did, I heard a change in the sound of the air as it raced through the airfoils. I pulled at the lines but didn't get a response. Yanked again. Nothing. Suddenly, we were veering to our left—eastward, directly toward Damascus—caught in a freak gust.

No way. I leaned forward and shouted in Avi's ear "Stay with me," and I put all of my energy and all of our combined weight into the right-hand steerage line to make it respond. I looked up. The right-hand foil was beginning to collapse on me. Not good. Not with this much weight, and an unbalanced situation.

I loosened up on the right-hand steerage line, and put my weight on both risers. Then, with my forearms, shoulders, back and legs taking every bit of the strain they could, I pulled, and dropped, pulled, and dropped, pulled, and dropped, trying to "shake" the chute so its foils would even out. I didn't care how cold the air racing past us was—I was sweating through this one, friends.

Finally, I felt the chute even out, and our eastward arc ceased. I swung us back onto course, hoping that Koby and Wonder hadn't experienced the same detour that I had.

0409. Two thousand five hundred feet. The descent had been slowed by a head wind—which managed to keep us higher than expected. That was fine with me. I wanted to assemble over the target, and then come down in slow deliberate circles, so that we could pick our landing spot.

That's the way I liked to practice when I had my guys do twenty, thirty, even forty HAHO jumps in a short period of time over the Arizona desert back in the US of A. Everyone forms up, and we come in nice and tight—a unit that's full of tactical integrity. Of course, in Arizona, we had miles and miles of open desert—all belonging to any number of government agencies, and nicely encircled by hundreds of miles of chain-link fence. Here, the ground was open, it was occupied by people who wouldn't mind slitting our throats given half a chance, and I had no idea what the fuck we'd find once we set our feet down.

0410:40. I could make out the ground now—two to three miles off to my left there were the lights of the Syrian airfield at Mezzeh. Below, a two-lane highway wove back and forth. I steered right. The landing point was a hilly, scrub-covered area out of sight of the highway, close to the same abandoned camp Avi and I had reconnoitered.

Piece of cake. No big trees. No tall buildings—I hate landing in heavily wooded areas. The fucking tree limbs beat the shit out of your body as you come in. Often, you can't flare and land—instead, you have to drop like the proverbial sack of shit—which is exactly how you feel when your tired, sore, hyperextended, and aching bones hit the deck.

I was just congratulating myself on a textbook approach when Avi started beating a tattoo on my gut with his elbows—jamming them into me *bam-bam-bam* as if he was running for his life. I looked down and saw that he actually *was* running—his legs were going a mile a minute. Then I looked ahead and realized why: five, maybe six hundred feet directly in front of us—and maybe two hundred feet below—a series of high-tension power lines crossed our trajectory path. Two hundred meters to our left I could make out one of the big support pylons. A hundred meters or so to our right was another. The lines hung between in a casual, lethal arc.

My friends, the reaction time in a situation like this one is zero. If you think, you will die. I did not think. I grabbed the starboard steerage line and hung on it with every ounce of Avi's and my combined weight. We went into a tight turn, the chute veered right, we began to pick up speed, and we descended at twice the speed at which we should have been moving. What am I talking about? I'm talking about a testicle-sucking thirty yards in about a second and a half. But it also carried us just under the lowermost of the high-tension lines.

The corkscrewing didn't help our landing either. I cut our combat packs loose at the very last second so we'd lose about a hundred pounds of weight. It helped—but not much: we spiraled in more or less uncontrollably—no way to flare or use the natural air-brake capabilities of the big flat chute. So the final fifteen yards of descent might be best described as sheer terror punctuated by potential trauma.

We hooked and dragged and landed in a fucking heap—Avi on the bottom, me atop him, and the chute covering everything. I reached between us to release the harnesses.

He groaned loudly, then went silent.

"Avi—what's up?"

He didn't answer. I threw the canopy off, rolled him over, and checked. His neck had pulse—so he was alive. I unstrapped the helmet, ripped off his goggles, and ran my hands over his body in a superficial search for broken bones. None. His face was white—no color at all. But he was breathing, and I couldn't see any blood. I'd probably knocked the sonofabitch cold when I'd landed on top of him.

I pulled the rucksack up, opened the valve on the Camelbak water container, drizzled some on my hands, and rubbed Avi's face. Finally, his eyes opened. "What the hell—"

"You just lived through your first HAHO, boychik," I said. "Welcome to the club."

"If this is living . . ." The Israeli tried to sit up, but he had a hard time doing so.

I pushed him back down. "Lie there. Catch your breath. Give it a few seconds."

He lay back, closed his eyes, and rolled an arm over his forehead. "Great idea. Wake me when this is all over, okay?"

I disengaged the tangle of harnesses, and had just begun to lock and load our weapons and run an equipment check when I heard movement to my left. I swung the AK around. Wonder and Koby came over a low rise through the scrub brush, bearing their chutes and equipment.

The big Israeli looked at Avi's inert form. "Just like always," he said. "But he's alive, right?"

I nodded.

"Did he throw up?"

"Not yet."

My answer brought a wry smile to Koby's creased face. "Then he's definitely improving as a jumper. So, congratulations, mister officer."

We'd begun on a good note: no equipment was busted, nothing had been lost during the long and bumpy ride down. Avi even turned on the cell phone.

"You can't receive anything here, can you?"

He listened carefully. "No, not here—not quite," he said. "But IDF keeps cells open right to the northern edge of the security area in Lebanon—that's less than thirty-five miles away. If we were five, ten, maybe fifteen miles closer . . ."

That, friends, should give you some idea about the distances in this part of the world. We were sitting on the fucking outskirts of Damascus and there were Israeli cell towers that we could almost use.

We buried the chutes, then pulled off our jumpsuits so that we looked a little more like civilians—although not many civilians go around with combat "Y" suspenders, pistol belts, rucksacks, and automatic weapons. But WTF—you do what you gotta do.

0438. Wonder took point. We'd actually landed twelve hundred or so yards south of the high power masts—more than four kilometers closer to our objective than planned. We were perhaps three hundred yards west of a two-lane highway, in a rocky, duned area punctuated by clumps of scrub brush and thorn bushes. If we paralleled the road, we'd come to our Magellan point in four kliks—or about twenty-five minutes of walking. But it was getting late—or early, depending on how you look at things, and I wanted to make some time. Daybreak was just after six in these parts—and despite a high cloud cover moving from the west, I wanted to get inside our target before it became easy to spot us.

So we jogged. Let me tell you something about jogging in sand. It is no fun. It is also hard on the calves, the thighs—and every muscle, joint, and tendon in between. After about six minutes, I realized that Steve and I might make it, but that Avi and Koby would be DBA—Dead Before Arrival. I changed the pace. Jog two hundred paces, walk three hundred. We covered the four kliks in twenty-one minutes. That's not bad for people carrying sixty or so pounds of gear on their backs.

Have I told you lately how grateful I am to the people who make the Magellan? Well, I am. We came up a small wadi, carefully bypassed a knot of ramshackle mud-cake houses that probably housed the squatters who'd taken over after the Palestinians had left, climbed across a low rise—and there, more or less directly ahead of us, was the compound the FORTE satellite had discovered. The accuracy of the fucking thing is within yards.

What I saw was an irregular—that is to say trapezoidal—four-sided compound, which seemed to be part of a larger, industrial-zone kind of arrangement. It reminded me of the way Herzliya looked before it became San Tropez. A well-marked side road led from the two-lane highway to the complex. And unlike the other roads which tracked to facilities in the zone, the road to our target had been well-paved to handle heavy trucks.

The site itself was deceptive. There was a single rolling chain-link gate, outside which sat a darkened wood gatehouse. Two large signs were posted on either side of the entrance. One was in English, the other in Arabic. They had the same artwork, so I gathered that they said the same thing. And what they said was

SAHID MEDACIN EQUIPPMENT COPMANY, LTD. As you can see, spelling is not a strong subject in Syrian schools. I hoped they'd done better in Arabic. Inside the fence stood a large, unremarkable two-story, flat-roofed building. The Arabic version of Sahid Medacin Equippment Copmany, Ltd., was painted on a huge billboard on the roof, along with a big bottle of liquid. The whole thing was slightly tilted, as if one of its supports had given way.

Of course, we were still some two hundred yards from the outer fence line. And three hundred yards from the inner perimeter. We dropped and began to reckon the possibilities. There weren't very many of 'em.

It was Koby who pointed it out.

"Look, mister officer," the big noncom said. "See how the wire is strung?"

I looked. "So?"

"When's the first time you ever saw wire strung like that?"

I gave the two perimeter fences a closer examination. Oh, I'd seen similar arrangements before—in Israel. But that wasn't the first time. The first time had been in Guatemala.

Yeah—I see your hand flapping out there. Guatemala, you say, but we're in the Middle East. Yes, we are. But in the early eighties, the United States cut off all aid to the Guats because of their large numbers of flagrant human rights violations in a very dirty war against a bunch of Communist-supported guerrillas. So, deprived of American assistance, guess who the Guats hired to build most of their security infrastructure for them. You got it—they hired Israelis.

I was currently looking at the same layout of the generic security perimeter that surrounds most Israeli military installations, as well as those that have been designed by Israel and built by Mossad contractors in such places as Singapore, Argentina, China, Senegal, Taiwan, South Korea, Jordan, and the Czech Republic. Was I surprised to see this system in place not thirty-five miles from downtown Damascus? Yes I was—but I wasn't shocked. After all, Ehud Golan was a part of this equation, and Ehud—traitor or not—was Mossad.

I scanned the site. All the lights faced outward: anybody approaching would be illuminated, while the defenders would remain in the dark. It also meant there'd be two lines of razor wire atop each fence. And there would be three lines of electronic sensors (they'd be on the fences, and scattered on the ground for sixty to eighty yards beyond the outer perimeter). And there would be watchtowers at every corner of the fence line, giving the guards overlapping fields of fire.

I recited what I saw and what I knew to Avi and Koby. "Did I miss anything?"

"Not that I can think of," Avi said.

Now, let me tell you right now that the Israelis design good security perimeters. But as you probably know by now, there is no security I cannot breach.

Let me qualify that statement. There is no security I cannot breach—given enough time. But at the moment, it was just past 0500, which meant that time was about to run out on me.

So subtlety, friends, was about to be out of the question. We'd go balls to the wall. Now before you start getting skeptical, lemme tell you about one of the most effective infiltration techniques I perfected when I commanded Red Cell. It was like this: I'd commandeer a fucking car, then simply fucking drive through the fucking gate of the fucking installation, and never do a fucking thing but wave at the fucking guards as I passed through. Are you catching on to this ironic use of the F-word here? Good. Also, you know and I know that Avi speaks just about every . . . (no need to use the F-word again, is there?) dialect of Arabic used in these parts. If something more elaborate than waving at the gatekeepers became necessary, we'd keep our mouths shut and let him do all the talking. And if that didn't work we had automatic weapons.

There is one other thing you should know about the site. It was way undermanned. They'd done it on purpose, too—I mean, if you have armed guards patrolling everywhere and machine gun nests every six yards, then the signs that tell the world you're making "medacin equippment" aren't gonna fool anybody, especially the Israelis and the Americans, both of whom have satellite capability. Oh, those two perimeter fences were more security than your normal everyday industrial plant might have, but not so much more that they stood *waay* out. And, as we scanned the watchtowers, we saw not a man in 'em.

Now, all we needed was a car.

Slight problem. There hadn't been a single bit of traffic in the six or so minutes we'd been watching the target.

I explained the problem. Koby frowned. "You wait," he said. He pointed at a sharp bend in the highway just out of sight of the turnoff for the industrial zone. The sky beyond it was starting to tinge that unique burnt rose color that you see only in this part of the world in the moments shortly before dawn breaks. "You wait close to there, mister officer." He dropped all of his gear except for the AK, and held his hand out. "I'll need a knife."

Wonder pulled a large Spyderco folder from the inside of his waistband. "Try this."

"Believe me, *gingi*, I will," Koby said. He turned to leave, then turned long enough to perform a respectable Schwarzenegger. "Dun't vorry—I'll be beck," he growled.

0522. We waited, back far enough from the road so that we wouldn't be noticed if traffic passed us by. No Koby.

0526. We waited. Avi cracked his knuckles. Each one. Slowly. Twice. Wonder's expression told me that he knew we'd gone all the way to FUBAR. Still no Koby.

0528. Approaching vehicle. No lights. Weapons ready, just in case. It stopped right at the point Koby'd indicated. He jumped out and waved us on.

I didn't bother asking how or where or WTF. No time for that. Besides, it wasn't much of a car. That is an understatement. Once upon a time I think it might have been a green Datsun—impossible to say without carbon dating—but it probably could be traced to the mid-seventies. At least I think it had been green once. Now it had one orange fender. Its doors didn't quite match—or fit. It lacked mirrors, and it was missing its rear window. It was the most beautiful car I've ever seen.

Chapter

22

WE FILLED THE TRUNK WITH OUR SUPPLIES, AND PILED IN. AVI DROVE. Koby and Wonder were crammed with the rest of our gear in what used to be the backseat. I rode shotgun. Avi put the car in gear and we drove away. At times like this, in case I haven't mentioned it before, your heart is going at a rate that cannot be calculated, adrenaline is flowing by the gallon, and sentences tend to become simple and declarative.

Lights on. Turned the corner. Up the road. Moved toward the gate and gatehouse. Eased up and almost stopped. There was stirring within. A man's head, his kaffiyeh askew, appeared behind the dirty, cracked panes of the gatehouse door. Avi waved at the fellah inside. He opened the door and shuffled out. Avi said something in Arabic. The man laughed, showing broken teeth, and responded. Then a second man appeared. Glassa coffee—no, tea— in his hand. The first man nodded to him. He set his glass down on the gatehouse window ledge. His sandals scuffing pea gravel, he ambled to the gate and began to open it.

My antenna sensed something going bad. First man having second thoughts? Maybe—he was checking a list. He brought it out to the car. Avi made a joke—fellah looked up. Avi shot him—one shot clean through the eye into the brain—with a suppressed

318

Beretta .22-caliber pistol. Where the fuck had he stowed that? I'd never seen him pack it.

The other man kept working on the gate. Dead man collapsed. Slid down to the ground without a sound. Lay at the side of the car against the door. Out of mind; out of sight.

The gate was now open. The man who'd opened it turned and came back toward us to wave us through.

Avi opened the car door—the fucking Datsun door currently wedged shut by the weight of the body up against it—Avi pushing harder now, straining, and all of a sudden things began to move very, very quickly and things started to happen and I opened my door and got out and the look on the man's face showed that he realized that he'd been screwed with and was about to get dead and he started to turn and shout but before he could do anything Avi put a bullet through his eye at seven yards with another marvelous shot and I wondered how the fuck had he improved so much and not told me.

Sometimes, friends, things are not simple and declarative.

We moved the bodies back inside the gatehouse, stuffed them under the small desk, removed the tea, and closed the door. Then we drove into the compound, leaving the chain-link gate open.

Okay—we were inside. The question was, now WTF? Avi solved that one—he read a sign that directed us to the executive offices. We took a left, drove behind the building, then made a quick right into a small U-shaped courtyard, and we were there.

Two black Mercedes sedans sat side by side in front of the entrance. Koby checked them out. Both had Lebanese plates—one from Beirut, the other from Sidon. I lay my hand on the hood of each. The paint was still slightly warm to the touch, which told me they hadn't been here for a long time.

I scanned the windows for movement and perceived nothing. If we were being watched, it was being done surreptitiously. This was a strange situation. I'd detected no movement. Except for the two men working the gatehouse, we'd seen no other personnel—no guards, no workers, none of the commotion one might expect to see in and around a plant that was manufacturing nuclear weapons components. In fact, there was no action of any sort—no whirring of mechanical machinery, or the hum of air-conditioning, or the whining of electrical motors and whomping of pumps—all the kinds of sounds one associates with a manufacturing facility. But here, there was nothing.

It was very disquieting, my friends. I mean, usually at installations like this one, there is some kind of activity at all hours. But here, it was like zip, zero, nada. The lights—that is to say radiation emanations—certainly were "on" at this place. The FORTE satellite had determined *that* fact for sure. But—Mercedes sedans aside—no one seemed to be at home.

Recon time. The front door was unlocked and we slipped inside. The foyer was about thirty by thirty, with two facing corridors that obviously led to opposite sides of the factory. The place was furnished in archetypal Middle East industrial. This, dear reader, is a polite way of saying that the accoutrements were dilapidated and everything was coated with a film of fine dust. There were dusty marble floors, sallow, dust-filmed mustard-colored walls, a dusty ceiling with a dusty ceiling fan, two dusty framed portraits of Haffez el Assad facing the front entrance, and a collection of dusty metal-framed furniture and dust-coated office equipment. Dead ahead, one narrow dusty stairway with ornate, decorative wrought iron railings led up to the first floor. Immediately to its left, another—this one had been cut into the building recently and had been designed in a more utilitarian manner—led down below ground level. Guess what it was coated with.

There were enough scuff marks on the floors to tell us that people had been using the place—and recently. Weapons at the low ready, Koby and I split right and left. We made sure the foyer was clear—it was—then the four of us separated into two pairs. Wonder and I took the port-side corridor, Avi and Koby went starboard. If we dry-holed, we'd reassemble at 0610. If one team engaged, the other would close on it as backup.

Wonder and I moved cautiously down the long, marble-floored hallway. The fluorescent lights gave everything a greenish tinge—surreal and unearthly. There was no air-conditioning—again, strange for a place where they were making nuclear weapons materials—but you could hear ceiling fans as they whirred behind the office doors. The doors in our corridor had milky glass upper panels and metal lower panels. We moved carefully, ducking under, checking back, opening the doors, and making sure no one was inside.

There are two kinds of tactical entries, friends. The one I prefer to use is dynamic. The name says it all—*wham-wham, blam-blam, the bad guys all get slam-slammed.* The other method is called slow and deliberate. It is used when stealth is necessary, or when you want to sneak up on your adversary and take him down *sans* violence. I do not prefer slow and deliberate because it is time-consuming, it takes a lot of concentration, and I have usually spent a lot of energy getting to the site in the first place. As in this morning.

0609. We worked the entire ground-floor left-hand side. We came up dry—I mean *dry*. Nobody in the executive offices. Nobody in the labs. Nobody anyfuckingplace. Not that they weren't expecting a crowd: three of the largest rooms had been converted to six-man dorms, complete with three bunk beds per room, and military-style lockers. A makeshift kitchen had been created in what had once been a lab. But there were few signs of inhabitation. The mattresses on the bunks were bare. There was food and booze— vodka and beer, to be precise—in the kitchen.

And guess what, friends? All the writing—from the labels on the booze and mattresses, to the heat 'n' eat instructions on the boxed victuals—was in Cyrillic. It was obvious that the technicians who were coming to assemble this installation were—ta-da—Ivans. I silent-signaled to Wonder. He nodded, and we started back the way we'd come.

We reconnected with Koby and Avi in the foyer. Had they seen anything? Their answer was the same as ours—no, although they'd seen indications that the place was going to be occupied soon, just as we had.

I pointed toward the "down" staircase. Koby nodded, Yes. I pointed at Avi and indicated that he was to remain behind and keep an eye on the ground floor.

Face it—you don't want to clear a floor, then go below, and come back to find that your adversary has set up an ambush for you.

I took point. I started down, one tread at a time, my feet moving carefully so as not to make noise. I kept my back to the wall, and my AK at low ready. Behind me, the muzzle of Koby's M-16 sat just above my left shoulder, providing potential cover if I needed it. Behind him, covering our butts, was Wonder and his AK.

Moving down stairs like this, friends, is a potentially dangerous tactic. You are at a disadvantage if someone is waiting in ambush for you—because he will most often see you before you see him. When I work slow, deliberate entries and there is a stairwell involved, I prefer to use a mirror on the end of a long pole to make my way around the turns.

But I didn't have a mirror. So I moved very cautiously, and very deliberately. Came to the first landing. Cut the pie—that is to say, I edged around the outside so as to give myself an ever-expanding field of vision (and fire!) as I moved down, around, and down again.

Still all clear.

The second landing was uneventful, too. From it, a short flight led to the basement floor proper. I signaled a halt. You don't want to bunch up at the bottom of a stairwell. A team that's all knotted up tightly can't react as well as one that's spread out.

0614. We worked our way into the basement proper. The illumination was minimal—one overhead in six was lighted. I signaled for Wonder to relieve me on point—I needed a break and it looked as if this was going to be as uneventful as our first leg.

Gentle reader, have I ever explained the Rogue's First Rule of Life to you? It goes like this: that phone call you've been waiting for all morning won't happen unless you're sitting on the pot and unable to answer. Here, too, shit happened: Wonder hadn't gone six yards when he silent-signaled me to stop dead in my tracks and motioned that there was "enemy ahead." I didn't see a thing, but I know Wonder well enough to follow his lead in situations like this one, so I stopped as instructed. Behind me, Koby froze, too. Obviously, he knew when to take "yes" for an answer.

I watched as Wonder *q-u-i-e-t-l-y* shifted his weapons—it's amazing how he can do it without making any noise whatsoever—unsheathed the knife that hung on his belt, and then, stealthy as a goddamn hungry lion, he began to move forward. Wonder wasn't greedy about it either. His progress was inch by inch as he moved up toward a huge, wooden shipping container—it must have been eight by eight by six—and slowly, surreptitiously, furtively turned the corner, moving out of sight.

I stopped. Behind me, Koby also halted. We waited, our breathing shallow. I could hear my own heartbeat and wondered if Koby could hear it, too.

Ahead, I heard a slight rasping sound, as if someone's feet had shifted position on the dusty floor. I waited, my AK ready to cover Wonder if he had to make a fast retreat.

There was only silence. Then Wonder's face reappeared around the corner of the shipping container. He silent-signaled us to move up quietly.

We did. When we turned the corner, I saw what had caused the shifting sounds. An inert figure lay on his stomach, a pool of blood widening on the concrete floor below his neck. Next to him on the cement lay an Uzi submachine pistol.

Wonder's hands told us that he was going to do some more hunting, and he moved off into the fluorescent half-light of the basement. Koby silently rolled the corpse onto its side and began to go through its pockets. Next to the body lay a sheaf of papers. The Israeli handed them to me. I examined them. They were waybills— and from the look of them they'd been stapled to the crates.

I saw that Koby had retrieved a wallet. From the front pocket he pulled a blue handkerchief, and a set of keys that were soundlessly rolled in the handkerchief to keep them from making ambient noise. The keys stowed, he opened the wallet and examined the inside.

His eyes went wide. He showed me what had grabbed his attention—it was a blue plastic identity card, with Hebrew writing on it. I shrugged as if to ask WTF.

Koby put his lips next to my ear. *"Meluim* card," he whispered. *"Tzahal.*[14] Reserve ID."

0618. Wonder pronounced the basement clear. Of people, that is. Equipmentwise, as many apparatchiks are fond of saying, it was jam-packed. There were scores of huge, wooden shipping crates down there—they'd been brought in down a huge, newly constructed concrete ramp. Inside those crates was the Syrians' dual-use equipment.

It hadn't even been unpacked yet. I examined the cases until I discovered the ones containing the hot freon tanks I'd first learned about in Andrei Yudin's dacha. I patted the rough wood—things were finally coming full circle. And yet . . . and yet, something bothered me. Bothered me deeply. There was a blip, a snag, a glitch, a flaw in this situation.

Can you guess what it was, dear reader? No? Well, let me elucidate for a few seconds. Remember back a couple of hundred pages when Avi told me Mossad was absolutely certain that the Syrians were building a nuke with the help of the Russian Mafiya?

Well, what if that information was actually what the KGB used to call "disinformation"? In other words, Mossad wanted everyone to believe that the Syrians were building a bomb.

---

[14]*Tzahal* is the Hebrew acronym for Israeli Defense Forces.

You say it doesn't make sense. You're right. Except, that is, unless the scenario being followed was the one I'd come up with a short time ago and passed onto Kenny Ross and Chairman Crocker: i.e., certain forces within the Israeli intelligence community, with the complicity of some Americans, probably at Langley, were conspiring to allow the Israelis to take the Syrians out of the peace process by way of a preemptive attack.

If you believe that scenario, then this empty plant and the unpacked crates make a lot of sense. It is called baiting the trap.

I silent-signaled Wonder to start rigging the crates with explosives. He gave me a thumbs-up and went to work with Koby. Yes, I know that Chairman Crocker had told me to be stealthy and not to make any waves. But goddammit, I wasn't about to let this stuff fall into the hands of terrorists. We already have enough problems. We don't need some fundamentalist assholes, or any other tangos for that matter, creating powerful, portable nukes.

0624. Avi snuck downstairs and interrupted Wonder's work. He pointed his index finger toward the ceiling and jabbed it rapidly. "I heard something," he whispered. "On the roof."

We made tracks. The ground floor was quiet. I took point again, and cleared the stairwell slowly and deliberately, until I reached the first floor landing. I went round the corner. There *was* movement— I heard it, too.

The hair on the back of my neck stood up. My breathing slowed. My whole body became a sensory device—every follicle was an antenna, seeking the source of the hint of sound I'd perceived.

Up the steps, one by one. I paused. Waited. The same sound again. As if something were being dragged across a floor, a few inches at a time.

Another two steps. Landing ahead. I signaled everyone to dead stop. I handed my AK off to Koby, who handed it back to Avi. Then I dropped as low as I could and crept ahead, using the stair rail to pull myself along. The ornate metal would camouflage my silhouette until I could see clearly what was going on.

Dear readers, do you remember that back in Paris I had a bad experience with a nasty section of wrought iron railing? You'd assume I'd have learned my lesson, wouldn't you.

Yeah, well, remember the old Rogue Warrior's Eighth Commandment of SpecWar—"Thou shalt never assume." It was doom-on-Dickie time. As I pulled myself along, the six-foot segment of railing on which I was pulling separated from its anchors and came crashing. Down. Onto my beautiful, perfect, Slovak puss.

Fuck me. I tossed it aside. Koby and Avi dodged just in time—it would have slammed into them—as it went careening past Wonder, shattering somewhere near the first landing.

Well, when you lose surprise there's nothing to do but ATTACK. God bless Koby—the man was a Warrior. He knew WTF to do. Never paused a millisecond but came charging up past my position, his M-16 ready to give covering fire.

At the top of the stairs he flung himself down, his rifle pointed toward an unseen target. I scrambled to my feet, grabbed my weapon from Avi, charged up the stairs to Koby's position, and dropped alongside him.

His M-16 was up and sighted—his finger was on the trigger. I looked down the sights of my own weapon and saw what he saw.

Werner Lantos and Ehud Golan were staring at us in obvious surprise. Lantos had his omnipresent cell phone. A small aluminum suitcase stood at his feet. Ehud had a similar suitcase in one hand. In the other was a semiautomatic pistol. It was pointed toward the floor, its muzzle vaguely in our direction. Behind them, two goons with Uzis slung across their chests—certainly weren't doing 'em much good hanging there, huh?—were in the process of moving what appeared to be a small, portable something—it looked like a generator?—bolted to a wood frame. They'd gotten it halfway through the open doorway that led out onto the plant's flat rooftop before we'd interrupted them. I guess what we'd heard was the frame being dragged across the roof.

Avi Ben Gal came up the stairs. He stopped just behind where Koby and I lay. "*Bokker-tov*—good morning, Ehud," Avi said. "*Manneh-sh'ma*—how's it goin'?"

"Not so bad, Boy Scout," Ehud said in English. The pistol in his hand moved slightly. Next to me, Koby's finger began to exert pressure on the trigger of the M-16.

Avi stepped past us. Bad move. You don't want to put yourself in front of your covering fire.

Except now that he'd done it I was able to see the Beretta in his hand. And he had the presence of mind to move to his right—giving both Koby and me a clear field of fire.

The muzzle of Ehud's pistol rose another few centimeters. Avi didn't say a thing—he simply shot the Mossad man directly in the left kneecap. Then he put another bullet in Ehud's right kneecap.

Then he put a third bullet four inches below the gold Gucci buckle on Ehud's trousers.

Ehud collapsed. That's an understatement. The sonofabitch went down screaming. The pair of Uzi-toters reacted—badly for them, as it turned out. They swiveled, grabbed for their weapons and tried to swing them up. They weren't going to bother aiming—this, they realized, was gonna be a spray-and-pray situation.

As you probably know, the M-16 has a sharp report—a whiplike *whaappaack,* as opposed to the AK's duller, chunkier, *thwack.* That's because the M-16 is basically a .22 on steroids, while the AK has chunky, much more conventional—even old-fashioned—bullet load,[15] which puts it well within the .30-caliber area.

Koby fired twice. *Whapp-ppak*—I know that because both of his red hot spent casings found their way down the back of my shirt. I fired once—a remarkable shot, given the fact that I was wriggling like crazy to keep the fucking hot brass moving so they wouldn't burn me any worse than they were already. But I managed to hit the asshole square in the chest and send him butt over teakettle. At thirty feet, the AK kicks ass like the proverbial mule.

Koby's eyes were still focused downrange to seek out any more threats. His cheek mold on the stock was still firm. But his finger had moved off the trigger. "Mine went down first, mister officer."

I really liked this guy—except for where he put his used brass. "Fuck you, *mister* sergeant. Your muzzle speed's faster than mine. Besides it took you two shots. In my Navy we learn not to waste ammo."

Meanwhile, Ehud didn't look much like a hood anymore. He was rolled up into a ball, moaning like the cocksucking coward he was. Coward? Yeah—people who get their kicks by torturing other people are basically cowards. People who set bombs that kill innocent people are basically cowards. And people who sell their countries out are cocksuckers. Ehud was both.

And Werner? He was just a cocksucker—a cocksucker who was jumping around like a fucking organ-grinder's monkey, waving his cell phone and screaming "Don't shoot" in five or six languages.

"C'mon—" I was on my feet and charging forward. I kicked the pistol from where Ehud had dropped it so it was out of everybody's reach. Then I slapped Werner onto the deck—he went down

---

[15] 7.62 by 39 milimeters, to be precise.

without too much protest—stomped his phone just in case he had an autolocator in it, and frisked him, thoroughly, top to bottom.

Wonder dealt with the two corpses while Avi and Koby worked over Ehud. They did a pretty job of hog-tying the cocksucker with their kosher duct tape, too. He looked like a fucking bleeding mummy when they finished with him.

Meanwhile, I grabbed Werner by the collar of his four-grand suit and dragged him over to the generator. Except, when I took a look at it, it wasn't a generator. It was a small insulated container with a pressurized, gasketed cap held in place by a series of wing nuts.

I nudged the device with my foot and looked at Werner. "What is it?"

He shrugged, as if to say he didn't know.

I backhanded him. He went down hard. "C'mon, Werner . . ."

He crawled onto his hands and knees, then struggled to his feet. The artery in his neck was throbbing more than it had in Paris.

I took him by the lapels with my left hand, squeezed tightly, lifted his feet just off the ground, then swatted him across the face half a dozen times with my right hand. "Werner . . ."

I released him. He wiped blood from his nose. "It's a chemical residue device."

A what? I'd never heard of anything called a chemical residue device. So I asked Werner to explain what it was in language that I could understand. I didn't say please, either.

But he told me anyway, in words of two syllables or less, just like I'd asked. Werner stopped speaking. I looked at him and he cringed, as if I was going to slap him around again. Oh, I thought about it, but why waste the effort.

Besides, I had other things on my mind right now. You see, dear reader, things had just become very, very clear.

What we'd discovered here, friends, was a form of hunting lure.

You see, when some people hunt deer, they use chemical agents to attract their prey. They spray themselves with doe scent—and hope that some very big and horny buck (sorry about that) will smell it, get all excited, and come charging blindly through the woods in search of doe pussy.

Well, same principle applies here. We all know that the dual-use equipment the Syrians bought is still in its crates in the basement, which means there's nothing that would attract a FORTE satellite. So Werner set a lure—this chemical quim—which FORTE, flying overhead, sniffed out. The satellite data would be fed through

Langley to the Israelis, who'd come and flatten the building. No wonder the CIA had caved on the FORTE so fast.

Now he was packing it up—absquatulating with the evidence just the way I absquatulated when I was taking Vynkenski, Blynkenski, and Nodyev to the cleaners back in Moscow. Why bother? No sense leaving anything that might be discovered later in the rubble.

But there was more. I opened the aluminum suitcases. Inside each was a battery-operated laser targeting device. They were the same sort of devices SpecWar operators had used during the Gulf War. A squad of SAS or Delta shooters would infiltrate Iraq, plant a couple of these gizmos close by a strategic target and turn them on, then skedaddle out of Dodge. Some hours later, an air strike would flatten the place with laser-guided weapons. Fire and forget, is what the pilots call it.

In fact, the Israelis had used the same technique when they bombed the Iraqi nuclear reactor at Ossirak back in 1981. The only problem back then was that the Mossad agent[16] who was responsible for setting the laser device didn't make it out of the plant and was killed during the raid.

But that was then and this was now, and it was crystal-clear obvious what was going on. Werner and Ehud had come to remove the lure, plant the targeting devices, then pull out before the Israelis hit the place.

Gentle reader, you know as well as I do what the obvious question is. Let's all say it together: *So, when will the Israelis hit the place?*

I posed the question to Werner—who had to know, since he was one of the folks placing the targeting devices. When he didn't answer I broke a finger—his, not mine—and asked him once more. This time he decided to tell me.

"Fourteen-thirty," he gulped, tears streaming down his face. "When the sun will make it more difficult for the Syrians to chase the raiders west."

I examined Werner's sorry puss closely. My own expression made it very clear to him that if he'd lied, he was a dead man. But the information he'd given me was tactically practical—it made the

---

[16]He was one of the European contract employees working on the installation. A piece of Ossirak trivia: the lead pilot on that raid was ultimately employed by Israeli intelligence to "run" the American spy Jonathan Pollard.

kind of KISS-sense Israelis are known for. It also gave us some time. But not a lot.

By now, my friends, you must be wondering WTF. I mean, this situation is very much like one of those Russkie *matryoshka* dolls you buy at the Izmaylovo art market in Moscow—the dolls that open up and there's a smaller one inside, and you open that one up, and there's another, and another, and another.

Well, what we have here is a sting within a sting. You say you don't quite understand? Okay—let me give you some gist.

- Item: Mossad constructs a sting, i.e., selling Russkie dual-use equipment to the Syrians, so that the new government can use the situation to trash the Syrians and take them out of the peace process. To accomplish this they use Werner Lantos, who keeps CIA informed—to a degree. But Werner is his own man. He's greedy and he's corrupt. And maybe he's a double agent as well.

So he convinces the Russkies to play. Well, that's to be expected: for them it's a win-win situation. They get hard currency for their dual-use material, and their people get a foothold back in Syria. I'd be willing to bet a buck or two there'd be some intelligence operatives along with the technicians.

So the sting is set up. But there's a glitch: Paul Mahon senses there's something awry. So Werner has Andrei Yudin the *vor* waste Paul and his family. That would have been the end of the story—except for the fact that Paul was my friend and my shipmate.

Okay. Segue to the present. Syria is hit by an Israeli air strike that levels this building and destroys all the dual-use equipment. What happens?

Well, first and foremost, as the news commentators are fond of saying, the peace process is stopped cold—with the Golan Heights still in Israeli hands. That makes the current Israeli government very happy.

But what about the bigger picture?

- Item: the world learns that the intelligence that Israel used to base its attack—the FORTE information—was provided by the United States.
- Item: the Arab world's negative opinion of the United States is increased.

And now here is the kicker.

- Item: Russia now steps in and offers its services to the Arab world as mediators, a move that will help to reposition it as a global power broker.

I see you waving your paw. You say you don't think the Israelis would bomb the site unless they had independent confirmation about the nuclear materials.

But they did have it—from Ehud the Hood. Which is why he and his fellow no-goodnik Werner Lantos were here up close and personal to place the targeting devices.

Well, it was time to toss a fucking SEAL wrench into the plot. "Wonder—finish planting the goddamn explosives. I wanna blow the hell out of this place."

"Aye, aye, Skipper." Wonder punched Koby's arm hard enough to make the tough Israeli wince. "C'mon, *mister* sergeant—let's go make the earth move."

I called after him. "And set it up to give us somewhere between twelve and fifteen minutes after we pull out."

"Gotcha." Wonder turned to leave. Again, I stopped him in midstride with my voice. "And set a booby trap on it." I didn't want anybody defusing Wonder's handiwork.

He paused, hands on hips. "Anything else, Captain Dickhead— maybe you'd like whipped cream and a cherry on top? Or can I get to fucking work already?"

I saluted *le prodige rouge* with my middle finger to remind him he was still Number One with me. "Get the fuck outta here."

I looked down at the bound-and-gagged Hood, who was still writhing in pain on the deck. "Avi—what do you want to do with him? It's gonna be hard to bring him along making all that noise."

Avi, who was shooting pictures with the autofocus camera, pulled his eye back from the viewfinder. His face was a mask. "Oh, I think Ehud should stand watch this morning," he said. "Somebody has to make sure that the demolition charges work properly."

We pulled out at 0745. Before we departed, we opened two dozen shipping crates in the basement and photographed the contents. We made sure that Werner and Ehud were in most of the pictures. We left everything behind except for a handful of documents Avi took from Ehud Golan's pockets, the thick sheaf of waybills from the dual-use material crates, the weapons, the pair of laser targeting devices in their suitcases, and a few other goodies. The five of us fit comfortably in Werner's Mercedes. It was also nice to see that Werner had been supplied with the kinds of papers that get folks through roadblocks. Avi looked them over carefully, then pronounced them authentic—and valid.

There was even a current road map in the Mercedes' glove compartment. We picked the route of least resistance—took the highway to Qatana, and from there straight up the mountain road to Burqush, on to Rakhle, and from there across the Lebanese border through one of the mountain passes just to the north of what the Syrians call Jabelech Cheikh, and the Israelis call Mount Hermon. It was not the most direct way—but it was the one least likely to arouse anyone's suspicion.

The route was Koby's suggestion—he'd finished his reserve duty less than a month before and had been assigned to the northern-most quadrant of the Lebanese security zone. His thick index finger pointed out the Syrian positions he remembered—positions just beyond the Israeli lines, across the international border.

So, instead of taking the most direct route, which would take us through those Syrian army checkpoints, we fishhooked north toward Dahr el Ahmar, then turned southwest at Nabi Safa, then put pedal to metal and drove hi-diddle-diddle, right down the middle, paralleling the Litani River—and headed straight for the Israeli Army headquarters just outside Hasbaiya. Avi drove, and I rode shotgun, just like the old days. Werner sat between Koby and Wonder in the backseat, riding the hump. He actually smelled like shit and I wondered whether he'd soiled himself. Not my problem. But we still opened the windows. We were maybe fifteen kliks from the plant when I heard the reverberation of the dull explosion. Werner Lantos winced at the sound. He was the only one who did.

We drove the first half hour in silence. Then Werner began to find his sea legs. He was a hell of a salesman, believe me. I mean, if I hadn't known what I knew, and if he hadn't smelled so fucking bad, I might have started half believing him.

He was one of the good guys. He'd put his life on the line for us—that's the Americans—and them—that's the Israelis—hundreds of times. Sure, he stole—but he never stole from us. Only from no-goodniks like Viktor Grinkov, or Andrei Yudin. Honest, he promised. The only people who were really getting screwed were bad guys.

I turned toward him. "Only bad guys."

He nodded. "Yes, yes." And you know what? The cockbreath probably believed what he was saying.

"What about my friend, Paul Mahon? What about his wife and kids? What about the enlisted Navy driver who died? What about the people in Paris who were blown up in those three bombings?"

That shut the sonofabitch up for a while. But by the time we were cruising up the long, curved road to Rakhle, he was at it again.

I finally told him to shut the fuck up. "Werner," I said, "I'm gonna make you an offer you can't refuse." I turned in my seat and draped my arms around the headrest. "If you flap any more lip during this drive, I'm going to start breaking your appendages. Joint by joint, starting with your right big toe and working all the way up to your left thumb. Got it?"

He looked at me and saw that I was serious. "Yes," he said.

"Good." I relaxed the intensity of my stare. "Now—because I am a tough man but a fair man, if we get where we're going and I haven't broken any more of your joints, I will let you try to convince my boss that you're on the right side, and I will abide by what he says."

"You are? You will?"

"Yes."

The dirty look Wonder gave me was unbelievable. But I didn't care. I knew what I was doing. You see, friends, there *are* times when—as Werner himself had explained to me in Paris—geopolitics plays a role in the outcome of situations, and you cannot allow personal feelings to interfere with a global weltanschauung. Besides, my remarks brought us some blessed peace and quiet for the next three-quarters of an hour.

I wish I could titillate you, gentle reader, with news that we had to run half a dozen roadblocks under fire, blast our way through a bunch of Syrian commandos sent out to pursue us, and generally outfox the whole Hizballah guerrilla organization in eastern Lebanon. But the fact of the matter is that we did not. Both in Syria and in Lebanon, one can, most of the time, move from one location to another with no interference, and very little delay. We saw two military police jeeps in Rakhle—but nothing else. Not even at the Lebanese line.

At the sleepy, one-man Lebanese border station a klik and a half inside the border near Kfar Oouq, the unarmed official motioned us through with a cursory wave and a pro forma *"ahlan v'Lubnan"*—welcome to Lebanon. Our only real problems began when we crossed the first of the SLA checkpoints, just north of Nabat, at 1015. The SLA—the acronym stands for the Southern Lebanese Army—is a creation of Mossad. It is made up mostly of Christian gunsels, who are paid, trained, and equipped by Israel. They are not nice people, and they have heavy weapons. Well, they have heavier weapons than we did.

And so we sat in the blistering sun for half a fucking hour while the CIC—that's *capo* in charge—went to find his *capo dei capi*, who in turn, had to go looking for his fucking *capo del tutti capi*, so that some provision could be made for escorting us the last ten or so miles to the IDF regional headquarters at Hasbaiya. There had been ambushes, the *capo* said. It was dangerous, he insisted. We needed protection, he emphasized.

And so we sat, and we waited. Koby excused himself and wandered into the SLA checkpoint, looking for coffee. Wonder went off to drain the lizard. Avi and I sat in the car, keeping an eye on Werner. Still, it occurred to me that maybe we shouldn't waste time, which was, after all, kind of precious. I turned to Avi. "Will your phone work here?"

He shrugged. "If we're far enough south to pick up one of the IDF cells." He reached down for the pack that sat between my feet.

"I'll get it—" I unzipped the rucksack and rooted around until I came up with the phone, put it to my ear, punched the keypad, and hit the "send" button. Nothing.

Avi held his hand out. "Let me see." I handed it over to him. He extended the antenna, and played with the switch but couldn't get the damn thing to work either. "Battery's dead," he opined. "I think I may have left it turned on."

Werner Lantos either had to take another crap real bad, or he looked like he wanted to say something. "Okay, Werner," I said, "Now, you can talk—what is it?"

"That's a Nokia—same as mine. I have a twelve-volt power cord in the console."

I opened the center console and found the cord, plugged it into the phone's receptacle, then jammed the power plug into the Mercedes's cigarette lighter. Immediately, the phone's lights came on.

"Why, thank you, Werner," I said.

"You're very welcome," he replied.

I handed the phone to Avi. "You want to try Tel Aviv?"

"I'd better, don't you think?"

I nodded. Avi punched a series of numbers into the phone and then hit the "send" button. He waited, silent, as the call began to transmit. Then, abruptly, he hit the "end" key and handed me the phone.

"I was just thinking," he said, "it's probably more important for you to get hold of your people than it is for me to get hold of mine. Besides, there's nothing I want to say on an open line. So, you make your call—I'll have a secure telephone as soon as we get to Hasbaiya—that won't be more than half an hour."

"You're right." I punched the international access code onto the keypad, followed by the country code, area code, and then Kenny Ross's number. Yes, I know it was way before normal business hours back in the U.S. of A. But I also knew that Kenny would be waiting to hear from me—and so would Chairman Crocker.

Kenny picked up on the second ring. "Ross."

"It's me."

"Where are you?"

I told him.

"Sit-rep?"

He wasn't wasting any words on me, so I didn't waste any on him. I gave him the requisite no-shitter.

I could tell from the tone of his voice that he liked what he heard. "Evidence?"

"Yup."

"Verification?"

"We have pictures."

"Great." There was a muffled *thwop* as Ken Ross cupped his hand over the receiver and spoke to someone in his office. Then he said, "We'll be able to take it from here, Dick." Then there was another pause on the line. Finally he came back. "Let me sit-rep you. First, I can tell you we acted on your faxed information from this end," he said.

That would be the $50 mil in Russkie money he was talking about. "And?"

The satisfaction in Ken Ross's voice was evident. "Without going into detail on this phone, Dick, I say that there are a lot more poor Ivans in the world today than there were yesterday—and they know enough about how they were ripped off to be mighty pissed about it, too."

That was terrific news. I love it when Russkies are pissed off. But there was another loose end I wanted to see tied off. "What about changes at our embassy in Moscow, Admiral?"

"The DCM with the trust account?" Ken Ross reported gleefully. "SECDEF showed your fax to the secretary of state, who went ballistic. That sonofabitch is looking for a job because of you."

My friends, there are times when one feels like celebrating, and this was one of 'em. But there was business to do first.

"Admiral," I said, "When I came out, I brought the project's prime contractor with me—a fella named Werner Lantos. Maybe you've heard of him?"

Ken Ross, who of course knew all about Werner Lantos, interrupted me: "Whoa, Dick. We don't want anything to do with Lantos—*anything*. At best he's a double agent. At worst—who knows."

I smiled encouragingly at Werner Lantos. "You're absolutely right," I said to Ross. "Which is why Werner wants to talk to you— to prove just how valuable he might be to us."

There was evident irritation in Ken Ross's voice. "As I just explained—"

"Precisely," I said, a soothing expression directed toward Werner. "Which is precisely why he wants so badly to speak with you now."

"I don't want a goddamn thing to do with the man," Ken Ross shouted in my ear.

I paid no attention to him. "And so, here he is—in person."

I put my hand over the phone's mouthpiece very loosely, so my words could be heard in Washington. "Werner," I said, "just like I promised, I am going to let you speak with my boss, Admiral Ross. You may even call him by his first name—Admiral. I want you to tell him everything. And I mean, everything. When you've finished, if you can convince him that your ass is worth saving, your ass may get saved."

I handed Werner the phone. He looked like the original drowning man who'd just been tossed a life preserver.

Then I opened the car door. Stepped outside. Stretched. Avi did the same.

It was, actually, a glorious day. At its best, Lebanon can look just like a layout in one of those glossy magazines about lifestyles of the obscenely rich—the ones that cost ten bucks a copy and are edited by people named Paige or Muffy. And it certainly did today. The sky was Kodacolor blue. Big, puffy white clouds moved regally, high over Mount Hermon. Deep blue-green cedar trees—those fabled cedars of Lebanon—dotted the rocky hillsides. I looked up the slope, beyond the checkpoint, to where a dozen or so sheep were feeding on thistle in an olive grove of gnarled trees that must have been a hundred years old. Make no mistake, friends, there is a reason that for more than five thousand years, people have been fighting over this patch of ground we currently call the Middle East. God, it was a perfect day.

At which point it occurred to me, in the way things that have nothing whatsoever to do with your present situation occur to you, that Paul Mahon would never, ever, experience a perfect day like this one. Paul was gone—forever. His family was gone—forever. My godson, Adam, was gone—forever.

Y'know, it's funny, the little things you remember about people. Like the time Paul and I had been ordered by our respective bosses to steal the Army mascot from the Pentagon lobby the week before the Army-Navy game.

What I remember was not the snatch—when we tackled the damn mannequin it almost broke in half—or the chase (we must have had twenty MPs on our tails, and lemme tell you, folks, that despite the fact that we were ossifers and they weren't, if they'd caught us they would have tried to beat the shit out of us). No, what I remember was right after we burst through the shiny mahogany double doors of the vice CNO's suite. The MPs couldn't follow because we'd made it to sacred ground—ground that was protected by Marines. Big Marines. Very, very big Marines.

Paul had the mannequin by its shoulders. I had it by the knees. He turned and looked at me, his lungs heaving from the long run, his uniform collar tinged with sweat, his hair in his face. And he had this gnomish, dumb smile on his face—it was really a totally dumb smile. A moronically dumb yet euphorically twinkly smile. And he said to me, laughing so hard that it gave him hiccups, "Do you know that it has cost the American taxpayers four and a half million dollars so far to train me"—then he hiccupped—"so that I could do . . . *this?*"

What I remember, friends, is that dumb, twinkly smile, and the hiccup.

The sun was bright. The sheep were grazing. I looked at Werner Lantos in the backseat of the Mercedes. He was gesturing, somewhat pathetically, it seemed to me, as he tried to convince Kenneth

Patrick Ross, Rear Admiral (Lower Half) and submariner, of the impossible. To wit: he, Werner Lantos, was one of the good guys.

I looked at Avi. He'd moved away, toward the checkpoint barrier, where he was impatiently staring south down the road.

I tapped on the Mercedes's window.

Werner Lantos looked up, an impulsive expression of annoyance flashing across his face. He cupped his hand across the mouthpiece, the artery in his neck throbbing, and he looked angrily over at me, as if to say, I'm *talking*, you twit.

Y'know, my friends, it occurred to me that, once an asshole, always an asshole. It occurred to me that we'd already put Werner's account numbers and passwords to good use. It occurred to me that almost all the scores I'd vowed to settle up, had been settled up.

And so, my friends, it occurred to me that it was time to get . . . personal. I reached into my pocket and extracted the detonator. With my left hand I released the arming safety.

It was at that point in what remained of his life that Werner Lantos realized what I was doing.

I smiled at him as I pressed the button.

It was actually a smaller charge than I'd thought. Very little noise, too. Werner's head—what there was of it—didn't even go through the window glass, although it did leave a shallow impression—a sort of quasi-death mask. But they were gonna have to hose the interior of that car down before they used it again.

I looked over at Avi. He started to say something, then stopped.

I tossed the detonator at him. He caught it, one-handed, and slipped it into a pocket.

Now it *was* time to move. "Yo, Avi, why don't you rustle us up some fresh transportation," I said. "We've got better things to do than stand around here with our fingers up our asses—Wonder's got a chief's test to study for, I've got to get my goddamn men back before they go soft on me, and you, hell—*you've* got dogs to walk."

Glossary

A² aforementioned asshole.

Admiral's Gestapo: what the secretary of defense's office calls the Naval Investigative Services Command. See: SHIT-FOR-BRAINS.

AK-47: 7.62×39 Kalashnikov automatic rifle. The most common assault weapon in the world.

AMAN: Hebrew acronym for *Agaf Modiin,* Israel's military intelligence organization.

ATS route: Air Traffic Service route. Commercial airspace.

AVCNO: Assistant Vice Chief of Naval Operations.

BAW: Big Asshole Windbag.

BDUs: Battle Dress Uniforms. Now that's an oxymoron if there ever was one.

ben zona (Hebrew): sonofabitch.

Beretta: .22-caliber semiauto pistol favored by Israelis.

BFD: big fucking deal.

BIQ: Bitch-in-Question.

byki (Russian): bodyguards.

BOHICA: Bend over—here it comes again!

Boomer: nuclear-powered missile submarine.

BTDT: Been There, Done That.

BUPERS: Naval BUreau of PERSonnel.

C-130: Lockheed's ubiquitous Hercules.

C-141: Lockheed's ubiquitous Starlifter aircraft, soon to be moth-balled.

C-4: plastic explosive. You can mold it like clay. You can even use it to light your fires. Just don't stamp on it.

C²CO: Can't Cunt Commanding Officer. Too many of these in Navy SpecWar today. They won't support their men or take chances because they're afraid it'll ruin their chances for promotion.

CALOW: Coastal And Limited-Objective Warfare. Very fashionable acronym at the Pentagon in these days of increased low-intensity conflict.

Cannon Fodder: See FNG.

c'est dommage (French): what a pity.

Christians in Action: SpecWar slang for the Central Intelligence Agency.

CINC: Commander-IN-Chief.

CINCLANT: Commander-IN-Chief, AtLANtic.

CINCLANTFLT: Commander-IN-Chief, AtLANtic FLeeT.

CINCUSNAVEUR: Commander IN Chief, U.S. Naval forces, EURope.

clusterfuck: see FUBAR.

CNO: Chief of Naval Operations.

Cockbreath: SEAL term of endearment used for those who only pay lip service.

COMINT: COMmunications INTelligence

CONUS: CONtinental United States.

crackers: CRiminal hACKERS—cyberpunk tangos.

CQB: Close-Quarters Battle—i.e., killing that's up close and personal.

CT: CounterTerrorism.

DADT: Don't ask, don't tell.

DEA: Drug Enforcement Agency.

DEFCON: DEFense CONdition.

DEVGRP: Naval Special Warfare DEVelopment GRouP, based at Dam Neck, Virginia. Current U.S. Navy designation for SEAL Team Six.

detasheet: olive drab, ten-by-twenty-inch flexible PETN-based plastic explosive used as a cutting or breaching charge.

DIA: Defense Intelligence Agency. Spook heaven based in Arlington, Virginia, and Bolling Air Force Base just outside Washington, D.C.

Dickhead: Stevie Wonder's nickname for Marcinko.

Diplo-dink: no-load cookie-pushing diplomat.

DIPSEC: DIPlomatic SECurity

Dipshit: can't cunt pencil-dicked asshole

Dirtbag: the look Marcinko favors for his Team guys.

Do-ma-nhieu (Vietnamese): Go fuck yourself. See DOOM ON YOU.

Doom on you: American version of Vietnamese for go fuck yourself.

Dweeb: no-load shit-for-brains geeky asshole, usually shackled to a computer or pencil.

EC-130: Electronic warfare-outfitted C-130.

EEI: Essential Element of Information. The info-nuggets on which a mission is planned and executed.

EEO: Equal Employment Opportunity (Marcinko always treats 'em all alike—just like shit.)

ELINT: ELectronic INTelligence.

EOD: Explosive Ordnance Disposal.

F³: Full Fucking Faulkner—lots of sound and fury.

FIS: Flight Information Service.

flashbang: disorientation device used by hostage rescue teams.

FNG: Fucking New Guy. See CANNON FODDER.

Four-striper: Captain. All too often, a C²CO.

frags: fragmentation grenades.

FUC: fucking ugly Corsican.

FUBAR: Fucked Up Beyond All Repair.

gingi (Hebrew): redhead.

Glock: Reliable 9mm pistols made by Glock in Austria. They're great for SEALs because they don't require as much care as Sig Sauers.

Goatfuck: What the Navy likes to do to Marcinko. See FUBAR.

GSG-9: Grenzchutzgruppe-9. Top German CT unit.

HAHO: High-Altitude High-Opening parachute jump.

HALO: High-Altitude, Low-Opening parachute jump.

HICs: Head-In-Cement syndrome. Condition common to high-ranking officers. Symptoms include pigheadedness and inability to change opinions when presented with new information.

HK: ultrareliable pistol, assault rifle, or submachine gun made by Heckler & Koch, a German firm. SEALs use H&K MP5-Ks submachine guns in various configurations, as well as H&K 93 assault rifles, and P7M8 9mm, and USP 9mm, .40- or .45-caliber pistols.

Hotti-ha (Hebrew; plural is *hotti-hot*): a real piece.

Huey: Original slang for Bell's AH-1 two-bladed helicopter, but now refers to various UH configuration Bell choppers.

HUMINT: HUMan INTelligence.

humongous: Marcinko Dick.

Hydra-Shok: extremely lethal hollowpoint ammunition manufactured by Federal Cartridge Company.

IBS: Inflatable Boat, Small—the basic unit of SEAL transportation.

IED: Improvised Explosive Device.

IMPOTUS: William Jefferson Clinton.

Jarheads: Marines. The Corps. Formally USMC, or, Uncle Sam's Misguided Children.

JSOC: Joint Special Operations Command.

KATN: Kick Ass and Take Names. Marcinko avocation.

KH: KeyHole. Designation for NRO's spy-in-the-sky satellites, as in KH-12s.

KISS: Keep It Simple, Stupid. Marcinko's basic premise for special operations.

LANTFLT: AtLANTic FLeeT.

M²: Mossad muscle. Israeli bad boys.

M-16: Basic U.S. .223-caliber weapon, used by the armed forces.

Mark-I Mod-0: basic unit.

MILCRAFT: Pentagonese for MILitary airCRAFT.

Mossad: Israel's intelligence organization. Equivalent to CIA.

MOTI: Ministry of the Interior.

NAVAIR: NAVy AIR Command.

NAVSEA: NAVy SEA Command.

NAVSPECWARGRU: NAVal SPECial WARfare GRoUp.

Navyspeak: redundant, bureaucratic naval nomenclature, either in written nonoral, or nonwritten oral modes, indecipherable by nonmilitary (conventional) or military (unconventional) individuals during normal interfacing configuration conformations.

NIS: Naval Investigative Service Command, also known as the Admirals' Gestapo. See: SHIT-FOR-BRAINS.

NMN: No Middle Name.

NRO: National Reconnaissance Office. Established 25 August 1960 to administer and coordinate satellite development and operations for U.S. intelligence community. Very spooky place.

NSA: National Security Agency, known within the SpecWar community as No Such Agency.

NSCT: Naval Security Coordination Team (Navyspeak name for Red Cell).

NSD: National Security Directive.

NYL: nubile young lovely. See: HOTTI-HA.

OBE: Overtaken By Events—usually because of the bureaucracy.

OMON: Russian acronym for *Otdel Militsii Osobovo Naznachenyia,* or Special Purpose Militia Detachment. SWAT team attached to the Russian Ministry of the Interior.

OOD: Officer Of the Deck (he who drives the big gray monster).

OP-06–04: CNO's SpecWar Briefing Officer.

OP-06: Deputy CNO for Operations, Plans, and Policy.

OP-06B: Assistant Deputy CNO for Operations, Plans, and Policy.

OPSEC: OPerational SECurity.

PDMP: Pretty Dangerous Motherfucking People.

POA: piece of ass. See: HOTTI-HA.

POTUS: President of the United States. See: IMPOTUS.

RDL: real dirty look.

RPG: Rocket-Propelled Grenade.

R²D²: ritualistic, rehearsed, disciplined drills.

RUMINT: RUMor INTelligence.

S²: Sit the fuck down and shut the fuck up.

SATCOM: SATellite COMmunications.

SCIF: Special Classified INtelligence Facility. A bug-proof room.

SEAL: SEa-Air-Land Navy SpecWarrior. A hop-and-popping shoot-and-looter hairy-assed Frogman who gives a shit. The acronym stands for Sleep, Eat And Live it up.

Semtex: Czecho C-4 plastic explosive. Used for canceling Czechs.

SES: Shit-eating smile.

SH-3: versatile Sikorsky chopper. Used in ASW missions and also as a spec-ops platform.

Shit-for-brains: any no-load, pus-nutted, pencil-dicked asshole from NIS.

SIGINT: SIGnals INTelligence.

SLUDJ: Top secret NIS witch-hunters. Acronym stands for Sensitive Legal (Upper Deck) Jurisdiction.

SMG: submachine gun.

SNAFU: Situation Normal—All Fucked Up.

SNAILS: Slow, Nerdy Assholes In Ludicrous Shoes.

SOCOM: Special Operations COMmand, located at MacDill AFB, Tampa, Florida.

SpecWarrior: One who gives a fuck.

Spetsnaz: Russian SpecWarriors who all too often don't give a fuck.

SSN: nuclear attack sub, commonly known as sewer pipe.

SSBN: nuclear ballistic missile submarine, commonly known as boomer.

STABs: SEAL Tactical Assault Boats.

SUC: Marcinkospeak for Smart, Unpredictable, and Cunning.

SWAT: Special Weapons And Tactics police teams. All too often they do not train enough, and become SQUAT teams.

Szeb (Arabic): dick.

TAD: Temporary Additional Duty (SEALs refer to it as Traveling Around Drunk).

Tailhook: the convention of weenie-waggers, gropesters, and pressed-ham-on-glass devotees that put air brakes on NAVAIR.

TARFU: Things Are Really Fucked Up.

TECHINT: TECHnical INTelligence.

THREATCON: THREAT CONdition.

Tiger stripes: The only stripes that SEALs will wear.

TIQ: Tango-In-Question

TMWTP: the man with the pin.

TTS: Marcinko slang for Tap 'em, Tie 'em, and Stash 'em.

U$_2$: Ugly and unfamiliar.

UNODIR: UNless Otherwise DIRected. That's how Marcinko operates when he's surrounded by can't cunts.

VDL: Versatile, Dangerous, and Lethal.

vor v zakonye (Russian): mafiya Godfather.

Wanna-bes: the sort of folks you meet at Soldier of Fortune conventions.

Weenies: pussy-ass can't cunts and no-loads.

WTF: what the fuck.

zapodlo (Russian): shady business.

Zulu: Greenwich Mean Time (GMT) designator used in formal military communications.

Zulu-5-Oscar: escape and evasion exercises in which Frogmen try to plant dummy limpet mines on Navy vessels while the vessels' crews try to catch them in *bombus interruptus.*

INDEX

All entries preceded by an asterisk (*) are pseudonyms.

349